A SELLSWORD'S MERCY

Book Six
of
The Seven Virtues
by
Jacob Peppers

This book is a work of fiction. Names, characters, places and incidents are either the product of the author's imagination or are used fictitiously. Any resemblance to actual persons, living or dead, or to actual events or locales is entirely coincidental.

A Sellsword's Mercy
Book Six of the Seven Virtues

This book is licensed for your personal enjoyment only. This book may not be re-sold or given away to other people. If you would like to share this book with another person, please purchase an additional copy for each person you share it with. If you're reading this book and did not purchase it, or it was not purchased for your use only, then you should return to the retailer and purchase your own copy. Thank you for respecting the hard work of the author.

Copyright © 2019 Jacob Nathaniel Peppers. All rights reserved, including the right to reproduce this book, or portions thereof, in any form. No part of this text may be reproduced, transmitted, downloaded, decompiled, reverse engineered, or stored in or introduced into any information storage and retrieval system, in any form or by any means, whether electronic or mechanical without the express written permission of the author. The scanning, uploading, and distribution of this book via the Internet or via any other means without the permission of the publisher is illegal and punishable by law. Please purchase only authorized electronic editions, and do not participate in or encourage electronic piracy of copyrighted materials.

The publisher does not have any control over and does not assume any responsibility for author or third-party websites or their content.

Visit the author's website:
www.JacobPeppersAuthor.com

To my son, Gabriel,

If you're a distraction,

Then you're the best kind

Sign up for the author's New Releases mailing list and get a copy of *The Silent Blade*, the prequel for The Seven Virtues, FREE for a Limited Time!

Go to JacobPeppersAuthor.com to get your free book!

CHAPTER ONE

Darkness lay settled on the woods like some great slumbering beast, the chill passage of the wind its restless exhalations as it threatened to awaken from its deep sleep. The watcher crouched fifteen feet up an ancient oak, the balls of his feet resting on a limb thicker than a man's thigh. He did not stir, did not so much as move, and anyone seeing him might have taken him for no more than some misplaced statue, pulled up into the tree by children, motivated by that unexplainable sense of fun which adults have long since forgotten.

The night was quiet, unnaturally so, as if even the insects and birds had abandoned their homes and shelters in the face of what stalked through the forest. The only sound was an almost imperceptible rustling of the dead leaves littering the forest floor, so quiet that a man might easily have convinced himself it was no more than his imagination. But the watcher knew better, knew well what the sound meant, what it foretold, and so he waited, motionless, peering into the darkness.

He didn't have to wait long. No more than a few minutes had passed before figures in faded gray robes appeared on the forest path beneath him. They slunk forward, their unnaturally long arms nearly dragging the ground upon which they walked, their stretched, mutilated features turning left and right as they scanned the darkness around them, making full use of their preternatural sight as they searched for signs of their prey.

The figure knew this, just as he knew that they would, inevitably, find that for which they searched. He and his brothers had trained for many years in the art of disappearing, of covering their own tracks, but their retreat had been made in haste, and they'd had no time to eliminate all traces of their passage. What few signs they'd left behind would have escaped the notice of even the best trackers the race of men had to offer, but those which walked beneath were not men but abominations, and sooner or later they would pick up the trail.

He shifted to keep the creatures in view as they passed beneath him. A silent turn, yet the one nearest him abruptly froze and cocked its head. He watched it, waiting for what would come, and there was no fear or excitement in his eyes, only a mild curiosity as he readied himself to draw the sword at his back, waiting for what would come. Even one on one, many of his brothers had fallen to the beasts, and he knew that, should the one notice him high in his perch and draw the attention of its comrades—if such creatures as this could be said to be comrades at all—he would soon be following his brothers into the great dark. So he watched. And he waited.

The creature seemed about to look up at the tree in which he crouched when, abruptly, its head snapped around with the unnatural speed of its kind to look back in the direction of its comrades. The watcher followed his gaze. The other abominations had frozen on the trail and were all standing in a semi-circle beneath a tree equal in size to the one in which he crouched.

There was a *whoosh* of displaced air and a moment later the one that had been standing beneath him huddled with the rest of its kind. The watcher raised his eyes to the dark-clad figure crouched high in the tree's branches. Despite the black clothing that covered him, leaving nothing but his eyes exposed, the watcher recognized him. He did not know his name, for they had all long since given up such things, but he knew him just the same, had known him since he'd been little more than a child and had first been brought to the Akalians. The man currently crouched in the distant tree had come the same year, and they had often trained together with all matter of weapons, the tally of their victories in the bouts almost always even, the watcher slightly faster, his brother the stronger.

Yet such strength or speed, they both knew, would avail a man little against such as these. The black-garbed figure looked up and, for a moment, their eyes met. There was no anger there, no fear or plea for help, only a purpose that had long since driven out all other concerns. It would only be a moment, the watcher knew, before the creatures looked up and discovered his companion's hiding place, and his brother knew it too. Without so much as a nod or a word, his brother drew the blade at his back and leapt from the tree, his sword flashing in the darkness.

Crimson flew as his blade cleanly severed the head from one of the creatures' shoulders. He spun, going for the next closest, but before he had a chance the tips of three slender swords erupted from his chest in a shower of blood. The man grunted, no more than that, and dragged himself further onto the blade of the nearest, getting close enough to use his own shorter sword and bring it down between the creature's neck and shoulder with his formidable strength.

The sword bit deep, and blood fountained into the air. A moment later, the creature collapsed to the ground, dead. Yet more silver flashed in the darkness, and the Akalian followed his own victim down. The watcher looked on in silence as the creatures gathered around his fallen companion, eerily quiet as their blades came down again and again. Soon, it was over. The creatures took no time to mourn their own dead only turned and started on their path once more as if nothing significant had occurred.

The Akalian watched them until they were out of sight then climbed down the tree and began the trip back to where the Speaker and the others gathered. He did not check on his companion, for he knew well enough that the creatures would not have left the thing undone, nor did he pay much attention to the direction in which the creatures traveled. After all, the man lying dead was not his only companion, nor he the only watcher.

CHAPTER TWO

The Speaker of the Akalians stood in the doorway of the small room, watching the sleeping figure. There were dozens of other such rooms in the place that had, for the last few months, served as a barracks for him and the others, many more than they needed after the deaths of the past two days. When they had erected the barracks, there had been nearly seventy-five of his brothers with him, but now no more than a dozen still lived.

He mused on how quickly things could change—even now, he thought he could detect the faint smell of freshly-cut wood still coming from the walls of the barracks in which he stood, while most of those who had helped build it lay dead in the forest.

The woman rolled restlessly in her sleep, but did not awaken, and for the first time since they built the barracks, the Speaker realized just how small the rooms were, with only just enough space for the simple beds—little more than pallets, in truth. He realized, too, how spartan they were—no paintings hung on the walls, no souvenirs or knick-knacks to tell the stories of those who lived here, nothing whatsoever to speak to the identity of the men who called it home. Such was the way of the Akalians. Such was *his* way. And yet, for the first time in a very long time, he felt the lack of such mundane things as a small, aching sadness in his chest.

Scared townsfolk called the Akalians monsters or demons, and though they were neither, in his darker moments the Speaker felt that either was nearer the truth than calling them "men." For in their dedication to their task, their purpose, they had long since abandoned all the trappings of men: fortune, fame, personal property. Love. The last thought sent another ache through him, yet had anyone watched him they would have seen none of the emotion he felt show in his placid expression.

He heard the soft sound of footfalls at the end of the hall—a courtesy he and his brothers showed to each other, when they could—and turned to see an Akalian approaching. The Speaker waited until the black-garbed figure came to stand within several feet of him, the figure's hands flashing in the intricate language known only to those of their number.

"They are close then."

Another flurry of hand motions.

"Yes," the Speaker said, nodding once. "He fought well. Go and tell the others—we leave in two days' time."

The black-garbed figure hesitated, as if he might say more. "Something troubles you?"

The figure's fingers moved slowly, as if still reluctant to share whatever he wished to say. When he finished, the Speaker nodded. "I understand. Yet for all their gifts, they will not find us so quickly as that, I think. We have two days, at least."

The figure nodded, no sign of whether or not he agreed showing in his eyes or posture, and that was no surprise. Akalians did not argue, they did not ask questions—they obeyed. The Speaker watched the man go, his expression as unreadable as ever, yet if one had looked closely enough, he might have seen the not-fully concealed worry in his eyes. "Two days," he muttered to himself. "We have that much time, surely. We must."

He turned back, once more watching the woman lying in the bed. For all her anger when awake, for all the vengeance she carried within her like some festering wound, in her sleep she looked almost at peace. Looking at her, taking in the lines of her face, he remembered a little girl, barely old enough to walk, and the wide eyes that had seemed to study everything, to question everything. She rolled in her sleep again, but aided by the herbs the Speaker had given her and the others to help overcome their shock at what they'd experienced, she would not awaken just yet, and he thought that for the best. For many reasons, not the least of which was because she had the look of someone who got little sleep.

He stood there another minute, watching her, then he eased the door shut. He took a slow, deep breath and turned, starting down the hallway. There was much to be done, and far too little time in which to do it.

CHAPTER THREE

Grinner sat at the throne room's finely appointed table, savoring the cool feel of the silk shirt against his skin. Since his injury, he experienced regular fevers, and no matter what medicines or potions the old fool of a healer gave him, he'd often wake screaming from confused, horrible dreams, his bed clothes soaked through with sweat, and on more than one occasion he had even experienced the shame of voiding his bowels in his sleep.

On such nights, he'd wake covered in his own filth, disgusted with himself beyond what he would have believed possible. Even worse, during such times, his body was so weak he could barely move, and he was forced to allow one of the healer's assistants to clean and bathe him. If he had not already seen to the death of Silent and the others, then the experience of having the heavy-set, simple-witted woman strip him and roughly lift him—as if he was some newly-born calf and she a farmer's maid—before carrying him into a waiting bath would have been ample motivation.

Yet for all the humiliation and loss of dignity, there was no denying that the bath water—so hot as to be nearly scalding—worked wonders on his weak muscles. "Heat to beat the heat of the fever," the healer had told him after the first such bath. It had not been the first or only time the crime boss had considered having the man killed, yet he had hesitated. For all his foolish talk and the uselessness of his medicines, the man was known as the best healer Perennia had to offer.

Besides, he consoled himself, though he might have suffered terrible wounds to his face—ones that, even now, he could not bring himself to examine in a looking glass—his enemies were all either dead or imprisoned. Hale and the woman, May, were the only two still alive, and they would be dealt with soon enough, as soon as he could convince the sow of a queen that the only answer to their treachery was death. She was close now, he knew. Another day, maybe two, and she would see the wisdom of his words.

He reached for his wine glass, bringing it to his mouth only to remember at the last moment that he wore the silver mask. He had spilled many drinks over the past days as he grew accustomed to its presence but this time, at least, he saved himself such embarrassment. He raised the mask with one hand—just enough to expose his dry, chapped lips—and took a long drink of the soothing wine. Before him sat a plate of fine food, the best cuts of meat, various cheeses, and breads, yet as usual, he had little appetite.

Since his injury, something as simple as chewing his food sent daggers of pain lancing through his ruined face, and he knew that he had lost weight. The old healer told him he must eat to regain his strength, but for all of that Grinner ate little, and beneath the fine silk clothes, his body grew frailer with each passing day. He had always been thin, but the lack of food was beginning to tell, and he thought it wouldn't be long before his arms became as skinny as a child's. Yet despite knowing this, he could not force himself to endure the pain of eating for long, and so he spent his days subsisting on thin soups and tasteless broths.

He glanced at the plate of sugared pastries on the table, and didn't bother to suppress the sneer that rose to his face—not that it mattered much, as the featureless silver mask he wore hid his expression. That was one thing, at least, to be grateful for, considering the amount of time he'd spent around the fool queen of late. Once, such pastries had been his favorite, yet now the thought of chewing on something even so soft as they made his skin go cold in anticipation of the pain that would follow. He closed his eyes against a brief bout of dizziness brought on by the fever, taking a slow breath as he waited for it to pass. He wanted nothing more than to go back to his manse and crawl into his bed, to close the door against the world and lie in the cool darkness until the pain lessened. Instead, he was stuck in the castle, for he dared not risk losing his growing influence on the queen.

And for all his suffering and his pain, there were things to be pleased with as well. The deaths and imminent deaths of his enemies, of course, but that wasn't all. While he spent his days seated at quiet lunches or dinners, his second-in-command, Eustice, sent his men throughout the city to every tavern and whorehouse within its walls. There, they drank, whored, and most importantly, subtly spread rumors of how Grinner foiled the assassination attempt on the queen as well how Silent and the others had abandoned Perennia right before battle with Kevlane and his armies.

Grinner was quickly becoming a hero to the populace, and it wouldn't be long before the names of Aaron and his companions would be used as curses. The crime boss was well on his way to the power that he so deserved, if only he could suffer through the queen's company a little longer. Once he was decidedly entrenched in the hearts of her and her people, there would, perhaps, be another attempt on the queen's life, one that, despite Grinner's heroic efforts, succeeded, leaving the city with no leader and only one man to fill the role. If, that was, he could keep his patience.

He regarded the queen where she sat on her throne, idly poking a slice of meat with her fork. Grinner had not been the only one changed by the events of the last few days. Queen Isabelle had never been beautiful in the classical sense—or any sense at all, so far as that went—yet she had always still taken great pains in her appearance, wearing only the finest dresses and perfumes, covering her skin's many imperfections with powder so thick it was a wonder she had been able to breathe.

But since her sister's disappearance, the queen had seemed to shrivel in on herself, and though she was still as fat as ever, there was a wasted, sick look about her. The fat on her face sagged as if she were some ice sculpture that had begun to melt, and the fingers holding her fork shook perceptibly. Her normally carefully-done hair was full of knots and tangles, and she put off a decidedly unpleasant aroma that reached Grinner even at the far end of the table. She smelled as if she hadn't bathed or used any perfume for nearly a week which—Grinner knew from the reports of the men and women he paid to keep an eye on her—was nothing short of the truth.

"Is everything okay, Your Majesty?" he asked, filling his voice with a concern he did not feel.

She didn't seem to hear him, her piggy eyes focused on the meat on her plate, studying it with some sick fascination the way a child might study a beetle being swarmed by ants.

Grinner cleared his throat, trying again. "Majesty?" he said louder.

She started as if woken from a deep slumber, knocking her plate—and the food piled high on it—off the table. "Oh, my," she said, blinking her eyes in that slow, dim-witted way that always reminded the crime boss of a particularly stupid cow. "Forgive me, Councilman Grinner," she said, "I'm afraid I was distracted."

"No forgiveness necessary, of course, my Queen," Grinner said, bowing his head as a servant scurried forward to clean up the mess. "I only wished to ask after your welfare."

"My welfare," the woman said as if she had never heard the word and had no idea of its meaning. Then she nodded slowly. "Yes, I understand. I thank you for your concern, Councilman. Tell me," she continued, finally meeting his eyes, a desperate, quiet terror on her face, "do you believe that my royal sister, Adina, will return soon?"

Oh, I am quite sure she will not, Grinner thought, smiling behind his mask. *Though, I suppose it is possible that some hunter might find pieces of her, but I suspect such a thing will be little comfort, you fat, worthless pile of dung.* "I assure you, Majesty," he said, injecting what he thought was just the right mix of grave solemnity and passion in his voice, "that I will not rest until Queen Adina is found. My men are scouring the city and its outlying regions, searching for any sign of your royal sister's whereabouts or those of the others."

"It isn't true, what they say in the city," the queen said, her gaze unfocused once more as she stared into space. "My sister would never abandon Perennia. Surely, you know the truth of that. And the others, General Envelar and all the rest." She paused, shaking her head. "It's ridiculous, surely. After all, General Envelar saved my life when Kevlane attacked. Had it not been for his intervention, the mage would have killed me and taken my place long before now." She shuddered, as if the very thought of the man sent a shiver of fear through her. "I mean," she continued, "why would Aaron do such a thing, Councilman?"

Grinner shook his head slowly, as if thinking the question over. "I do not know, Majesty. If there is a man within Telrear wise enough to know the minds of men, I am afraid that I'm not he. Regarding your royal sister, please believe me when I say that what few men are not out searching for her whereabouts are doing what they can to determine the source of these vile rumors. I will do everything within my power to put an end to them and deal with whoever is fool enough to speak evil of one of the royal blood. I, of course, believe none of the nonsense about your sister, as Queen Adina always struck me as a woman with courage and resolve beyond any, save, of course, yourself."

The queen nodded, her expression lifeless despite the compliment and the fact that, in normal times, she would have partaken of it with as much relish and vigor as she did the sweet meats she loved so much. "And General Envelar and the rest?" she asked. "What are your thoughts on them, Councilman Grinner?"

Grinner gave a helpless sigh. "Forgive me, Majesty, but I just don't know. As you say, General Envelar saved you from one assassination attempt already, and it is hard to believe fear would drive him to abandon you in your greatest hour of need. Still," he said, shrugging sadly, "I have heard of stranger things. I have heard stories of soldiers who have fought in dozens of battles suddenly being struck down with fear for no discernible reason when facing far easier odds than they have in their pasts."

The queen seemed to consider that, then finally gave a slow shake of her head. "No," she said in that lifeless, toneless voice. "General Envelar did not strike me as such a man—he was many things, but a coward was not numbered among them."

Grinner sneered and, once again, was thankful for the mask he wore. *Whatever else he was, the bastard is dead now,* he thought viciously, *and that is no less than he deserved for all his mocking, for all his threats.* "I'm sure it is as you say, Majesty," he said. "For I have known Silent long myself, and he has never seemed a coward to me. Yet," he added, as if just having the thought, "if he did not flee in fear, then he must have left the city for some other reason…"

He waited, giving her plodding mind time to consider it. "You mean treachery," she said finally, her eyes wide.

Grinner shook his head slowly. "I don't know what I mean, Majesty. I hesitate to call anyone a traitor without proof, but then, some might say the proof is clear enough now that he and the others are gone. The rumors say he is in league with Boyce Kevlane himself—I know, I know, a terrible thing to consider, one I can hardly credit. Yet, in all my years of city life, Majesty, one of the things I've learned is that rumors rarely exist without some reason."

The queen nodded slowly, her head moving on her body as if of its own accord, and she looked to Grinner like some ill-used marionette. "Yes. I thank you, as always, for your wisdom, Councilman Grinner. I am grateful that you, at least, have not abandoned m—the city."

Grinner smiled at that. "Of course not, Majesty. My loyalty is, first and foremost, yours to command. I wish only to serve you as best I may and to do my small part to keep you—and the people of this fine city—safe. As to that," he said, leaning forward in his chair, "I believe it might be wise to discuss the woman, May, and Councilman Hale."

The slightest frown creased the queen's heavy features. "They are both imprisoned, are they not?"

"Indeed they are, Majesty."

"They have been questioned," she said. "Captain Gant did it himself. He believes them both innocent of any wrong doing." She glanced at Grinner, one corner of her mouth tilting up in an almost imperceptible half-smile. "He even expressed some doubts about your own sincerity in wanting what is best for myself and Perennia."

Grinner stiffened in anger, and hoped she would take it for no more than hurt. "I do all I do to serve you, Majesty," he said, not having to feign the emotion in his voice, "and would sacrifice more than just my looks, such as they were, to keep you safe." It would be good, he thought, to remind her of what he had given up for her, of what saving her had cost him, but he was surprised by how much rage rose in him at the thought. He took a moment, forcing himself to stay calm. "Still," he continued, "if it is your will, I will leave Perennia and take my men with me—the last thing I want is for you to doubt my loyalty."

"Forgive me, Councilman Grinner," the queen said, her voice almost wheedling now, "I did not mean to offend you. I know well the sacrifice you made for me—Captain Gant is a brave man and a great soldier, but he would be the first to admit that he does not do as well with people as might be desired. A simple man with a soldier's understanding of the world. Still," she went on, her expression troubled, "we will need such men in the coming days."

Yes, Grinner thought, making a mark on the mental tally he kept of anyone who'd wronged him, *a simple man, and one who must be dealt with soon.* "Of course, my Queen. I don't believe anyone could question the captain's loyalty or military knowledge, and he is no doubt a great boon in these troubling times. Still, if you might trust me enough to touch upon the subject of May and Councilman Hale once more..." He hesitated as if awaiting her pleasure, leaving just enough hurt in his voice.

"Oh, of course, Councilman Grinner," she said, "please do not take offense at the captain's words, truly. His opinion is not one I share, for I saw your courage well enough in the courtyard when you risked your own life to slay the two assassins who had come for me."

"Very well, Majesty," Grinner said, bowing his head, "and I am most grateful for your kindness. I was only thinking about the rumors regarding Silent and the others. It seems to me that, if Hale and May *are* traitors, no one would be more likely to know the whereabouts of the sellsword and—perhaps—your sister, than they. I wonder if it wouldn't be too much to ask for you to allow me to interrogate them personally. Though I hold nothing but the highest respect for Captain Gant, such a noble, upstanding man as he may not be as well-versed in the subtleties of criminals and criminal enterprises as my unfortunate life of the streets has taught me—and my men—to be."

The queen nodded thoughtfully. "And you believe that, in questioning them, you might discover some information regarding my sister's whereabouts?"

Grinner didn't miss the childlike hope behind the question. "I cannot know for certain, Majesty," he said, "but I think it worth the effort."

"Very well," she said, "I will tell the captain to allow you, and those men you deem necessary, access to their cells."

"Thank you, my Queen," he said, bowing. "And, if I may, there is one more thing—if, in my questioning, I discover that Councilman Hale and Lady May *are* guilty of treason, what do you wish to have done with them?"

The queen hesitated, looking around as if hoping someone—her royal sister, perhaps, or that bastard Envelar—would appear out of thin air to tell her what to do. "I..." she began, "I don't know." She swallowed hard, not a queen at all, in that moment, but a child waking from a nightmare and looking to an adult for comfort. "What would you have me do, Councilman Grinner?"

Grinner took a moment, as if considering the question, then shook his head slowly. "Given the recent disappearances of so many of the city's leaders, the people are worried, Majesty. They are afraid at a time when we need them to be brave, and they question at a time when they must follow orders. If we are to have any chance of success in the coming battle with Kevlane, we must reassure them that their leader cares for them and, more importantly, is willing to act decisively to protect them. Besides," he added, as if it was no more than an afterthought, "we do not know how many were involved in the conspiracy on your life or, for that matter, the disappearance of your royal sister."

He sighed, meeting her eyes. "Forgive me, Majesty, but I fear that, should my questioning discover the absolute truth of Councilman Hale and Lady May's guilt, we must put our own personal feelings aside and show the people that we are steadfast in our resolve." He shook his head slowly, sadly. "We must execute them both, and it must be done publicly, so the people might see that their leaders do not sit idly by while treachery and death run amok in the city."

"Execute them?" Queen Isabelle breathed, as if the idea had never crossed her thoughts and, given what few thoughts her fool's mind seemed to have, Grinner didn't doubt it. "But surely..."

"I understand your hesitation, Majesty," Grinner said, taking a calculating risk of interrupting her. When she didn't call him down, he smiled once more behind his mask. "Indeed, I share it, for I have known Councilman Hale and Lady May for many years, and despite the fact that our positions have often put us at odds, I think of them both as friends, no doubt as they do myself. In truth, I applaud your hesitation, for it is a demonstration of that unending compassion for which you are known throughout the kingdom of Telrear. Yet, if we should discover they are traitors…"

Queen Isabelle let out a heavy breath and nodded. "Then they must die. The people must be made to feel safe again."

"I fear that it is so, my Queen."

"Very well," she said, reluctantly, then turned to the crime boss and some small bit of strength, of resolve, returned to her face. "But only if they are found to be guilty, Councilman Grinner. I will need unquestionable proof before any action is taken."

"Of course, Majesty," Grinner said, his grin widening behind his silver mask. *And proof you will have. I will make sure of it.*

CHAPTER FOUR

May had been born on the streets, into a life of dubious prospects where, odds were, that before her sixteenth birthday, she would be dead at worst or, at best, become some man's property. She had been born without privilege, without coin or a family name to protect her, yet despite all of that, she had flourished.

The poor girl had grown into a woman, a woman who had spent most of her years not only outmaneuvering two of the city's most powerful crime bosses, but also leading a secret rebellion against a prince. She had made it her life's work to protect the people of Avarest, those unfortunate souls who could not protect themselves. She had even had some success, rescuing more than a few young women—inevitably pretty and also inevitably half-dead inside from the terrors their tormenters had subjected them to—from the clutches of perversions and evils she would not wish on her worst enemy.

In all those years, she had been cautious and careful, aware of the many dangers that lay around every corner, cognizant of those who watched from the shadows, waiting for her to make one fatal mistake, one grievous error in judgment so they might pounce and rid themselves of the meddling woman once and for all. She had been aware of the dangers, yet she had not been afraid.

She was afraid now. Her cell was barely large enough to lie down in which, in truth, was probably just as well. If it were any larger, she would have spent the interminable hours pacing the cell, wearing a furrow in the dirt floor with her worry. As it was, she only sat in the corner, her arms wrapped around her knees, unable to keep herself from starting at every sound. She knew how she must look—filthy, hopeless, her gaze full of a quiet terror, and she hated herself for it. Yet, for all her knowledge, for all her self-loathing, she could not still the tremors of fear that shook her frame from time to time.

The air smelled of dirt and sweat and excrement, a sickening melding that, seemed to her, the stench of hope's decaying carcass, for those who filled the dungeon had long since given up any dream of being saved. Even the cries for help that arose from those cells around her were done without conviction or expectation, more a litany of despair than any true plea for salvation. Scared she might be, but she did not send her own voice up into that tormented chorus, for she knew that to do so would be to sacrifice the last bit of her dignity, to drag a red blade across the throat of her own hope. So instead, she only sat in the corner in silence, save for the sporadic, quiet whimpers that escaped despite her best efforts.

But since being imprisoned, May had been forced to learn some hard truths, and one was that it was only a matter of time before her cries echoed with those of the others, only a matter of time before reason and logic bowed down before desperation and fear, and she believed that, at that moment, she would be truly lost.

She scratched at her itching head, hating the greasy, tangled feel of her hair, and wondered what Thom would think of her now, wondered if news of her imprisonment had even reached him. She prayed to the gods that it had not, for though the first mate was normally kind enough, he had a temper that, when roused, was not easily put to bed, and she feared what he might do if he learned that she was being held in the dungeons. *Like as not the fool will get himself killed.*

The thought sent a fresh shiver of anxiety through her, and a sound somewhere between a whimper and a moan escaped her. She wondered, too, about Silent, about Adina, and the others. She wasn't sure how long she'd been in the dungeons, as there was no means of marking time there save, perhaps, for the arrival of the gruel that served as the prisoners' meals. Yet she had grown to believe that even the food was not brought on a regular basis, as if being unable to mark the passage of time was only one more facet of their punishment.

"*Gods,*" she said, in a voice that was scratchy and tortured and unrecognizable even to her own ears, "*let them be okay.*"

"You're worried about the lad."

May considered pretending she hadn't heard, but knew from experience that if she ignored him, the man would only keep talking, so she raised her head, looking across the dirty, well-paced hallway that ran in between the cells to the one opposite her own. Hale sat with his back propped against the wall of his cell, his massive frame reclined and looking as at ease as if he lounged on a cushioned divan in some brothel instead of in a cold dungeon. The poor, flickering orange light of the dungeon's randomly placed torches did little to reveal any of the crime boss's features, but what May could see of his mostly shadowed face reflected a calm she couldn't credit.

"Of course I do," she said. Normally, she would have snapped the words out, adding just the right amount of acid and venom to keep the man on his toes and show what a foolish statement it was, but she didn't have the energy, and her words came out toneless and dead.

The shadow shifted slightly in what may or may not have been a nod. "Figured as much. Still, I wouldn't."

"Why?" May asked, hating the hope in her voice, the need for reassurance. "You believe he's safe?"

The big crime boss grunted in what might have been a laugh. "How in the name of the Fields would I know, lass?" His thick shoulders moved in what she took for a shrug. "Still, I don't reckon there's a fella out there with more practice at not gettin' dead than our friend Silent. I don't s'pose it'd be wrong to say he's made a career out of it."

May felt some small bit of her usual indignation return, and she rolled her eyes. "Thanks so much for your input," she said.

If the crime boss noted her sarcasm—and he'd have had to be deaf not to—he gave no sign. "No problem," he said. "Anyway, while you're prayin' to the gods, why not put in a word for me and see if they can't bring Bella here, for a spell." He grunted. "Now, there's a whore a man might think of marryin' and turnin' into an honest woman. If, of course, he was the marryin' kind."

May let out her breath in a hiss of frustration, "What is *wrong* with you? We are, in case you haven't noticed, in a *dungeon,* and I doubt very much if Grinner will let us idle here long before he decides to have us killed in whatever manner suits him best."

"Yeah," the giant agreed, "the little bastard's got a heart to match that new face of his." He laughed, a great, bellowing laughter that, despite everything, somehow made May feel calmer. "Anyhow, I might not be the quickest bastard sometimes, but the cell bars did kind of give the dungeon bit away."

"*Damnit,*" May said—practically yelled, in truth. "Don't you take *anything* seriously?"

"Gods forbid," the big man said, "and why would I? Seems to me the world takes itself seriously enough without my help." He leaned forward then, his massive bulk shifting so that his face was only inches from the bars of his cell. "Not to offend you, lady love, but I got a bit of advice I might share with you, if you've a mind to listen."

May opened her mouth to tell the man in no uncertain terms just what he could do with his jokes and his advice both, but she found herself hesitating. *Ah, why not?* After all, however annoying the crime boss might be, his voice was better than the silence, better than listening to the screams for help that would never be answered. She shrugged. "I'm listening."

"Let. It. Go."

May stared at the man, waiting for him to say something else, but he only remained silent, his shadowed form studying her. "What?" she said finally. "Let *what* go? What kind of stupid advice is that?"

"Oh, I think you know well enough what I'm talkin' about, lass, but if you want to play the fool, I won't begrudge you it. Your worry, your thoughts, your *wisdom.* Let it all go. Normally, those things are what give you strength, I know it well enough, and it's those same things as have made you such a burr in my ass over the last years. But they'll only hurt you here. Oh, you hide it well enough, but I reckon I've seen men on the headsman's block less ate up with worry than you."

"Well, forgive me for *worrying*," May snapped. "It's just that, oh, I don't know, I'm in a dungeon, my friends are missing, and a wizard from ancient times is creating an army of monsters to destroy the whole world. I guess maybe I'm just a touch out of sorts."

"Maybe," the crime boss said, "but I don't think so. Seems to me that worryin' and frettin' over this thing or that is one of the biggest reasons why you're as formidable a woman as you are. Always analyzing, always second-guessin' every decision you make, then third-guessin' that. You ask me, you got worry in you right down to your bones."

A shiver of fear and uncertainty ran through May at the man's words. She'd dealt with Hale often enough in the past years, and despite his own prodigious—very nearly legendary—strength, she had always consoled herself with the fact that he was, by all accounts, not particularly intelligent. A man who would have been at home swinging a bloody axe on some ancient battlefield, covered in the blood of his enemies, one who would have been equally comfortable in some tavern, drinking until he passed out, or in some brothel spending a fortune on prostitutes. A warrior, a drunk, a philanderer. But the image of Hale the Scholar had never occurred to her—had seemed, in truth, utterly ridiculous.

Sure, she had thought the man possessed of some animal cunning—after all, a man couldn't rise to the top of such a powerful criminal enterprise as he had without some survival instincts and a sense for where danger lay. But wise? Intelligent? Capable of discerning a secret she had always believed she'd managed to hide except from those closest to her? No. That, she would not have credited him.

To think that all these years he had understood her in a way that few others had, that he had somehow seen past her posturing and her veils to the truth of her was a fearful thing to imagine. "I don't know what you're talking about," she managed finally.

The man shrugged his thick shoulders again, and May was put in mind of massive boulders shifting against each other. "Have it your way, lass. I s'pose every man or woman's got a right to their secrets, and I wouldn't think of refusin' you yours. Yet, my advice ain't changed."

"Let it go," she repeated, unable to keep the mockery from her voice. "And how exactly am I supposed to do that anyway, Hale? In case you haven't noticed, things aren't exactly going according to plan right now."

The crime boss let out another of those great, bellowing laughs. "In my experience, woman, things never do. As for how you let go of all your worries and your fears, I don't know, and I don't much care. But you'd better let 'em go just the same. They might serve you well enough out there," he said, waving his muscled arm in a vague gesture to indicate the world outside the dungeon, "but they've no place here. Forget what'll happen tomorrow, or what happened yesterday. One's a book already written, and the other a book you'll probably never get a chance to read. You just keep your mind on right now. The sun'll rise tomorrow, or it won't, and your worryin' about it won't do you any good—not here."

May frowned. "That's an easy enough thing to say, but not so easy to do. And I don't think that the answer to our problems is going to be in sitting here refusing to think."

Hale grunted. "Any of those thoughts of yours gonna open up these cell doors for us?"

The club owner's frown deepened. "Well, no, but—"

"How 'bout the guards then?" the crime boss pressed. "Any of your worryin' and thinkin' gonna get them to come on in here and apologize, tell us it was all a mistake, and they're ever so sorry for the bother?"

"*No, damnit,*" May hissed. "But what's your solution then? Just sit here and wait until Grinner finds some excuse to have us killed? Just march to our executions—if he even allows us to leave our cells alive, that is—with smiles on our faces? Gods forbid you do some *thinking*. Best we just let whatever is going to happen happen—no use putting up a fuss, is that it?"

In the flickering orange torchlight, the crime boss's eyes seemed to shine with hunger. "Oh, no, lass. I didn't say that—not at all. I reckon that, when the time comes, I'll put up a fuss right enough."

CHAPTER FIVE

Wendell yawned as he made his way out of the Akalians' barracks and into the night. Though he'd been awake for nearly two hours, he felt as if he could fall asleep standing, a natural enough side effect, according to the Speaker, of the herb Wendell and the others had received. His vision felt blurry, his feet uncertain beneath him as if he'd spent a long night drinking. He'd always heard—and said it himself, of course—that a man ought to have a hair of the dog that bit him to keep the worst of the hangover at bay, but he figured that whatever dog had latched on to him with the herb the Akalians gave him had damn near swallowed him whole.

Of course, that hadn't stopped him from finding some more of the herb—crushed into a fine powder and stored in one of the few cabinets the barracks had—and eating a handful shortly after waking. Now, though, he felt even more tired, almost felt as if he weren't in control of his body at all, and he reflected—not for the first time since the impulse to take more of the herb had come and gone—that maybe there was a reason why the wisdom of drunks was theirs and theirs alone. No one else, he figured, was stupid enough to believe it.

But despite the powerful urge to sleep, the sergeant refused its embrace. For one, he'd seen more comfortable "beds" than the ones the Akalians offered in alleyways and, more importantly, despite the princess's earlier words, he wasn't completely convinced that the Akalians didn't eat people, and what better

A Sellsword's Mercy

time to take a bite out of a man—if you've a mind to—than when he was sleeping? Oh, he'd checked himself over as well as he could when he woke, but there'd been no looking glass in his room, so he couldn't be sure, and being eaten, so far as Wendell was concerned, wasn't the type of thing a man took a chance on.

So he walked out into the night, concentrating on putting one foot in front of the other as he made his laborious way toward the tree line. He'd no sooner made it there than a shadow separated itself from among the trees, and he tensed as one of the Akalians, dressed all in black, stepped out to move in front of him.

Ah gods, Wendell thought, *here it comes.* "Hi there, fella." The Akalian didn't answer. *Probably trying to decide which bit looks the tastiest.* "Pleasant night, ain't it?" Wendell ventured, trying again.

Still, the Akalian did not speak, only stared at him with those unreadable eyes, and Wendell frowned, his mind racing. "Anyway," he said, as off-handed as he could manage, "I ain't nothin' but blood and bone. 'Case you were wonderin'. Not enough fat on me to feed a mongrel dog."

The black-garbed man turned and walked back in the direction from which he'd come, his inscrutable gaze resting on the forest beyond. "Not much for small talk," he muttered, unable to decide whether he was offended that the man hadn't responded to him, or grateful that he must have already eaten. "Suits me fine, anyway," he said to himself. "I've got to piss like nobody's business."

With that, he pulled his trousers down and suited actions to words. He had only just gotten a good start when a voice spoke from behind him. "They don't actually eat people, you know."

Wendell started, fumbling his grip. "Damnit," he said, turning to see the youth, Caleb, walking up. "Oh, it's the kid. How's it goin' with you?"

"I'm okay," Caleb said, staring off into the woods. Then, as if it was an afterthought, he turned to Wendell. "How are you?"

"Damp," the sergeant muttered, fastening his trousers. "Anyway, how do you know they don't eat people? Just 'cause you ain't seen it don't mean nothin'. I ain't never seen a woman take a sh—err...do her necessaries. But that don't mean it don't happen."

The youth shrugged, as if it wasn't worth speaking on any further, his eyes still locked on the forest. A strange kid, but

Wendell wasn't surprised. Every smart person he'd ever met had been a little strange, and it seemed to him the more they knew, the stranger they got. If the Virtues were as powerful as everybody seemed to think, then he figured the kid might be the smartest person in the world. The poor bastard. "Anyway," he said, stifling a yawn, "anybody else up yet?"

Caleb shook his head. "They weren't when I awoke at any rate. The herb the Akalians used did its work well, I think. I asked what it was called, but they would not tell me, and I'm not surprised. I've never heard of a sedative as efficacious as this one." He made a thoughtful sound in his throat. "I wonder if it is only more potent in its natural form or if it is noxious. Perhaps, it is important to dilute it into some..."

The kid went on, but he might as well have been speaking a different language for all Wendell understood of it, and it seemed to him that each word the youth spoke made his vision blur even more. "Well," he said, nodding thoughtfully. "Pleasant night, ain't it?"

Caleb turned to him, cutting off his monologue midstream—thank the gods. Then he looked up at the sky as if noticing it was dark for the first time. *Poor bastard,* Wendell thought again. "I suppose so," the youth conceded.

Wendell heaved a sigh of relief. Apparently, the boy spoke the common tongue, after all. "So," the sergeant ventured, "you reckon the general and the others will be up soon?"

"The others, yes," Caleb said, nodding. "As for Aaron...his dose was considerably higher than ours, judging from what the Speaker told me. I suspect on an order of four to five times as much, though I can't be sure. Also, it must be considered that liquid has a faster absorption rate, as well as a higher optimization rate, than other forms. In truth, I went to visit General Envelar first, upon waking, fearing that so large an application of a soporific such as the Akalians used might put him in danger. Thankfully, however, he seemed well."

Wendell blinked. "Right. So...do you reckon he'll wake up soon?"

Caleb turned and looked at him for several seconds, then finally shrugged. "I don't know."

And why couldn't you have just said that in the first place? Wendell thought. He considered saying as much, but the youth had already turned away again.

"They're out there," Caleb said in a frightened voice, and for the first time he sounded like a kid instead of some dusty scholar who'd spent his life bent over ancient tomes.

Wendell grunted, putting his hand on the boy's shoulder. "They'll keep for a while yet, lad."

The youth turned to him, studying him with wide eyes. "How do you know?"

The sergeant smiled. "My ma used to say that the world has its own truths, and most of those can't be found in a book." Wendell considered that, his smile slowly fading, then shrugged. "Never really understood what she meant, to tell you the truth. But one thing I do know is they won't find us until the general and the others have woken, so you can rest easy on that score."

"But how do you *know?*" the youth pressed, clearly wanting to be comforted.

Because if they do, we're all dead. But, somehow, Wendell didn't think that was what the youth needed to hear, so he met the boy's eyes, his own expression as solemn as he could make it. "Do you really want to know?"

The boy nodded eagerly, and Wendell glanced around as if someone might be listening, then leaned in close. "Because, lad, last night…I dreamed I was a bird." The youth blinked at him, and Wendell gave him a wink, patting him on the back.

"A…bird?"

"That's right," the sergeant said, deciding to leave out the fact that he had actually been a chicken and that, in his dream, the Akalians had been fighting over who got to eat him. "Now," he continued, deciding he'd best make his retreat before the boy had time to think it over, "I'm for bed. Goodnight, lad."

"Goodnight," Caleb said in a halting voice, clearly still mulling over the sergeant's words.

Wendell turned and started away, grinning as he did. Let the boy's mind work on that for a while. He'd only taken a few steps when he decided he'd best ask the Speaker if they had a wash basin somewhere. *They'd better not find us,* he thought, wincing at the damp feel of his trousers with each step he took, *not tonight, at any rate. I'll be damned if I die covered in my own piss.*

CHAPTER SIX

Aaron surfaced slowly into consciousness, buoyed on the gently lapping waves of a dream he couldn't quite remember. He yawned, opening his eyes to find that he was in a room he didn't recognize. It was small and unfurnished, reminding him of the barracks back in Perennia. Normally, the fact that he had no idea where he was or how he'd come to be there would have been cause for concern, but his mind felt filled with a fog, one which dampened his emotions and left him with nothing but a vague contentment he could not explain.

He *was* curious—in an unfocused, distracted sort of way—but he felt no particular urgency to assuage his curiosity. There was a strange lethargy seeping through his body and his mind both, one that made it difficult for him to remember all of the things that he should be worried about, that made it difficult, in fact, for him to worry at all.

He thought about getting out of bed and doing some exploring to figure out where he was, but he decided against it. The bed beneath him was soft, the covers warm, and he couldn't summon the energy to leave them just yet.

"It's the drug," a voice said from beside him. "Again, I am very sorry about that."

There was a man standing beside the bed. "Hey," the sellsword said, his thoughts fuzzy. "You were in my dream."

The man was dressed all in black, but his face was uncovered, and Aaron could see the slow smile that spread across it. "That is, perhaps, one way of looking at it. Though, in truth, you were awake when last we spoke."

Aaron nodded, more because it seemed required than anything else. "As you say," he mumbled, then he closed his eyes and felt himself drifting down to sleep.

A hand settled on his shoulder, and he reluctantly opened his eyes once more. "Forgive me," the man said, "but I fear that our time grows short, and there is much I must tell you—much you must understand."

"Of course," Aaron said, studying the man's serious, somehow sad expression. He realized there was something odd about the man's face, a sort of timeless quality to his features, and Aaron couldn't even guess at his age. He could have been anywhere between twenty and eighty years old. His voice, though, spoke of great experience, of the wisdom that only comes from a long life full of joy and sadness both. The sort of voice that...

He woke to someone shaking his arm and frowned slightly. "Just going to sleep a little, is all," he muttered. "Wake me later."

"There's no time," the man said again. "Many people are in danger, and even now their lives hang in the balance. You must awake, Aaron Envelar, for there is much for you to learn and little time in which to do it. The fate of the world hangs in the balance."

Aaron yawned. "The fate of the world always hangs in the balance."

"Perhaps," the voice answered. "And Adina? What of her?"

Aaron snapped fully awake at that, the events of the last few days crashing down on him in rapid succession. He remembered flames dancing in the darkness, the silver streak of blades in the night. He remembered Kevlane's creatures and their captives, his friends, staked to the ground in a clearing as if waiting for their execution. He sat up in bed, glancing around the small room. "My sword," he said. "Where's my sword?"

"It is safe. Now, please," the man said, "you may relax here. You are in no immediate danger."

"Relax?" Aaron demanded. "Are you out of your damned mind? Look," he said, remembering the Akalians carrying him away from the battle, "I don't know why you took me or what your plans are, but if you get in the way of me helping my friends—"

"Your friends are safe," the man assured him.

"Safe?" Aaron said. "What in the name of the gods do you mean? I don't even know where Adina is, and the last I saw of the others they were staked to a clearing—"

"Not any longer," the Speaker of the Akalians interrupted. "They are as safe as any can be in these times. They are here, in the barracks, where they have been for the past three days. As is Princess Adina."

Aaron breathed a heavy sigh of relief at that, but then something the man had said struck him. "Three days? What are you talking about?"

The Speaker sighed, nodding. "I'm afraid that you have slept for three days, Aaron. The fault of the herbal mixture in the darts which struck you. Normally, we do not use so much, but you were particularly resistant to the effects, and we were forced to take drastic measures. In truth, I was not sure when you would wake, or if you would wake at all."

Aaron studied the man, frowning. "Particularly resistant. Yeah, not the first time I've been drugged. But that means…my dream…it was real."

"Yes."

"Then there really are eight Virtues," Aaron said, "not seven as everyone believed."

"Yes."

The sellsword grunted. "I think it best you show me to Adina and the others—then I'll have some questions for you that need answering."

Co? he asked silently, *are you there?* There was no answer, and his frown deepened.

"If you are wondering at your Virtue's absence," the Speaker said as if reading his thoughts, "then I can assure you that she is, at least, safe. Once assured of your well-being, she has spent these three days with her father, Lord Caltriss. It is a reunion that has been thousands of years in the making, and one that I dared not begrudge them."

Aaron nodded, rising from the bed. "Adina and the others—show me."

***

The Speaker led Aaron past rooms appointed similarly to his own, eventually stopping in front of a doorway with a small window built into it. On the other side of the door, he could see Adina, Leomin, Gryle, Caleb, and Wendell. They were all eating, save for Adina herself, who was speaking to one of the black-garbed figures standing at the side of the room. Aaron couldn't hear what she was saying, but he knew that expression well enough—it was the face she got when she thought he was being particularly stupid and had it in mind to educate him. Though Aaron felt a great surge of relief at seeing her and the others safe, he didn't much begrudge the Akalian the tongue-lashing he was no doubt getting. But if Adina's anger bothered the black-garbed man he gave no sign, only standing and weathering the princess's tirade without comment or reaction.

Aaron reached for the door, but the Speaker grabbed his arm, forestalling him. The sellsword turned with a frown. "Look, I appreciate what you did, saving them, but if you don't let go of my arm right now, we're going to put that legendary skill of you Akalians to the test."

"I understand your desire to see her and the others, to speak to them," the Speaker said, his voice calm, "but on the blood of my brothers who gave their lives to rescue you and your companions, I ask that you allow me to show you something first."

"The blood of your brothers," Aaron said, remembering the black-garbed figures that had appeared in the torchlight, striking down several of Kevlane's creatures before they had a chance to react and then staying and battling it out with them. Despite their impressive skill, the Akalians had stood no real chance of victory. *But, then,* he realized, *they never meant to win.* They hadn't fought the creatures with the hopes of defeating them, but only so Aaron and the others might be rescued. They had fought, and they had died, for him and the others. "How many?" he asked, his voice low and harsh.

The Speaker took a moment to answer, and Aaron thought he saw some great emotion pass through the man's eyes, but it was gone in another instant. "Sixty of my brothers began their journey to the long dark in the forest clearing."

Aaron nodded slowly, feeling numb. "And how many of you are there left?"

"Less than two dozen of us remain," the Speaker said, and though his expression did not change, Aaron thought he could hear some of the pain, some indication of the true loss the man had experienced beneath the surface of his words.

"Why?" It was the only thing Aaron could think to ask, for he found that he needed some explanation, some reason why those men might have thrown their lives away.

"For you," the Speaker said. "And for the others."

"A bad deal you made for me, at least, Speaker," the sellsword said, his voice nearly too low to hear. "But I thank you for saving the others."

"You are wrong, you know," the speaker said. "You still do not understand the role that you will play. How important you are."

Aaron grunted. "I'm not worth this—maybe there are those who are, but I'm not one of them." He couldn't resist glancing back through the window then, watching Adina. As angry as she clearly was, he had never seen anything so beautiful, so perfect. *There*, he thought, *there is a woman worth fighting for, worth dying for.* "You should go back to wherever you came from, Speaker," he said, still watching Adina. "I thank you for what you did, but you should take yourself and the rest and go back to the others."

"The others?"

Aaron turned then. "The rest of you. The other Akalians."

The Speaker frowned, and there was a profound sadness there of which that frown was only the barest glimpse. "You misunderstand, Aaron Envelar. There are no others, no home to which we might go. We, here, are the last of the Akalians."

Aaron stared at the man in shock. "Gods, you can't be serious. Well, then you *have* to go! Get out while you still can, while there are any of you left to escape."

The man gave a slow smile at that, and he shook his head. "Forgive me, Aaron Envelar, but the mission of the Akalians is not to survive—it never has been. And not even you might tell us where we will go, for we are not finished here—not yet."

"Not even me?" Aaron said. "What does that mean?"

The Speaker nodded. "Come," he said, beckoning Aaron to follow. "I will show you."

The sellsword hesitated, glancing through the window once more at Adina and the others. May was not with them, he saw, and that was something, at least. She, it seemed, had been smart enough to stay away. Anyway, it was clear that whatever the Akalians wanted from Aaron and the others, they didn't mean them any harm. *Sixty men.* "Okay," he said, turning back to the Speaker. "Show me."

***

The Speaker led Aaron past empty room after empty room, each identical to the one in which he'd awoken. "What is this place, anyway? Where are we?"

The Speaker glanced at him, continuing to walk down the hallway. "As for where we are, we are still within the forest outside of Perennia, though, admittedly, some distance from where you fought the Lifeless."

Aaron frowned. "The Lifeless?"

"It is what we call the magi's creatures. In truth, there is some little life left, but only enough that one might gaze upon them and feel the absence of what is missing. The magi, in his incredible power, shapes them, ripping out those things that make them human and leaving, in their place, an ever-hungry void."

Aaron grunted. "Lifeless, huh? Well, as good a name as any for them. Still, if this Boyce Kevlane is as all-powerful as you say, it seems to me that he would be better off sending the dead at us. These things aren't easy to kill, sure, but they *do* die."

"You speak of reanimation," the Speaker said, his voice dark, "of creating perversions that are the antithesis to life itself. Boyce Kevlane is a magi of the ancient order, the most powerful of his kind in the history of the world...yet, Shadow be praised, such workings of the Art are beyond even such as he."

"Are you sure?" Aaron asked. "Because it seems to me that he's been learning some new tricks. There was one in the forest, one that was different from the others—"

"Yes," the Speaker said, the slightest bit of worry entering into his normally placid tone, "the abomination. He is unique, but he will not be for long. You see, the magi is, in some ways, like an artist. A sculptor, perhaps, or a painter—"

"I think you might have Kevlane all wrong," Aaron interrupted. "As far as I know, paintings rarely come to life and start killing everyone around them, and sculptures don't move faster than a galloping horse."

The Speaker nodded his head as if to concede the point. "Yes, but, like Kevlane, a sculptor or a painter's work only has as much potential as the materials he uses. A man cannot build a house from sand, nor can a sword be fashioned from water. In this, they are the same, for though Kevlane's Art is powerful, his workings cannot exceed the materials upon which he uses them."

"People," Aaron said. "You mean people."

"Yes."

Aaron considered that, thinking back to the creature in the clearing, the one who had been stronger than the others and, with a shock, realized that, despite the scarring that had covered its face, something about it struck him as familiar. It took him a moment, but finally the face—and the name—crashed into his mind. Savrin. The man who he had left at the gate when they escaped the city, the man who he had told to go back to his sister. Apparently, the man had not listened. *The poor bastard.*

He rubbed at his eyes, feeling suddenly very weary. "So you're saying that he hasn't been able to create more like Savrin because, what? The people he has to experiment on haven't been good enough?"

The Speaker shrugged. "Good or bad—how may one man judge the worth of another in such a way? Say only that water has its uses—to a man in the far reaches of the desert, there is nothing of more value and, to such a man, water is a savior. It is water that gives life to plants, to the animals of the forest and plain and, in the end, to us. Yet, a carpenter who chooses to fashion a house from it is a fool, for there are other mediums he might use, ones better suited to the task. Say, then, that the people on which the magi has been working his Art aren't 'bad'—only that they are ill-suited for his purposes."

"Shit," Aaron said, freezing in the hallway. "Kevlane is planning a tournament—if what you're saying is true—"

"Yes," the Speaker agreed. "Very soon, the magi will have all of the warriors he needs to create an army of creatures greater even than those which we now face."

"Exactly," Aaron said, feeling impatience rise in him. "That's exactly why I and the others have to leave. Now. Don't you understand that with each moment we delay, Kevlane grows stronger? The tournament is set to start any day now, and if we don't make it to Baresh before that—"

"The tournament has started already," the Speaker said. "Yet still warriors flock to Baresh by the score in search of fame and fortune."

"Damnit man," Aaron said, "then don't you get it? You have to let us go."

The Speaker shook his head. "It does a man no good to rush to the battle only to find that he has no weapons with which to fight, to realize that he doesn't even know *how* to fight."

"And what?" Aaron said, unable to keep the annoyance out of his voice. "You're going to give us weapons?"

The Speaker shook his head again. "You already have the weapons—I'm going to show you how to use them."

Aaron sighed. "I don't want to sound like an asshole here, but if I don't know how to use weapons after all this time, I never will."

The Speaker stopped walking and turned to him. He reached out with a speed that was shocking and grabbed Aaron's wrists. He pulled upward so that Aaron was looking at his own hands. "You know how to use these," the Speaker said. "With them, you might slay many men, many of the Lifeless but, in the end, you will fall." He let Aaron's hands drop and pointed at his mouth. "This weapon, too, you know well the use of. With it, you would command thousands of blades, would bring the full force of them to bear on Baresh, on the magi and his armies. Those soldiers would follow you willingly, conquered by the power of your speech, and they would follow you to their deaths."

Aaron frowned, forcing himself to remain calm. "Well, if what you're saying is true, then we're all fucked anyway—but know this, Speaker, if I'm going to die, I mean to do it with a blade in my hand."

"Spoken like a true warrior," the Speaker said in a voice which held no emotion. "A true fool."

Aaron grunted at that, and opened his mouth to retort, but the Speaker went on. "Whether you die with a sword in your hand or without, you and those who believe in you would be dead just the same. No," he said, slamming his open hand on Aaron's chest hard enough to make the sellsword take an involuntary step back. "*This* is the weapon you must use—this is the one for which you have no understanding. You are like a child swinging naked steel—you like the feel of it in your hands, but you have no understanding of what it means when the blade cuts."

"My heart? Is that what you mean?" Aaron said. "Because, in my experience, a sword is more use in a fight any day."

"Yes," the Speaker said, a slight smile rising on his face. "In your experience. Still, there is time, if only a little. And do not believe yours is a unique problem, for many men go through life never understanding what power lies inside them, hordes of children each swinging their own swords and then acting surprised when someone is hurt. You, though…" He leaned close, meeting Aaron's eyes. "You are different. If other men carry swords, then you have an army of thousands of them. You cannot afford to continue as you have, cannot afford to ignore the best weapon you have, for while other men might, in their ignorance and lack of understanding, leave one or two wounded and bleeding from the passage of their life, you, if you do not learn, will leave thousands, not wounded, but dead."

"No pressure then," Aaron said sardonically. "Anyway, you were going to show me something?"

The Speaker studied him for a moment then nodded. "Yes. This way."

They continued deeper into the barracks, passing one empty room after another. They saw a few other black-garbed men as they walked, but not many, and the truth of their sacrifice was brought home to Aaron anew. He was still walking after the Speaker when a form lying in the bed of one of the rooms they passed caught his eye, and he stopped, staring. "That woman…" he said, remembering when he'd entered the clearing. "I've seen her before."

"Yes," the Speaker said, and though his voice was still calm and collected on the surface, Aaron thought he detected a hint of what might have been impatience underlying his tone. "What I want to show you is this way. If you'll follow—"

"Hold on a minute," Aaron said, casting his mind back to the clearing, remembering the woman on her hands and knees, bloody but not quite unconscious. Nor, he recalled, had she been staked to the ground like Leomin and the others. He turned to the Speaker. "Who is she?"

There was a definite tenseness to the Akalian's posture now, but when he spoke his voice was calm enough. "Only another that was saved from the Lifeless; she need not concern you. Now, if you will—"

Aaron frowned. He'd grown up in the Downs, had spent his life dealing with criminals, and he'd grown proficient in detecting lies or half-truths. The Speaker was hiding something. "Just wait. From what you've told me, I think I can understand why you saved me and my friends, and maybe I am a bumbling child swinging a sword around, but I know deceit when I see it." He pointed a finger at the sleeping figure, his gaze never leaving the Akalian. "In the clearing, the night the others were taken, she was there."

The Speaker's expression was, as usual, unreadable, but there was a stiffness to his jaw that Aaron thought hadn't been there before. "Yes."

"'Yes?'" Aaron repeated. "That's it? A minute ago, you couldn't seem to talk enough, but now all of a sudden you've nothing to say?" He shook his head. "Look, I appreciate what you and your men did—the sacrifice you made to save us—but people I care about have suffered, some have even died, because I didn't know enough of what was going on. Now, I'm not following you anywhere before you tell me who she is and why she's here."

The Speaker sighed. "Will you not take my word that she is of no danger to you or your friends, and that she will in no way impede your fight with the magi and his minions?"

Aaron considered that for a moment, then shook his head. "No. I'm sorry, but no. I've had enough of secrets in the past few months to last me a lifetime. I know you helped us, and I'm grateful, but I'm not taking another step without some answers. All I know is that she was in the clearing with the others and that she looked as if someone had struck her over the head. I may not understand as much about Kevlane and his followers as you seem to, but I know enough to know that he loves treachery and betrayal. I've nearly lost count of the number of assassination attempts I've witnessed since I came to Perennia, and it seems to me that a clever bastard like Kevlane might just place a wounded 'innocent' with the others, on the off-chance that she gets into a position where she can betray us or kill one of those people I want to protect."

The Speaker's face twitched, a crack appearing in his seemingly unflappable composure. "She is *not* one of Kevlane's creatures, nor is she in his employ."

Aaron shrugged. "Not good enough. You can say that, but I know what I saw, and it is suspicious enough. How can you be sure that she isn't—"

"*Because she's my daughter!*" the Speaker roared, his voice thick with emotion, and the mask of calm fell away completely, leaving a face twisted with fear and untold grief.

Aaron studied the man. "Your daughter."

The Akalian took a slow, deep breath as if gathering his calm once more, but he was not fully able to banish the emotion from his face. "Yes."

"I didn't think the Akalians *had* children."

The Speaker turned away as if unable to meet the sellsword's gaze and studied the young woman lying in the bed, fast asleep despite his shouting. "We do not."

"You're going to have to explain," Aaron said, sorry for the pain that thoughts of the woman caused the Speaker, but not sorry enough to risk the lives of Adina and the others.

The Speaker sighed heavily. "You will not be satisfied that she is of no consequence in your quest and leave it at that?"

Aaron didn't answer, only watched him, and finally the black-garbed man nodded, a sadness gathering in his eyes that was hard to look upon. "Very well. If you must know the truth of it, then I will tell you, but I warn you that I have never told anyone else of these things—not anyone—and the telling of them will be...difficult."

Aaron nodded. "In my experience, most things that matter are."

"Yes," the Speaker said, still studying the girl. "You are right, of course."

Still, he hesitated, and the sellsword only stood in silence, waiting for the man to recall the memories which seemed to cause him such pain. Finally, the Akalian began to speak, and his voice seemed to come from a long way off, as if some physical part of him were being pulled back into the past. "Thirty years ago, I and some of my brothers heard rumors from the southern reaches of Telrear, rumors of monsters that wore the skin of men, ones that felt no pain and attacked anyone who came close."

"Kevlane's creatures," Aaron said thoughtfully.

The Speaker nodded. "Yes. Or so we thought. Had it been only one voice speaking such things, we might have dismissed them, but there were many, and so three of us went to investigate, to discover the truth of things." His gaze grew distant as he looked back on that time so long ago. "As we traveled south, we began to hear more and more talk of the monsters, and where the rumors we had heard to that point had all been of a man's, wife's, cousin who had a friend who'd seen the creatures himself, or something equally uncertain, now we met several who claimed to have laid eyes on them personally. Or, perhaps 'met' is the wrong word, for then, as now, my brothers and I are viewed with fear or open hatred by the people of Telrear.

"Still, over the years, we have learned how to see without being seen, how to hear without being heard, and soon there was too much evidence to believe the claims anything but the truth. And so we traveled on, sleeping in the forests, while forests there were, crossing mountains, sheltering on the desert plains, and never coming too close to any human settlements—growing fewer and further between as we journeyed—that we came upon.

"It took over two months of traveling, but finally we came upon the village from which the rumors had originated. It was a small place of only a few hundred, its people carving out a living in the desert, subsisting largely off of the flesh of reptiles and bugs and what few plants would grow in that sand-covered wasteland. They were a people as hard as the sand-scoured mountain upon which they'd built their homes, not given to idle speech or entertainment, for all their energy was spent scraping out a living in a place that seemed, to me, wholly unwelcoming to the step of man."

Aaron grunted. "Seems to me that they should have looked for a new place to live—if the sands wanted the village, I say let them have it."

"Do you?" the Speaker asked, as if genuinely curious. He made a thoughtful sound in his throat. "And what of your own life, I wonder? A life spent with one eye always to the shadows in search of some killer or thief who may or may not be there, a life spent always looking over your shoulder, never able to trust those you would call friend." He noted Aaron's surprised expression and nodded. "Yes, Aaron Envelar, I know much about you, but let us leave that, for now. I will say only that as hard as the lives of the people of that village might have been, they were lives, at least, that they understood, and the dangers ones with which they were long acquainted. Sufficient reason, I suspect, for most men to remain where they are, for though the world beyond their own might hold wonders beyond any they have known, it might also hold terrors, ones that their lives have not prepared them for. The same reason, I suspect," he said, meeting Aaron's eyes, "that you chose to remain in your own world with its own terrors."

"Alright, alright," Aaron said. "So what happened?"

"We saw nothing amiss upon our arrival to the outskirts of that village, and we could not gather our information in the normal way, for, as I've said, the people of that place spoke little and gossiped less. They were a practical people, and would have had little time for wiling away the hours in some tavern, drinking and sharing stories, even had there been such a place for them to meet, and there was not. So, my brothers and I took the only option available to us—we waited. We stayed outside that village for nine days, far away, hidden by the scorching sands well enough that we might not be discovered, but close enough, or so we hoped, that we might be made aware when the creatures came back.

"I will not waste your time describing the difficulty of those nine days spent surviving off only what little sustenance the sands would provide. For though we have many talents, we Akalians knew little of how to live in such a harsh environment as the one we now faced. I will say only that, on the eighth day, one of our number fell and did not rise again—though whether from hunger, thirst, or simple exhaustion I could not say for sure. We two that remained were weakened greatly, our well-honed muscles, trained over years spent in practice, were flaccid and weak, our disciplined minds, strengthened by years spent in prayers to the Shadow, were ravished and frail. Even our eyes, once so keen, were blurred by days spent looking at the shifting, sun-battered sand.

"Our ears, though, worked well enough, and so it was that we heard the screams—roars of anger, more than anything else—from the distant village. Not that a man would have needed particularly good hearing to pick them out, for there was little else to hear in that desert save the wind and the constant susurration of the shifting sands, a sound not unlike the warning hiss of those poisonous snakes which called that place home. We set off immediately, our hearts full of sadness for the people but also full of relief that we might be able to complete our mission, that we might discover the truth of that place's evils and put those lonely mountains and dunes of sand behind us. I will not say we ran, for our weakened bodies were capable of little more than a crooked, desperate shamble, yet shamble we did until finally we came upon the outskirts of the village itself.

"The people of that village had many enemies, but those enemies were starvation and thirst, baking heat in the day and freezing temperatures at night. They had no mortal enemies, for they had nothing worth taking. This was the reason, then, why the village had no walls except for those only a few feet high that served not as a barrier against enemy forces but against the driving sand which always threatened to bury the settlement of people that had dared take up residence there, returning to the desert what was rightfully its own. They were hard men, but they were not warriors.

"So they were not ready for what came upon them. By the time my companion and I made it to the village, two of its menfolk lay dead on the ground, their blood steaming on the sun-baked sand. We thought that, surely, we had come upon our enemy at last, had found him where he'd hidden so far away from the world, yet when we made our way into the village square, such as it was, where the carnage was still taking place, it was not the Lifeless which had set upon the villagers, but more than twenty men and women gone mad from the desert heat and a great sickness which had come upon them.

"For these, we saw, were victims of the wasting sickness, their faces shriveled, their gazes fevered and mad, and when we closed with them and drew near enough to give battle, we found that even their flesh was hot to the touch, nearly enough to leave blisters on any who came into contact with them. Still, I understood at once why rumors of monsters had reached so far into Telrear, for they did not fight like men but like beasts—they carried no weapons save for those the gods had given them, nails and teeth, and they showed no concern for their own welfare as they attacked, three or four dragging down the more unfortunate of the villagers and feasting upon their flesh even as my companion and I slew them.

"They did not show any concern for our blades, and when wounded they gave no sign, for the Wasting Sickness had combined with the madness to drive out any understanding of pain or self-preservation. Our task was made more difficult still by the fact that the villagers, with cries of "demon" attacked us as well as their persecutors, and we did what we could to fend them off without giving them serious injury."

"Gods," Aaron breathed, picturing in his mind what must have been mass-confusion as the two exhausted Akalians fought against the mad while, at the same time, being forced to defend themselves against those they'd come to save. "It must have been terrible."

"Yes," the Speaker agreed. "It was. The battle, if battle it might be called, lasted no more than half an hour, if that, but in my weakened state it felt an eternity." He paused for a moment, sighing heavily. Just when Aaron thought that he wasn't going to go on, he began once more. "I do not know when my companion was brought down, do not know even whether it was the occupants of that place or those given over to the madness which gave him his death. I know only that we fought together for a time, he at my back, and that once, when I had a moment to glance behind me, he was no longer standing as he had been, but lying on the ground, still as only the dead can be.

"I remember little of that time, only the weight of the sword in my hand, heavier than I could have ever imagined, the burning, feverish wounds in my flesh where the mad ones had scored it with teeth and nails and, more than either of those, the grief I felt as my sword did its bloody work. For despite what men think of us, we Akalians are not monsters, just as those I fought were not monsters, only men and women driven mad from sickness and suffering. Yet there could be no reasoning with them, for what the desert had left of them was not human any longer, but only cruel, unthinking beasts.

"When the last was slain and lay dead on the sands, I turned to those villagers for which my brother had given his life and saw, in their faces, only hatred. They cursed me, naming me demon and worse, and I left with what speed I might, driven on despite my wounds and, in many ways, because of them, for I knew that to be vulnerable there, among those men, would be as good as death, and I was not yet ready for the True Dark.

"I do not know how long I walked into the desert, any sense of where I was or where I was going lost to the fevered pain which afflicted me. I know only that I walked, putting as much distance as I could between myself and the villagers with their hate, between myself and those poor souls I had slain as well as my dead brother. Yet for all my reasons for walking away, for all my knowledge of what would happen to me should the villagers find me in my weakened state, my body finally used up the last of its strength, and I collapsed to the ground, unable even to move my face off of the burning sand on which it lay.

"I waited, then, for my death to come upon me, to hear the footsteps of Salen at my back, accompanied by Akane, the Dark Watcher, there to ensure the treatment of his loyal servant. But when the footsteps came, they belonged neither to the Death God or my own, but to a woman. She spoke to me, though in my delirious, dying state, I knew not the content of her words, only their tone—soft, caring words spoken to calm and reassure, words that, it seemed to me, did not belong in such a place, in such a wilderness.

"I gave no answer to them, for I could not, and the last thing I remember before unconsciousness took me was the taste of cool water upon my lips, a feeling greater and more powerful than any I have felt before or since."

"She saved you," Aaron said.

The Speaker smiled then, and it was a fragile thing, one of joy and pain both. "Yes, and in more ways than one. When I woke, it was dark, and I lay inside a small tent, large enough to accommodate me with only a little room to spare. I was covered in blankets which did much to drive away the night's freezing cold, and a water skin lay beside me. I do not lie to say that I drank heavily of that skin—too heavily, as it turned out, for soon I threw up much of what I had taken. Yet I could not stop, for the cool moisture felt like the touch of the gods themselves in that scorched, barren place.

"She returned a short time later with food to eat. She was beautiful, Aaron Envelar, even as sick and fevered as I was, I could see that. Possessed of a beauty that somehow reflected the wild, loneliness of that place, yet held a softness as well, as if she was born of two worlds, and I remember thinking that one such as she did not belong in that place, that one so perfect might not, in truth, belong in this world at all."

He shook his head as if to banish some errant thought. "I will say no more of her than that, only that, for the first time in my life, I felt a need for something more than the training to which my life had been dedicated, to the purpose for which my brothers and I strove. And I will not recount for you the time she and I spent in that tent as she snuck away from her village—the same one I had left—to minister to me and bring me back to health. I will say only that, over those days and nights when we were together, we grew to care for one another, and I grew to love her more than anything in my life. Where once I had worshipped the Shadow God, now I worshipped her."

He paused, and Aaron watched a range of emotions flicker across his face, joy and pain intermingled so tightly that one could not be separated from the other. "In time," he went on, "I grew stronger, and regained some of my old self. And as my health grew, so too, did our love for one another, and I decided I would renounce my dedication to the Shadow God, would abandon my brothers and our cause, for my love of her made all else without purpose. I thought it no great matter, for the brothers who had accompanied me on that journey had both ventured to the long dark of death. It was, then, believable enough that I, too, might have met the same fate."

He smiled. "Time passed, as it always does, and I made us a home hidden from the villagers just as our love was hidden, for in all the places that I have been in my life, of all the peoples I have met, none hated my kind as much as those living in that cruel place, and we left them to believe that I had died somewhere in that scorched wilderness. It wasn't long before she bore my child, a young daughter in whose perfect face our love was brought to life and evidenced."

"Her," Aaron said, staring at the woman in the bed.

"Yes," the Speaker said. "We lived a life of solitude, the two of us, yet in our love we never felt lonely, for we had each other and our newborn child. Yet, for all that, my wife—for so she became—was forced, from time to time, to travel into the village in search of supplies, for no man or woman can live in such a place alone. As our daughter grew, my wife would take her along on her trips; the villagers believed that my love carried a great shame, that she had produced our daughter out of wedlock with some stranger, yet none believed it to be me, for they all thought me long dead."

The joy that had crept onto his expression as he spoke vanished now, and his normally timeless face seemed to somehow transform to Aaron, becoming tired and haggard. "It was not perfect, for she was shunned by the villagers when she visited, yet it was manageable, and most importantly, we believed ourselves safe. After all, the villagers had never seen my face, garbed as I was in the black clothes of the Akalians, clothes which we had long since disposed of. There was nothing to mark me as a follower of Akane any longer. Nothing, save, for the Night Coin, the mark by which one Akalian might know another." He turned to Aaron. "You know of this thing?"

"Yes," Aaron said, remembering the black coin Adina had found in the castle courtyard. "I have seen one before."

The Speaker considered that and nodded. "Few have, you know. It is the mark of my kind, but it is not one that we share with outsiders willingly. I, myself, kept mine close to me, knowing the danger it represented in giving away my identity, yet not quite being able to rid myself of it and, in so doing, rid myself of the life I once led." He shook his head slowly. "Oh, if only I could go back now, could tell myself to throw the coin away as fast as I could, to let the swirling sands of that place bury it as if it had never been...but time is a river upon which a man is carried, and he may not turn back to visit once more that which has passed.

"I did not bury the coin, did not discard it. Instead, I hid it in the false bottom of a small chest which my wife had purchased for me as a surprise on one of her visits to the village. I put it there, hidden, and I thought no more of it. Not," he said, his voice growing hard, "at least, until I saw it carried in the hands of men who meant death to me and my family."

"You see, Seline, our daughter, was clever; even at little more than a year old, she was curious about everything, and our one regret was that our small tent afforded little room for her to explore and play. I suppose, looking back, that it seems obvious enough that she would go through my chest as there was so little else to occupy her, yet at the time I thought nothing of it. Not, that was, until my wife returned with our daughter from town one day, filled with worry, for, you see, my wife had only taken her eyes off Seline for a moment as she shopped, but it was long enough for my daughter to take out the shiny coin—no doubt a worthy trinket to one so young—from where she'd hidden it and begin playing with it. My wife said that she didn't think anyone noticed before she snatched the coin away and led our squalling daughter from the village, but knowing the world as I do, I had my doubts."

"And so what if they did notice?" Aaron asked. "As you said, not many people know what the coin means—what are the chances some desert villagers would know of it?"

The Speaker nodded. "Normally, I would agree with you. Only, my brother died in the village, remember, and I did not have the strength or opportunity to gather his body and take it away from there. And he, like all Akalians, had such a coin."

Aaron grunted. "Shit."

"Yes," the Speaker said, a smile coming to his face, but it was a weak, frail thing and it withered as he began speaking once more. "I kept a special watch on our camp at night while my family slept, reasoning that they would most likely choose to come in the darkness, if they intended to come at all. Three nights passed without sign, and I began to believe that perhaps my wife had been right after all, that they had not noticed the trinket my daughter had carried." He sighed heavily, and in that sigh was a regret and pain so deep that Aaron wondered how the man wasn't swallowed up by it.

"I often went out to hunt for food at night, for in the desert there are lizards and snakes that, while hidden in the heat of the day, will rouse themselves in the cool darkness to come out and hunt, and they tasted surprisingly good when prepared well, as my wife knew how to do. Such was my hope, to find some morsel to break our fast on the morrow, when, on the fourth night, I saw torches in the distance. Fifteen or more, perhaps as many as twenty, but not more than that. When I saw them, I knew well enough why they had come, and so I went out to meet them.

"As I said, these men were not warriors, and the weapons they carried ranged from machetes to stout lengths of wood. Yet, despite that, I knew the look in their eyes, understood well what was meant by the set of their jaws, for I have seen such looks before. They had upon them the look of men prepared to do murder, and so for all their lack of training and proper weaponry, I approached warily, my own blade strapped at my back. When I stepped out of the darkness, several of them started toward me, as if to attack, but the one in the front, a wizened old man whose skin was leathery and tough from years spent in the sun, held up a hand, forestalling them.

"I was surprised at that, and had some faint glimmer of hope rise in me, until he began to explain that demons such as my kind would not be tolerated in their lands, and that the woman and the babe must die as well, for one was the spawn of a demon, and the other corrupted by it. I knew at once that there would be no reasoning with them, for though the old man had not stepped forward to attack as the younger ones had, I was familiar with the irrational hate in his eyes. After all, I had seen it before.

"I am ashamed to say that I considered slaying them then—true, they were many, and I only one, but, as I've said, they knew little of the art of war, and I thought my chances at least even of coming out the victor."

"Ashamed?" Aaron said. "Why the fuck would you be ashamed? Those bastards came to kill you and your family—you would have been well within your rights to do what needed doing."

"According to who, Aaron Envelar?" the Speaker said, meeting his eyes. "You? I thank you for the sentiment, but there was a time before then, remember, when I served Akane, the God of Shadow, and despite what many think of him and those who follow him, the Dark God abhors violence for its own sake, or without just cause, and who was I, one man, to judge whether my cause was worthy or not?"

Aaron frowned, still not convinced, and the Speaker shook his head slowly. "Still, I believe I would have attacked those men anyway, would have fed their blood to the ever-hungry sands, if I believed my chances of victory better, but even odds are hard to take when the lives of one's wife and child hang in the balance."

Aaron nodded slowly. "So what did you do?"

"To understand that, you must first know that the peoples of the desert are, without exception, terrified of fire. They fear it in the same way sailors fear rogue waves or kings fear betrayal. For, you see, there is little water in the desert to put fires out once they are begun, and though they made their houses from clay and not wood, that meant only that they would become little less than ovens if the fire took them. And a life in the desert without shelter from the elements is a short one indeed."

"So," he said, lifting his burn-scarred hand up so that Aaron could see, "given the threat poised to my wife and daughter, I did the only thing I could think to do. If they believed me a demon, then I would be a demon in truth, one who felt no pain or fear, only vengeance, and before they could react I stepped forward and grabbed the burning brand of the leader's torch, extinguishing its blaze with my flesh. I did not cry out—though the Dark One knows I wanted to—nor did I release that torch until the flame was extinguished. They looked in awe at me then, and I feigned to be without pain as I stared at them, their expressions twisted with fear and revulsion in the light of the remaining torches. I would go, I told them, but the woman and child were to be left alone, and should I ever hear of harm coming to them, I would return with those of my kind and wreak such vengeance upon them and their families that people would speak of it for generations."

"Damn," Aaron breathed, staring at the man's scarred hand. "What did they do?"

The Speaker shrugged. "What could they do? Men such as they who were not warriors but survivors? They agreed, promising vengeance of their own should I ever come back to plague their people, then they left." A tear wound its way down the Speaker's face, but he met Aaron's gaze, unashamed. "And I left with them, abandoning my wife and daughter to a world which cares little for the innocence or beauty of a thing except to see that innocence despoiled, that beauty destroyed." He seemed to wither, to shrink in on himself, and he shook his head slowly. "To my great shame, I left them."

"But you didn't have a choice," Aaron said. "You saved them."

"So I thought at the time," the Speaker agreed, glancing back at the woman—his daughter—lying asleep in the bed. "But for what? So that she might live a life bent on vengeance, twisted by hate? So that the woman I once loved would spend her years wandering cities that were not her own, hoping for mercy from a world which has none? Perhaps I saved them, Aaron Envelar, but in doing so I damned them both."

Aaron wanted to comfort the man, but he could not find the words. Nearly thirty years the man had spent away from his daughter and the woman he loved, all in an effort to protect them. He did not ask the man why he did not go to them when they left the desert and came to the cities, for he knew well enough. The desert villagers may have hated them, but they were not the only ones who looked at the Akalians as demons—far from it—and as long as he was with them, they would never have been safe. What could one say to a man who had suffered such as that, who'd had his entire life and everything that he loved taken from him?

"Have I now satisfied your suspicions regarding her?" the Speaker asked, and though his voice was without emotion, Aaron could see the pain of the awakened memories in his eyes.

"Yes," the sellsword said, not trusting himself to say more.

"Very well," the Speaker said, his expression growing unreadable once more. "This way, then, and I will show you one of those things I believe you must see."

They didn't have to walk long, and in a few minutes they arrived at another room. The Speaker withdrew a key from a chain hung about his neck and unlocked the door, stepping inside. Aaron followed warily, not sure what to expect, then let out a hiss of surprise as he noted the figure lying on the bed.

Manacles on her wrists and ankles secured her to the four bedposts. Her hair was in disarray, tangled and knotted. Her face and the pale skin of her arms that showed on top of the bed covers were covered in red, bloody welts, as if some cruel torturer had dragged a knife across her flesh for the sheer joy of it. Despite the blood and hair covering much of the woman's face, Aaron immediately recognized Tianya, the leader of the Tenders.

"What have you done to her?" he demanded. The woman had attempted to kill him, but seeing her there, so badly abused, sent a wave of anger washing through him. "Why is she chained?"

The Speaker shook his head. "We have done nothing to her, only cared for her as best we may. The wounds you see upon her flesh are not our doing, but hers, and the manacles are necessary. When we first retrieved her, half-mad with grief and shock from the forest outside Perennia, we gave her a room much as the one you used with no such constraints. That night, she tried to kill herself for the first time—there have been several more attempts since, and we have been forced to take drastic measures to preserve her life."

Aaron stared at the woman in disbelief, remembering the last time he'd seen her. She had meant to kill him, to take the Virtue of Compassion from him and, with it, flee as far away from Kevlane as she could. But one of Kevlane's hulking brutes had come upon them, slaughtering the Tenders who followed her, and Tianya herself had vanished into the woods. In fleeing and abandoning the rest of her order, leaving those she led to die, she had preserved her life, but one of the lessons Aaron's own life had taught him was that no matter how fast a man—or a woman—ran, no matter how great a distance, they could not outrun themselves, could not outrun their own shame.

The leader of the Tenders, once a woman of great will and confidence, lay on her back in the bed, her eyes open but staring at the ceiling above her without recognition, and she did not so much as stir at the sound of Aaron and the Speaker's voices. "What's wrong with her?" he asked.

The Speaker shook his head. "I do not know. My people are skilled in many ways, and though we are all trained in medicine and the treating of wounds, we are taught to heal the hurts of the body. Hers, I believe, is a hurt of the mind, and our knowledge is of little use in such matters." He turned to Aaron. "I had hoped you might help her."

"Help her?" Aaron asked. "Gods, man, I'm no healer, and even if I was, I doubt there would be anything I could do for her. I wouldn't even know where to begin."

"No," the Speaker agreed. "But given your bond with the Virtue of Compassion, you might be able to see into the dark places of her mind in which she huddles, might be able, perhaps, to pull her out of the shadows."

Aaron grunted. "Look, Speaker, I don't know how much you know about the Virtues—I'll have some questions about that later, I promise you—but I've never done anything like that."

"Nor has a first-time mother birthed a child before," the Speaker said, giving Aaron a small smile, "yet her body knows what to do just the same. This woman carries the Virtue of Perception within her, Aaron Envelar, and if you are to do battle with the magi and his minions, you will need what gifts it provides."

Aaron shook his head, wanting to tell the man that he could do nothing for her, but the steady, confident gaze with which the man studied him coupled with Tianya's terrible condition decided him. "Once I get Co back from her reunion with her dad, I'll try. I won't promise anything, but I'll do what I can."

"Yes," the Speaker said, nodding. "And that is all any man can do."

"Well," Aaron said, unable to take his eyes from the wretched form of the leader of the Tenders. "What now?"

"Now, I believe, we should find Lord Caltriss and Lady Evelyn, for there is much to discuss and little time in which to do it. Your companions should already be waiting for us."

Aaron nodded, for he had been thinking much the same. If everything was going according to plan, the armies of Perennia and the other kingdoms should already be on the march toward Baresh and, with any luck, he and the others might catch up with them before they reached the city walls. "Lead on."

***

Adina and the others were already seated when the Speaker led Aaron into the large room. A table sat at the room's center, maps and papers scattered on its surface, and Aaron's companions sat around it, talking quietly. When Aaron closed the door behind him, they turned, and Adina hurried toward him. "Thank the gods you're okay," she said, pulling him into an embrace.

"I'm alright," Aaron said, holding her tight despite the pain that ran up his wounded arm.

A Sellsword's Mercy

Finally, after what might have been a moment or an eternity but was, either way, too short, Adina pulled back from him, looking him up and down. "I came to see you as often as they let me—they said they believed you'd be okay but..." She trailed off, tears gathering in her eyes, and Aaron cupped her face in one hand.

"I'm okay, Adina. Really."

"Good to see the general decided to wake up from his nap, sir," Wendell said, grinning as he came to stand beside Adina, bringing his fist to his chest in salute. "Though, if it was beauty sleep you were after, I think maybe you got up too soon."

Aaron laughed. "You're one to talk, you ugly bastard." The sergeant started to say something else, but Leomin, Gryle, and Caleb rushed up to shake Aaron's hand, and he found himself touched by how excited they all were to see him up and around. *Damnit, Firefly, you're making me soft,* he thought.

Sure, Co said, her voice brimming with happiness no doubt from being reunited with her father, *you're about as soft as a razor.*

Aaron paused to clear his throat, looking at each of his companions in turn. "I'm glad to see you're all okay."

"Yes," Leomin said, smiling and flashing his white teeth. "And I assure you, Mr. Envelar, that we are all quite glad to *be* okay."

Adina glanced to the two Akalians that had taken position on either side of the door then to the Speaker who was making his way to a chair at the head of the table, flanked by two more of the black-garbed figures. "Do you know what they want?" she asked, her voice quiet.

"A little," Aaron said. "I think we're about to find out more now. The man seems to know what he's about, and I think it best we trust them. After all, if they wanted us dead they wouldn't have even had to draw a blade to do it—Kevlane's creatures would have done the job for them happily enough."

"*Trust?*" the Parnen said, his eyes wide in mock disbelief. "This coming from Aaron Envelar, the sellsword of some ill repute who, I suspect, emerged from his mother's womb only to scowl at her and ask her what she was on about?"

Aaron snorted. "Yes, you bastard. Now, let's have a seat and see why we're still alive."

The others started toward the table, and Aaron followed after. *I, also, am glad that you are alright,* Co said.

I'm glad that you're okay, too, Firefly. Now, don't go getting all mushy on me.

I wouldn't dream of it, the Virtue said, but he heard the amusement in her tone. *Truly, though, I visited you every day.*

And I thank you for it, Aaron thought back, pulling up a chair beside Adina and sitting down. *Now, before you get me all weepy, let's see what these guys have to say, why don't we?*

Very well, the Virtue responded with reluctance, *but I must admit that I do so enjoy seeing you weep.*

Aaron scowled at that and chose not to respond, instead turning to the Speaker of the Akalians. "Alright, we're all here. Now, what do you want of us?"

"No," the Speaker said, looking up at the door even as one of the Akalians stationed there motioned to him with their hands. "Not all of us have gathered, not yet, but soon, I think." He gave the black-garbed man a nod, then the Akalian unbarred the door and swung it open.

The woman, Seline, stalked in, glancing at the two Akalians at the door with open hostility. For his part, the Speaker did an admirable job of keeping his expression calm, but Aaron saw the powerful emotions turning just beneath the surface as he watched her make her way further into the room.

"Seline?" Leomin asked in a shocked voice.

"Now then," the Speaker said, "since we are all here—"

He'd barely gotten the words out when there was a rush of displaced air. Aaron, who'd been watching the woman, saw little more than a vague blur as she moved with an impossible speed, and when he turned back to the table he saw that the Speaker had risen, and the woman stood directly beside him, a blade poised at his throat. *Well, shit,* he thought. *I guess that explains where the Virtue of Speed went after Beth.*

Yes, Co said, her voice worried, *and she does not seem happy to be here.*

Despite the blade at his throat, the Speaker's expression remained calm, and if he felt any fear, he did not show it. "Seline," he said in a soft voice, barely more than a whisper. "It is very good to see you."

"Don't you say my name, you *bastard,*" the woman spat. "Don't you *dare.*" The two Akalians standing on either side of the table started forward, their hands going for the blades at their backs, but the Speaker motioned them away.

"It has been long since I saw you last," he said, meeting his daughter's gaze.

"You mean since you *abandoned* us?" she hissed, her hand shaking with a rage that Aaron knew all too well. "Yes, *Father*, it has been very long since you left me and my mother alone. Do you have any *idea* of what we went through? Of what we—what *she* suffered because of you?"

The Speaker didn't answer, only watched her. "*Answer me damn you!*" she screamed, jerking the knife closer, and a line of blood formed on the Akalian's throat.

Aaron jumped up from his chair. "Just hold on a damn minute," he said. "Just re—"

"Stay out of this," she said. "I don't know what lies he's told you, but this man is a monster. The cruelties he's done, that he's *allowed* to be done—one such as him deserves to be killed."

Aaron held up his hands, showing her that he meant no harm. "Maybe he is a monster and maybe he isn't, but either way, you would have been dead without him and the other Akalians." He gestured around the room. "We all would have. And I might know more than you think."

"And what, exactly?" she demanded, turning back to the Speaker, her eyes flashing with fury. "That's supposed to somehow make up for a lifetime of suffering the cruelties, large and small, that he could have prevented?"

Leomin swallowed hard and rose. "Seline, I confess that I don't know what this is about, but perhaps if we were to talk ab—"

"Stay out of this, Leomin," she said. "I don't want to hurt you, but I will if I have to. Nothing is going to keep me from giving this bastard what he deserves."

The Speaker stared at her, and there was no fear in his gaze, only a deep, abiding sadness. "I am truly sorry, daughter, for how I have wronged you."

"You're sorry?" she asked in a voice that was half a scream. "You're *sorry*? And *stop* looking at me like that! Do you think it will somehow save you?" She shook her head. "No. Nothing will save you now—for years, I have been hunting you, following any rumor, any sign, and no matter what happens to me after, you will die for what you've done."

"You will not be harmed, Daughter," the Speaker said. "Come what may."

"Stop that, *damn you!*" she screeched, her hand shaking in earnest now where it gripped the blade. "Do you think I won't do it? That I don't have it in me? I have killed before, *Father,*" she spat. "Men who deserved it much less than you."

"I know," the Speaker said. "For the truth of it is in your eyes. It is no easy thing to take a man's life." He studied her, his face full of compassion. "I am so very sorry, Daughter, for what has been done to you—for what you have had to do."

"I don't need your damned apologies," she said. "I needed a father."

"Yes," the Speaker said. "Yet I am Akalian, young one. We are no one's family—we are merely shadows, not part of the world and its cities, and could not be even if we wished it. Kill me, if you must. If you believe it will heal that which is broken inside you—I will not resist."

It's as if the bastard wants to die, Aaron thought, frustrated. He saw the woman's hesitation and, through his bond with Co, felt it the moment she decided. "Wait!" he yelled, and she froze, turning her head to look at him.

"This is none of your concern." Seline said through gritted teeth.

Aaron met the Speaker's eyes and saw the pleading there, saw him begging him, without words, to keep secret the words that had passed between them. He grunted, suddenly angry. "Look," he said, turning to the girl. "The world's treated you bad. Well, what of it? You're young, lady, so maybe you haven't figured it out yet, but that's what the world does. It allows us to be born, so it might come up with new ways to torture us, new ways to use us. What, you think you're the only person here that life's fucked over?" He snorted. "Woman, you're not the exception—you're the rule. There's thousands of assholes just like you, *millions,* each with their own sob story, each nursing some grudge, blaming someone else for the shit hand life's dealt them."

Her eyes snapped wide at that, as if he'd struck her. "You...how dare you—"

"Because I'm just one more asshole," he said. "That's how." He glanced at Adina and the others, strangers only a year gone, yet now he would have given his life for any of them. "Only," he said, meeting the woman's eyes once more. "The difference is that I was a bigger prick than you've ever thought of being. I walked around each day with my grudges stacked high on my shoulders, so high I could sometimes barely move for the weight of them. I turned my life into a quest to wrong not just those who had wronged me, but everyone, everything, that I came into contact with."

"Let me guess," she sneered, "you met some friends, maybe a woman, and decided that the world wasn't such a bad place after all, is that it?"

Aaron laughed. "Lady, the world is a shithole. It always has been, and it'll continue to be long after you and I are dust in our graves. But you're not far wrong. I did meet people. A woman. Friends. And they showed me that though the world might be cruel, that didn't mean I had to be. They showed me that there's another way. A better way. That there are people in the world just like me, doing what they can to survive and that, what's more, many of those people are *good* people, the kind who reach down to help a stranger to his feet, if he falls." He turned and met Adina's gaze. "The kind who treat a man like a person, no matter how much he acts like a monster."

"Nice speech, but that doesn't change what *he* did," Seline said, the knife shaking in her hand once more.

"No, it doesn't," Aaron admitted, reaching out tentatively with the power of his Virtue, more carefully than normal, for the woman was in a high state of stress and, what's more, had obviously bonded with the Virtue of Speed. He'd learned over the time spent with Leomin and the others that those who'd bonded with a Virtue of their own proved particularly resistant to the influence of the others.

Still, light touch or not, it was enough for him to feel the roiling cloud of emotion within her, like some ever-raging storm threatening to destroy everything in its path. "Listen to me, Seline," he said, allowing the barest hint of the power of the bond to be carried on his words. "Life isn't easy—no one ever said it would be. And we can always find someone to blame, if that's what we're looking for. A man who trips in the street might blame the cobbler who fashioned his shoes, might blame the city officials for their poor roads, or any of a thousand other people. But what serves the man best is picking himself up and getting back on his way—whatever way that is."

A portion of the wild rage left her eyes as she listened to his words, as the power of his bond with Co did its work, and her gaze softened a fraction. "I don't have a way...without this, without *him*," she said, gesturing with the blade to her father. "I don't know where I'm going—I don't even know who I am."

"Well, welcome to the world, lady. Few enough of us know who we are, and none of us know where we're going. What I've learned over the last few months, though, is that all we can do is try to hurt as few as we can while getting there, leaving what small good we can behind us when we've gone."

"You sound like a priest or a monk," she sneered. "Too scared to tread on the grass, lest you accidentally step on some bug and kill it."

Aaron laughed at that—he couldn't help it. He laughed long and hard, and it felt good. He'd been called a lot of things in his time—few enough of them good—but he'd never been called a priest or a monk before. "Lady, you've got me all wrong." He sobered slowly, wiping at the tears the laughter had brought to his eyes. "Anyway, I'm not saying you should just roll over and let the world take what it wants, because the world wants everything you've got and then some, and the only way to keep any of it to yourself is to hold on tight, to fight when you have to. And sometimes you *do* have to. For all I said about most people just trying to get along, to survive the best way they know how, there are monsters walking among us—I should know. I've met them. And when a reasoning man—or woman—meets one such as that, the only thing he or she can do is fight. But whatever that man is," he said, gesturing to the Speaker, "and the truth of the matter is I'm not sure myself, I know enough to know he's no monster."

She stared at Aaron in silence for several long moments, no one else daring to speak. Then, she seemed to shrink in on herself, to somehow become smaller, become *less*. The arm holding the blade fell limply to her side, and the knife clattered to the floor. Then, without a word, she turned and walked out.

Leomin made to rise, but Gryle grabbed his hand, stopping him. "Forgive me, Leomin, but perhaps now isn't the best time to—"

"Let him go," Aaron said, suddenly very tired. The chamberlain turned a questioning look on him, and the sellsword nodded. "I'd tread lightly, Leomin," he said to the Parnen. "She won't want to have anyone around right now." That he knew for a certainty, for he recognized some bit of himself in her, saw reflected in that broken gaze the same hopelessness that he had carried for so long. Leomin needed no more permission than that, and in another moment he was hurrying after the woman.

"But," Gryle said, obviously embarrassed at even coming this close to arguing with Aaron. "If you know she doesn't want people around..."

"Right now, what she wants and what she needs are two very different things, Chamberlain. Trust me—I've visited the dark place she's in. Shit," he said, sighing, "I lived there."

He turned to the Speaker then, meeting the man's gaze, and he found that he was more than a little angry. The Akalian had stood there willing to die, willing to let his own daughter murder him, to keep his secrets, and for what? "You should have told her," Aaron said. "Damn you, she could have walked out of here with her head held high, with a *father,* instead of slinking away like some beaten dog."

If the Speaker noticed the anger in Aaron's tone, he did not show it. Instead, he only nodded. "Yes, but it is best this way."

"*Why?*" Aaron demanded. "Why is it better that your daughter thinks her father has always hated her than for her to know the truth? Why are you so worried about your own fucking secrets that you won't even spare her the pain she's feeling? You could have given her her father back, damn you."

"Yes," the Akalian said, his voice sad. "But I would give him back to her only to take him away again, and I am not so cruel as that."

Aaron frowned, caught off-guard. "What are you talking about?"

The Speaker swept the room with his gaze, taking in Aaron and the others, apparently unconcerned with the trickle of blood running down his throat. "You have all decided, together, that the magi must be defeated, and you are right in this, for if left to his own devices, he will not stop until all of Telrear is brought low beneath him. It is for this reason that I and my brothers—" he paused, gesturing to the Akalians in the room, "—have dedicated our lives to stopping him, to ferreting him and his followers out wherever they hide and doing what we must to keep the world safe from the horrors they would visit upon it."

"Wait a minute," Adina said, her surprise clear in her voice. "Do you mean that, all along, the purpose of the Akalians—"

"Has been to stand against the magi and his evil. Yes," the Speaker said. "It is a charge which my people and I have taken upon ourselves since the days of Caltriss, since the magi, in his madness at the loss of his friend and, in his broken vanity at the spell's failure, cast himself from the castle's parapet to be shattered upon the ground beneath. To shatter, but not to die, for as I think you know well, he is a difficult man to kill."

Aaron snorted. "Saying he's a difficult man to kill is like saying fish have a hard time flying, but I take your point. Still, that doesn't explain why you left the girl in the dark, and what you meant by saying you would take her father from her."

The man gave him a small, sad smile. "Because soon, Aaron Envelar, I will die. I and what remains of my brothers will pass from this world into the realm of Shadow, and the Akalians will be no more. For thousands of years we have battled the magi and his twisted creations, the Lifeless, but we will not survive to see another year pass, I think."

"Your god tell you that, did he?" Aaron demanded, annoyed. It seemed the man had a death wish, and he was bound and determined to see it through. "Or maybe all Akalians are just fortune tellers, is that it? If so, I've got a friend who'd love to invite you to accompany him for a game of cards or two."

Wendell grinned. "That'd put a frown on that bastard swordmaster's face right enough."

"We are not fortune tellers," the Speaker said calmly, as if the sergeant had never spoken. "Nor, has the Dark One forewarned me of my death, for such knowledge is too great for mortals to bear. Now, you would march upon Baresh. You have sought some means of entering the city without bringing death to those innocents who are imprisoned within its walls, have you not?"

Aaron rubbed at his temples where a headache was beginning to form. It seemed that the man couldn't stay on one topic, and he was reminded of the first time he'd met Leomin. "Yeah, but what does that have to do with anything?"

"Everything," the Speaker said. "At least, that is, so far as myself and my brothers are concerned. For it is we who will open the gate for you."

"Oh yeah?" Aaron said. "All two dozen of you, is that it? While you're at it, how about you just go ahead and defeat Kevlane and his armies, save us all a trip? There's no way to get the gate open from the outside short of battering it down. It's reinforced all to shit. We'd be better off trying to break a hole in the outer wall."

"He's right," Caleb said, speaking up for the first time and glancing timidly around at those gathered as if waiting for someone to call him down. When no one did, he went on. "The gate has been reinforced with metal plates, and flanking towers sit on either side. Any man approaching the gate will be forced to endure withering crossbow fire and, I suspect, much worse than that, given what we've seen of the force Kevlane can bring to bear."

"I know well of the gate, and the difficulties it represents," the Speaker said, bowing his head to the youth. "And I thank you for your input. You carry the Virtue of Intelligence well. Yet, even so, we *will* open the gate—it has been done before. I myself led the party which opened the gates of Yasidra and razed it to the ground."

The youth's face grew pale, and he made a strangled sound in his throat. The chamberlain reacted similarly, his face twisting in confusion. "But...that can't be right. That...that's impossible."

"See?" Aaron said, turning back to the Speaker. "Look, I've seen your men fight, and if it was a matter of skill with the sword, I wouldn't doubt you for an instant. But the gate will not be broken, and the city walls are fifty feet high or more, and I don't doubt that the battlements will be crawling with Kevlane's—"

"Yasidra?" Gryle breathed, staring at the Speaker with an awe-filled expression on his face, apparently unaware that Aaron had been speaking at all. "Did I hear you wrong?"

"No, strong one," the Speaker said, turning to the chamberlain. "You did not."

"What difference does it make what castle it was?" Aaron asked, frowning as he looked between the two men. "That doesn't change anything about Baresh. It's still impossible."

"You...forgive me, Mr. Envelar," Gryle said in a voice little more than a whisper, "but you don't understand. Yasidra and its razing are famous—or, perhaps, infamous is a better word. You see," he said, glancing at Caleb who nodded, looking as if he might be sick, "the lord and lady of the castle were minor noblemen at the time with no fortune or powerful army to speak of. Yet they were rarely ever accosted and, for the most part, they were left to their own devices. This because their castle was believed impregnable. It was also, as it happens, the reason why its lord and lady had no fortune, for what fortune they had—a significant one, I assure you—they spent on the fortress's creation and maintenance, and it boasted walls higher and thicker than any fortress before or since. Still, for all its reputation of being unconquerable, the castle itself sat in a particularly infertile part of the land, surrounded by scant woods and bogs which made growing any crops or raising livestock difficult."

"Not that I don't appreciate the history lesson, Gryle," Aaron said, turning to look at the Speaker, "and not that I'm not impressed, but no matter how defensible the castle was, it wasn't filled with creatures that can run faster than a horse can gallop, or others that could throw the same horse the way a child might throw a pebble, if they had a mind."

The Speaker nodded his head to Aaron as if to concede a point, but Gryle wasn't finished. "You are right, of course, Mr. Envelar. There is no proof." He glanced at the Speaker as if seeing if the man would correct him before going on, "nor is there any indication that such creatures as Kevlane's succored behind its walls. But those that did were cruel enough." He cleared his throat, his face taking on a greenish tinge. "You see, Mr. Envelar, as I've said, food was scarce in that region, and at some time—nobody knows exactly when—the lord and lady of the house began to...supplement what the farms and livestock of the villagers were able to provide."

"Supplement?" Aaron asked. "What in the name of the gods are you talking about, Gryle? Supplement *how*?"

But the chamberlain's hand was held to his mouth as if he might be sick. "With the villagers themselves," the Speaker said, and this time there was a hardness in his tone that spoke of an old burning anger, one that had not yet been extinguished by the passing of time.

Gryle nodded, clearing his throat and seeming to master himself. "Perhaps, the lord and lady of the house first started..." He paused, taking a slow breath before continuing. "...*Partaking* of the villagers out of what they deemed necessity. Some theorize that in such an infertile region, they would have had little choice. Still, no one knows for sure—all we know is that the people of Yasidra soon became livestock themselves, and though the city's army was not formidable, it was enough to keep any man, woman, or child from escaping its walls. Regardless of their reasons, it is agreed that the lord and lady of the house became quite mad, glutting themselves daily on the flesh of those subjects they were meant to protect."

He shook his head sadly. "Yet their atrocities remained hidden for many months until, finally, a guardsman fled from the city, bringing news of the terrors being visited upon its people to the outside world. At first, the king doubted the man's claims, and why not? For though Lord Wayren, the ruler of Yasidra, was not often seen at court and did not rank high on the king's list of favored noblemen, Lady Wayren was his cousin, and it is said he had many fond memories of her from when they were children. In any event, letters were promptly sent to inquire after the veracity of the guardsman's tale. It would have been an easy enough thing, I suspect, for the lord and lady to put on airs, to disguise those terrible crimes which had been committed within the city's walls, but they were too far taken by the madness by then, and no response—nor the messengers themselves—ever returned."

The chamberlain turned and looked at the Speaker as if the Akalian was some alien creature which he had never seen before. "In any event, the king began to marshal his armies, preparing for what would no doubt be a long siege—yet before they had even begun to march, word reached them of Yasidra's destruction. It was said that the fires of its burning could be seen from miles away."

"An evil place," the Speaker said, "of evil deeds. Even after the infection had been excised, the villagers let free, the ghost of what had happened there lingered and could only be cleansed with fire." He turned to Aaron. "The magi is capable of great evil, has what tools he needs to bring it upon the world, but for all the danger he represents, his evil is one that has been seen before."

"I understand," Adina said, and they turned to her. "And I'm thankful that you saved those people and did what you had to do with the lord and lady but...I don't understand what this has to do with Baresh."

"Plenty, I suspect," the chamberlain said, his eyes never leaving the Speaker, "for, as I said, the fortress was thought to be unassailable. Yet, that is not what strikes me about his words the most."

"Then what?" Adina asked. "It is a terrible story, truly, but why is it that you and Caleb look as if you have both seen a ghost?"

"Forgive me, Princess," Gryle said, bowing his head, "but if I seem...discomfited by the Speaker's words, it is because the razing of Yasidra took place over five hundred years ago."

Aaron and Adina both jerked as if struck and, for a time, neither could speak. Then, finally, the sellsword turned to the Speaker. "Five hundred years?"

The Akalian nodded slowly, bowing his head to Gryle and Caleb. "Yes," he said, meeting Aaron's gaze. "I was young then, only just named the Speaker of the Akalians, yet it is a time I cannot forget." He sighed. "Some images, some memories, it seems, stay with you no matter the passage of the years."

"But how is that possible?" Aaron managed.

The Speaker gave him a small smile. "*Will*, Aaron Envelar. We spoke of it before, do you remember?"

"Yes," the sellsword said uncertainly. "I thought I was dreaming."

"But you were not," the Speaker said. "Still, many others have claimed much the same after feeling the power of the Will upon them, for it is not so very different. After all, in dreams, we feel as if we are not in control of our own bodies, our own minds, do we not? And I, of course, apologize for exercising the bond against you, but I thought it best, given your recent...episode."

Episode, Aaron thought. *A kind enough way to describe being taken over by a murderous rage that makes a man want to destroy anyone or anything he sees.* "Never mind that," he said, waving it away. "You were right to do it, but I can't say I love the idea of my control being taken away from me. But I want you to answer me something else, Speaker—just how old are you?"

"I am six hundred and fifty-three years old," the Speaker said. "The day of my birth will come in little more than a month's time, but I will not be here to see it. My time will soon end."

Adina and the others gasped in surprise at that, but Aaron only studied the man in shock. It seemed so long ago now that Co had first bonded with him, that she had explained that the Virtues would make a man live longer, but over six hundred years...*Is that possible, Firefly? Can the Virtues really make a man live so long?*

I do not know, Aaron, she said back. *The longevity given by the bond of the Seven is not so long as that. At least, I have never heard of it being so, but, then, I did not know that my father had become as I am either. Still, I would not be overly troubled, for I do not detect any deceit within him.*

Nor do I, Aaron answered, *and that's exactly* why *I'm troubled.* It was one thing to know that there was an evil, ancient mage out there who'd been alive for thousands of years and was set on the destruction of the world—a hard thing to understand, to imagine, but he thought he'd come to grips with it. But here, before him, stood a man that, by all evidence, was as mortal as he himself, yet generations had been born and died while he lingered upon the earth. Aaron wondered at what such a man must feel, dedicated so completely to the impossible mission he had set for himself that he had not even allowed himself to die. Still, the newfound knowledge at least explained the timeless look of the Speaker's features, and Aaron's inability to even hazard a guess at his age.

He stared at the Speaker with awe, imagining the things the man must have seen, imagining how the world must have changed during his unusually long life. And all the while he was looked down upon by those who he would save, treated like some monster from a children's story. "Gods," he said finally, "that must have been terrible."

The Speaker smiled then, and the expression lit up his features. "It has been...interesting."

"Alright," Aaron said, since none of the others seemed capable of speech just then. "You've sold me—I believe you can open the gate. Now what?"

"Now," the Speaker said, an unmistakable strength in his voice that had not been there before, and Aaron thought that he felt the touch of the man's Virtue as it floated on the man's words. "Now, we must prepare. You are all great warriors in your way," he said, meeting each of their eyes in turn, "and you have fought valiantly, stood gravely against the darkness. Yet, for all your courage, you have been incomplete, and for all your honor, for all your sacrifice, if you continue as you have, you will fall. And the world will fall with you."

He turned, locking his eyes on Adina, and such was the power of his gaze that she seemed transfixed, and it looked to the sellsword as if she barely even dared to breathe as the power of the Virtue, of Aaron Caltriss's Will, fell upon her. "You have been like a knight riding to battle, yet afraid to guide your horse as it must be guided, for you fear some unknown danger, some unseen pit or trap that might snare your mount and steal its life."

Adina opened her mouth to reply, but no words came out, and the Speaker was already turning to Caleb in any case. "You are an archer with great skill, knowing the wind like no other, one with the bow in your hands, yet still you hesitate, for fear that your shot will fall short, that it will not be enough." His eyes seemed to flash a bright, brilliant white for a moment as he stared at the youth. "That *you* will not be enough."

The youth's face twisted with emotion, and his gaze turned to his feet, but not before Aaron saw the defeated expression that arose on his features. The Speaker was already looking to Gryle though, and the chamberlain watched him with wide, frightened eyes like a deer cornered by a wolf. "And you, strong one. There is pain in you, for that which you have lost, for what you see as your failure. Yet, you carry within you the heart of a warrior, one you have buried beneath doubt and uncertainty, choked with your belief that you will fail, that surely you *must* fail. Yet for all your efforts, it still beats within your chest, begging for the release that you so refuse."

Then the Speaker turned to Wendell, who fidgeted nervously, looking as if he would have rather been anywhere besides sitting in that room just then. The Akalian studied the sergeant for several seconds. Wendell winced as if expecting a blow, but to Aaron's surprise, the Speaker only grinned. "Ah, but here is one with great wisdom. A coarse sort, no doubt, like some precious gem covered in dust, buried deep in the ground. But like that gem, of incalculable value, if one only takes the time to excavate it, to wipe it clean and see it as it truly is."

The scarred sergeant made a strangled sound in his throat then looked behind him as if the Speaker must surely be talking about someone else, but the Speaker only grinned wider, his expression only sobering when he turned to Aaron. "As for you—"

"I know, I know," the sellsword interrupted. "A child swinging a sword."

The Speaker grinned wider. "Just so." He looked at each of them in turn then. "You have all demonstrated a courage few possess. You have sacrificed much for the good of others, and you will sacrifice more before it is done, yet without belief in yourselves, without understanding your *true* selves, you cannot win."

"Then what are we supposed to do?" Caleb's voice, sounding weak and afraid.

The Speaker raised his head, and though Aaron didn't notice any more of a change in his stance than that, suddenly he seemed much taller, *larger* somehow. "You must find the courage not only to face the magi and his abominations, but to face yourselves. You must find your *will*." Aaron studied the expressions of his companions, saw the doubt there, a reflection of his own, but the Speaker only smiled.

"Do not worry," he said, his eyes flashing again, and this time there was no questioning whether Aaron saw what he thought he did, for the man's eyes blazed white. "You will find it. I will show you." He turned back to Wendell once more, the sergeant still with a stricken look on his face. "If you would be so kind, wise one, you may leave us, for there is nothing I might tell you about yourself that you do not already know."

The sergeant nodded solemnly, but Aaron didn't miss the childlike grin of relief that broke on his features as he turned and walked—practically jogged, in truth—to the door. Once he was gone, the Speaker turned back to the others. "I will show you your will," he said again. Then he raised his hands to either side, and suddenly the blurry, white form of Aaron Caltriss, the long dead king, appeared beside him. And when next the Akalian spoke, it was not with one voice, but with two. "*We* will show you."

CHAPTER SEVEN

"You…will…tell us what you know," Grinner panted, collapsing onto the stool in the corner of the dungeon cell. He let the leather whip he held rest on the floor as he stretched his arm, rubbing a hand across his sweaty forehead.

Hale, the other crime boss of the Downs, and Grinner's long-time rival, watched him with emotionless eyes. His wrists were manacled to a bracket on the ceiling to keep them in place, and his feet dangled so that only his toes could touch. A normal-sized man would have been left with nothing to support his feet at all, but the crime boss was bigger, taller than most.

Shirtless, he reminded Grinner of some great bear, thick with muscle and sinew, his chest covered in dark hair that resembled fur. But if the man was a bear, then he was a poorly treated one, for his chest, back, and sides were striped with bloody wheals where the whip had scored his flesh. Yet despite what must be terrible pain, the giant of a man showed no sign of his suffering on his face, only watched Grinner with eyes that seemed to carry no emotion, yet they were even more disturbing for all that, and Grinner sneered, angry at himself for the fear and uncertainty they caused him.

"You think yourself tough, is that it, Hale? You stand against the pain, against the truth, and for what? You suffer needlessly. All you need do is admit that you were in league against Queen Isabelle and the kingdom of Perennia, divulge the plans you formed with May and the other conspirators, and your pain will end."

Hale didn't answer, and despite his own exhaustion, Grinner jerked himself up from the chair, baring his teeth behind the silver mask he wore. *"Damn you,"* he yelled. "You stand in my way!" He paused, glancing at the two guards who had accompanied him into the dungeons before turning back, forcing a calm he did not feel into his voice. "You stand in the way of Queen Isabelle, and for what purpose?"

Hale hocked and spat out a mouthful of blood, then he turned to the old man and gave him a bloody grin. "A man doesn't take a stand because he has something to gain by it, Grinner. That's one thing you never seemed to understand. A man stands because that's what a man does, that's all. And as for my pain bein' brought to an end, I don't reckon that's true of anyone, save the dead. Now, why don't you bring that toy whip of yours over here again and get back to work? I'm tired of listenin' to your blather. Or," he said, grinning wider, "are you not quite finished with your rest?"

Grinner sneered and motioned sharply to one of the guards. "Perhaps fists will find the truth where reason cannot."

The guard hesitated, glancing at his fellow. "Sir, are you sure—"

There was a grunt from Hale that might have been a laugh, and Grinner felt his face flush with anger. *"Yes, I'm sure!"* he screeched. "Or do you think to question your queen's orders?"

"O-of course not, sir," the guard stammered, "it's only..." He glanced at Hale's bloody form. "I don't know how much more he can take, sir..."

Grinner opened his mouth to speak, but Hale beat him to it. "You go on now, son," he said to the guard, then he paused to wince and spit out some more blood. "It won't be the first beatin' I've taken, and I don't expect it'll be the last. Besides, I reckon I've got it comin' and then some, even if it ain't for the reasons this bastard'd have you do it."

The guard hesitated another moment, swallowing hard, then he stepped forward, beginning to remove his armored gauntlets as he did.

"No," Grinner said, smiling cruelly at the big crime boss. "Leave them on."

The young guard's eyes went wide at that, and he glanced between Grinner and Hale. The big crime boss rolled his shoulders, stretching his neck from side to side. "Best get it done, boy, before I fall asleep. All this talkin's makin' me tired."

***

May listened from her cell opposite Hale's own as the torture—which Grinner dubbed as questioning—continued. She had long since looked away, for despite all the horrors she had seen in her life, all the terrible things to which she had borne witness, there was something about watching Hale hanging senseless as that thug Grinner had his way that turned her stomach and brought tears to her eyes.

She listened to each meaty *thwack* of gauntlets on flesh, cringing at each pained grunt from the big crime boss, not even bothering to wipe the tears from her eyes any longer. How had things gone so wrong so quickly? She had always known that she balanced her life on a knife's edge, that, at any moment, a single slip would be enough to bring it all crashing down around her. She had known, but somehow she had never believed it would happen, and she'd certainly never had any inkling that the man who would cause her destruction would be the aging crime boss, Grinner.

She thought that she should be, if not pleased, at least ambivalent at the torture Hale was being forced to undergo. After all, he and his men had posed a danger to her and her operations for many years. Yet try as she might, she could find no satisfaction or contentment in his suffering, only pity and more than a little awe. For whatever else he might be, a self-admitted cheater, liar, murderer, and more, there was something somehow noble about the giant crime boss, something deserving of respect. It was as if he had entered into the wrong calling, had been born into the wrong age, for May thought he would have been more at home on some ancient battlefield, fighting against—or with, on this point she wasn't sure—hordes of barbarian savages bent on civilization's destruction.

In such a place, such a time, a man like Hale would have been respected, honored, and she believed that men would have followed him with a loyalty and dedication that few others could engender in their troops. He was a man built for a bloody age, yet now it was he who was bleeding. *And you too scared to even so much as look, woman,* she scolded herself. *No matter what he has done in the past, he was your strength when you had none of your own—the least you can do is bear witness to his suffering.*

And so she turned, resisting the urge to snap her eyes closed as she took in the crime boss's battered form. His head hung low, his lank hair dripping with sweat, but it was his chest, his stomach, and arms that drew her attention, for they were covered in blood and fresh bruises from the guard's attentions. *Gods help him,* she thought. *He may not be a good man—though I'm not sure about even something so simple as that any longer—but he is a man, and he does not deserve this.* What's more, she knew that to no small degree, the crime boss was taking the beating for her. Of course, they *hadn't* collaborated to plan the queen's assassination or the fall of Perennia, or whatever other evils Grinner was now trying to lay at their feet, but if Hale decided to tell Grinner what he wanted to hear anyway, then his suffering could have been over. All he needed to do was lie, and it wasn't as if he hadn't done that much and worse before, yet the giant only hung in silence, drooling blood and grunting with each impact of the guard's fists.

"Alright," the big man said finally, the word grating out with the sound of two great boulders shifting against one another. "I'll...tell you."

The older man made a pleased sound in his throat, and May felt her heart flutter in her chest. Still, she could not blame the giant, for he had suffered far more pain than most would—more than she would herself, she was certain.

Grinner held up a hand to the guard, and the man stepped back, panting heavily and resting his hands on his knees. "Oh?" he asked. "Have you finally been made to see reason then, Hale? Will you finally admit the truth of what you and those others—May Tanarest among them—were about in plotting the assassination of Queen Isabelle and the downfall of her kingdom?"

"*Yes,*" Hale grated in an agonized tone barely loud enough for May to hear. "But...closer. Hurts...to talk."

Grinner slunk forward, every bit of his posture screaming his pleasure at the other crime boss's agony, and May was reminded of some great spider, cruel and malicious for no other reason than its own enjoyment. "Yes?" he asked when he was close, leaning forward with his ear cocked to the giant. "You have something to say? Some truth you would finally like to impart?"

"*Y-yes,*" Hale managed, slowly raising his face. It was covered in blood, bruised and swollen to a point that May couldn't believe the man was able to talk at all. But he wasn't just talking—he was grinning. "The truth is," he said, his voice still full of pain but louder now, confident, "you're an asshole."

Grinner recoiled in surprise, a whimper of fear escaping, but not fast enough to avoid the bigger man's thick legs as he swung forward, planting his feet solidly in his stomach. The air exploded from Grinner, and he flew across the cell, slamming against the bars with a bone-rattling crash. The two guards stood as if frozen, staring in wide-eyed wonder at the crime boss's crumpled form as if they had no idea of what to do.

Then a low moan escaped the old crime boss as he shifted on the floor, his head rising in a jerking twitch, as if each movement was agony. He tried to speak, but at first what came out was no more than an unintelligible sound somewhere between a mewl of pain and a growl. He started to climb haltingly to his feet, and belatedly one of the guards rushed forward, helping him up.

With a hiss, Grinner slapped at the man, and the guard backed up as the crime boss rose, one arm clasped around his stomach, his shoulders hunched. As he stood, May saw that his mask had come off, and she gasped at her first view of his terrible wounds.

For their part, the two guards only stood staring with what might have been a sick fascination. "Well?" Grinner wheezed breathlessly. "W-what are you…fools s-staring at? You s-saw him strike me. Puni…punish him."

"Oh," Hale said from where he hung, smiling past his swollen face, and if May could have made the man shut up, she would have, for anything he said would surely only incense the old man further. "The real…punishment's about to start then? Good I was…starting to get bored. As for why they're staring…" he continued, each word no doubt a pain but keeping his smile well in place for all that, "that most likely…has something to do with they've never…seen anyone so ugly before."

The few parts of Grinner's face that weren't scarred twisted in confusion at that, and one of the guards reached down and picked up his mask from where it had fallen on the cell floor. "Excuse me, sir," the guard said, holding it out, "but you dropped this."

Grinner stared at the proffered mask as if it had betrayed him, his ruined face seeming to crumple in upon itself, and, for a moment, a silence descended on the dungeons. It was a silence May knew all too well, for she had heard such a silence before, while living in the Downs. It was the kind of silence that demanded to be filled with screams and cries for mercy. But Grinner's face showed no mercy. Instead, his ruined features filled with an insane rage, one that spoke of no reason or logic, only the wish to visit pain upon someone.

The old crime boss took the mask with a shaking hand. He slipped it over his face then turned to regard Hale. "Kill him."

He spoke the words in little more than a whisper, but they seemed to echo within the dungeons for all that, and there was such hate in them that May felt a chill run up her spine. "Grinner," she said, speaking for the first time, "wait, surely—"

"Quiet, *woman*," the crime boss hissed, not even bothering to turn away from the guards. "You're next."

The two guards only stood staring at Grinner as if he'd spoken a different language. Finally, one cleared his throat. "But...sir, we were only meant to question—"

"*Never mind what you were meant to do!*" Grinner screamed, his voice breaking, "Kill him now!"

The two guards recoiled at the naked, unreasoning fury in the crime boss's voice, their troubled, wary stares locked on Grinner as if he were some wild animal that might attack at any moment. One of the two went so far as to grab the handle of his sword, sliding the blade halfway out of the sheath at his waist, though it was unclear whether he intended to follow the crime boss's orders, or planned to use the sword to defend himself should the old man charge him.

May couldn't blame him either way, for though the mask covered the crime boss's face, she could see his eyes dancing with a fevered madness beyond all reason. "*Well?*" the crime boss demanded, his fists clenched at his sides, and May noted, troubled, that blood seeped from his hands where the nails of his fingers dug into his flesh, but if Grinner noticed, he gave no sign.

"Sir," one of the guards tried again in a voice one might use to soothe a wild beast, "Queen Isabelle told us to question them to determine whether or not they're guilty. She would not be pleased—"

Hale laughed at that, a great bellowing laugh, and Grinner shook with rage. *Shut up, you idiot,* May thought furiously. *Can't you see he's mad?* But either the giant crime boss could not see it, or did not care, for the laughter continued, and a strangled, tortured sound came from Grinner's throat. Finally, he stalked toward the nearest guard—the man whose blade sat half out of its scabbard—and ripped the sword free himself. "*Fine,*" He hissed in a voice that was at once both frightening and pitiable, "I'll do it myself, if you lack the nerve."

He turned to where the giant was strung up, and Hale left off his laughing to study the old man with a bloody grin. "Well?" he said. "You going to do something or just stand there, you old bastard?"

The blade shook in Grinner's hand, yet still the crime boss hesitated.

"Come…on then," the giant grated, each word full of pain. "Or…is it that…you're afraid to get your hands dirty?"

A horrible keening rose from Grinner then, a sound that could not have come from any sane man or woman, and he stalked closer to the other man. For his part, Hale seemed to tense, leaning his body forward as if almost eager.

"*Kill you,*" Grinner muttered. "*Kill you…kill you…*"

"Stop him!" May screamed at the two guards. "You've got to do something!"

But the two men only stood and watched as Grinner stalked closer to Hale, and she might as well not have spoken at all for all the reaction they gave. "*Grinner, stop!*" she tried again, but the old man gave no sign that he'd heard her as he moved forward in hitching steps, like some marionette under the guidance of a particularly unskilled puppet master.

"*Stop in the name of the queen!*" came a new voice, and the authority of it, the *demand* in it, made it past Grinner's madness, and he froze, turning. May followed his gaze to see Captain Brandon Gant marching down the dungeon hallway.

"Put the blade down, Grinner," he said, stepping inside the cell. "Now."

Some of the rage faded from the crime boss's countenance, and when he spoke his voice sounded nearly human. "Captain Gant. You overstep yourself—Queen Isabelle has given me leave to question the two prisoners regarding their involvement in the conspiracy for her death."

The captain's mouth worked as if he'd swallowed something sour. "So I've heard, but in my experience questioners rarely do their work with swords."

The crime boss started and stared down at the sword as if only now realizing he carried it. "A tool to induce fear, Captain Gant, in the hopes of motivating him to tell what he knows. Nothing more."

Brandon Gant glanced at the bloody, battered form of Hale before turning back to Grinner. "Well, Councilman, if his smile is anything to go by, it isn't working."

Grinner studied him for several moments then finally let the sword fall to his side. "Very well, Captain, as you say." He walked to the stunned guard and handed him back the blade before looking to the captain once more. "Still, there are other ways to question him, other tools that we might use, and let me assure you, we shall have the truth before the day is out, and Queen Isabelle will be sa—"

"No," Captain Gant interrupted, "you're done." He gestured to the giant crime boss, "Dead men tell no secrets, and a fool could see that anymore of your *questioning* would kill him."

"You do not have the authority to..." Grinner began but cut off at the sound of the captain's blade leaving its scabbard.

"I would not question what authority I have, Councilman Grinner," he said. "Unless, that is, you wish to make use of that sword after all, only against an opponent who is likewise armed." He leaned forward then, a small, eager smile on his face. "Do you?"

The crime boss hesitated, glancing at the two guards as if trying to decide which side they would take, should it come to it, and there was a pregnant pause, one in which May didn't dare to so much as take a breath. Then, after a moment, some of the tension seemed to leave the old crime boss's body, and he nodded. "Very well, *Captain*," he said, making the last word a curse, "But

Queen Isabelle will hear of your meddling, this I assure you. I suspect that she will not be pleased with one of her own getting in the way of the truth."

"Perhaps," Brandon Gant said, "but, then, I'll hear those words from the queen herself—not from a sniveling coward who only finds his courage when his opponent is unarmed and chained."

Grinner tensed, and May thought that he would attack the captain, after all, but he only stood, his body trembling. "You have made a mistake, crossing me, Captain. I will see your position revoked. Before I am through, you won't be allowed to even so much as muck out the queen's stables. Come," he barked, turning to the two guards before stomping out of the cell.

The two men hesitated, glancing at their captain uncertainly, but he only gave them one sharp nod. "Better follow him, lads. Whatever evil may come, let it come to me only."

"*Sir,*" they said in unison, then they started away after the rapidly departing old man.

"One more thing, boys," Captain Gant said without turning away from his study of the big crime boss. "Leave the manacle keys."

"But, sir," one said, "are you sure that's wise? They say he fought like a demon when taken. He nearly killed poor Jessum. He'll never walk right again, that's for—"

"Leave them," Brandon repeated, his gaze still locked on the giant who watched him with dark, unreadable eyes.

"Yes sir."

They tossed the keys at the captain's feet, and disappeared down the dungeon corridor, following in the furious Grinner's wake.

Once they were gone, the captain picked up the keys before making his way to the giant. "Am I going to have any trouble out of you?"

Hale's jaw worked before he turned and spat out a mouthful of blood. "Reckon I've... been about as much trouble as I mean to today."

Captain Gant gave a sharp nod and set about unlocking the man's bonds. When his arms came free of the ceiling, the crime boss stumbled, and Brandon was forced to catch him, grunting with the effort of holding up his weight. "Big bastard, aren't you?"

"Been...told as much," Hale grated. "Though normally the ones who tell me are much...prettier than you."

"I don't doubt it." Slowly, the two men worked their way to the corner of the cell, Captain Gant hissing with strain, Hale grunting in what May could only imagine was unimaginable pain. Finally, they reached the corner, and Captain Gant released the giant where he half-sat, half-collapsed on the cell's dirt floor.

The captain took a step back, panting. "Gods, but I'm too old to be lugging the likes of you around."

The crime boss, however, didn't answer. The moment he sat, his head slumped onto his chest, and May would have thought him dead had she not been able to see the almost imperceptible rise and fall of his chest. Brandon turned to look at her with something like wonder in his eyes. "I think he went to sleep."

May nodded, forcing her gaze away from the crime boss's bloody, broken form. "Yes," she said sadly. "That's a blessing, at least."

Captain Gant nodded and withdrew a key from his waist, locking the cell door behind him as he stepped back out into the corridor. "He'll suffer more, before it's done. Unless, that is, he tells what he knows."

May's eyes went wide. "Captain, surely you don't think it's true? That we—"

Brandon Gant shook his head. "I trust you, May, no matter what that snake Grinner says. Princess Adina and General Envelar vouched for you, and that's enough for me. As for him, though..." He turned, studying the unconscious crime boss before finally shaking his head. "I don't know—the man's a criminal, after all, and though I despise Councilman Grinner and his methods, I've little trust for Hale. Men, I've found, will act according to their natures, and his nature is clear enough for any with the eyes to see it."

May started to tell the man that she was little more than a criminal herself, but decided that now, locked within a dungeon cell, might not be the best time to risk turning the one person who seemed to be on her side against her, so instead she only nodded. "A week ago, I would have said much the same. But now...I'm not sure." She shook her head slowly. "Anyway, whatever faults Hale has—and there are many, I admit—he is not a man known for subtlety of this kind."

"About as subtle as a battle axe, from what I've seen," the captain admitted. "But that doesn't change the fact that it was his men who tried to assassinate the queen."

May decided to leave that for now; after all, she wasn't sure how she felt about the crime boss herself, only that she was confident he'd had no hand in what had happened. But a hunch was pitiful enough evidence, and wouldn't do anything to convince the captain. "As you say, Captain. Tell me," she said, shuffling toward the cell door, hating the desperation in her voice but unable to quell it, "what of Silent and Adina? Has there been any news?"

The captain's expression could have been carved from stone, but she could see the worry beneath the surface of it, could hear it in his voice when he spoke. "Nothing. I fear for them, May, but what's more I fear for all of Perennia. Without her sister and General Envelar by her side the queen is…" He hesitated, finally shaking his head. "I do not know what will happen in the coming days."

May frowned. "The army. Has it reached Baresh?"

The captain met her eyes with an obvious reluctance. "No. It has yet to march, and now I am not sure that it even will. The queen is…" He paused again, and on his features, May could see his loyalty to Queen Isabelle warring with his concern for the city. "She is worried," he said finally. "Now, it seems, she is hesitant to make any move, lest it be the wrong one."

"But, Captain," May said, grabbing the cell bars. "The army *has* to march. The tournament in Baresh will begin any day now—if it hasn't already. Kevlane will—"

"I know, May," he said. "I know. I have spoken to Queen Isabelle of this, but still she waits." He gritted his teeth, and when he spoke again the club owner could hear the frustration in his voice. "And for all my threats, that snake, Councilman Grinner, probably has the right of it. Since he 'saved her life,'" he said, his tone making it clear what he thought of that, "the queen has kept Grinner close to her side, refusing any counsel but his. I suspect she won't be overly pleased when she hears I have come in the way of his questioning."

May stared at the man, stunned. "But...but surely she understands that Grinner is a monster. She has to know that he cares nothing for anyone but himself, that he'd kill his own mother, if she stood in the way of what he wanted."

Brandon nodded. "I have told Her Majesty as much but..." He shrugged. "I just don't know, May. And it is not only the queen, I fear, who has been beguiled by the councilman and his lies. Many in the city, too, believe that you and Hale are traitors. There are whispers that even General Envelar and Princess Adina herself were in on the conspiracy, and I've lost count of the amount of tavern brawls that I've had to see put down over the matter. The city is...tense. Even now, I can hardly walk down a street corner without seeing a mob of people shouting about Princess Adina and General Envelar's treachery, screaming for justice."

May heart skipped a beat. Justice, to such men and women, she suspected, meant not only her and Hale's execution, but also hunting down Silent and the others. And if they returned to the city when it was in such a state? "Gods, Brandon," she said, "if they come back..."

The captain gave a sharp nod, his expression troubled. "I know, May. I know. I've got my men—the ones I'm sure are loyal—scouting outside the city in search of them. Not as many as I'd like and, so far at least, they have found no sign. I'm afraid if Aaron and the others don't come back soon..."

"Relax, Captain," May said with a confidence she didn't feel. "Aaron and Adina know how to take care of themselves."

He met her eyes, scratching at the gray bristles of his beard, "It's not them I'm worried about, May. At least not mostly."

May studied him, saw in his gaze the truth of how bad things in the city were becoming as people, scared and uncertain, chose anger over fear. Not an uncommon reaction—she had seen it a thousand times before—but, this time, that anger might well see her and Hale to their deaths, and the city to its own soon after. "What of Thom?" she said, afraid to hear the answer but needing to know.

"He's alright," the captain said. "For now, anyway. As is Balen, before you ask. That one's clever enough, for it seems he saw what was coming before I did."

"Why do you say that?" May asked, a sinking feeling rising in the pit of her stomach. "What's Balen done?"

The captain shrugged. "He's disappeared, that's all. And wherever he went, it seems he took the youth Michael, and Bastion with him. It'd be my guess that, wherever they are, Thom's with them, and if they're smart, they'll keep their heads down for a while. With the city how it is, it's best if any confidants and friends of General Envelar and Princess Adina stay out of sight. I don't know that they'd be attacked but, May…I don't know they wouldn't be either. Grinner, at least, seems to have forgotten them—too busy trying to whisper poison into the queen's ear, I suspect."

"Thank the gods for that, anyway," May said. "It's good to know they're safe."

"As safe as anyone can be in such times," the captain said. "Still, the situation in the city is deteriorating each day that passes without sign of the general or the princess. There aren't armed mobs patrolling the city in search of anyone connected with the general—not yet—but I think it's only a matter of time before they go looking, and May, when they do…"

May nodded, swallowing. "Balen and Thom are sailors, Bastion was wounded and the boy's too young to know what's going on. Balen and Thom will take them where they feel safest. To the ships."

"Yes, I suspect they will," the captain agreed. "And it won't take a genius to search for them there."

"Gods," May breathed, as troubled by the captain's obvious worry as anything else, for Captain Brandon Gant had never struck her as a man easily disturbed. "We have to do something, Captain."

"Yes. But what?" Brandon asked, and May found she had no answer to give him. All her knowledge, all her network of informants and spies was of little use so long as she remained in this cell.

The captain must have read her thoughts on her face, for he sighed. "I'll do what I can to get you out of here, May, but I can make no promises. The queen still listens to my counsel, but she does not seem to hear it, and I get the feeling she only does it to humor me. It is as if she's in shock or…" He shook his head, frustrated. "I don't know. Only that bastard, Grinner, seems able to get through to her. Still, I'll try."

May nodded. "Thank you, Captain. That's as much as anyone can ask." He started away, but paused when May spoke again.

"Captain...about Hale. I know how it looks, and I can't explain it, but I don't believe he was involved in this."

The captain turned and considered the giant crime boss where he sat, his head drooping on his chest. "I'll send a healer to look at his wounds. That much, at least, I can do."

"Thank you, Brandon. I know things look dark enough now, but everything will work out in the end. You'll see."

He grunted. "I wish I had such faith."

So do I, May thought. But she forced a smile she didn't feel. "And I wish I had a bath, but the gods will what they will. And don't concern yourself, Captain—I have enough faith for the both of us."

She watched him walk away, and it was all she could do to keep from screaming out, to stop herself from begging him to come back, to not leave her alone. When he was gone, she let out a heavy breath, sinking down onto the floor of her cell and leaning her head back against the wall. There had been a time, days ago, when she'd worried over the filth and dirt that covered her, when she'd been appalled at the smell that was most definitely beginning to gather around her, but she thought little enough of it now. Not, she suspected, a good sign.

"That was a...good job. With the captain."

May's head shot up in surprise. Hale sat where he had before, but he'd raised his head, and he studied her with eyes that looked black in the torchlight. May snorted. "Not subtle, indeed. And just how long have you been awake?" she demanded.

The crime boss grunted in what might have been amusement or pain. "Never slept. Seems it don't come as easy when...I don't have a good whore to send me off. Tell me, woman," he said, leaning his face forward, "you scared?"

May rolled her eyes. "Let me guess—this is the part where you tell me I shouldn't be afraid?"

His laugh was interrupted by the pained hiss of a sharp intake of breath. "Hardly. Only a fool feels no fear when the blades come out, and they're out in truth now, make no mistake. My question for you is, when they get here—and get here they will—what will you do? Will you run or beg? Will you fight?"

May considered the question. She thought of Aaron, of Adina and the others, all in danger now, if they weren't dead already. She thought of Grinner, so confident in his newfound power, and she realized that though she was still afraid, she was also angry. Angrier than she ever remembered being in her life. She felt her upper lip twist into a snarl. "I'll fight, alright. And when I find out who is behind this, I'll kill every last one of them."

The crime boss grinned. "Now, that's good. Fear won't do us much good, not now. But anger…now that we can use."

CHAPTER EIGHT

He found her at the edge of the clearing, her back to him as she stared off into the surrounding woods as if searching for something. As he drew closer, he noted a slump to her shoulders, one that had not been there before. It gave her a broken, defeated look he did not like, one at odds with her usually confident, self-assured manner.

She turned as he approached, wiping an arm angrily at the tears streaming down her face before turning away once more. "Leomin. What are you doing here?"

He came to stand beside her, following her gaze out into the woods. "They are out there, yes? Those creatures of Kevlane's, what your fa—what the Speaker calls the Lifeless."

She shot a look at him. Clearly, she had expected him to say something else, and she nodded slowly. "Yes, I suppose they are," she said, looking out at the woods. "Though, I take it you have more experience with them than I."

"Something about which I take no pleasure, I assure you."

"What are they, Leomin?"

"Once, they were men and women. Children. Now, though, I suppose 'Lifeless' is as good a term as any, though even that is not quite right, for it is that small spark of life remaining inside them that makes them so terrible to behold. They are fast, and they are strong, and, if the magi is given time, they will number in the thousands. If, that is, they do not already."

"I saw them," she said. "In the clearing. The Akalians are known as the best fighters in the world, yet I watched two or three of them fall for every creature that died."

"Yes," Leomin said. "They are terrible indeed." He resisted the urge to ask her how she was, to see if he could find words to heal some of that pain she so obviously carried inside her. She would not thank him for the attempt, he knew, would only withdraw further into that place of agony and grief that she had erected around herself.

"And yet..." she said, her voice little more than a whisper, "you are going to fight them."

"Not alone, lady," he said. "Were it so, I do not think you could even call what would follow a fight."

"You and the others then. You will follow that General Envelar into battle."

"Yes."

"I saw him in the clearing, too. He is a cold one, Leomin. Cold and hot all at once."

"Yes," the Parnen said. "He is. And he is my friend. Aaron Envelar is no simple man, lady, but then, these are not simple times."

She grunted. "That's true enough, anyway. But what of it? I saw your Aaron Envelar fight, Leomin, saw the way he reveled in it, the way he enjoyed it. Maybe he *is* complicated, but he is no hero out of a storybook—that much I know."

"Forgive me, lady, but heroes do not live in storybooks. They never have. I will admit Aaron Envelar is no knight in shining armor but who is? He is only a man, with his own faults, his own weaknesses, but he is a man with a skill in combat unmatched by any I have ever seen, even our black-garbed friends here. Still, it is not his talent with a blade that makes him a hero—Aaron Envelar is possessed of a will greater than any I have ever known. He is not a man who loves easy, but when he does he would take on the gods themselves to protect the people he cares for."

"Then he is a fool, for what chance does any man have against a god?"

Leomin considered that for several seconds and finally he nodded. "A fool. Yes, Aaron Envelar is a fool, Seline. But then, all men who have shaped history were thought so in their time. All courage contains within it foolishness, and if the world should survive what's coming, then it and all the people within it will owe our foolish general a great debt, for it will be he who has made it possible."

"Pretty words, Leomin," Seline said, "of course, you have ever had a way with words, as you have had a way with lies. Tell me, if you have such faith in General Envelar, are you *truly* willing to die for him?"

Leomin laughed. "Dying is easy enough, lady. Wise men or fools, we all share that particular talent. But yes, if you must hear it, then I am willing to die for Aaron Envelar. But more importantly, I am willing to live for him, am willing to follow him in what he believes needs doing."

She snorted. "Well, I doubt you'll have to worry about living for him long. If Kevlane really does have many more of those creatures, the general and everyone who marches with him will be dead soon enough."

"Perhaps."

For a time, the two said nothing, thinking their own thoughts as they gazed out at the interminable depths of the woods. There was beauty there, yet danger too, slinking around the trunks of the massive oaks, lurking in the shadows. It had not found them yet, but it would. That was a thought, a truth, they both shared.

"I'm coming with you."

Leomin was startled and, seeing his shock, she shrugged. "I've spent nearly my whole life hunting death, Leomin, expecting it. I've wasted years tracking a monster, sniffing out his trail, following what few signs there were—rumors and rumors of rumors. I took this quest on, but I never expected to survive it. After all, anyone who goes hunting for monsters has to accept not just the possibility, but the certainty of her death, for monsters are not made to cower, but to kill. Yet, when I finally found my monster, I realized he was only a man after all. No better than other men…but no worse either."

Leomin studied her for some time before finally speaking. "That explains why you did not bring the blade home when you held it at your father's throat, lady, but it does not explain why you would accompany us."

"Maybe I'm bored?" she said, trying for a smile. When Leomin only watched her, saying nothing, she finally sighed. "Very well, Leomin. It seems you will know all my secrets, after all. I've spent the time since I was a child focused on death, seeking it, in truth, not just for the man I hunted but, I think, for myself as well. It would be…I believe I would like fighting for life instead."

Tears gathered in her eyes, and it seemed to Leomin that she was like a dam holding back a raging river of emotion. It would break, sooner or later, and when it did he hoped only that he would be there to see it. There would be sadness, of course, but he thought that, within those currents, there would be joy as well. Still, he had some idea what dangers lay ahead of them, more than she, and his first instinct was to grab her and shake her, to scream that she must be insane, that she should get as far away from him and the others as possible. Though all lives led to death, the task which he and the others undertook was almost certainly the quickest path to it.

His second thought, though, was to embrace her, to see if he might in some small way erase the pain and loss he saw etched into her face. Vengeance was a cruel master, but the abandoning of it left a hole in a person's soul that was not easily filled. He wanted to tell her he was glad she was here, with him, that he was overjoyed that she would be with him and the others whatever came.

But instead, he only nodded, doing his best to school his features to avoid betraying his own mixed feelings. "And your father?" he said, hating himself for asking but knowing it was a question that should—no *needed*—to be asked.

"Not my father," she said. She held up a hand to forestall his comment. "Oh, do not look so scared, Leomin. I will not kill him, but neither will I claim him. He abandoned me long ago, made of me a stranger—doing that was his choice, not mine. I will not hate him, but neither will I love him. He is nothing to me but a man I might pass in a busy city street and never see again—no more, no less."

"But, Seline," Leomin said, unable to resist moving forward and putting his hands on her shoulders, for she looked so vulnerable, so small in her grief. He thought at first that she would knock them away, but she did not. "Your father," he said, his voice soft and low as if speaking to a wounded dog, afraid that it might bolt at the slightest provocation. "I'm sure he had his reasons."

"All men do," she agreed, looking into his eyes. "But his reasons are not mine, Leomin. I will come with you and the others, will help however I can, but do not ask me to love him. Do not ask me..." She trailed off, tears streaming down her face, and Leomin pulled her against his chest.

"I will not, lady," he whispered. "And I swear to you that if ever I might save you hurt, I will do it. I will not abandon you."

She nodded against his chest, and he felt the wet, but not unpleasant sensation of her tears soaking through his shirt. After a time, she backed away. "What will you do now, Leomin of the Parnen?" she said. "You know all my secrets—they are laid bare before you."

He smiled, and somehow the smile felt more real on his face than thousands that had come before it. "I will cherish them, lady. You are beautiful. You know that, don't you?"

She gave a sardonic grin. "More pretty lies."

"No, Seline," he said. "No more lies between us. Remember?" He started to say something more, but paused as he felt something from behind him in the Akalians' barracks, a surge of power akin to that given off by the bond of the Virtues. He turned, frowning. "Did you feel that?"

"Yes," she said, her own expression troubled. "I...what was it? Is it...*them?*"

Leomin had no need to ask what "them" she meant, for his first thought had also been of Kevlane's creatures, that they had somehow already found them here, but using his own bond, he reached out tentatively to that surging power then finally shook his head. "No," he said. "Not them. I think it is your father and the others. And...I think that we should go to them." He turned back to her. "Will you come?"

"In a moment," she said. "I think...I would like to be alone for a time."

Leomin frowned, thinking, and she sighed. "Oh, don't look at me like that, Leomin. I'm not going to hurt myself, if that's what you're thinking. And do you really think you could stop me, if I meant to?"

"Lady," Leomin said honestly, "I have seen you move. If that was what you wanted…I doubt my eyes would even be fast enough to see it."

She smiled. "They're something aren't they?"

"The Virtues?" Leomin asked, and she nodded. "Yes. They are something." He glanced back at the barracks from which that power still radiated.

Seline laughed behind him. "Oh, go on then, Leomin. I will follow soon enough."

Leomin smiled at her. "I'll be waiting."

***

Seline watched the Parnen walk toward the barracks, the usual swagger in his step that she suspected he didn't know he had. Not that his lack of knowledge would keep her from teasing him about it the next time they spoke. She felt…strange. Lonely, tired, sad, all of those things, but most of all she felt *lighter*. It was as if a great burden had been lifted from her shoulders, and though she had carried it long enough that she might never walk properly again, still she *would* walk, and at least she was done carrying its weight.

Leomin had only just disappeared inside the barracks when the Virtue of Speed materialized in front of her, a glowing ball of yellow light that swirled and danced as if it contained within it some great storm. "You said nothing of how you feel for him."

"No," she said. "I did not."

"Then, perhaps you have not told him all your secrets, after all."

She smiled. "Perhaps not." But she thought that, given time, she would. She glanced back at the forest where, somewhere not so far away, those creatures hunted her and the others. She would tell him. Given time.

CHAPTER NINE

"...Just don't make no sense, is all. Why would they off and disappear like that? And right before we go marchin' to war, too." The man shook his head as he leaned back in his chair, glancing at his four companions seated around the table. "I tell you, it just don't make sense."

"Don't it?" another spat. He was a big man, his stocky frame thick with muscle, and if the scars on his face—a nose that had been broken more than once, and an ear that looked like a lump of misshapen wax—were any indication, Darrell suspected he was a man who had little time for words, a man who preferred to finish his arguments with fists instead of rhetoric. "I ask you," he said, glancing around at the others seated, "what type of fella is it that runs off right before the blood lettin' starts? Seems to me there's only one kind—a coward."

Darrell watched the reaction of the man's companions from where he sat in the corner of the tavern's common room, his hood pulled down to cover his face, and was dismayed to see them nodding slowly in agreement. All but the first man who shook his head slowly. "Just never would have thought it of the general, is all."

"Yeah?" the big man answered, a challenge in his eyes. "Well, I never would have thought I'd see you get knocked on your ass by a woman in the practice grounds neither, Lemm, but thinkin' a thing don't make it true, does it?"

The first man colored at that and looked as if he would argue, but remained silent.

"There is another possibility though," a new voice said, and Darrell bared his teeth as the man spoke, for this was the man he had come to listen to, the one he had painstakingly followed through Perennia's streets.

"Yeah?" the big man said, as if daring the other to contradict him.

The one who'd spoken only shrugged. "Could be you're right, and I can't say as it'd surprise me none. Lot of folks are brave enough when the swords stay in their sheaths, or when they figure it's other folks'll be doin' the bleedin' instead of them. But those same ones'll trample you into the dust if you're in their way when they take it in mind to run."

The big man grunted. "That's what I said, ain't it?"

"So it is," the other agreed, "so it is. And put it mighty good you did, too. Only, you asked what kind of man runs right before the fightin' starts. Well, seems to me that there's two kinds. Cowards, like you said, and one other..." He hesitated for effect, glancing around as if expecting that they might be overheard. Not that it mattered—Darrell had listened to many such men in many such taverns over the last few days, and he knew well enough what he would say. Knew, too, that those who would disagree with the sentiment were growing fewer and fewer every day. "Well, the other's a traitor. Far as I'm concerned," he said, pausing to eye each man in turn, "a fella like that is the worse of the two. Sure, a coward might discover on the day of a battle that his legs ain't good for nothin' but running, but a traitor, well, a fella like that never meant to fight at all. He's the kind that won't meet you blade to blade, the kind'll sneak up on you when you're abed and slice a smile in your throat."

Darrell felt himself tense at that. He knew that he should remain calm, that the last thing he needed was to draw attention to himself. After all, it was only by luck that he hadn't been taken captive with May and Hale. He'd been following Grinner's men, as Adina had asked him, when he heard of the club owner and the crime boss being taken prisoner. He'd been distracted by his worry for Aaron and the others and hadn't thought through what such a thing might mean before he rushed to the castle meaning to learn the truth of it. It was only chance that had sent him practically barreling into Balen, Michael, and a giant soldier named Bastion as they hurried away from the castle.

The sweating, breathless first mate had told Darrell everything he knew about what had taken place, about Grinner's sudden rise to prominence, before begging the swordmaster to accompany him and the others to the ships where he thought they would be safest, should the worst come to pass.

Grinner. Even thinking of the man made Darrell's hands clench into white-knuckled fists. He had accompanied the others to the boats, helping Balen with the giant who was clearly wounded and unable to stand, let alone walk, without help. But then, against Balen's wishes, he'd gone back out again to do what he could. First, he'd traveled to the inn where he'd been staying, remaining outside, hidden in the shadows of an alley, and he hadn't had to wait long before a squad of soldiers had shown up asking after him.

Darrell had thought to go hunting for Aaron and the others, had even been on his way to do so when he'd remembered what Adina had asked of him, to investigate Grinner to discover what, if any, hand he had in the disappearance of the others. Besides, he knew that Captain Gant had men out searching for Aaron and the others, and he, at least, was no traitor.

So instead of rushing off to find Aaron as he'd wanted, Darrell had spent his time following Grinner's men, listening to them spew their vile lies to any who would listen as he tried to follow the rumors back to their source. He hadn't learned as much as he would have liked, but he knew enough now to know that Balen was right: the worst *had* come to pass. From what he'd seen and heard, Grinner had managed to insinuate himself deeply into the queen's counsel, and all over the city, rumors were spreading of Aaron, Adina, and the others running away on the eve of battle. Cowards at best or, at worst, siding with the ancient mage, Kevlane, and turning against Perennia and its people.

Although he knew he would be of no use to Aaron and the others locked away in some dungeon, that there were soldiers out, even now, searching the city for him and Aaron's other companions, he could not help the anger that rose in him on listening to the man's filth. "Traitor, is it?" the big man said, his mouth drawing into a frown as he considered it. "Well, now, might be that's the case, but I don't know it matters much one way or the other. Far as I'm concerned, once they're found they should be executed, and let the Death God sort 'em out."

"I just don't know," the one named Lemm said, finally gathering up his courage. "General Envelar was tough on us, sure, but he never struck me as no coward. Just about as far from one as you could get, you ask me. And traitor?" He shook his head. "Naw. That just don't sit right with me."

Darrell watched Grinner's man study the others at the table, gauging their reactions. When they frowned, he leaned forward, eyeing the man who'd spoken as if he'd just drawn a blade before glancing at the others, his gaze finally settling on the big man. "They say General Envelar weren't workin' alone. Said there was other folks helpin' him."

The big man frowned in thought. "You mean the princess, right? I've heard the same, and so far as I'm concerned, they can put the headsman to work on her, once he's done with that bastard Envelar and those other two they've got locked away." He barked a harsh laugh. "Not that I'd mind if they let me spend a little time with her first, that is."

"Princess Adina is royal blood!" Lemm said. "You can't talk about her like that—she's King Marcus's daughter, for the gods' sake, not some whore you picked up in a brothel."

"Not just the princess, anyway," Grinner's man said as if Lemm had never spoken. His gaze was still locked on the big man who was scowling at Lemm. "Ordinary folks. You know, folks like tavernkeepers or clerks or…" He paused, turning to look at the one who'd challenged his story. "Or soldiers."

Darrell felt his stomach drop as he watched the big man and the other two at the table think it through, saw as they turned to stare at the man who'd stood up for Princess Adina with open hostility on their faces. "You a traitor, Lemmy boy?" the big man said. "That it?"

Lemm's face went red again, and Darrell could see anger and fear warring on his features. *Just let it lie, Lemm,* he thought desperately. *Just leave it alone. A stand is all well in good, but one that ends in a pointless death is of no use to—* "No I ain't!" Lemm said, rising out of his seat, his hands knotting into fists at his sides.

"Seems to me you all are the traitors, sittin' here bad mouthin' the queen and general as if they've already been proven guilty and all that's left is the axe."

"*Ware!*" Grinner's man shouted, jerking out of his own chair and backing up. "He's goin' for his sword!"

Lemm wasn't, of course—Darrell saw that clear enough—but his hands were close to his sides and, thereby, close to the hilt of his sword. Not that the swordmaster suspected it would have much either way, for the soldiers had decided they had a traitor among them even before Grinner's man spoke, and his confirmation of danger was all the excuse they needed.

Lemm stood stupefied as the big man rushed him, his own thick-fingered fist crashing into the stunned soldier's nose with a spurt of blood. Lemm was apparently tougher than he looked, however, and he didn't go down. *Leave it, please,* Darrell thought, *just apologize and—*

But Lemm didn't leave it. He stepped forward, swinging his fist in a left hook at the big mn—who was apparently so surprised that Lemm hadn't gone down on the first punch that he wasn't ready for a counter-attack. Lemm's fist took him square in the chin, and he stumbled, nearly falling himself. The smaller soldier's second fist struck him in the gut, and the big man's breath left him in a *whoosh.*

Instead of pressing the attack, Lemm only stood, his chest heaving, blood trickling down his nose, as he studied the big man who was bent nearly double, gasping for breath. "Now, look here," the smaller soldier said, "I ain't no traitor, and that's that. Damnit, Celd, you *know* me. Me and you grew up together, and you know I'm the queen's man through and through. And just who the fuck is this stranger anyway, with all his talk of traitors? I ain't never seen 'em before, and—" But whatever Lemm had been about to say was cut short as one of the other soldiers came up behind him and brought one of the wooden tavern chairs crashing down on his head.

Lemm didn't stumble, and whatever he'd been about to say went unsaid, as he collapsed to the ground in a heap. "Son of a bitch," the big man, Celd, wheezed, righting himself once more. By now, everyone else in the tavern had turned to watch the proceedings. Maybe it was his embarrassment at getting the worst

A Sellsword's Mercy

of the brief scuffle, or maybe Grinner's man's words had had their desired effect. Either way, whatever relationship Celd and Lemm had shared held no place in the fury twisting his face. "Son of a bitch is a traitor!" The big man said to the room at large. "Workin' with that bastard Envelar and Princess Adina to assassinate our queen."

Darrell saw a mixture of emotions on the faces of those in the common room then, shock, doubt, and more anger than he would have liked. But the worst of it was that none of those who seemed to doubt the big man's words made any move to intervene as he gave the unconscious man three hard kicks with his booted feet.

On the third, Darrell thought he heard something crack, and he grit his teeth together, knowing that to get involved would be useless. Such scenes would be playing out in taverns all across the city now as men who were angry and scared lashed out at those around them. The best help he could give Lemm—and those others in the city—would be to follow Grinner's man when he left, to try to learn as much as he could and present it to the queen. She would listen—she had to.

He looked back at Celd and noted that, now that the fight was done and his "traitor" unconscious at his feet, the big man seemed unsure of what to do. He only stood there, frowning down at the man before finally turning to look around the room. But if he was looking for Grinner's man, he was going to be disappointed, for Darrell realized with a flush of guilt that the man had disappeared sometime during the scuffle, and he'd been so distracted by his own anger that he hadn't even noticed.

"*String him up!*" someone in the crowd shouted, and though Darrell craned his neck to try to discern if it was Grinner's man, he couldn't see past the circle of people that had gathered at a relatively safe distance around the scene.

"*Kill the son of a bitch!*" someone else yelled, and this one, at least, Darrell could see, for he stood in the front row of the circle. Not Grinner's man at all, this one, but a chubby man dressed in a tunic and breeches fine enough to set him apart from many of his fellows and to mark him as a fairly well-off merchant.

Darrell turned back to the big man, hoping against hope, but he saw the unthinking anger return to his gaze, and he bent and lifted the unconscious soldier from the ground as if he weighed no more than a child. He slammed him against one of the thick wooden beams that served as a support for the tavern's ceiling, and Lemm let out a low groan slowly regaining consciousness. The big man, Celd, turned to one of the two soldiers standing with him. "Come on. Gut this fucking traitor."

Darrell had to let it happen—he knew that. As evil as it was, as terrible as it was, him risking getting captured himself would only hurt the city, in the long run. With Aaron and the others gone and no idea of when they'd be back, it was up to him to find out what exactly Grinner and his men were up to and bring news of it to Queen Isabelle. It was the right thing. The smart thing. So it was with no small amount of surprise that he found himself standing, his feet carrying him away from the small, corner table at which he'd sat and toward where the scene was taking place.

"Let him go." He moved toward the big man, but three others from the crowd stepped in his way.

"Just let it happen, friend," one said.

"Yeah," said another. "We ain't goin' to put up with no traitors in our city."

Darrell met their eyes, saw the anger and blood-lust there, and thought it unlikely he would be able to talk them down. Perhaps, given time, he might have done just that, but with each moment that passed, Grinner's man could be getting further and further away from the chaos he'd instigated. It had taken Darrell several days to work his way up to this man, one who, from what he'd gleaned, stood higher in Grinner's pecking order than the others, and he'd hoped—*still* hoped—that the man might lead him to, if not proof, at least the one who was organizing everything for the crime boss while he drank and dined in the castle and whispered poison into the queen's ear. It was a hope that was quickly diminishing with each second that passed.

"Please move," Darrell said, but the men didn't listen. At least, that was, until he drew his sword from the sheath at his back. "Now."

They moved quickly enough then, stumbling out of the way, the blood-lust in their gazes replaced by fear as they realized that the blood they sought could come from them as easily as another. An opening appeared as others tried to get away from the man carrying naked steel in his hands, and the big man, Celd, and his two companions turned to Darrell. "Who the fuck are you?"

"It doesn't matter who I am," the swordmaster said, throwing his cloak over his shoulders to free up his arms. "What matters is that you are about to murder an innocent man—a friend, judging by what he said."

The big man sneered. "Traitors ain't no friends of mine, old timer. Now, you'd best get out of here before you piss me off."

Darrell sighed. "That's exactly what I'm trying to tell you, Celd, if you'd listen." He gestured to the half-conscious Lemm who was only starting to open his dazed eyes. "You have known this man nearly all your life, have you not? Yet at a few words from a stranger, you are prepared to murder him, without any proof of guilt?"

He saw the big man thinking it through, considering it, and he was growing sure that things would work out alright after all, when someone from the crowd pointed an accusatory finger at him. "Hey, I knew I seen him before! That's one of the bastards is on all the flyers been handed out in town square!"

Darrell watched whatever reason had begun to assert itself on Celd's face fade once more. "Yeah, hold on just a damned minute. I do recognize you. Why, there's a warrant out for your arrest!"

"Things are not always as they seem, Celd," Darrell said, trying one last time but with little hope. "We have, all of us, been deceived. Councilman Grinner is the real traitor, and it is he who is orchestrating—"

"*Councilman Grinner?*" one of the other guards barked. "You should have chosen a different scapegoat, you old bastard. Everyone knows Councilman Grinner saved the queen's life not a week gone."

"Yes," Darrell said, forcing himself to remain calm and gathering what ragged patience he had left. "From an assassination that, I suspect, he himself—"

"*Kill the traitor!*" someone from the crowd screamed. "*Kill them both!*"

And then words were no longer of any use, for the two soldiers standing with Celd drew their blades and rushed forward. They were competent enough, men who'd spent the last weeks or months of their lives training with the blade, but Darrell had lived longer than either of them by far, and he'd spent the majority of those years honing his skill with the sword, perfecting it. Time and age had robbed him of some of his strength, some of his speed, but the knowledge and experience remained, and he parried the first man's blade easily enough, dodging a wild swing of the man's companion as the soldier rushed forward.

Darrell kicked a leg out as the man passed, and the soldier gave a yelp of surprise as his feet went out from under him, and he crashed to the ground. He started to rise, but Darrell put the tip of his sword at the man's throat, and he froze. "It doesn't have to be this way," he said to the other, nearest soldier. "You have made a mistake, but it is not too late to fix it. Nothing has yet been done that cannot be undone."

But the soldier's blood was up, and he was in no mood to listen. He gave an angry shout and charged, apparently oblivious to the blade held at his companion's throat. But the last thing Darrell needed was to draw innocent blood, even if it was a fool's blood, so instead of letting the blade do its work, he kicked the prone man hard in the face before narrowly avoiding the overhand swing of his companion. The sword crashed down into the prone man, cutting a deep, bloody furrow in the man's arm, and he screamed in agony.

"That son of a bitch traitor is killin' 'em!" shouted a voice from the crowd. "Someone call the guard!"

Darrell had no time to concentrate on the man's words though as the soldier, apparently unaware or unconcerned that he'd wounded his own comrade, rushed forward again. Darrell didn't meet the man strength to strength. Instead, he stepped back, letting the tip of the man's blade pass so close that he felt the wind off of it. Before the sword had completed its course, however, he lashed out with his own, pivoting to lend the blow force, and struck the man's blade, taking advantage of the soldier's own momentum to send the swing wide, and its wielder stumbling, wrong-footed, after it.

Before the man could right himself, Darrell stepped forward and planted a boot on the seat of his pants, sending him crashing into a nearby table. Ale mugs toppled from the wooden surface, shattering on the ground around the man as he fell, and Darrell moved in behind him, striking him in the back of the head with the flat of his blade.

It had all happened in a matter of moments, and when he looked up to see if the big man was coming for him, Celd was still standing as he had been, staring at the swordmaster with wide, shocked eyes. "Leave it, Celd," Darrell said. "You aren't doing yourself or the city any favors by accusing innocents. Take your men and leave."

But the big man didn't. Instead, the confusion and surprise slowly faded from his expression, replaced by anger. "How the fuck do you know my name?" he roared, and with that he seemed to forget about Lemm, the previous object of his ire. He released him and rushed at Darrell, his sword leading.

Celd was big, no doubt used to being able to overpower those he fought, and it only took a moment for Darrell to see that, as was so often the case, the man had turned his greatest strength into his greatest weakness. During his time with the army, his commanding officers would have showed Celd the proper footwork, would have drilled him on the importance of combining technique with his prodigious strength. But in his fury, the big man abandoned whatever lessons he'd learned and reverted to a street tough, swinging the sword more like a club than a blade, intent on battering Darrell down with it.

Yet for all his lack of grace, the big man was surprisingly fast and that, coupled with the fact that he showed no concern for his own well-being, meant that Darrell was forced to dodge when he could and parry when he could not in a frantic effort to keep the man's wild swings at bay. Each parry sent a jolt of pain up his arm, for a fool Celd may have been, but he was also possessed of a fool's strength. And while he seemed to care nothing for his own safety or that of those around him, the last thing Darrell wanted was for more innocents to be hurt, and he was forced to parry several strikes that—though they had no chance of hitting him—would have cleaved a bloody path through several of the onlookers that were too engrossed in the show to grasp their peril.

If those lucky few he saved appreciated his intervention, they gave no sign, continuing to shout for his death and his blood, cheering Celd on like some demon chorus bent on destruction. The swordmaster made a desperate lunge, knocking aside yet another strike that would have split a pig-faced merchant's head in two, but before he could retreat, the big soldier caught him in the jaw with a fist that felt like it was made of stone.

The blow only clipped him, but it carried such power behind it that Darrell's vision blurred, and he stumbled back, his mouth filling with the coppery taste of blood. The big man's untrained but undeniably effective attack left him open, and in his bewildered state the swordmaster very nearly took advantage of it, stopping his own blade only at the last moment before it pierced the man's chest and drove through to his heart.

Instead, he left the blade there, panting, blood seeping down his chin, and met the big man's eyes. Celd stared down at the steel inches from his chest as if it was no more than some offending branch on a walk through the woods. Darrell hoped that would be the end of it, but the soldier was in the full grip of what he thought was his righteous anger, intent only on his opponent, and he swatted the blade aside with the flat of his hand.

Before Darrell could react, the big man tossed his own sword aside and charged, tackling him and driving him into another of the tavern's supports with bone-rattling force. Darrell wasn't sure if the room did in fact shake from the force of the impact, or if it was only his vision, and it didn't matter much in any case as the big man followed up the tackle with a fist to his ribs.

Darrell grunted and an immediate, sharp pain let him know that if one of his ribs wasn't broken, it was at least cracked. He tried to push the soldier off with his free hand, but the man was far too strong, and he took another fist in the shoulder that made his arm go numb. In a normal fight, under different circumstances, Darrell would have brought down his sword—the one he still held—and ended things fast enough. This time, though, killing the big man would only make matters worse, so he weathered blow after blow as he tried desperately to bring order to his dazed, confused thoughts.

Finally, it came to him, and he slammed his head forward into the other man's nose. Celd brayed in agony, his grip loosening enough for Darrell to free his sword arm from where it had been trapped by the big man's body. Then, before the soldier fully recovered, Darrell brought the handle of his sword crashing down on the back of the man's head one, two, three times. The first blow elicited a grunt from the big man, the second sent him stumbling, and on the third he collapsed to the wooden floor in an unconscious heap.

Darrell stared at him, his chest heaving, aches and pains riddling his body that told him in no uncertain terms that he wouldn't enjoy moving around for the next few days. When the big man made no move to rise, the swordmaster glanced around him and was greeted with dozens of hostile stares. For the moment, none of those in the crowd had worked up the courage to attack him, but he knew it was only a matter of time. What was he, after all, but a clearly wounded old man with a sword? It was one of the very few times in his life where Darrell wished he looked like more of a threat than he was instead of less.

Still, there was no time to worry about that just now, and he turned to where the soldier, Lemm, was beginning to work his way to his feet. The swordmaster shuffled toward him, his blade held at the ready in an effort to discourage any in the crowd from attacking. The soldier was standing by the time Darrell made it to him, though he was wavering drunkenly, and his gaze was unfocused. His back was also curved as if in pain, no surprise after the kicks he'd taken while he was unconscious, and Darrell's own ribs ached sympathetically. "Lemm."

The soldier didn't seem to hear him, running an arm across his bloody face, his head swiveling from side to side with a confused expression like a man waking with no idea of where he was or how he'd come to be there. "Lemm," Darrell said again, louder this time. "Look at me."

Darrell had seen men take such head wounds and never regain their senses, so it was with some relief that he watched the soldier sway around until his gaze, more or less, met his own. "W-who are you?"

"Not important," Darrell said, glancing around at the angry crowd. *Mob might be a better word,* he thought. Or, at least, it soon would be. "What is important, Lemm," he continued in a voice little more than a whisper, "is that in a few seconds, these people here are going to decide that twenty on two is pretty good odds, and your bad day is going to get much worse." Not that he'd had a particularly fine one himself, but it was best to keep things simple to someone who'd suffered a head wound.

Lemm slowly nodded. "I don't...what should I do?"

"Walk to the door," Darrell said, still eyeing the crowd. "*Walk*, don't run, you understand?"

"I...yes. I think so."

"Good, and Lemm?" Darrell grabbed the man's shoulder with his free arm and winced at the ache in his shoulder.

"Y-yeah?"

"Don't return to the barracks—don't report to any of your officers unless it's Captain Brandon Gant himself, do you understand?"

Lemm frowned. "But...why?"

"Why?" Darrell asked, keeping hold of the man's shoulder and gently pushing him forward. "Because they've decided you're a traitor, Lemm, and—"

"*I'm no traitor,*" the soldier said, and Darrell was glad to hear the strength in his voice, if not particularly happy with the anger coloring his words.

"I know that and you know that," he said, leaning over and speaking directly into the man's ear. "And, maybe, deep down *they* know that, but right now they *feel* that you are. Maybe they'll regret it later, after our corpses have cooled, but that won't bring us back from the dead."

"You want me to hide," the soldier said in a half-accusing tone, but thankfully he allowed himself to be guided toward the door.

"Yes," the swordmaster agreed. "I want you to hide, and I want you to live."

The crowd followed silently in their footsteps, an army of demons ready to drag them down into the depths. A man started forward, his face twisted with anger, and Darrell brought his sword up. The man sneered, but he stopped advancing, so there was that at least.

"How long?" Lemm asked, apparently still not realizing the danger they were in. "How long am I supposed to hide like a coward?"

"Not long, Lemm," Darrell said, reminding himself to be patient. "Whatever is going wrong with the city, it will be fixed before too long—you have my word." It was the first lie he'd told in a very long time, but it got the man out the door of the tavern and into the street.

"What now?" the soldier asked, standing outside the door and looking to the swordmaster who still stood in the doorway.

"The first to follow us dies," Darrell said into the tavern. Then he slammed the door closed, turning back to the soldier. "Now you run, Lemm." The soldier still hesitated, as if unsure. "Now, Lemm!" Darrell said. "Run as fast as you can!"

He started at Darrell's shout and the swordmaster let out a sigh of relief when the man turned and began running down the street. His relief was short-lived, however, as someone tried to throw the tavern's door open. It hit him hard, nearly knocking him from his feet, but he managed to force it closed again.

"*Hey, you!*" His shoulder pressed against the door, grunting with the effort of holding it closed, Darrell looked up the street in the opposite direction from where Lemm had gone and saw four city guardsmen running toward him.

He bit back a curse. If he let go of the door, those inside would be on him in a moment, and in his weakened state he didn't think he'd be able to make it away in time. On the other hand, if he only stood at the door, the guards would reach him and, if he were lucky, he would be thrown in the dungeon with May and Hale. No choices but bad ones then. He glanced at the sword still in his hand and a thought occurred to him. He could use the forged steel to jam the door closed, buying himself a precious few moments, but then he would be weaponless, defenseless in a city that wanted him dead.

He hesitated, but not for long. After all, he could get another sword—he only had the one neck. So with a grunt of effort, he rammed the blade down and at an angle through the slit at the bottom of the door as hard as he could, piercing the wood. He gave it a testing pull, but it was stuck fast.

Then, with one more glance at the approaching guards, Darrell turned and ran, venturing out into a city that held nothing but hate for him, alone and defenseless.

CHAPTER TEN

"Gods curse it, man, let me through!" Brandon Gant bellowed. He stood at the stairs leading to the queen's quarters. He'd come nearly a dozen times in the last two days, seeking audience with the queen, yet he'd been turned away each time, always given the same answer.

In normal times, the castle guards would have jumped to obey their captain's commands. Now they only stared at him with expressionless faces. "Forgive me, Captain," one said, "but you know we can't do that. Queen Isabelle has said she needs rest after these last trying days, and that she is not to be disturbed."

"Queen Isabelle," Brandon repeated, a sneer on his face. "Councilman Grinner, you mean. Now, let me through, or I'll force my way in."

"Sir," one of the guards said, alarmed, "please, don't do that. We would have no choice but to take such an action as a threat to Her Majesty."

"Threat?" Brandon asked, so stunned he could barely speak. "*Threat?* Gods man the threat is already here! Can't you see that? I'm trying to protect the queen."

"Nevertheless, sir," the other guard said, "we cannot allow you to pass. Her Majesty herself explained to us in no uncertain terms that she was to be left alone and without visitors."

Brandon Gant bared his teeth, and despite his better judgment was about to try to force his way past them anyway when suddenly the door opened, and he looked up to see Councilman

Grinner standing there. The mask he wore hid his expression, but the captain didn't miss the unmistakable amusement dancing in his eyes.

"Oh, Captain Gant," he said in a merry, almost welcoming tone that seemed strange and out of place coming from behind that silver mask. "I had not expected to see you today. How are you?"

"How am I?" Brandon demanded. "I think you know well enough, you snake. What have you done with the queen?"

"What have I done?" the crime boss asked, his tone one of genuine curiosity. "Why, I have done nothing but look after Her Majesty's welfare, of course, Captain. I would think that you of all people would appreciate that."

"The only person's welfare you've ever looked after is your own," Brandon said, his voice full of venom. "Now, will you let me see the queen or not?"

"Oh, I'm terribly sorry, Captain," Grinner said, his voice full of regret, "but I cannot. You see, Her Majesty is resting now. I'm afraid the last few days have been very trying, even for one of her royal stature. I have only just come from her presence, in fact."

"Is that so?" Brandon said. "And if she's resting then why does she need you there, I wonder?"

The councilman shrugged. "I do not think to question my queen's wishes, of course, but only to serve her as best I may. Still, if you have some message you would like me to bring her, I would be more than happy to deliver it once she wakes."

"Why you smug son of a bitch," Brandon growled, starting forward but halting as the two guards—men he'd known for years—reached for the handles of their swords.

"Now, now, Captain," the Councilman said, and though his voice held only concern, Brandon noted the laughter dancing in his eyes behind the silver mask. "That is really no way for one loyal man to talk to another. After all, we are both servants of Her Royal Majesty, are we not? There is no reason why we should not be on the same side. Come," he said, stepping out of the door and closing it behind him. "Walk with me." He put a hand on the captain's shoulder and started to guide him down the hallway.

"Sir?" one of the guards asked, and Brandon felt a fresh bloom of anger rise in him as he noted that the man had addressed the question to Grinner.

"Oh, there is nothing to worry about," the crime boss said, waving a hand dismissively, "I am sure I'm quite safe in the captain's company. Isn't that right, Captain?"

Brandon frowned. "You'd best not walk us by any high windows."

The crime boss chuckled as if Brandon had just shared some jest, then began leading him down the hall once more. "I understand you are upset with me, Captain," Grinner said in a voice loud enough to be heard by the guards, "though for what reason I cannot imagine."

Brandon gritted his teeth. "Can you not?" he said. "You have wormed your way into the queen's graces for now, Grinner, but I know what you are up to and it will be my distinct pleasure to attend your execution when the truth comes out."

Grinner waited several minutes before he spoke and when he did they were far outside the hearing of the castle guards. "Truth, Captain?" he asked, with that same amused tone in his voice that made Brandon want to strangle him. "You sound like a priest now. So caught up in the truth, looking at the world in black and white. But the world is *not* black and white, Captain, but full of grays, and the truth is as malleable as clay to those who know how to work it."

"No, Grinner," Brandon said. "That's where you're wrong. The truth is not water to be contaminated with a drop of poison, it's not clay to be shaped in your hands. It's steel that will not bend, that keeps its form no matter what else may occur. It is strong and sharp, and sooner or later, it will cut those who think to toy with it."

The crime boss chuckled. "Ominous words, Captain, but only words for all that. Words that hold no power and therefore, are ultimately meaningless."

Brandon gave the man a vicious smile. "It may be the executioner's axe that takes a man's life, Councilman, but it is words that put his neck on the block in the first place. I would remember that, were I you."

"Quite," Grinner said, his tone bored. "Speaking of the headsman's block, I regret to inform you that my questioning—though not quite finished—has begun to reveal some disturbing revelations. It seems that, indeed, Councilman Hale and May

Tanarest conspired against Queen Isabelle in an effort not only to assassinate her but to hand Perennia over to the mage, Kevlane."

"*Lies,*" Brandon spat, grabbing two fistfuls of the front of the man's tunic and jerking him close. "You conniving bastard, if you've hurt May—"

"She is quite well, I assure you," Grinner said, holding up a hand to forestall the guards at the end of the hallway who had started forward. "I have, thankfully, not been forced to resort to physical pain in order to get the truth from her. Well..." he continued, his voice amused. "Not much, anyway. Still, I would be careful, Captain." He paused to stare meaningfully down at where Brandon's hands still clasped his shirt. "An attack on the queen's personal advisor is paramount to an attack on the queen herself, and when the headsman's axe begins to fall, there is no telling who might find themselves in its path."

"Is that a threat, Councilman?"

Grinner shrugged. "Call it a bit of friendly advice." He glanced down the hallway and then leaned close, speaking into Brandon's ear, his voice full of venom and anger. "Know this, Captain. May and Hale are doomed, both of them. Their fate is sealed, and no word you might speak or action you might take will save them. And should Envelar and the others return or be found alive—something I very much doubt—they will share the same fate. It would be wise of you to start looking after your own interests and stop meddling in others' affairs."

Brandon's lip curled into a snarl, and he shoved the crime boss away. "If you so much as think about hurting Princess Adina or any of the others, I will cut you down, and damn the consequences. You might believe you are in control now, Grinner, but so might a man breaking a wild horse. What he feels—what *you* feel—isn't control at all, only the illusion of it, one that will be shattered easily enough when the beast begins to kick. Whatever else happens, you will regret adding me to your list of enemies."

"Enemies, Captain?" the counselor said, tilting his head to the side. "I have no enemies." He turned and started back toward the stairs leading to the queen's quarters but paused, looking over his shoulder. "None living, anyway."

CHAPTER ELEVEN

The man sat alone in the poorly lit corner of the brothel's main room. He did not speak, and unlike most of the other men in the room, he was not accompanied by a lady of the night. In truth, he had not even been propositioned as most men would, upon entering the place, for the women who worked within the brothel's walls were better judges of mens' characters than many would believe. By necessity, they had learned, over months and years spent in their profession, to tell by looking whether a man was kind or not, whether he was the type of man who liked pain with his pleasure, the kind who hit.

They knew such men on sight just as they knew those who would try to weasel their way into more than they had paid for, or those who were simply lonely and would spend good coin for nothing more than the opportunity to talk and have someone there to listen, to show them the respect they did not receive in their own lives. It had taken such women, well-versed in reading people, little time to realize they wanted nothing to do with the cloaked stranger. He did not seem like a man who was quick to anger and prone to use his fists to solve his problems, yet there was an aura of menace, of danger, about him that was more unsettling by far. This man was no bear but a serpent, gliding through life's shadows until such a time when he decided to sink his fangs into something—or someone.

And so the man sat alone, sipping the ale the bartender had cautiously set before him before quickly retreating. The stranger

A Sellsword's Mercy

felt it just as well he was not bothered, for he had not come to talk but to listen, not to pay but to receive, and the scantily-clad women in their lacy dresses who draped themselves on the other men in the room could not provide what he sought.

"I tell you, it was bullshit is what it was," came a voice from the next table. The speaker had a whore draped across either shoulder like a shawl, and so the man sitting at the table could not see him, but he did not need to, for he had marked him upon entering the brothel and knew he was the one he was after.

"Well, sure it was, Greg," another man answered from the other side of the table, raising his head from where he'd had it stuffed in his own prostitute's cleavage. "Gods alone know what the folks holdin' the tournament were thinkin', lettin' women fight." He grinned wickedly. "Still, she was a pretty enough thing, and I don't reckon I'd mind takin' a turn at her, if'n she wanted to put down that thin little sticker she carried and let me do the stickin' instead. That way, I figure she could spin and twist all she wanted to, and I'd applaud just as loud as the crowd did when—" He cut off, realizing what he'd been about to say and turned to look at his companion, the one named Greg. "Well, you know."

Greg was not a particularly big man, but he was skilled with the two short swords he carried, and everyone who knew him knew that he was a mean, cruel man with little mercy in him. So when he leaned forward, a scowl on his face, it was no great surprise to see his companion's face go pale. "No, maybe I don't know what you mean, Richard. Why don't you tell me? Like the crowd cheered when *what* exactly?"

"Well," the other man said, swallowing hard, and the stranger noted the sweat glistening on his forehead in the lamplight. "When she fought, is all. That's all I meant, Greg."

Greg grunted and took a long pull of his own ale, then slammed it down on the table much harder than was strictly necessary. "They cheated me, is what they done. That bitch didn't even come close any of the three times they called it. Shit, even if she *had* somehow got lucky and managed to hit me, what of it? That little toy sword she carried wouldn't have done nothin' but piss me off."

"You're right, Greg," Richard said, eager to get back in his friend's good graces. "Of course, you're right. Gods, a little sword like that, can you believe it? All the fancy foot work and flipping around in the world ain't going to help you none, if you show up to a fight with at toy, and that's just what she had. Why, I imagine—"

"Why don't you just shut the fuck up?" Greg said. "I'm tired of hearin' you run your damn mouth."

"Alright, Greg," the man said, hurt and scared at the same time. "I didn't mean nothin' by it. I was just agreein' with you is all, just sayin'—"

"Never mind what you were saying. I don't give a shit."

"I think she was great," murmured one of the prostitutes hanging on Greg's shoulders, nibbling playfully at his ear.

"Yes," her companion said from the other side, and either they were new, or they trusted in their safety here in the common room of the brothel, or they were not as good at telling a man's mood as their companions, for they seemed oblivious to the anger building in Greg's face. "She was so fast. Like lightning come to life."

"Yes," the first said in a soft voice, her hand reaching below the table onto Greg's lap. "Just like that. She was like a storm, so fast I almost couldn't follow her. And the way she moved, flipping around..." She shook her head in wonder. "It was amazing."

Greg grunted. "What are you then, a couple of whore poets?" he asked, his voice hard and full of menace. The other man, Richard, blanched, studying his friend's face the way a man might study a wild animal, expecting it to attack at any moment.

"Now, now, that's not nice," one of the prostitutes said. "You were great; she was just better, that's all."

"Yeah, honey, there's nothing to be worried about," the other said, pausing to run her tongue along his neck before continuing. "We don't doubt your manliness, not for a moment. Still, maybe it would help if you showed it to us...upstairs."

But Greg didn't seem to hear her. Instead, he turned to look at the first, and she must have seen something in his gaze, for her playful demeanor was gone in an instant as she seemed to realize her danger. "She was just fucking better, that's all. Is that what you said to me?"

"I-I didn't mean anything by it, sweetie," she said, her voice not afraid, not quite, but not far from it either.

"To the Fields with what you meant!" he roared, and the woman gave a shout of surprise as he backhanded her across the face. Her head was rocked by the force of the blow, striking the wall with a *thump* but the man wasn't done yet. "*Fucking whore,*" he sneered, giving her a violent push that sent her crashing to the ground.

"Greg, hold on," his companion began, "she was just kidding is all, man. You don't want to—"

"Not another word," the angry man said, pointing a finger at him. "Might be you're okay with havin' whores talk to you like they're smarter than you, but I don't intend to sit here and listen to it." He stalked toward the prostitute lying dazed on the floor, blood flowing from her nose and mouth. "Is that it, whore?" he demanded. "You think you're smarter than me?"

"*N-no,*" she gasped, "I don't—" Whatever she'd been about to say turned into a scream as he grabbed a fistful of her hair and jerked her off the floor, only to slap her back down.

"Leave her alone, you asshole!"

Greg turned to look at the other woman who'd been sitting with him, his eyes flashing dangerously. "You'll want to keep that whore's mouth of yours closed until I pay you to open it. Unless you want to be lyin' next to your friend here. She's in need of some disciplinin' and I aim to provide it. Now, you want the same education she's gettin'?"

The woman stared at him with open hate in her eyes, but she said nothing, and he grunted. "Well, well. Seems you can teach an old whore new tricks, after all. Now, then," he said, turning back to the woman lying half-senseless on the brothel floor. "Where were we?"

He gave the woman a kick in the midsection, and the air exploded from her in a *whoosh*. "Better than me, was she?" he demanded. "*Better?* The judges cheated—anyone with eyes in their heads could see as much, and I ain't goin' to sit here and be talked down to by no whore."

The stranger watched calmly as the man delivered a second kick to the woman's midsection, and if he felt any emotion at all it was only a small sense of contentment, for he had come to the right place, had followed the right man. Instead of being satisfied by his own display of physical superiority, the angry man only seemed to grow further enraged, and the stranger realized— without feeling one way or the other about it—that, if someone didn't intervene and soon, the woman would die. He'd seen such anger many times before, and it was not easily quenched.

He'd no sooner had the thought than the barkeeper—along with two thickly-muscled men who served as the brothel's bouncers—appeared from out of the crowd who'd gathered to watch the spectacle. "Greg, I'm gonna need you to leave the lady alone."

The man and the moaning prostitute turned to the barkeeper, Greg with a sneer of anger on his face, the woman with an expression of desperate hope as if gazing upon her savior. "You callin' me out, Edder?" Greg asked. "That it? I beat that bitch fair and square and anyone watchin' woulda known it."

The heavy-set barkeep raised his hands to show he meant no harm. "Ain't nobody callin' anybody out, Greg. I don't think that woman belonged in the tournament anymore'n you, and the gods alone know what they were thinkin' lettin' her in. You had her and every swingin' dick here knows it. But I'm gonna have to ask you to stop beatin' on the whore. Ain't nobody gonna want to pay a coin for her, her face all smashed up."

"Ain't my fault she don't know when to shut her fuckin' mouth," Greg said, and some of the anger was gone from him now, replaced by defensiveness. "I come here all the time, Edder, and I deserve better than this shit."

"Naw, it ain't your fault. She ought to know better, and I aim to teach her," the barkeep said, looking down at the bloody woman who was staring at him now not as a savior, but a demon come to whisk her away to Salen's Fields. Finally, he looked back up at the man. "But what lessons she needs to learn, I'll be teachin' her, Greg. Not you."

"Or what?" Greg sneered, some bit of his rage returning. "You'll set those two big fuckers beside you on me, is that it, Edder?"

"If I have to," the barkeep agreed, "but I'd just as soon it not come to that."

Greg frowned, glancing between the prostitute and the barkeep. "What then? Because if you're expectin' an apology out of me, Edder, I can tell you now that we're goin' to be seein' whether or not those bastards are worth what you're payin' 'em."

"Apology?" the barkeep said, giving a chuckle. "And what next, I'll have you apologizin' to that chair over there? Maybe the table? Naw, Greg, she's a whore is all—wouldn't know what to do with an apology if'n you gave it to her. She's property, just like that floor there's got blood on it," he continued, gesturing to the crimson stained wood underneath the woman. "Difference is it's easier to mop a floor than mend broken flesh. Now, I figure you pay me for the damages, maybe take the rest of the night somewhere else until you cool off, and we'll call it square."

Greg thought it over, and despite the difficulties it would cause should the man refuse the barkeeper's request, the stranger found himself hoping he would. What followed would make his job a little harder, but it would also make it a little more interesting. So it was that he felt some small sense of disappointment as Greg withdrew his coin purse and began to pay the barkeep.

The show done, all of the brothel's patrons and workers went back to their own business. After all, there was coin to be spent and coin to be made, and one busted-up prostitute wasn't enough to keep them from either. All of them went back to their own affairs, that was, except the hooded stranger in the corner who watched the two men finish their transaction, watched with unblinking eyes as Greg started for the brothel's door.

Once the man was outside, the stranger rose, checking to make sure that his hood still covered his face, then followed after him into the night, and without knowing they did, everyone in the brothel breathed a little easier once he was gone. He paused at the mouth of a nearby alley, and a vague form, cloaked and hooded as he was himself, moved forward, staying within the darkness of the alley. "He's made too much of a fuss of himself," the man told the figure. "Kill those inside and burn it down."

The figure vanished into the shadows once more, going about its task, and the stranger gave a small smile as he started after Greg. "Hey! Excuse me, sir!"

The man, turned to look back at the approaching figure, his face twisted as if ready to fight. *Good,* the stranger thought. *He's got plenty enough fight in him, that's sure.*

"The fuck do you want?" the man demanded.

The stranger smiled. "I saw you at the brothel back there—saw you in the tournament too. You were splendid. I just wondered if I could, perhaps, buy you a drink."

A look of distrust passed across the man's face at a hooded stranger appearing out of the night to offer him a drink, but it was quickly banished. Men such as he, the stranger knew, took it as a point of pride that they were afraid of nothing. To such men, reasonable caution was all too close to fear. "Well, why not? You got somethin' in mind?"

Oh yes, the stranger thought, giving another small smile beneath the hood he wore. *I have something in mind, alright.* "There's a nice brothel two streets over—much finer than that flea pit we just left. If you'd like, it would be my pleasure to...coordinate your night's entertainment."

Greg considered that then finally smiled. "Well, alright then, fella. You've got my attention."

Yes, Caldwell thought, his smile growing beneath his hood. *And I'll have much more than that before the night is through. I am quite certain, Greg, that we will see just exactly what fear looks like on that face of yours.* "This way," he said, starting down the street at a fast walk. After all, the night was still young and—now that the tournament had begun in earnest—there was much work to do.

CHAPTER TWELVE

They stood on a vast mountain top, so tall that beneath them they should have seen nothing but clouds. Instead, the whole of the world lay spread out before them, and when Aaron concentrated, he could make out individual cities in that great vastness, could even make out individual people as they went about their daily lives. He felt a vague sense of peace settle over him, one he recognized from the conversation he'd had with the Speaker the night the Akalians saved him. For the first time he could remember, he felt no fear of the future. Nor, he realized, did he feel any cold which was strange, considering the height. And the wind—that surely should have been a frigid, driving force—was instead no more than a light breeze upon his face. "Am I dreaming?" he asked the man standing beside him.

"No, Aaron Envelar," the Speaker said, his face, stripped of the black wrappings he often wore, a welcoming, kindly one. "This is no dream. You, like so many others, have been dreaming nearly your entire life. Now, though, you must begin to awaken. You must open your eyes and *see*."

"See?" Aaron said. "See what?"

The Speaker smiled. "Yourself."

"I don't know what that means," the sellsword said, turning once more to stare out at the entirety of the world and all its people stretching out before them. "It's so big. There's…there's so many of them."

"I did my best to protect them," a new voice said. "But I failed." Now, the gray, misty form of Aaron Caltriss, the long-dead king, stood beside him on the precipice. The ancient king turned to regard Aaron. "You must protect them. You must save them where I could not."

"Protect who?" Aaron said. "Save who?"

"Everyone," Caltriss said. He shook his head sadly, gazing out at the world. "Boyce Kevlane was not always as he is now. Once, he was my closest friend, my most trusted confidant."

"Well, Your Majesty," Aaron said. "He changed."

The ancient king grew silent then, and it was the Speaker who answered. "Did you know," he said, "that there is a small sect of desert tribesmen who venerate their children the way most people venerate the gods? They believe that those newly brought into the world are, at their moment of birth, without flaw. That the place from which they came—the place to which we will all return—is a perfect place, of perfect creatures, and it is only by coming into this world that we lose that perfection."

Aaron grunted. "People are free to believe what they want, Speaker, but I don't know that I would call something that shits itself and would starve without its mother 'perfect.'"

"No?" the Speaker asked as if genuinely curious. He shrugged. "Perhaps. Perhaps not. Either way, these men and women of the desert spend their lives trying to reach that perfection to which they are born. They do not fight, nor make war. There is, among them, no deceit or artifice, for such things are most often caused by greed and envy, and these things we learn as we grow older."

"So what are you saying?" Aaron asked. "That we should be more like them? Because I'm afraid I've got to be honest with you here—I somehow doubt Kevlane and his creatures will lay down their weapons just because we ask them nicely. Sometimes, blood is the only way."

The Speaker smiled. "Yes, you are afraid, Aaron Envelar. As we all are. You are afraid you will lose those you have come to love, are afraid they will look to you to guide them, and you will be unable. You are afraid you will fail. And because of this fear, you question yourself. You question and you doubt, and you hesitate when you should act."

"And here my old swordmaster has been telling me my problem is that I always act without thinking. Now, you're telling me the exact opposite."

"Reacting and acting, Aaron Envelar, are not the same thing. You are a man who follows his emotions, who reacts to the world around you, when what is needed is a man who guides his emotion, a man who leads and acts upon the world. Still," he said, giving Aaron a wink, "you are a good man for all that, and there is hope."

Aaron sighed, gazing out at the world, at those cities full of people, most with no idea of the evil threatening to destroy everything they loved. And the only thing that stood between them and that certain doom was him and his companions. "I'm not feeling particularly hopeful just now, Speaker."

"I could hear their screams," a voice said, and they both turned to stare at the misty form of Aaron Caltriss, his gaze locked on some past time, some past tragedy. *"I was dead or nearly so, yet still I could hear their screams when the gates were breached, when the hordes came upon them. My people...my wife."* The apparition did not turn to acknowledge the two men, and it was as if he had forgotten they were there at all as he relived that moment when his life, his world, had come crashing down around him. *"Blood ran in the streets, blood and fire, though I had no nose with which to smell it, I did. The smoke in my lungs was suffocating, crushing, the screams of those I'd sworn to protect like jagged glass tearing at my soul."*

Aaron looked away from the wretched grief on the apparition's face, meeting the Akalian's eyes. "Hope, Speaker, is in short supply."

The Akalian's normally calm expression was troubled. "You believe you understand that Virtue which you carry within you, Aaron Envelar?"

The sellsword shrugged, caught off guard by the change of topic. "I believe I know enough about her to understand that she's a major pain in my ass, most of the time."

The Speaker nodded. "And with the power of your bond with her, you are able to discern the feelings of others, to in some ways, know their thoughts, are you not?"

"Yeah," Aaron said, thinking back to all those times when Co had allowed him to know how a conversation would go before it did, what a man or woman was thinking before they knew it themselves. "It's come in handy a time or two."

"I imagine so," the Speaker agreed. "And in all the years since the creation of the Virtues, none have wielded Compassion with such power and strength as you. Yet, for all that, you still have not understood the full extent of what it is you carry."

Aaron frowned. "How so?"

"The greatest strength of compassion, Aaron Envelar, is not in the feeling it arouses within those who have it. Instead, it is in the power it has over others, for with compassion, *true* compassion, men might be made to become better, might be given hope. Or," he said, turning to look at the misty form of Aaron Caltriss who stood gazing out at the world, tears gliding silently down his cheeks, "at its inverse, they might be made to despair."

"Wait a minute. Are you saying that I caused *that*?" he said, gesturing to the weeping king.

The Speaker nodded. "Is it so hard to believe? You have done it before, have you not?"

Aaron was just opening his mouth to tell the man he was wrong, when he remembered Belgarin's attack upon Perennia, recalled leading the Ghosts out against that army, fueling their own rage and hunger for blood with the power of the bond. He swallowed. "Yes."

The Speaker sighed. "There are not many in the world who know the truth of the Virtues' existence, Aaron Envelar. And very few among those who understand their dual natures—you, though, understand them well enough, I think."

"Yeah," Aaron said, remembering the feel of the rage burning inside him as he fought Kevlane's creatures, remembering how he'd joyed at each life his blade had taken. It was the same as when he and the Ghosts had fought outside the gates of the city. The same rage. The same joy. "But I wish I didn't."

"It need not be so," the Speaker said. "Understand, Aaron Envelar, that *you* are the one who guides your bond with the Virtue, and it is you who controls what shape it will take."

"Wait a minute," Aaron demanded. "Are you saying that I *wanted* that? That I wanted to take joy in killing those men, those creatures?"

The Speaker shook his head slowly. "Want has nothing to do with it. You did, and that's all that matters. You felt angry, betrayed, scared for yourself and those with you. You reacted and, through you, the Virtue reacted as well. You have great power within you, Aaron Envelar. Even without the Virtue, you are a man who can inspire thousands, one they will look to for guidance. With the Virtue, however, you have the power to save the world." He turned to stare out at the miles and miles stretching out below them. "Or," he said, "to destroy it."

Suddenly, the wind picked up, and Aaron thought he smelled a faint trace of smoke, as if a campfire burned not far away. He was just about to remark on this when the smell intensified a hundred fold, so powerful that he began to cough. There was another scent mixed in with the smell of smoke, one of burning, charred meat, and a third that he knew all too well—blood.

Aaron frowned down at the world stretched out before them and gave a strangled gasp. Beneath him, the world burned. The cities had become great pillars of fire reaching toward the heavens, and by some trick of the dream, he could see each individual person as they burned or lay dead in the streets. He looked to Perennia and there, too, the flames raged. Hundreds, thousands of corpses, but the fire was not responsible for killing them all. Walking among them were cloaked figures, some matching the massive, brutish frames of those creatures of Kevlane's he'd seen with impossible strength, others showing the too-slender frames that marked them as those possessing incredible speed.

"*No,*" he grated. "It can't be." He turned to the Speaker to tell him to make it stop, but the man was gone and so, too, was the long-dead king. "Why?" he demanded. "Why would you show me this?" But he realized even as he asked it that the Speaker was not responsible. The tragedy playing out beneath him was a creation of his own fears. His gaze was pulled to Perennia once more, and he wanted desperately to look away, but found that he could not. A moment later, his eyes were drawn to a figure walking in the streets.

The figure wore a cloak, but the hood was thrown back and even though Aaron could not see his face, he recognized him. Several corpses were scattered around the figure, and Aaron felt a mixture of shame, terror, and revulsion as he saw that the bodies were people he knew. Leomin lay only a few feet to the cloaked man's left, his throat a bloody ruin, his eyes staring sightlessly up at the sky. Gryle lay nearby, the youth Caleb's form beneath him as if he had tried to shield him, but they were both as still as only the dead could be. *"No,"* Aaron breathed. "It can't...*I* can't..."

And there were others there, too. So many others. Darrell, a bloody hole in his chest, Balen, his neck bent at an impossible angle, May sitting slumped against a nearby building, a look of astonishment on her face as if even in death she could not believe the doom that had come upon her.

"Aaron!" The familiar voice made his blood run cold, and he looked ahead of the cloaked figure to see Adina lying in the street, propped up on one elbow. There was a deep gash in one of her legs, and she was trying to rise but seemed incapable of doing so.

"I'm coming, Adina!" he yelled. "I'm coming!" But try as he might, Aaron could not move, his legs would not obey his commands.

"Aaron, please!"

"I'm trying, Adina!" He was desperate now, his breath ragged in his throat. "Gods, help me!" But the gods, if they heard, gave no answer, and his body continued to refuse his commands as he watched the cloaked figure stalk closer to her, a bared sword in his hand.

The princess tried to crawl away, but her wound had stolen her strength, and it took but a moment for the figure to reach her. It raised its sword, the blade stained with the blood of Aaron's closest friends, above its head. Then, as if sensing his presence, the figure froze, turning and looking up into the sky, directly at where Aaron stood on the mountain's peak.

The sellsword gazed upon those features, ones he knew well, and screamed, a terrible, tortured wail that echoed like thunder in the air. Adina had not been screaming for his help, had not been begging him to save her, for the face that stared back at him, a cruel, hungry smile on its lips, was his own. The eyes that studied him, full of malicious glee, were his eyes. She hadn't been begging for him to help. She'd been begging for him to stop.

"*Noooo!*" A last plea of his own, a last denial, but the figure's sword descended and, as it did, the vision, and the world, vanished.

***

Aaron's eyes snapped open, and he realized he was screaming. An inarticulate sound of rage and terror, of pain and loss.

"Aaron, it's alright. It's okay."

He managed—barely—to strangle the scream, as he felt hands on his shoulders. The Speaker was crouched before him, his normally calm features creased with worry, and Aaron realized that he'd somehow fallen to his knees away from the room's table. His hands ached, and looking down, he saw they were knotted into fists. They opened reluctantly, and he noted that blood stained his palms where his fingernails had dug into the flesh. "What happened?" he asked the Speaker breathlessly.

"I don't know," the man said, sounding unsure for the first time that Aaron had heard. "I have never been rebuffed so…completely before when using the Virtue of Will. I had not…I had not thought it possible."

"Where are the others?" Aaron asked, casting his eyes about desperately in search of some proof that his vision, his dream, had been no more than that.

"They are all sleeping," the Speaker said. "They finished their part in this many hours ago, and it is the early hours of the morning now."

Sleeping? Aaron thought wildly. How long had he been there, standing upon that mountain-top that didn't exist, watching the deaths of his friends and everyone he loved? Still, as troubling as such thoughts were, he couldn't help but notice that the Speaker sounded winded himself, and he looked old. Tired. Aaron understood well enough, for despite the fact that the vision had vanished, none of the emotion, the pain of it had left with it, haunting him more vividly than any dream upon waking.

"We must try again," the Speaker was saying. "There is little time, and we must—"

"No," Aaron said, shaking his head. Even the thought of reliving such a tragedy as the one he'd seen was enough to send shivers of cold fear running through him. "No." He rose on shaky legs, wiping his arm across his sweaty brow. "I'm done, Speaker."

"Done?" the man asked, as if the sellsword had spoken in a language he didn't understand. "But, Aaron Envelar, we must continue. Time is against us and—"

"*No, I said!*" Aaron yelled. "I won't see that again, I won't..." He shook his head desperately, trying and failing to banish the memory of the feel of the sword in his hands, a sword slick with the blood of his friends. He took a slow breath and met the Speaker's eyes. "I'm nobody's savior, Speaker. I'm no knight to vanquish the monsters. I *am* the monster."

The Speaker of the Akalians stared at him with a shocked expression, and Aaron turned, walking toward the door.

"Aaron, please!" the Speaker called after him. "We must continue. We must—what did you see?" he yelled as the sellsword reached the door and threw it open. He rushed through it, slamming it shut behind him, but the Speaker's words followed him down the hall.

"*What did you see?*"

CHAPTER THIRTEEN

"*Gods curse it, Thom, we're not soldiers!*" Festa's frustrated bellow normally would have been enough to send terror into anyone unlucky enough to find themselves on the receiving end of it, but Balen saw that, today at least, it wouldn't be enough.

The overweight captain stormed back and forth on the deck of his ship, his thick jowls red with the cold, covered in so many mismatching furs and coats that it looked to Balen as if at least half a dozen animals had died for him to feel some semblance of warmth. The crew went busily about their tasks—ones they often made up on the spot when the captain's temper showed, for, docked as they were, there were only so many things they needed to do. Yet still they managed, several men setting to mopping a deck that already looked clean enough to eat from, others—perhaps wiser than their companions—deciding to check on the ship's stores below decks. Balen even saw one sailor purposefully spill something—out of the captain's sight, of course—only so he might clean it up.

Thom, though, would not be so easily moved, and he stared at Festa with a determination that seemed to be a surprise even to the captain. "Captain, how long have I served under you?"

Festa frowned. "If this is you lookin' for a raise, Thom, you can forge—"

"How long?" the older man persisted, and if he felt any fear at interrupting the captain—Balen knew that men had been thrown overboard for less—he didn't show it.

Festa sighed. "Seventeen years, Thom. Seventeen at least."

"Twenty-one, in fact," Thom replied. "And during that time, have I ever asked for more than was my due?"

"Well, no..." the captain began.

"And have I ever balked at any duty asked of me? Have I ever caused you difficulty?"

"Fine," Festa snapped. "You want a raise? I'll give you one if it'll stop you stabbin' me with words like a damned woman. You're a good first mate, Thom, the best a captain could ask for. Is that what you want to hear? Now, how much is it goin' to take, eh?"

Thom shook his head, meeting the captain's gaze. "I don't need coin, Festa. I need your help."

The captain's expression—normally so hard and foreboding—gave a twitch, and it seemed to Balen that it threatened to collapse altogether, but Festa took a slow breath as if to gather himself, then hocked and spat on the deck. A sailor who'd just finished whatever makeshift job he'd found for himself rushed forward with indecent haste to clean it up, but neither the captain nor the first mate seemed to notice. "Damnit, Thom, don't you know what you're askin' me? It ain't as if I don't want to, but these lads," he said, gesturing around at the crew, "they ain't soldiers. Shit, most days it seems to me they ain't even sailors."

"Neither is she," Thom said, and Balen felt his heart go out to his friend at the sound of the older man's voice breaking. "She's in a dungeon now, Captain, and the gods alone know what they're doing to her in there. She doesn't belong there, not any more than a fish belongs on the shore, and her chances of making it out alive aren't any better than the fish's."

"Don't you think I know that, Thom?" Festa roared. "And just because you been the one slippin' below decks and dippin' your wick every chance you get, that don't mean you're the only one likes that red-headed she-devil. If it was in my power, I'd have her out of that dungeon even quicker than your—no doubt disappointing—tussles in the bedroom. But it *ain't* is all. I'm no knight with a white horse, and even if I *had* such a horse, I'd probably break my neck trying to climb my fat ass up on it. And what of these lads here? How you reckon they'd do in a scrap against armed soldiers, trained in fightin'? I've seen such a match before—I won't call it a fight, for the gods know massacre'd be

more fittin'. It didn't end pretty for the sailors, you can take my word. And why would it?"

His voice softened some, and he stepped forward, placing an arm gently on the first mate's shoulders. At another time, under different circumstances, Balen would have been shocked at such an uncommon display of compassion from the gruff captain, but just then he was too busy staring at Thom's face, seeing the fear and hurt there and wishing there was something he could do to take it away. "Men like us, Thom, we ain't made for armor and longswords, not built to go chargin' through castle hallways to slay our enemies. Our only enemy is the sea and the goddess that rules over it—friend and enemy both, mind, and she can be a big enough bitch that I don't reckon I'm too keen on searchin' for another."

"So you won't help," Thom said. His voice was little more than a whisper, but Balen could hear the desperation, the despair in it. He stepped forward and put a hand on Thom's other shoulder.

"It ain't that he won't help, Thom. It's that he can't. Surely, you see that."

The older man turned to look at Balen, and there was such pain in his eyes that it was all Balen could do to keep from bawling like a baby. He held it in, but only barely, and that was just as well. Being known as Balen Blunderfoot was bad enough, but even he had to admit that Blubbering Balen had a certain ring to it.

"I love her, Balen," the first mate said simply. "I don't know why that's been so hard for me to say, even to myself, but it's the truth. And the gods alone know why, but I think she loves me too. Truth to tell, I thought this sort of thing was long behind me, and I didn't feel the lack much, figured love was a young man's game and one that he always lost. Now, though..." He snorted, rubbing an arm roughly across his eyes. "Well. Maybe I was right about that last bit." He shook his head slowly. "I don't know what I'll do if something happens to her, Balen. I really don't."

"Nothing is going to happen to her, Thom." Balen said. "At least not yet—she's in a dungeon, sure, but that's all. Shit," he said, trying for a smile that withered almost as quickly as it grew, "I reckon there's been times on the sea I wished I had such fine accommodations as a prison cell. You too, I imagine."

Thom nodded slowly, but Balen could see his mind working the problem over anyway, not willing to give up the idea of charging in and rescuing her. "We might not be soldiers," he said, a glimmer of hope in his eyes, "but that big fella, Bastion, is. Maybe...if he could show us how to fight or..." He trailed off, no doubt coming to the same conclusion that Balen had himself, but Balen thought the older man needed to hear it anyway.

"He's one man, Thom, and a wounded one at that. Shit, he can barely stand, let alone fight, and even if he could, so what? Oh, I don't doubt he'd make a show of it like he did with those five fellas in the inn the chamberlain was stayin' at, but remember he was near dead when I found him. Besides, those were outlaws, sneakthieves, and men as do their killin' when their opponents are sleepin', if I was to wager. Not trained soldiers in armor. And if we decide to storm the castle there'll be a lot more than five of those fuckers in our way, I can guarantee you that."

"But we've got sailors enough," Thom said, desperate now. "If he were to train us..."

"Then maybe we'd at least die on our enemies' swords as much as on our own," Balen finished, hating himself but knowing that he had to dissuade the first mate from such a reckless course of action. "It'd be suicide, Thom. Even with a year to train, these boys here wouldn't be any more ready to fight trained soldiers than they'd be ready to take off and fly."

"So what, then?" Thom said, glancing between the two men. "We just leave her there in that cell? Just let that son of a bitch Grinner do whatever he wants?"

"Yes," Balen said. "For now. You and I both know that's what May would tell you, if she were here."

"But she *isn't* here," Thom said, gritting his teeth.

"No. She ain't. But she ain't dead either, and neither are we, not yet. There's still time for this ship to right itself, Thom, but you gettin' yourself killed ain't going to help nobody."

Thom sighed. "I hear you, Blunderfoot. I do, but I won't sit back and watch her die, that much I promise you."

"None of us are," Balen said, squeezing the man's shoulder. "You know that. Now, why don't you go on below decks and check on Michael and Bastion?"

Thom scowled. "Alright, but we ain't done talkin' about this."

"No. No, I don't expect we are."

Balen and Captain Festa watched the first mate shuffle toward the stairs, looking as if he'd aged twenty years during their conversation. "You think he'll be alright, Captain?"

Festa grunted. "If I got anythin' to say about it he will be, I'll tell you that much." He turned and bellowed at two nearby sailors, "*Eric, Pater, get over here!*"

The two men hurried up, but Balen didn't miss the nervous expressions that appeared on their faces before they managed to banish them. "Yes sir?" one asked.

"Eric, I want you to go into town and find the swordmaster, Darrell. You know the man I mean?"

"Yes sir."

"Good. He might not be too easy to track down—the gods know the queen's soldiers haven't managed it yet, though I suppose that ain't sayin' much. Stuffin' their heads in those tin cans like they do, it's a wonder they can see to take a piss. Anyhow, find him and tell him that whatever he needs from me to help our mutual friend, he's got it. Let him know we'll be here when he needs us."

"Yes, Captain," the man said, then he started away at a jog.

"*Eric,*" Festa yelled, and the man stopped and turned. "Find him, you understand? And if I learn you been lookin' for him in a whore's bed, I'll make sure it's the last one you'll ever need visit. Ain't no part of a man can't be taken off with enough determination, you hearin' me?"

The sailor swallowed hard. "Yes sir." Then he was off again, running faster than what Balen thought was strictly necessary.

Balen glanced at Festa in surprise, and was about to say something, when the captain went on. "Pater, I want you to visit some of the city's taverns," the man's eyes lit up noticeably at that, and Festa frowned. "Go ahead and have yourself a drink, if you've a mind, but no more than one, for if you draw any attention to yourself I'll use you for practice for the operation I intend for Eric, should he fuck it up." The sailor sobered at that, his face growing pale. Festa studied him for a moment, then, apparently deciding the man was properly chastised, he continued. "You go find you some of the queen's soldiers—I gotta think they catch quite a thirst walkin' around in those ovens all day. You chat 'em up good and find out all you can about where they're keepin' the lady May. Make a friend—Pater, shit, make a few of 'em. You clear?"

"He makes friends easy enough, Cap!" another sailor—Balen couldn't help but notice he was well out of throwing range if Festa decided something needed throwing—yelled. "You can ask Benjy's sister about that."

Another sailor—Benjy, Balen assumed—snarled and gave a scowl at Pater that said the one who'd shouted wasn't just yelling nonsense, and whatever wound he'd exposed wasn't healed quite yet.

For his part, Pater's face went a deep shade of red. "It was only the one time, Cap," he said to the frowning Festa, "and I didn't know it was his sister, honest to the gods. She was—"

"I don't give a damn what she was, or if she was Nalesh, the Father of the Gods, own sister, Pater. Far as I'm concerned, you can swab her deck all you want to, on your own time—though seems to me Benjy might have a bit to say about it. But on your *own* time, you understand?" The sailor nodded, risking a glance at the still scowling Benjy before deciding that, between the two, Festa was less likely to kill him out of hand just now, and turned back. "If you fuck this up, Pater," the captain went on, "I'll make what Benjy aims to do to you look like a holiday by comparison. Now, get your ass on before I decide to send him with you."

The sailor took off at a run, and Balen watched him go, amused and confused all at once. He turned back to Festa who was staring after the man, a troubled frown on his face. "I thought you told Thom you weren't going to help."

The captain hocked and spat. "And probably we won't be no help at all, Blunderfoot, so it weren't no lie. Like as not we'll all end up gettin' our fool asses killed, buried in some field full of worms and what all, and wouldn't the Sea Bitch be pissed off about that? Anyway…" He shrugged, fidgeting uncomfortably, an embarrassed expression on the his face. "Thom's a good man, a good mate, and that woman of his is filled with fire to match her hair—a good match for that old bastard, if ever there was one. Had my way, I'd keep her around just for the way she makes him squirm."

He grunted a harsh laugh at that then glanced to where Balen stared at him with open surprise and more than a little gratitude on his face. "Well?" the captain demanded. "What the fuck you lookin' at, Blunderfoot? If you ain't got nothin' to keep you busy while your own Captain Leomin's off on holiday wherever the shit he went, I imagine I can find you somethin'."

"No sir, Captain," Balen said quickly, but he was unable to keep the smile from his face, "I suppose there are some things I need to be about."

Festa gave a sour snort. "Well then?" he said. "Get on about it, Balen, 'fore I decide to throw your grinnin' ass overboard."

Balen laughed. "Yes sir, Captain. And…Captain?"

Festa raised an eyebrow, and more than ever he reminded Balen of some great big bear, hard and temperamental, but kind enough when it came to her cubs. "Just wanted to say…you're a good man. Sir."

Festa barked a laugh. "Gods forbid," he said. "Now, get on Balen before people start believin' your bullshit, and I have to kill half my crew to convince 'em otherwise."

"Yes sir," Balen said, bowing his head, but he didn't miss the slow, pleased smile that rose on the captain's face before he turned and hurried away.

CHAPTER FOURTEEN

Her face was soft and peaceful in her sleep, and from time to time she made almost imperceptible, contented sounds in her throat. Whatever dream she dreamed, it was not the visions plaguing Aaron, that much was sure.

The sellsword stood in the doorway of Adina's room, a storm of emotion raging inside him. It should have made him feel better, to see her there, peaceful and safe, but it did not, for the image of her lying in the street, begging her killer—begging *him*—to stop was not so easily banished.

He had thought—had *hoped*—that the irrepressible rage created by his bond with the Virtue had been quelled, that he had somehow mastered it. A fool's hope that had turned out to be, and he needed only remember how he'd felt in the clearing when facing Kevlane's creatures, thirsting for slaughter, to know it. And according to the Speaker, the rage wasn't the fault of his bond with Co at all, not really, but a fault within himself.

He wanted to argue, to tell the Speaker he was wrong, a fool, but he found that he could not. After all, had anger not been the driving force of his life for as long as he could remember, ever since his parents were murdered? He saw now that it had been. He had thought that, perhaps, by stepping into the light, by finding those people for whom he'd grown to care so deeply, that he had somehow slain that beast within him, had somehow vanquished the fury that had controlled him. He had been wrong. And his vision, as brutal as it had been, had been a much needed reminder of the truth of that.

It had been nice, believing he could be a man who loved and was loved, to imagine there was a world, a future, in which he could become a man of peace, one who was known for more than just his ability to kill. But as nice as the dream had been, it was only that, for though even monsters might, from time to time, step out of the shadows to feel the sun upon their skin, that did not change what they were, *who* they were.

"I'm sorry," he whispered, though whether he spoke to himself, to Adina's sleeping form, or the world in its entirety, he could not have truly said.

But Aaron, Co said, *you have done nothing for which you must apologize. They love you.* She *loves you.*

And that is, perhaps, my worst sin, Firefly. There are insects whose shape and features allow them to blend in to the world around them, to look like a leaf or a twig, and it isn't until their victims draw close enough, sure of their safety, that such creatures strike.

And you think that you are like those insects, then? Co demanded.

Yes. I did not set out to be, but then neither did those creatures—they are, in the end, only as nature made them. I have seen such insects when they turn on their unsuspecting prey, Firefly, and it has always seemed to me that the ones doing the killing are often as surprised as those being killed. For a time, we monsters think we can be just a leaf, can be only a good man, but the truth of what we are asserts itself, sooner or later.

Then become something better, Co said. *If you believe yourself to be a monster, Aaron, then change. And if you want to speak of insects, then what of caterpillars and butterflies? Or do you only pick and choose your truths to suit you?*

Aaron frowned. "Change?" he whispered. He considered that then finally shook his head. "I don't know how."

Yes, you do.

Through the bond they shared, Aaron knew the meaning of her words, and he grunted. "You mean Tianya."

Yes. She is one who has caused you nothing but pain and grief, yet you have a chance now to help her, to bring her back from that world of darkness she has erected around herself. You can save her, Aaron. It would be a mercy for her, but for you as well.

Aaron nearly laughed out loud at that, would have, had he not been aware of Adina sleeping peacefully only feet away. *Save her? Firefly, I can't even save myself, and whatever world she has made for herself, I would be doing her no favors to rip her from it—even if I could—only to bring her into mine. That would be no mercy. There is always a darker place.*

And always a light with which one might banish the darkness.

Aaron sighed. *They're nice words, but that doesn't make them true. If pretty words ruled the world, Firefly, then poets and philosophers would be kings and treated as such instead of spending their hours in dusty libraries reading through moldy books and writing words that only a few—if any—bother to read.*

So what then? the Virtue demanded. *If you're a monster then will you go and fight for Kevlane? Will you make your vision a reality in truth and kill all those who depend on you?*

"Of course not!" Aaron growled, and Adina rolled over in the bed. He winced. "I'd never do that, and you know it," he said, keeping his voice lower. "I'd never—"

Exactly, the Virtue said. *You'd never. The vision was only a projection of your own fears, nothing more. You are no monster, Aaron, unless you choose to be. Monsters are not born—they are made. If our dealings with Kevlane have taught you nothing else, they should have taught you that. Now, are you done feeling sorry for yourself, or do I need to slap you to make your brain start working?*

Aaron grunted, surprised by the grin that rose on his features. *Slap me, eh? That'd be a trick considering you have no arms.*

And most of the time I'm sure you have no brains, so yes I imagine it would be tricky indeed. They need you, *Aaron—not a man too scared of what he might do to do anything, but a leader, a friend who will walk before them and show them the way.*

And if I get us all lost? If I fail?

Then we were lost already so what difference would it make? And if you fail—though I am confident you will not—then you will not be the first. Good men fail as much as evil men, Aaron. But good men try.

Aaron watched Adina sleeping, thought of Gryle, Leomin, and Caleb, even of Sergeant Wendell and the Speaker's daughter, Seline. He thought of all those thousands back in Perennia who did not flee despite the threat they faced, of all those hundreds of thousands throughout the world,few of whom knew how close they stood to destruction. He could tell himself that there were other, better men who should be in his place, and he knew it was true, but they weren't there to take it, so what difference did that make? *Good men try.* He took a deep breath and let it out. "Alright," he said, turning away from the princess's room. "Let's go see Tianya."

***

The Akalians had obviously done what they could to take care of the wielder of the Virtue of Perception, cleaning the walls and feeding her, but for all that there was a slight odor of sickness in the room. He walked to the side of the bed where the woman lay, her eyes open but seeing nothing, her wrists and ankles still manacled. He studied her, frowning. He had only seen her a day before, yet it seemed to him that she had somehow withered in that time, as if whatever madness infected her was eating away at her body with each passing moment. "She's dying."

Yes, the Virtue answered. *Hers is a sickness not just of the body but of the spirit.*

Her voice was full of sympathy for the woman, and despite the fact that Tianya had done her level best to have Aaron and his companions killed, he found himself sharing it. After all, Tianya may have acted like a fool, but she'd had good intentions, however misguided her actions might have been. And how many could actually claim even that much? Not Aaron himself certainly—or, at least, not for the majority of his life.

We are what we choose to be, he reminded himself. "What do I do?" he said. "I don't know how to help her, Co. Somehow, I don't think a rousing speech is going to be much use here."

"You must touch her," the Virtue responded. "That will be a link enough for you—for us—to travel into her mind. But Aaron..." The Virtue hesitated before continuing. "There is danger."

The sellsword grunted. "Of course there is," he muttered. "Like maybe she'll break loose of her bonds and decide that killing me is still the best option."

"No, you don't understand," Co answered. "It is more than that. When you open yourself to her feelings, her emotions, you will become part of her world, her madness. There is no telling what threats may present themselves in such a place. You might...become lost."

Aaron didn't much care for the sound of that, but he only nodded, staring at the skeletal woman in the bed. Losing her Tenders, those she had led, had been too much for her, and she had chosen madness instead. He owed her nothing, and if he somehow *did* manage to save her, she would most likely thank him for it with a knife in the back. All that aside, there was apparently a very real chance that he would fail and be stuck in whatever nightmare world she found herself in—not exactly a pleasant thought. *Good men try.*

He sighed heavily. "You better not make me regret this," he said to the senseless woman. Then he reached out his hand, gathering the power of the bond around him. And he touched her.

***

It felt as if he were plummeting through space. Wind buffeted him as if in an effort to push him away, to drive out the unwelcome stranger who had come to its world. Darkness gathered around him as if trying to smother him. And he fell. He saw nothing, and he heard nothing but the wind in his ears, felt nothing but the touch of the darkness, tangible and somehow greasy, unclean.

The darkness was more complete than any he'd ever experienced, without even the vaguest hint of light to give the world shape or substance. Yet, for all that, he felt despair well up in him, a terrible, crippling sense of loss, for which he had no explanation. He cried out in surprised pain as talons—shaped from grief and self-loathing—tore at him from out of the shadows. And he fell.

A second could have passed, or an eternity, for time had no meaning in that place of darkness and despair. It was if he existed inside a void, one which held no future, no present or past. In such a place, nothing seemed real at all, and soon he began to feel as if he was not even real himself, could almost feel himself drifting apart in the persistent rush of wind, pieces of him falling away like tattered rags from a beggar's cloak.

He began to feel light-headed, his limbs growing numb as if from cold, and still the talons reached out of the shadows, pulling at him, tearing at him. No matter how he flailed in an effort to defend himself, the talons—and those to whom they belonged—always seemed just out of his reach.

You must hold on to yourself, Aaron, the Virtue said, a desperation in her voice he didn't like. *You are being torn apart.*

"Yeah," Aaron said through gritted teeth, the word falling dead into the air as if the sound even of his voice was somehow dampened, weakened, in this place. "Got a…knack for pointing out the obvious, don't you, Firefly?" Another clawed hand shot out, another piece of him fell away, and Aaron gave a shout of anger, reaching for the offending limb only for his grasp to come up empty, holding darkness and nothing more.

Her world, her despair, asserts itself. You must hold on to who you are. You must keep yourself!

"And just how the fuck do I do that?" Aaron snapped, swinging his arm wildly in a vain effort to keep his unseen attackers at bay. Another piece of him was snatched away, this one bigger than those that had come before it, and he felt some of his unease fall away as a great hopelessness settled over him like a cloak. There was no point in fighting. The darkness would consume the world just the same—had already consumed it, and what light remained was only an echo, only the final, dying spark from a campfire that had long since been snuffed out.

You must remind yourself, Co screamed, and even her voice seemed smothered and weak, as if it came from a great distant away, *you are Aaron Envelar. Say it!*

"I'm…Aaron Envelar," he said past lips that had grown numb from some inner cold, but the words held little feeling, little meaning.

And why are you here, Aaron? Why do you exist at all?

The voice sounded even further away than it had before, as if the speaker were moving away from him, or as if he were moving away from it. He felt a vague sense of alarm at that, but no real urgency, for that could not make its way past the numbness that inundated him, filling him up as if his blood itself had gone cold.

Why am I here? He asked himself the question with genuine curiosity. He had come for a reason, he knew, yet just then, he could not seem to think of it, and it did not seem to matter much in any case. He was here, that was all, and the world was a cold, dark place, without hope or joy as he had always known it to be.

Remember, Aaron—the voice said, and it was so quiet now that it might have been no more than a figment of his imagination, some random thought coming into his mind—*remember...Adina.*

At the name, Aaron felt some of the numbness that had been gathering around him slough away, the way some reptiles cast off their old skin. "Adina," he said, and, once more, at the sound of the name—*her* name—he felt power begin to rise in him, a hope and a passion that stood in opposition of that despairing, sad place. "I am Aaron Envelar," he said through gritted teeth. "I am my father's son...*and I am no monster!*"

He screamed the last, his voice powerful and alien in that place, and he heard what he took to be moans of pain from the darkness around him, felt some great body—or many, he did not know for sure—retreat. Then, unexpectedly, his feet struck the ground with such force that he fell to one knee, and for a time he knelt there panting, his head hanging as the feeling returned to his limbs. "Why am I not dead?" he said. "A fall from that far—however far it was—should have surely killed me."

"This is not the world as you know it, Aaron," the Virtue said aloud as she floated in front of him, a glowing ball of magenta light, ever shifting with a thousand different patterns and hues. "This world exists within Tianya's mind, and so has its own rules, its own laws."

Aaron grunted, looking around him and aside from the light of the Virtue, there was nothing but vast, unbroken darkness. "Must be a law against lights," he muttered. "I don't know what I'm looking for here, Firefly, but it's going to be a pain in the ass to find it, if I've got to stumble around in the dark."

"This is Tianya's place," the Virtue said, "and so its rules are her own—or, perhaps, it might be more accurate to say that it is the world of her madness, and here despair rules. Yet, we are here too, and so we might exert some small influence."

With that, the ball of light shifted and blurred and, in another moment, she was gone. In her place, now resting at Aaron's feet, was a lantern that gave off a distinct—and familiar—purple light. "So you're a lantern now," Aaron said. "That's a nice trick. Tell me, what happens if I drop you?"

"Do *not* drop me."

The sellsword sighed. "You know, Firefly, you've really got a way of taking the fun out of visiting the shadow world of a woman's madness." He grabbed the lantern by its handle and held it aloft. "Now what?"

"Now you walk," Co said as if he were a fool. "I'm sure you remember how."

Aaron grunted. "Any particular direction I should go? Or should I just follow the damned signs?"

"Just walk," the Virtue repeated.

"For how long?"

"As long as it takes," Co answered simply. "You see, Aaron, in this place, there is no true distance, no true time—at least, not as you think of such things. It is not a matter of walking from one place to another, but from one state of *being* to another."

"What in the name of the gods are you talking about?" he said, but he started out, into the darkness.

"Right now, you are being alone—you are also being a bit of a bastard, if you want to know the truth. You must continue until you are no longer alone, but are with Tianya, in whatever shape she might take here."

"Whatever shape?" Aaron said, struggling to follow the Virtue's nonsensical words. "And just what does *that* mean?"

"As I have tried to explain to you," Co said, clearly having difficulty in keeping her own patience, "this is not the world as you know it, and it does not obey that world's rules. In your world, Tianya is a middle-aged woman. But here, in this place, she might be anyone—or anything."

"Like a lamp," Aaron said, grinning as he felt the Virtue's surge of annoyance through the bond.

"Yes," she said, her voice sounding as if she were gritting her teeth despite the fact that she had no teeth to grit. "Like a lamp."

Aaron walked on, pleased with himself as he felt the Virtue seething, then a thought struck him, and he frowned. "Wait a minute—if she can be anything she wants to be, does that mean she could be, I don't know, a dragon? Because that would really ruin a day that's already starting to turn to shit."

"I suppose," the Virtue said thoughtfully, "though, I find that unlikely. Mythic dragons, you see, were always shown as creatures of power, of strength. Though this is her place, Tianya does not feel powerful or strong. It is for that reason that she is trapped here, within her own mind. I doubt very much that she will manifest herself as a dragon."

"That's not a no," Aaron said, but he walked on. The magenta light of the lantern shined brightly, yet it seemed that wherever he looked, he was surrounded only by inky blackness, and he could not say with any certainty what even comprised the ground on which he stepped.

Eventually, he began to hear sounds that might have been moans coming from up ahead, though they were so quiet at first that it could have been nothing more than his mind playing tricks in a place made for them. "Did you hear that?" he said, cocking his head and listening intently.

"Yes," the Virtue said, her voice solemn. "It seems that some part of Tianya has taken note of our presence here, that she has allowed—against her will or with it—for us to enter into her true place."

As if on cue, the moaning grew louder, a desperate, piteous sound that made Aaron's skin grow cold. Healthy, living things didn't make such sounds—they were, he thought, the cries of the dead rising up from Salen's Fields. Slowly, something seemed to take shape in front of him. He squinted his eyes, realizing that what at first he'd taken as no more than a shadow among thousands of them was, instead, a great tree, larger than any he had ever seen, thrusting into the dark sky. It was still in the distance, and he could only make out its outline, but it seemed to stretch on forever without end. It was from the tree—or somewhere near it—that the moans came.

Aaron had heard such sounds before; they were not comforting. The only people who made those sorts of piteous, desperate moans were the dying, or those who wished they were. As he drew closer to the tree, he realized that the sound was coming from the other side of its massive trunk and whoever—or whatever—was making it was blocked from view.

He did not want to go around the tree, did not want to see what could make such cries. But then, like so much in his life, what he wanted had little to do with it—he was going, that was all, and if there *was* a dragon on the other side of the tree, well, then his rescue—such as it was—would be considerably short-lived.

Aaron reached behind his back from habit, only to find that his sword was not there. *Great,* he thought. *Here I am about to face a nightmare dragon, and I'll have to kill him with nothing but words and mean thoughts.*

If it helps any, the Virtue said, *listening to you makes me want to kill myself all the time—if I could, anyway.*

Aaron sighed and started around the tree, taking each step carefully, but he realized after a moment that he might as well not have bothered. Whatever the ground was made of, it made no sound when he tread upon it. In fact, he heard nothing at all save for the moans of whatever creature shared this nightmare with him.

He stuck close to the tree as he moved around it, reasoning that if something *did* attack him, at least he'd know he had something solid at his back. It wasn't much, but then, he'd seen men live—or die—because of less. He'd known the tree was big when he saw it from a distance but now, so close that he could touch it, he realized that "big" didn't begin to encompass the size of the thing. Even "massive" fell far short. He thought maybe "imposing" worked better. Such a word might be used to describe a mountain or some great body of water, some prominent, awesome display of nature. The kind of display that always made Aaron feel small and insignificant while, at the same time—and for reasons he never understood—also made him feel somehow comforted. Perhaps it was because knowing that something so incredible was out there, that it would be out there long after he—and his worries—went to the grave, helped to put things into perspective.

The tree was imposing in that same way—a force of some incredible power, a creation which stood as mute testament against any who might argue against the existence of the gods, for surely such a creation demanded a creator. But unlike an ocean or a mountain range, the tree did not comfort him. Instead, it seemed to radiate sickness, and the side of Aaron that faced it as he moved around its trunk seemed warmer. It was not the kind of warmth that reminded a man of a campfire on a cold night, but the kind that made him think of fevers, of madness, and death.

He was trying to pinpoint what exactly was causing the feeling, was so focused on it, that he swayed closer to the tree than he intended, and his shoulder rubbed against its bark. A brief touch, no more than that, but it was enough for him to trip in surprise at the feeling of revulsion that suddenly overwhelmed him, and before he could think better of it he reached out and caught himself on the shadowed trunk. There was a spongy, fleshy feel to the bark, and his fingers sunk into it. The tree seemed to writhe beneath his fingers, slick and oily like thousands of snakes shifting restlessly, and still possessed of the sickening, burning heat he'd felt before.

Aaron winced and let out a grunt of disgust as he tried to pull his arm away. At first, it didn't want to come, and there was a distinct, unsettling *tugging* sensation, as if the tree were reluctant to let him go now that he'd made the mistake of touching it.

He pulled harder and finally his arm came free with a sickening *squelch*. "What in the name of the gods *are* you?" he said, frowning at the tree.

But the tree did not answer, nor the gods, and that was no surprise, for it seemed to him that such as they had no place here in this world of shadow and darkness. Frowning, Aaron continued around the tree, careful to keep a little distance between himself and the tree lest he accidentally touch it again.

Whether he walked for an hour or a year, he could not have said, for in that place of perpetual night, time passed strangely, as it often did in dreams. It was as if time was some lazy but arrogant watchman, napping on the job one minute only to forcefully make his presence known the next.

Still, he made progress, and the moans grew louder with each step he took. At first, he couldn't make out the source of the cries, but then he saw a figure huddled against the base of the tree. Judging by the size, it was a child, but it was hard to tell for sure, as the figure was dressed in rags and pressed up against the tree so that he could only see its back. Its body was curled around itself as if in expectation of a blow, except for one hand which was pressed against the tree. He couldn't see the hand itself as it appeared to have sunk into the tree's spongy bark, but the wrist and forearm were visible, and he saw black, striated lines running along the figure's skin, pulsing with what he thought must have been each beat of the figure's heart.

At first, Aaron was so disturbed by the sight of those dark lines that he said nothing, only stared in grim fascination. He had seen a lot of terrible things in his life, had witnessed pain and horror on a scale most couldn't imagine and wouldn't want to even if they could, but he had never seen anything so terrible as the sight of that huddled, wretched figure. Finally, he took a slow breath. "Hello?" His voice fell flat upon that shadow world, weak and insignificant, and he cleared his throat, trying again. "Hello?"

It could have only been his imagination or a trick of the darkness, but the figure seemed to shift slightly in response to his voice. "The tree is dying." A little girl's voice, sad and afraid all at once. "It's been dying for a long time."

She shot a quick look at him before turning back to the tree once more, but it was enough. She was young here—five or six, certainly no more than that—but Aaron recognized her. "Why is it dying, Tianya?" he said, crouching down near her but not so close, he hoped, as to startle her.

"Everything dies," she continued, and he could not have said whether she was talking to him or only to herself. "It's in pain now. I wish there was not so much pain."

"Why is it in pain?"

She gave him a quick glance, this one lasting a fraction longer than the last before she turned away. "Because it's dying, silly," she said, but there was no playfulness in her tone, only an emptiness Aaron didn't like.

Aaron grunted. "Can we help it?"

"No," the girl said sadly. "No one can."

Shit, Aaron thought. *What now, Firefly?*

Don't you see, Aaron? the Virtue thought back. *The tree isn't just a tree—it's Tianya. Or, to be more accurate, it is how she envisions her soul, her will to live.*

Aaron frowned, remembering the feel of its bark beneath his fingers. *And it's dying.*

Yes. But you have to save it.

Aaron sighed. *Gods, Co, what do I know about saving a tree? I'm no gardener or groundskeeper, and even if I were, I suspect such skills would do me little enough good in this place. I might not be an expert, but even I know that trees need sunlight to grow.*

So give it sunlight, the Virtue responded as if it was the simplest thing in the world.

Oh? Aaron thought back sarcastically. *And how do I do that? I've no idea.*

He rubbed at his eyes. *Thanks, Firefly. You're a big help.*

The girl let out a cry of pain, and Aaron was sickened to see her wrist disappear into the tree's surface, as if it were eating her alive. He rushed to her, grabbing her with the thought of pulling her away, but her skin was burning to the touch, and he recoiled, letting out a cry of surprised pain.

Whatever you plan on doing, Co said, her voice troubled, *you had better do it quickly. There isn't much time.*

"You...should not have come," the girl said, her voice little more than a harsh whisper. She turned to look at him once more, and this time she did not shy away. In the magenta light, her eyes looked black. "Now, you will die here too."

"I'm not quite ready to die yet, Tianya," he said distractedly, trying to think of some way of freeing her. Maybe if he covered his hands... "And when I do die, it won't be in a gods forsaken place like this."

"You don't understand," the girl said, shaking her head sadly. "This is the dying place—it is what things come here to do."

Suddenly, the world exploded in a sound that reminded Aaron of a wolf's howl, or a bear's angry roar. But the truth was it sounded like neither of those things. It was possessed of a strange, alien quality, a sound made by nothing that lived in the world of men, and it exuded such menace, such terrible finality, that it was all Aaron could do to keep from running away as fast as his legs could carry him. He turned in the direction from which he thought the sound had originated—no easy thing as it had seemed to echo from all around him with the strength of a thousand lightning strikes—but he saw nothing but shadow and darkness.

"They are coming," Tianya said in that hopeless, wretched voice. "They do not sleep—they do not rest."

Aaron swallowed at that. "What are they, Tianya?"

"They are those who have done battle with this place, who assail it. It is they who kill the tree."

Right. It would be fighting then, and him without a sword. Still, at least fighting was something he understood, some anchor to hold him in this strange world. "And let me guess," he said, studying the darkness around them in search of any sign of movement, "they're winning."

"No," the girl answered, meeting his eyes. "They've already won. Soon, they will feast."

He didn't like the sound of that, not at all. Whatever had made that roar had to have been massive, for it sounded as if a mountain had let loose a cry of war. Something like that would not easily sate its hunger—he was sure that he'd be little more than a snack—but he thought he knew well enough what such a thing, such a creature might eat. He glanced back at the tree, its dark fleshy bark pulsing almost imperceptibly. Not a snack he'd choose, but then, it wasn't a place he'd choose either.

He bared his teeth, struggling against the despair that threatened to overwhelm him. "It's not over yet, Tianya. We can still fight."

"You will not run even now?" she said, and in her voice, Aaron thought he heard some small bit of the woman he'd known, some fraction of her resolve.

There was another alien roar from the darkness, one that shook the very ground upon which he stood, followed by another and another, and Aaron's free hand clenched into a fist at his side as he held the lantern up higher in a vain effort to see the source of the sound. "The thing about running, Tianya," he said, "is that once a man—or a woman—starts, it's damned hard to stop."

"You will die then," the girl said, her voice holding no emotion, "and your death will be only the prelude to the tree's own."

"Maybe," Aaron admitted and, in truth, if those creatures in the darkness matched their cries he thought there was little chance of anything else. "But one of the world's hidden truths, Tianya, is that a man has never really lived until he has stood up for something he cares about, even when—perhaps *especially* when—there can be no hope of victory."

"You know this?" the girl asked curiously.

Aaron thought of the vision he'd seen, of his blade slick with the blood of his friends, of Adina staring at him as if he was a monster. *Good men try.* "No. But I'm starting to."

She nodded solemnly. "You are a brave man. A brave fool. It will be sad to watch you die."

A shiver of dread went through Aaron at that, but he forced it down. *Co,* he thought, *what's coming?*

I don't know, the Virtue said. *There is no telling what shape they might take, for what you will face will be representations of Tianya's fears, the despair and grief that have led her to this madness.*

Wait a minute, Aaron thought, having difficulty wrapping his mind around the Virtue's words. He turned to see the young girl staring off into the distance in the direction from which the cries were originating, a terrible fear twisting her child's features. *Do you mean to say that she, what,* makes *them? That she controls what they will be?*

Yes, the Virtue answered. *Though she knows it not. Tianya, like most of us, creates the demons that—borne of fear, grief, loss, anger—haunt her. This is her world. Though she feels powerless within it, she is the only one who has any true power here.*

That wasn't a comforting thought. "Will you not run while there is still time?" the girl asked. "They are closer now, and I will not be able to stop them from doing what they will. No one can. They are always hungry."

"No, Tianya. I won't run—I won't leave you."

The girl met his eyes, and there was a hint of what might have been gratitude in her gaze. "You are a brave knight, sir. I believe that you will fight well, never mind that it will make no difference. I would wish you luck but..."

"Right," Aaron said, "it would make no difference."

The creatures—whatever they were—were closer now. He could just make out faint movement in the darkness up ahead. It seemed to come from all around him, in every direction he looked, and when the unearthly roars began again, they were so loud as to drown out all sound, all thought, and he felt his teeth rattle in his mouth.

"Good luck, brave knight," the girl said. "I will mourn you."

Suddenly, Aaron felt something change, and he grunted in surprise as he realized there was a sword in his hand. It blazed a brilliant white that was painful to look upon. "What the fu—"

She sees you as her protector, Co said. *And a knight, after all, is no knight without the trappings of his class.*

Aaron looked down to see that he now wore white armor shining nearly as brightly as the sword itself. A gold cloak hung from his shoulders. A nickering sound drew his attention, and he turned to see a horse the color of marble staring at him as if in expectation. "You've got to be fucking kidding me," he said. "Gods, but I must look like a fool."

Well, Co said, *she is a child, after all. It is no surprise that she might envision her protector as one of those heroes from a child's storybooks.*

I don't suppose there's much hope of her imagining me an army, huh?

Unlikely.

Aaron sighed. "Well," he said, walking toward the horse, "I suppose this is better than nothing, and at least I've got a sword."

He threw himself into the horse's saddle, expecting the weight of the unaccustomed armor to drag at him but was surprised—and more than a little relieved—to find that he seemed able to move as well wearing it as if he had nothing on at all. Something in the darkness caught his eye, some massive shadow shifting, and he followed its movement up for what felt like hundreds of feet until he lost the shape of it in the gloom. "You've got to be fucking kidding me," he said again. "What is that thing?"

I do not know, Co said, *only that each creature you will face is a manifestation of Tianya's fears. The greater the fear, the despair, the more strength it will have.*

Great, Aaron thought. Now that he knew to look higher, he saw the vague outlines of many approaching figures, their forms only just visible in the darkness. It was as if mountains had begun to move toward him in attack, so great was the height and shape of them.

"Sir Knight," the girl said, and he turned to see her studying him with a worried expression. "They're—"

"Coming," Aaron finished. "I know."

"No," she said, shaking her head rapidly in a sudden panic. "They're not coming. They're here."

Another series of unearthly bellows shook the ground beneath his feet, and Aaron's horse had to step lively to keep from falling. "Well," he said, slamming down the visor of a helmet that had only just appeared on his head. "Let's go out to meet them." With that, he gave his horse a kick, and they charged forward, a brilliant white streak in the darkness.

I would be very careful, Aaron, the Virtue said.

Thanks for that, Firefly, he thought as he rushed forward, *I tend to be when I'm in a fight for my life.*

Yes, the Virtue said, *but remember, Aaron. This is Tianya's world. It is she who breathes life into it, who gives it shape. And she expects you to lose.*

CHAPTER FIFTEEN

Darrell's body ached with each step, but he followed the man down the city street, his mouth set into a perpetual grimace of pain. This early in the day, the lanes were crowded with all kind of merchants out hawking their wares, many of which were of decidedly dubious quality, but this didn't seem to stop the crowds of men and women that gathered to listen to the merchants' pitches.

Darrell was forced to move around them, losing sight of his quarry for a moment only to pick him up again, in the distance. He'd only just managed to escape the guards the night before, but he felt the absence of the sword he'd lost in the process keenly, though, perhaps, not as keenly as he felt the bruises that covered his body—evidence of his tussle with Celd and his companions. He'd woken this morning in a little-used alleyway, his entire body aching and stiff as he'd known it would be. Age might grant a man wisdom and experience, but it also made his body slower to recover from fights like the one he'd been in last night. It was as if his body, disgusted with him, thought he should have learned to avoid such foolishness long since and decided to teach him a lesson.

It hadn't been a pleasant night running from the guards, hurting and weaponless, but even worse he'd lost Grinner's man, the one whose words had been responsible for the violence in the tavern. Still, despite the fact that he had to struggle to repress a groan of pain with each step he took, Darrell had risen from the alley and forced himself onward. He'd stopped at a tavern in Perennia's poor quarter—more to rest his aching, abused body than to find any information—and had been shocked to see the same man from the night before sitting and chatting with several soldiers. Darrell didn't venture close, afraid that he'd be recognized, and whatever lies the man told the soldiers these, at least, didn't end with them turning on one another. Which was just as well—the swordmaster doubted his body couldn't handle another night like the one just passed.

He'd been relieved, then, when Grinner's man had risen from the table, excusing himself to its occupants and leaving the tavern. Darrell had followed, shuffling along in the man's wake, careful to keep his distance. It was how he'd spent the last half hour, the man seemingly traveling the streets at random with no obvious destination in mind, and the swordmaster hoped he stopped soon, or else Darrell would have to pay a cart driver to push him after the man. Somehow, he suspected that would draw more attention than he wanted.

Up ahead, Grinner's man turned down an alleyway, and Darrell hissed in frustration as he pushed his way through a particularly large crowd gathered to watch some sort of play. The swordmaster only gave the stage a quick glance as he passed, but it was enough to sow disquiet in his heart, for the puppets, though ill-done, were accurate enough for him to recognize Aaron, Adina, and one dark-skinned man that could only be the Parnen, Leomin. Currently, the one representing Aaron lay with his puppet's head dangling over a chopping block while another figure—dressed in the dark colors and mask of an executioner—stood over him, his toy axe raised menacingly.

Darrell didn't stay to see how the story ended—he thought he knew better than he would have liked. Instead, he continued to force his way through the crowd, ignoring the shouts of anger from those he pushed out of his way. His sense of unease grew as he feared he was going to lose the man and that he would have spent the last half hour of agony for nothing, so the swordmaster broke into a shuffling run in the direction he'd seen the man go.

He slowed down as he neared the alley's entrance and eased around it, wary in case the man should choose to look behind him. He needn't have worried, for the man was a little over halfway

A Sellsword's Mercy

down the alley and was far too busy accosting some poor woman to pay the swordmaster any attention. The woman was dressed plainly enough, in a peasant's woolen dress, and though she was not particularly pretty, Grinner's man seemed drawn to her just the same. She screamed as the man pawed at her, crying out in pain as he pushed her against the alley wall.

Darrell clenched his jaw, hesitating. The man's intentions were clear enough as he tore at the sleeves of the woman's dress, but the swordmaster knew that, should he make his presence known now by stopping the man, he would most likely lose any chance of tracing him back to his boss and learning who was responsible for the rumors being spread throughout the city. The woman screamed again as the man tore at her clothes and a piece of her dress ripped away exposing a bit of pale breast. *"Help! Someone please!"* she screamed.

That decided Darrell, and he rushed down the alleyway as fast as his battered body would carry him, each step a small agony all its own. "Unhand her!" he yelled, feeling like some knight out of a melodrama. Except this knight was old and tired, full of aches and pains—all of which he couldn't blame on the fight of the night before no matter how much he might wish to—and should have long since retired, spending his time bouncing his grandchildren on his knee and leaving the fighting to younger, dumber men.

Grinner's man turned at the sound of his voice, and as Darrell drew closer he saw an angry sneer on the criminal's face. "Get the fuck out of here, old man, before I teach you a lesson," he said, drawing a knife from his tunic and brandishing it in Darrell's direction in an unnecessary demonstration of what sort of lesson it would be.

"I'm afraid I can't do that, lad," Darrell said, moving closer, his hands up to show he meant no harm. "Now, why don't you just leave the woman alone and go on about your day? There are plenty enough places in the city where women would be all too happy to be pawed in such a way, provided you have the means of paying for the privilege."

"And what if I say no?" the man demanded.

Darrell sighed. "Then I suspect both of our days are going to get a whole lot worse. Look, I don't want any trouble, and I think there are things we'd both rather be doing just now than spilling blood—or having our own spilled—in some abandoned alleyway."

A reasonable argument, he thought, but the man disagreed, and he made that disagreement clear enough when he gave a shout of anger and charged Darrell, the knife leading. Tired, battered, and old he might be, but the swordmaster had spent his long years training in combat, so it was no great trouble to sidestep the man's awkward stab. Before he could try again, Darrell struck with the ridge of his hand at the man's wrist, and the knife clattered to the alley floor even as its wielder gave a shout of surprise and pain.

"You son of a bi—" he began, but cut off as the ridge of Darrell's other hand caught him in the throat. The man wheezed in surprise, his throat emitting a breathless, pained rattle, as he stumbled backward, his hands at his neck. The wind pipe wasn't crushed—Darrell had made sure of that, for the last thing he needed was having the guards called down on him again—but he knew well how much pain such a strike caused, so he wasn't surprised when the man fell to the ground, pawing at his throat as if it had caught fire and he was trying his best to put it out.

Darrell barely managed to keep his feet, as the woman barreled into him, her arms wrapping him in a tight embrace. *"Thank you so much, sir!"*

"Ma'am," he managed, wincing, "there's really no need to—"

"Oh, but there *is*," she said. "You saved me from that...that..." She trailed off, burying her head in his shoulder, and Darrell was forced to stand there awkwardly, patting her softly on the back as she cried.

"It's okay," he said, "you're safe now, but you should really—" The words froze in his mouth, his body going rigid with shock, as the blade went in. He stumbled backward as the woman let him loose, and he stared down at the knife sticking out of his side in shocked confusion. "What...I don't..."

"Did you really think we were just going to let you meddle in our master's affairs without any consequences?"

Darrell's vision had gone blurry, and he looked up, blinking. The woman stared back at him, a cruel, amused grin on her face. "But...I thought..."

A Sellsword's Mercy

"Of course you did," she said, and though his vision was slowly fading, Darrell didn't miss her roll her eyes. "Men. I swear, the gods never made bigger fools. Worried that he was going to steal my virtue, was that it?" She laughed. "Whatever virtue I had has been gone for a long time now, you silly old man."

There was a grunt of pain and anger, and they both turned to see the other man climbing to his feet. "Son of a bitch," he croaked. "You'll pay for that."

"Oh, let me do it, Shen," the woman pleaded, pouting like a child begging for a treat.

"Shut up," the man said. "The gray-haired bastard damn near broke my throat, and I aim to make him beg before it's done."

The woman folded her arms across her chest, frowning and looking like nothing so much as a young, spoiled girl, sullen and angry because she didn't get her way.

Darrell backed away from the two slowly, his legs as sluggish and unwieldy as his thoughts. "Where you going, fella?" The man sneered. "What, you thought I didn't see your ass followin' me, like I didn't notice you were the same son of a bitch that stuck his nose in where it didn't belong last night at the tavern?"

The man stalked closer, keeping pace with Darrell as he backed up, and the woman laughed. "Careful, Shen. This one's a swordmaster, they say."

"*Swordmaster*," the man hissed, hocking and spitting. "Well, I reckon it's good for me he ain't got no sword then, ain't that right, old man?"

Under normal circumstances, it would have been a small enough thing to deal with the man and woman too, but Darrell could feel what little strength the previous night had left him draining from his body as blood escaped the wound at his side. It galled him, but he decided the only option was flight, so he turned, shuffling toward the alleyway, not particularly surprised to see two more men blocking his escape. They were both grinning, but it was the knives in their hands that caught the swordmaster's attention. No way out then, at least not that way. He looked back and, sure enough, two others were making their way toward him from the woman's end of the alleyway.

"You're a slippery little fucker," the man said, lunging forward as if to attack. Darrell grunted, stumbling backward, but the man came up short, laughing at the swordmaster's reaction to the feint. "We been lookin' for you for some time now, old man. Imagine my surprise, then, when I saw you at the tavern last night, watched you keep that traitor from getting what was coming to 'em."

"He was...no traitor," Darrell managed.

The man shrugged. "Maybe, maybe not. It don't matter much either way, does it? Those folks in that tavern believed it readily enough, and *that's* what matters."

"But *why?*" Darrell demanded, not liking the whistling wheeze that accompanied his words. "Surely, your...master...must know that he dooms himself as well. When Kevlane—"

"Gods, but if I hear another word about this fucking magician or whatever he is," Shen said, shaking his head. "Look, old man, even if there *is* such a man as that out there, capable of all the bullshit I been hearin'—something I doubt—then the boss'll either kill him or bring him on side. He won't be the first legend I've seen bleed."

Darrell shook his head and suddenly a fresh wave of dizziness swept over him. The world tilted strangely, and the next thing he knew he was lying on his side on the alley floor. "Tired out, is that it?" the man was saying. "Well, I guess I ain't surprised—a man of your age, why, you ought to be at home in bed, gettin' some rest. Ain't no help for it, I suppose, but you can take comfort in the fact that you'll be gettin' rest aplenty when I'm done with you."

He crouched down beside the swordmaster, and Darrell reached out a weak hand, going for the man's throat. The younger man sighed, slapping his arm away then bringing the knife up into Darrell's face. "I want you to apologize for hittin' me, old man. Only, my ma, she always told me that actions speak louder than words. So, the way I figure it, it wouldn't mean a whole lot, you sayin' you were sorry." He grinned. "Instead, I think I'll carve my apology out of ya."

Darrell blinked, his vision so blurry that it seemed as if there were two of the man, both crouched down in front of him, both of them holding the blade out with deadly promise. "So stop talking and...get it done." *Forgive me, Aaron,* he thought. *Adina. I tried. The gods know I tried.*

"With pleasure," the man said, raising the knife, but before he brought it home there was a shout of surprise from somewhere

A Sellsword's Mercy

down the alley. Shen turned, as if to see what had caused the scream, and an instant later his body gave a twitching jerk. He wavered drunkenly for a second then collapsed on top of the swordmaster, and Darrell let out a grunt of surprise as the unexpected weight fell upon him. Warm liquid seeped onto him, and blinking his blurry eyes, he saw a long, thin wooden shaft sticking out of the man's back. He frowned at it for several moments, struggling to get his confused thoughts in order. One moment, he thought he faced certain death, and the next his would-be killer was laying on top of him with a wooden *arrow*—that's what it was—protruding from his back.

Now that his slow thoughts had begun moving once more, Darrell realized he could hear the muffled sounds of fighting around him. Perhaps Grinner's men—and woman, don't forget that, for it was she who'd nearly killed him—had turned on each other. Perhaps, the city guard had shown up, drawn by the sounds of violence or by some unseen witness. Either way, Darrell had to get away as quickly as possible, for what the city guard had in store for him—if that was in fact who had come upon the scene—would be little better than the death he'd faced at the hands of the criminals. The only difference was that it would take longer.

One chance, then, to sneak away while the others were busy fighting. One chance, but not a good one, for Darrell's body was weak from blood loss, and the corpse lying atop him leaking warm blood onto his chest felt as heavy as if a mountain had come and perched upon him.

Hissing with the effort, Darrell pushed at the corpse, coaxing his failing muscles into action. By the time he was finally able to lever the body off of him his breath was ragged, his face covered in sweat. He lay there gasping for air, struggling against the darkness gathering at the corners of his vision, threatening to overwhelm him.

Then, believing he was as recovered as he would be, he stood. Or, at least, he tried. What actually happened was that his legs gave the slightest twitch, and his back raised a couple of inches off the ground before he collapsed in a panting heap once more. *One chance?* he thought sardonically. *No chance at all, old man.* It seemed like maybe he wouldn't get to die sitting and watching the sunset, after all. But, then, he'd never really expected to. Still, dying was one thing, but giving up was quite another, so he gathered what little strength remained to him, envisioned it in his mind, pictured waves of energy rushing toward him. Then, after a moment, he tried again.

He was still trying when several figures walked up to gather around him, staring at him where he lay writhing on the ground. "Well, by the gods, if it ain't the swordmaster," came a gruff voice.

"I told you it was, Urek, didn't I?" said an eager voice. "I told you, remember, I says, Urek, I'm pretty sure that's the—"

"Alright there, lad, alright. You told me, sure, and it was well done. Hold on a second," the man said, and through his blurry vision Darrell was just able to see the man squat down next to him. "Well, shit, old man," he said. "You've got a blade buried in you."

"My...thanks," Darrell managed, "for being a fool." He didn't know who these men were, or what they wanted, but he wouldn't go to his death a coward. Not if he could help it.

The man grunted. "Well, then you got off light. A bad one, but I've seen men survive worse. Shit, come to that, I've seen the boss take wounds quite a bit worse and keep on knockin' heads like he was in a contest and meant to win it." He barked what might have been a harsh laugh. "'Course, if the boss was here, he'd say he'd had bigger scratches on his eye."

"The boss..." the swordmaster said, what little hope he'd had of rescue dwindling each moment. "I guess you mean...Grinner...then."

"*Grinner?*" the man spat, his mouth twisting as if he'd just eaten something sour. "Gods no, man. I ain't got no more time for that old bastard than I do a whore with swords for legs." He paused, then shrugged. "Well, truth to tell I'd take my chances with the whore and call it a day." He gave a gesture and one of the other men knelt down beside Darrell, and it wasn't until he was close, his head bent to examine the wound, that Darrell realized he wasn't a man at all, but a woman, though one that was bigger, more muscular than most men, including the one who'd first spoken.

"In deep, but not too deep anyway," the woman murmured in a voice that was surprisingly rough even given her appearance. "Any deeper, and I imagine you'd be havin' this conversation with the Death God himself." She leaned in closer, her hand wrapping around the knife, and she glanced at Darrell. "This is going to hurt."

The swordmaster swallowed, nodding. "I'm ready."

"You sure?" she said, throwing him a wink that seemed completely out of place on that hard face. "'Cause, if not, I imagine I could find some way to distract you."

Darrell swallowed again, though this time for a very different reason. "I'm...sure."

She grunted, her thick shoulders shifting into a shrug. "Your loss, though it's probably for the best. I'd break you."

"No offe—" he started, then his words turned into a sharp hiss of pain as she jerked the blade free.

"None taken," she said, grinning at him and displaying a mouth in which several teeth were missing. "Now, shut up and let me work, unless you fancy bleedin' to death in this shit-stained alleyway."

Darrell was about to thank her but decided he'd best let her concentrate. Besides, the wound in his side was throbbing terribly, the sharp pain of her removing the blade having done much to dispel the comfortable—if deadly—numbness that had begun to seep into his limbs, and he didn't think he could have managed the words anyway. He vaguely saw the woman reach into a pouch at her waist, saw her retrieve a handful of something from within it. "Still awake?" she asked, glancing at his face.

"Still...awake," Darrell managed.

She sighed. "Too bad—here we were gettin' along so well. I don't imagine you'll appreciate my beauty so much after this."

Darrell frowned. "Wha—" he began, then she dumped whatever she'd been holding on the wound in his side, rubbed it in, and it felt as if she'd just poured liquid fire onto him. He tried to scream, but what came out was little more than a dried, hacking croak as he strained in the grip of an agony he would not have imagined possible for a man to feel and not die. The last thing he saw before the darkness took him was the blurry, indistinct face of the woman as she leaned close to him, and he wasn't sure in his current state, but she seemed to be wearing an apologetic expression.

"I know it hurts," she said, "but you've lost a lot of blood, and there was no choice. Healing...always...hurts." And then Darrell was drifting, and as he was carried further out to sea on the gently lolling waves of unconsciousness, the pain lessened by increments.

And though he did not know much about these people, wasn't sure whether they were friend or foe, he was grateful for that, at least.

***

Urek stared down at the old man then hocked and spat. "Gods, Beautiful, but if I ever take a wound, and the only way you have of bringin' me back is that fire powder or whatever the fuck you call it, you let me die, understand? Just seein' you use it is enough to give a man nightmares."

The thickly-muscled woman looked up at him from where she was bandaging the swordmaster and gave him a wink. "If it's good dreams you're after, I might have the remedy you're lookin' for."

Urek grunted. "I don't doubt that," he said, "but somehow I've got a feelin' your solution'd kill me as quick as an axe to the throat. Ian ain't walked right since you took it in mind to show him your 'remedy,' the poor fool."

She sniffed, and despite her thick frame and manly appearance, it was a surprisingly dainty sound. "Ian is a baby and too small by half—at least in any way that matters. I can't help it if he can't handle a real woman."

Urek snorted. "I'm not sure there's a man born can handle you, Beautiful." *A bear, maybe,* he thought, but wisely left the last unsaid. Beautiful was kind enough—and he'd take her home cures over any healer's, excepting the fire powder, of course—but she had a temper that, when roused, would have made a bear's pale in comparison.

She smiled at that, putting her missing teeth—evidence of the fact that she liked to fight as much as she liked certain other activities—on full display, and Urek made himself smile back. "Finished?" he asked.

"Aye," she said, "I'm finished." She studied the old man lying unconscious in the alleyway. "He's a bit wrinkled, I'll admit, but there's something...*distinguished* about him, isn't there?"

One of the other men in the alley barked a laugh. "Sure, Beautiful, just so long as you like your men like you like your wine—old and bitter."

Several of the men laughed, but Urek held up a hand, silencing them. "That's enough of that, now," he said, scowling at the six others sharing the alley with them. "Unless, that is, you lot want to hang around this alley until the city guard get here. If what we been seein' lately is any indication, I don't expect they'll be apt to listen to any explanations until after we're dead."

"B-but Urek," Osirn, the youth, said in that always-eager voice he had, "w-we couldn't explain anything if we were dead on, on account of, well, we'd be…you know. Dead."

Osirn was the youngest of the crew, and sometimes Urek had a hard time imagining what the boss had been thinking, taking him on. Still, he had to admit he'd never seen anyone with faster fingers, when it came to picking a lock or jimmying a door. The boy worked like he talked—fast. "Yeah," Urek said, reminding himself to keep his patience, "I suppose we would."

He looked back to where Beautiful still knelt over the old man and frowned as he saw her running a hand gently across his face. *Poor bastard. If the wound don't kill him, she will.* "Alright then, lads, we hang around here much longer we'll have grown roots by the time the city guard arrive, and I don't plan on giving these stupid bastards any company," he said. He gestured at Grinner's dead men—and woman, Urek and his men being equal opportunity murderers—laying scattered about the alleyway. He turned to one of the men. "Shits, grab him, and let's get out of here. The rest of you keep your eyes open, and remember what the boss always says—we ain't safe till we're dead."

The man, Shits, stepped forward, scowling. "Aw, come on, boss. Why not let Beautiful carry him? She's clearly taken a liking to him."

Urek shot a glance at Beautiful and saw the anger building in her face like dark clouds gathering before a storm. He swallowed hard and looked back at Shits. "Beautiful ain't gonna carry him on account of carryin' a heavy load is a man's job, and Beautiful is a lady." It said something about the wisdom of those men in his crew—wisdom learned from hard experience thanks to a couple of poor bastards that were no longer breathing—that no one even so much as cracked a smile at that. "You know, Shits," Urek said, "you think you got your name due to that one time you went out drinkin' more than any fool with any sense would with somewhat predictable results, but the truth is you got it on account of that's just about the only thing that comes out of your mouth—shit. Now, get him before I lose my patience."

Shits muttered under his breath at the laughter of his fellows, but he went, and that was all well enough. Urek never begrudged a man his right to bitch and moan, just so long as he did what needed doing, and a glance at Beautiful showed him, to his relief, that she'd been pleased at his comment.

Shits grunted with the effort of leveraging the old man onto his back. "Gods, but the bastard is heavier than he has any right to be."

"Yeah," Urek said dryly. "Well, I've always heard the years sit heavy on a man, and now I guess we know the truth of it. Now, if you're done with your cryin' I think it's time we got out of here."

CHAPTER SIXTEEN

Adina awoke feeling groggy and out of sorts. For several panicked moments she could not remember where she was or how she'd come to be there. Then her memory returned and, with it, a feeling of confidence, of courage that she was surprised to find. It was as if she had turned over a cushion she'd searched before only to see that, this time, a gold coin waited beneath her questing fingers. She didn't remember much of her meeting with the Speaker, and what little she did recall seemed to make no sense: her standing on a mountain top, the Speaker of the Akalians beside her, his voice soft yet powerful, insistent.

She couldn't remember the man's exact words, but she remembered well their meaning—*you are enough.* A simple thing, really, yet her fate and that of her people might depend on her understanding it, *believing* it. For all her life, Adina had always measured herself against those around her, and had inevitably found herself wanting. She was not as wise as her father, not as compassionate as Eladen. Nor, either, was she as clever as Ellemont, or as wild, as bold as her sister Olivia had been.

Tears gathered in her eyes, but she was slow to wipe them away. Though the memory of the family she'd loved so dearly was painful, there was also joy there, joy and, more than that, comfort. So she allowed herself a moment, lying there in the Akalian barracks, to remember her father's easy smile, Olivia's, wild, somehow freeing laugh. She remembered too the half-grin, arrogant and self-deprecating at the same time, that her brother,

Ellemont, so often gave her. As if the world were full of fools and he knew it, yet he knew just as well that he was one of them. She remembered Eladen, standing tall against her—and the rest of her siblings—recriminations and warnings, doing what was right not because it was easy but simply because it was how he was.

The world was a darker place now that Olivia's laughter was no longer in it, now that Eladen's hope, and her father's wisdom had been wasted and squandered. It had been done the way a child, knowing no better, might discard some precious gem because it was covered in dirt only to pick up a river-smoothed rock instead and think themselves lucky in the bargain.

The world was that child, rushing along the river bank, charging headlong across a fallen log that spanned the rapids beneath, unaware that the fallen tree upon which she ran was cracking beneath her. Adina did not know if she and the others could hold that makeshift bridge together long enough for the child to cross, thought it all too likely that the youth would be swept away in the torrent that was Kevlane's cruel quest, but she would try.

She didn't have her father's wisdom, nor her brothers' cleverness or compassion, yet *she was enough*. Enough to see the battle through to whatever might come, enough to stand against the coming darkness, and if she could not save the girl from her precarious perch, then she would at least stand on the other side with a lantern in hand, showing her the way that she must go and, she hoped, giving the girl—giving the *world*—the strength they needed to reach the other side.

She wondered idly what the others had experienced when the Speaker touched them with the power of the Virtue of Will, wondered if they felt as she did—somehow lighter, as if a great burden had been stripped away from her. They all had departed the meeting room at nearly the same time—Gryle, Caleb, even Leomin and the woman Seline who had shown up moments before Adina had been lost in her own vision or dream or whatever it had been. They had walked out together, and yet Adina had not thought to ask them of their own experiences with the Speaker, had not even stopped to wonder how the man might have touched all of them at once with such power—or even if he had. She had been exhausted and elated and possessed of a contentment that most often only came to one in dreams, when the worries and fears of the waking world stood on the other side of a barrier of sleep, unable to penetrate into the dream in which she found herself.

And whatever the others had experienced, they, too, seemed reluctant to speak, to break the power of the dream that still seemed to hang over them. They had each made their way to their rooms separately with no more than small, knowing smiles. All, that was, except for Aaron. For the first time since she'd wakened, Adina felt a twinge of worry. The sellsword had not walked out with her and the others. When she'd left, he and the Speaker had both been sitting, their heads against their chests, their eyes closed, so still that, had she not seen their chests rise and fall, Adina might have thought them dead. She had considered asking the Speaker if everything was okay, but had decided against it as she had not wished to interrupt whatever vision the two men shared. Now, though, with the power of her vision no longer as strong and all-encompassing, she felt a niggle of worry that Aaron had not left with them, nor had he come to see her when he'd finished as she'd been sure he would.

That doesn't mean there's anything to worry about, Addy, she thought, and started at the nickname her brother Eladen had given her when she was a child. She had not thought of it in some time, not since Eladen's death at the least, and it was odd that it would invade her own thoughts so naturally. Still, old nickname or not, surely she didn't have to worry about Aaron. It was no great surprise that it would take him longer to hear and accept the Speaker's message, for while he was the most capable man she knew, he was also the most stubborn. Add to that the fact that Aaron was the general of her sister's army, and that it would be he who would led the battle against Kevlane and his creatures, and it was no real surprise that the Speaker's message to Aaron had taken longer to impart—or to receive—than it had for the others.

But for all her logic, Adina couldn't rid herself of the uncertainty that had disrupted her otherwise happy mood. She rose from her bed and dressed, all the while telling herself that everything was okay, that Aaron was okay. Not that it did her much good. With each moment that passed as she hurriedly threw on her clothes and boots, Adina grew more and more certain that something had happened, that something was wrong. By the time she was finished dressing, her fear had crystallized in her mind, and she left the room at a run.

She hurried down the barrack's hallway to the room Aaron had been given. *He'll be fine,* she told herself as she knocked. *He'll answer the door, exhausted from lack of sleep, but fine otherwise.* But no one answered her first knock, or the second. She tested the door and it swung open. Aaron was not there. The barracks had no windows, and so she couldn't be sure what time it was, but she didn't think she'd slept overly long. She felt certain it was still dark, most likely the very early hours of the morning.

So then where *was* he? *There's still no reason to panic,* she told herself. *He just stayed in the meeting room with the Speaker, that's all.* That made some kind of sense, surely. Even now, the two men were no doubt bent in conversation, most likely over how the Akalians would breach Baresh's walls to open the gate, and what to do once they had.

Adina hurried down the hallways toward the meeting room. Two Akalians stood on either side of the door, and if they felt any surprise or confusion at a woman practically sprinting toward them in the middle of the night, the black cloth wrapped around their faces concealed it. "I need to get inside," she said, pausing to pant for breath.

Without a word, one of the Akalians disappeared inside and reappeared a moment later, swinging the door wide so that she could enter. The Speaker sat in the same chair in which he had hours before, his face uncovered.

"Princess Adina," he said. There was a note of exhaustion in his voice and dark, purple circles under his eyes. Whatever power his bond with the Virtue of Will gave the man, it was clear that exercising it took a toll on him. "I had not thought to see you again until tomorrow."

"Sorry, but I was looking for Aaron."

The Speaker frowned. "General Envelar left a few hours ago—I had thought he went to rest. I'm sure he's in his room, for experiencing the power of the Virtue of Will is, I'm afraid, an exhausting prospect not just for me but for he—or she—who it is used upon. I myself, I must admit, had fallen asleep in my chair before—"

A Sellsword's Mercy

"He's not in his room," Adina interrupted, aware that she was talking over the leader of the most-skilled—and most feared—warriors the world had to offer, but too concerned for Aaron to care. "I checked. And he didn't..." She paused, stopping herself from saying that he hadn't come to see her, as she'd thought he would. The Speaker might have saved her and the others, but that didn't mean her relationship with Aaron was any of his business.

Adina watched the Speaker's expression grow troubled, mirroring the fear she felt in her own heart. "Did something happen?" she asked.

The Speaker seemed in deep thought, and he started when she spoke. "Forgive me, what did you say?"

Adina took a step further into the room, her fear making her bold and more than a little angry. "Aaron didn't leave with me and the others. When I left, you were both still in here doing...well, whatever it was you were doing. Now, I can't seem to find him, so I'm asking you—did something *happen?*"

The Speaker frowned. "Aaron Envelar is a powerful man—not even he understands the true strength he commands. I had expected such a joining of the bond to be...difficult. But conquering one's fears is never easy and—"

"What did you do?" Adina demanded, her jaw clenching.

The Akalian shook his head slowly, seemingly lost in thought. "It is not what *I* did, Princess, but what Aaron Envelar did."

"And just what was that?" she managed, her patience a frayed, pitiful thing.

"He banished me," the Speaker said, as if he still didn't quite believe it. "Never before have I experienced such a...rejection as I did at his hands when exercising the power of my bond. In truth, I had not even known such was possible. General Envelar somehow took over the vision—my vision—and made it his own, throwing me out of it, the way an innkeeper might expel a customer behind on his payments."

He shook his head in wonder that such a thing could happen, but Adina cared nothing for the man's surprise, only for Aaron and finding out where he was. "So what was the vision about then?"

"I...don't know," the Speaker said, and he held a hand up to forestall Adina before she could speak. "That is to say that, before Aaron banished me from it, the vision was much the same as those you and the others experienced. Of course, the message was different, as it had to be. What he might have seen or felt afterward..." He shook his head slowly. "I do not know, but he seemed greatly troubled at the vision's end and, during it, I was forced to restrain him lest he hurt himself. He called out your name, this much I know, but after he woke he said little before departing. Only said something about being a monster and—"

"Wait a minute," Adina interrupted, her heart racing in her chest, "he said he was a monster?" She'd heard the sellsword say such before, when his bond with the Virtue of Compassion caused him to go into one of his uncontrollable rages, and she had thought—had hoped—that those days were behind him.

"Yes," the Akalian said, obviously concerned. He rose from the chair in which he'd been sitting. "I think, perhaps, I will help you find him, if you will have me."

"Fine," she said, already restless to be moving, to be searching for him. "Aaron has felt this way before, thought that the only way he could protect me and the others was to get as far away from us as possible. We'll have to go into the woods to check—"

"There is no need," the Speaker said, "for I know that General Envelar has not ventured into the woods and away from the protective perimeter my brothers have established. I would have heard news, had he done so."

"You're sure?"

"Without question, Princess," the Speaker said, "for my brothers believe in the importance of Aaron Envelar in the coming battle as much as I do—or nearly so."

Adina hissed. "Where then? The barracks isn't that big. If Aaron has reverted to believing that he's a monster, he'll want to get as far away from me and the others as he can."

The Speaker frowned, considering. Then, finally, his eyes went wide. "Oh gods, let it not be so," he breathed.

"What?" Adina said, her stomach fluttering with apprehension. "What is it?"

"Perhaps it is as you fear, Princess, and General Envelar has sought to put as much distance between himself and you and your companions as possible. But the circumstances allow him little enough movement and, such a man, without the ability to flee in fear of the monster he believes himself to be, might choose another course."

"What course?"

"He might choose to prove to himself that he is not a monster, after all. *Gods*," he breathed, this in little more than a whisper. "*He is not ready.*"

"Not ready for *what?*" Adina demanded.

"Follow me," the Speaker said, heading for the door at a jog. "Perhaps, there is still time."

***

"Why did you bring her here?" Adina demanded, her fear making her angry as she and the Speaker walked through the barrack's hallway. "You know she tried to kill Aaron before, don't you?"

"Yes," the Speaker said, "I know, but though Tianya was misguided, her intentions were good—I would not wish anyone such a death as Kevlane would visit upon her, should she be captured. And even if mercy was not enough to compel me to help her, surely practicality would have been, for Kevlane covets the Seven, and should he bond with even one more, he would be all but unstoppable." He stopped in front of a door and nodded to her. "She is within."

Adina pushed her way inside the room, not bothering to knock, for if what the Speaker had told her was true, Tianya would not have answered in any case. The door swung open, and she felt a great sense of relief flood through her when she saw Aaron knelt beside the woman's bed. Her relief was short-lived, however, for she saw that the sellsword's eyes were closed—as were Tianya's—and he was not moving.

"Aaron?"

He did not answer, and Adina hurried to the bed. As she drew closer, she saw that he clasped one of Tianya's too-thin hands in a white-knuckled grip. "Aaron?" Suddenly the sellsword let out an angry hiss. Adina knew that sound, had heard him make it before. He was in pain.

As she watched him, a line of blood began to trickle from his nose. That decided her, and Adina rushed forward, meaning to jerk the sellsword away from the wasted form in the bed and whatever pain he'd subjected himself to. She'd only just grabbed his shoulders—shocked at how hot they felt to the touch even through the thick shirt he wore—when the Speaker stepped into the room.

"*Do not,*" he said, in a voice that was at once commanding and full of fear.

Adina froze, though whether by her own will or that of the Speaker's bond forced upon her, she could not have said for sure. She turned to him, her lips twisting into a snarl. "Why not? Can't you see that whatever it is, whatever he's doing, it's *hurting* him?" As if to illustrate her point, the sellsword let out a low, almost imperceptible moan, and his breathing sped up until he was nearly panting. "Damnit, what's happening to him?"

The Speaker shook his head slowly. "Aaron Envelar has entered into the woman's madness, Princess. He is in her world now, her mind, and there is no way of knowing what horrors he faces within it."

"Well," Adina snapped, studying the sellsword, troubled at the rapid rise and fall of his chest as he sucked in shallow, desperate breaths, "then get him out of it. Surely, there must be a way to—"

"No," the Speaker said. "There is not. Believe me, Princess, I beg you. Aaron's being is now a part of Tianya's mind, and should you sever the connection…" He shook his head slowly, and Adina's heart skipped a beat in her chest.

"He'd be lost," she said in shock. "Lost in her mind."

"Yes," the Speaker agreed. "Should you separate the connection before it is finished, the Aaron Envelar you know would not return. His body would still live on, but without his mind to guide it, it would be little more than a sack of flesh."

"But *why?*" Adina demanded. "Why would he do this? He knows as well as I what Tianya is capable of, what she was willing to do to him. Why would he possibly risk his life for hers?"

The Speaker winced. "Because I asked him to."

"You did *what?*" Adina screamed.

The Akalian's face was troubled, but he did not look away from where he studied the sellsword. "The war with the magi and his minions comes, Princess, and even with all of the Virtues gathered together, even with their combined might, victory is far from certain, for there are other magics in the world. Dark magics which the magi uses even now to raise an army against us the likes of which Telrear has never seen and will not see again, whatever comes."

"And?" Adina hissed. "Somehow that gives you the right to ask Aaron to risk his life for a woman who tried to kill him? And why couldn't you do something yourself, like with the visions you showed me and the others?"

The Speaker was shaking his head before she was finished. "The power of my Virtue is dependent upon a person's will. Even if that will is a weak, frail thing, it might still be strengthened by the bond. But the woman you know as Tianya is too far gone for such measures, Princess, for she has almost fully succumbed to her madness, her grief, and in doing so has given up whatever will she once possessed."

"*Almost* fully," Adina repeated, glancing back at Aaron and the wasted, frail thing in the bed. To her, it looked as if Tianya were moments away from death, and it was a wonder that a person in her condition could even draw breath into her lungs. "What happens when she does succumb completely?"

The Speaker met her eyes. "Then she will die, Princess."

"And Aaron?" The Speaker did not answer her, only studied her silently, and Adina realized she didn't need him to. She thought she knew the answer well enough—if Tianya died then so would Aaron. She took a slow, deep breath. She would do the sellsword no good, if she gave in to the panic that threatened to overwhelm her, so she forced herself to slow down, to think. "So what can we do?"

The Speaker's face twisted with frustration, but he clearly made his own effort to calm down. He shook his head. "We can only wait."

"And pray Aaron is strong enough," Adina said, nodding and taking at least some comfort in that, for Aaron was the strongest man she had ever met.

"Not only Aaron, I'm afraid," the Speaker said. "You see," he continued, noting her confused expression, "General Envelar is within the woman's world, and though I do not doubt his courage or his resolve, he will be facing Tianya's madness, her fears. And though others might lend their aid, in the end, we each must conquer our own demons."

"So there's nothing we can do," Adina said, her voice little more than a whisper.

"We can hope, princess," the Speaker said, coming to stand beside her and putting a hand on her shoulder. "We can hope."

They lapsed into silence then, studying the two motionless figures as if their attention might somehow cause them to rouse. They remained still, however, the line of blood still winding its way from Aaron's nose. Adina wanted to reach out, to wipe it away, but she was afraid to even so much as touch him now, afraid she might inadvertently break the connection between Aaron and the woman on the bed, leaving him trapped in her world, her mind. So instead she only stood, helpless, listening to the occasional, nearly inaudible moan or grunt of pain from the sellsword, her body tensing with each sound.

***

The Speaker of the Akalians stood stoically, and had some other person been there to see it, they might have marveled at his calm as he watched the sellsword's desperate battle. But they would have known nothing of the storm of emotion raging inside him. He marveled at the sellsword's inner strength, wondered at the fact that he was here at all, for the man who had walked—almost fled—from the meeting room had been a man without hope or belief in himself; yet now the same man risked his life to save a woman who had caused him nothing but grief and pain. It was a wonderful, terrible thing to watch, yet it was his to witness, so he remained still, waiting for what would come next and knowing that the fate of Telrear hung in the balance.

It had been long years since he had felt the darkness so close, since he had questioned so strongly his own beliefs, his long established course. In that moment, the fight for the world took place not on a battlefield or at castle walls but in a small, unassuming room that still smelled of freshly-cut wood. Beneath his placid exterior, the Speaker of the Akalians raged at himself, berated himself as a fool for asking so much of the sellsword. He raged, he despaired, and for the first time in a very long time, the Speaker of the Akalians felt doubt, a doubt that threatened to make a mockery of all that he had thought he'd accomplished in his long years, one that, in a moment, might make ash of all his preparations, all his plotting and scheming.

Yet in our moments of greatest despair, there is still hope.

The Speaker turned to see the misty form of Aaron Caltriss, the world's greatest king, standing beside him. The form did not shift or stir, only stood silently regarding the two figures by the bed. Studying the old king's visage, the Speaker was reminded of his troubled words within the vision they shared with Aaron Envelar. The sellsword had not realized, even then, that it was his own despair, his own concern that had so affected the dead king. The Speaker had not thought such a thing possible himself, for a bearer of a Virtue to—intentionally or unintentionally—effect another of the Virtues so directly.

There is hope, then? the Speaker asked in his mind.

The misty apparition didn't turn so much as there was a subtle shift in the smoky haze that constituted his form. One moment he was staring at the two figures by the bed and, in the next, he was studying the Speaker. *There is always hope, Raenclest,* the dead king said. *While a man lives, there is hope and…sometimes…* His mouth slowly turned into a small smile. *Sometimes, even when he is dead.* It had been long years since anyone—the Virtue included—had used the Speaker's given name. It sounded strange to his ears, though not unpleasant. The man, Raenclest, was long dead, subsumed by the identity of the Speaker, of what he had needed to become. Still, there was something vaguely pleasant, reassuring about the sound of it, and he took the Virtue's use of the name of the man he'd once been for what it was—a gift. It was as if he'd detected an aroma that, though he could not place it or remember the time at which he'd first smelled it, still harkened back to some joyful memory.

Thank you, King, the Speaker thought, *but I am that man no longer.*

But you are, the apparition said. *You are what you have always been, yet you are more, too. That is one thing that Boyce never understood—a man cannot change completely, cannot be made into something new, for though he might change his clothes and his hair, even his body and his thoughts, what comes is always built upon what was there in the beginning.*

It was always a slight source of discomfort to the Speaker when the Virtue spoke of the magi as if he were just a man, for the Speaker himself had spent his many years thinking of him almost as a force of nature, a terrible doom that must be stopped. *But if that is true, King, then the magi would still be the man you once knew, the friend you once knew. The Lifeless, those poor souls upon which he visits his horrors, would still be men and women with hopes and dreams instead of unrecognizable monstrosities bent on death and destruction.*

There was a subtle shift and the Virtue's face was only inches from his own, the dead king's hand on the Speaker's shoulder, a feather-light weight. *But they are all the same men, Raenclest. We all are, and though you think that you must be more than you once were, though you fear that remembering might be a source of weakness, it is, in truth, your greatest strength, for it was the man,* Raenclest, *who committed to stopping Boyce and his abominations. It was Raenclest who took over the role of Speaker for the Akalians and convinced them of the coming danger.*

And the magi? the Speaker thought, not yet ready to concede the point. *The Lifeless?*

You think them monsters, unrecognizable from the men and women they were, the Virtue said. *You think Kevlane, in his folly, a monster, too, beyond hope of redemption, and you are right. But you are right for the wrong reasons. It is not Boyce's dark soul that makes him irredeemable, not his cruelties and malicious intents, not our inability to recognize the man he once was within him, that make him beyond saving. Instead, it is his inability to recognize himself. He is lost, unable to find his way back to the man he once was, because he has forgotten who that man was—would not recognize him even should he walk past him in the street. Too long has he sustained himself on hate and revenge—hate for me and mine for abandoning him in our death, revenge on a world that he feels has wronged him. It has corrupted him, changed him, and the most terrible part of that change is that he does not even remember what he has lost.*

The Speaker frowned, considering. He did not like to think of the magi as a man, for a man might be pitied, might be, in some way, understood, yet he felt the unmistakable ring of truth in the dead king's words. He thought, too, that some great knowledge, some great secret that might lead to victory, lay hidden within them. He was just opening his mouth to question the Virtue further when the door began to open, and the misty form of the king vanished, the shifting fog that comprised his form fading into nothing.

The Speaker nearly called him back, desperate to finish the conversation, for over his long years bearing the Virtue of Will, he had never heard the dead king speak so plainly or so much, and he thought that that, too, was significant. But he remained silent, for the Virtue was no servant to appear when called. Besides, the need for comfort was a quality of normal men, and though the man, Raenclest, might have been right to seek it, the Speaker of the Akalians was more—and less—than normal men.

So the Speaker pushed his doubts, his uncertainties and questions aside, and turned to see one of his brothers standing in the doorway, studying him silently. The newcomer took in the figures at the bed and the princess standing beside them. Another might have been forced to wonder at the Akalian's thoughts, but the Speaker could see his own concern mirrored in his brother's eyes. He gave a nod to tell him to go on with his report, and he watched, a dread building in him as the Akalian relayed his message through the hand signals unique to their kind.

Finished, the man bowed, and the Speaker returned it before watching him depart as silently as he had come. Then he turned back to where the princess knelt by the bed, hating the news he would be forced to tell her, for the choice she would have to make. It was a choice much like the one the man, Raenclest, had made many years ago, glancing back over his shoulder amid the swirling sands of that distant land and seeing, for the last time, the small tent he'd shared with his wife and daughter until it vanished over the horizon as if it had never been. There was nothing more terrible, he knew, than being forced to forsake one love for another, to abandon one duty in the effort of fulfilling a second. It was a terrible choice, a crushing one. And it was one the princess would have to make—and soon.

CHAPTER SEVENTEEN

Darrell was greeted back to consciousness by a variety of aches and pains, most of which he was long-acquainted with. Not friends, exactly, but familiar anyway, a group that had grown to a crowd over the years, each demanding his attention. A shoulder that had been knocked out of socket one too many times whispered quietly, stiff fingers murmured their own entreaty, his lower back spoke louder to be heard over the others, and his knees nearly shouted to be recognized. Aches and pains and scars he'd gathered over the years that never failed to make themselves known when he first awoke, proof of battles fought and battles won, but no less painful for all that. But today there was a new, fresh voice in the chorus, one that the passage of time had not yet lowered to the susurrating drone which the others shared, one that screamed, making itself heard over the din.

A sore shoulder rotated and stiff fingers reached out, gently exploring the ache in his side, and he found that someone had taken the time to bandage it. That, at least, was something. He felt no joy at adding another voice to the symphony of a life hard lived, but better that than the song being done altogether. He was not quite ready to hear those final notes, the end of the melody—soon, perhaps, but not yet. Not when so much was left undone.

He opened his eyes warily and winced at a bright light, turning his face away.

"Ah," a voice said, "seems you ain't gonna die, after all. I'll take my gold now, Shits."

A Sellsword's Mercy

There was a muttered curse at this, and the swordmaster heard the unmistakable *clink* of coin changing hands.

Darrell blinked slowly, enduring the sharp stabbing sensation in his eyes as they grew accustomed to the light without complaint. After all, nothing taught one the ability to endure like growing older, and though the years were sometimes a harsh teacher, they were always thorough.

When his eyes grew used to the light, he regarded the figure looming over him. At first, he couldn't place who the man was, his thoughts scattered and uncertain as they often were upon waking. Then, after a moment, he recognized him as Urek, the man from the night before. "You…saved me," he said, the words coming out in a croak from a throat unaccountably dry.

The man grunted, "I had a hand in killin' those bastards right enough, as we all did. But it was Beautiful did the savin'."

Darrell cast his mind back, following the foggy, shifting path of his memory to the woman with hands of fire that had set his side ablaze. A plain face, missing teeth, and shoulders wider even than the thickly-muscled Urek. "Yes," he said, "I remember."

The big man grinned, and at once the menace and coldness vanished from his hard face. "Aye, I imagine you do, you poor bastard."

"I…I would like to thank her, if I could."

The big man's grin grew wider, and he held his hand out to his side, palm up. The man called Shits shuffled forward, scowling, and dropped several coins into the waiting palm. "You see," Urek said by way of explanation, "Shits here figured there weren't no way in Salen's Fields that any man would thank a woman for subjecting him to what you went through night afore last." He leaned in conspiratorially. "He's young still, and stupid the way only the young can be. He don't understand age teaches a man to be grateful for the little things and that pain is just a matter of course."

Darrell opened his mouth to respond, but swallowed instead, trying to get some of the dryness out of his throat. Urek winced, grabbing a mug of cool water from the nightstand and offering it to the swordmaster, who drank it greedily.

"Sorry for that, friend," the big man said. "Beautiful'd have my hide she knew I was sittin' here gloatin' and runnin' my mouth without offerin' you a drink. It's the fire powder, you see. Works wonders on all matter of wounds—some of the lads think eatin' enough of it would turn a man into a god, but I don't believe it, and wouldn't try it even if I did. Likelier than not, the silly bastard'd shit fire until he burned up, and even if he didn't, I've seen enough of the powder doin' its work to know godhood just ain't worth some things."

Darrell studied the man as he downed the rest of the water—his throat was still dry, but now, at least, it didn't feel as if he were trying to swallow past a mouthful of gravel and dirt. He realized that he still didn't know what had motivated the man and his companions to save him—he'd been too busy dying to ask. "Friend?" he wheezed.

"Well, sure," Urek said, winking. "I'm old enough to know a fella can always use another friend—my experience, they got a way of dyin' on ya so it's a wise man keeps around some spares."

"Who...are you?"

The big man shrugged. "Just one more useless son of a bitch in a world full of 'em, I reckon. But if you're meanin' who are me and the lads here, and why did we find it in our hearts—not kind hearts, mind, no matter what lies folks tell—to pull your old wrinkled ass from Salen's door, well, that's another matter entire."

"I prefer...well-aged," Darrell managed, finding a smile coming to his face despite the pain—quieter now but still there—in his side. There was something about the big man's affable nature that made him nearly impossible not to like, though judging by the scars on his sinewy forearms—knife scars, and Darrell had seen enough to know—some people still found a way.

Urek barked a laugh at that. "Sure, and I'd prefer makin' women swoon to makin' babies cry when they have a look at me, but preferrin' a thing don't make it so. I like you, swordmaster. You seem like a fella knows how to keep perspective. Some folks, findin' themselves all banged up, surrounded by a group of no good criminals like ourselves...well. Let's just say we go through sheets quicker than a brothel as folks end up findin' out their below-works ain't quite as dependable as they thought."

Darrell gave a weak laugh. "My...below-works haven't...been dependable for some time."

The big man chortled in answer. "Well, sure and why not? But, then, you got all those wrinkles to show for it, ain't ya? Not a fair trade, maybe, but as fair as we poor mortals can expect."

"You…still haven't…said who you are."

Another man stepped—practically leapt—forward to stand beside Urek. He was a thin youth, no more than seventeen, and his thin, sharp-featured face twisted into a smile the way a young child's might when he finds, unexpectedly, that he knows the answer to his tutor's question. "We're Hale's army, that's who we are, ain't that right, Urek?" he said, turning to the big man but continuing before he had a chance to answer one way or the other. "We're the boss's men, through and through and—" He froze abruptly, his body tensing as if in expectation of a blow.

"That's alright, lad," Urek said, shaking his head at Darrell in a long-suffering, almost fatherly way. "Beautiful's out getting more medicine for our friend here, so it seems you've a reprieve from meetin' Salen face to face. Still, my old sergeant used to say a man ought not practice holdin' a sword the wrong way anymore'n he'd practice holdin' his pecker crooked. He was a real son of a bitch, but he was right enough in that, I think. Bad habits with the blade'll get a man killed quicker'n anything, and I reckon the same could be said of our Beautiful."

The kid nodded, his eyes wide as if he'd just received a death threat which—according to the sober looks of agreement from the other men in the room—seemed the prevailing opinion. "Yes sir, boss, sorry, boss. That is to say," he said, turning back to the swordmaster and visibly concentrating on each word before he spoke, "we are Hale's men and *women* through and through." He finished, breathing a sigh of relief.

Darrell felt a vague twinge of unease at that, but not much of one, for he had come to suspect as much while listening to the men talk. Still, he found himself frowning as he glanced around the room. Four men here, and if he recalled the night before correctly—no way to be sure as he'd been concentrated, mostly, on the blood pouring from his side—then there were no more than ten in total.

The content of his thoughts must have showed on his face, for the man Urek let out a sour grunt of agreement. "Sure, swordmaster. I imagine a fella of your profession ain't much impressed by an army the size of our'n, and I can't say I can blame you. We ain't of a number to go marchin' against no castles or standin' in front of armored men swingin' swords and the like, and the only time the ground shakes when we're on the move is if Shits here had beans the night before." He winked. "Young and dumb, as I've told you, and the young take longer to learn their lessons than us old bastards. 'Course," he said, shrugging, "they got more time to learn 'em too, so I suppose that's alright."

"But...how so few?" the swordmaster asked, rubbing at his dry eyes.

"Ah, head hurts, does it? And the eyes too?"

Now that he thought of it, Darrell realized that a headache was beginning to form in his temples, one that had gone unnoticed with all the other aches and pains he felt. "Yes."

"That'll be Beautiful's fire powder. Wreaks havoc on the eyes, I'm told, makes everythin' brighter, painfully so, as an after effect." He shook his head "You ask me, swordmaster, there's some things are worse than dyin', but we needed you alive, so there's no help for it." He motioned to the man, Shits. "Get the swordmaster another glass of water, will you, Shits?"

"Why me?" the man asked. "Why not have the kid do it?"

"Well, Shits," Urek said, giving the man a hard look. "On account of I ain't heard you complainin' for the last few minutes and decided I missed it, figure it'd be best if I gave you somethin' to bitch about. Now, go on." The man did, muttering all the way as he grabbed the empty glass and stepped outside. Urek watched him go before turning back to Darrell and shrugging. "I know he seems like a pain in the ass—truth is, he *is* a pain in the ass—but for all his bitching and moaning, Shits is a good man to have beside you in a scrap. A mean son of a bitch when the mood's on him, and one you can count on to cover your back for ya."

Darrell was still focused on something else the man had said. "Why do you need me?" he asked. "I'm not sure what I can do to help you."

"We'll get to that," Urek said. "First, I reckon it best we talk about what's goin' on in the city, and why our numbers are so down as you've clearly noticed. See, that bastard Grinner has the boss locked up in the dungeons—you've heard as much?"

"Yes," the swordmaster said. "May has also been imprisoned."

"The fire-headed she-devil, is it?" Urek said. He grunted. "Yeah, I'd caught a rumor or two about that." He shook his head as if in wonder. "I tell ya, swordmaster, ain't nobody this side of the grave caused the boss as much trouble as she has. Been a thorn in the boss's ass—in all our asses—since I signed up. Ain't a woman I know—save maybe Beautiful, that is, and don't you tell her I said no different—to match her. There was a time—few years gone, now—when one of the boys took it in mind to kill the she-devil, thought maybe it'd get him on the boss's good side. He failed, of course—the man was a fool through and through, and his not knowin' the boss's mind on the subject any better'n he did was just a symptom of it, not the evidence. Still, word of one of his men makin' a move on May Tanarest reached the boss's ears, and it weren't long before Hale figured out who was responsible. If you've met 'em, then you know that when the boss starts askin' questions a man with any sense left in 'em will do whatever he can to answer."

Darrell nodded. He'd only seen the towering crime boss a few times, and had exchanged no more than a dozen words with him, but he knew of what Urek spoke. There was a quality to the man—a very rare quality—that projected dominance, power. Even resting with his feet up as he so often had in the queen's meeting chamber, the crime boss had seemed like a lightly-dozing lion, relaxed but ready, at the least provocation, to lash out. "I think I understand that much."

Urek nodded, grinning. "Sure. See, most folks think the boss is just a big brute that solves his problems with his fists and reckons why trouble yourself with a door when there's a perfectly good wall to walk through."

Darrel smiled back. "And you're saying he's not?"

"Gods no," Urek laughed. "He's a brute all right, and I pity the wall as stands in his way. Thing is, the boss also has a soft spot—don't tell 'em I said so, or I imagine I'd have some soft spots of my own before he was done correctin' me—but he does. Got it for women and kids, mostly, and the lady May, well, she ain't no exception. Shit, if anything, she's the cause of it, one way or another."

He leaned forward, scowling at Darrell. "Now, I don't want you thinkin' the boss has any sort of designs on her, nothin' like that.

He loves his whores as much as the next man, and he's got little use for a wife and all the shit that comes attached to her. Anyhow, point is, once the boss figured out who it was as went after her, he was as angry as I've ever seen him and intent on havin' a talk with the fella responsible." He shook his head. "Swordmaster, I don't mind tellin' you I'd rather face a she-bear protectin' her cub than the boss when he's of a mind to have a conversation of that sort. Well, I never saw that poor, stupid bastard again, and May Tanarest went right on doin' what she'd been doin', confoundin' the boss and that old bastard, Grinner, as much as ever."

"Why do you tell me this?" Darrell asked.

Urek shrugged. "Sometimes, I get to talkin', swordmaster, and there ain't no stoppin' me. But I guess I tell you this on account of I want you to understand that if there's a way to save the woman, me and the lads here'll do it. Wouldn't do us no good to get the boss out of that shit hole the queen's thrown him in only to have him beat the shit out of us first thing. You might think we're a bunch of bastards that'd stab you in the back and take your purse as soon as talk to you—and, on most days, you'd be right, mind—but we're on your side here."

Darrell considered that, but it didn't take long. After all, if the man had wanted him dead, he would be. They wouldn't have had to do anything but wait, and Grinner's thugs would have taken care of it soon enough. "Very well," he said, "and I thank you. But, tell me, what happened to the rest of you? I was under the impression that Hale had a significant criminal empire. No offense but…" He trailed off, not sure of how to finish.

"But we're only a few swingin' dicks and a woman whose cures are worse than the disease," Urek finished, nodding. "Well, you're right enough there, swordmaster. See, the thing is, we're criminals, just like all those other bastards that followed the boss. And when news got out that the boss was thrown in prison, and his men were bein' hunted down for questionin'…" He shrugged as if it was of no great concern, but Darrell saw anger hiding in the big man's eyes. "Well, folks started to ask themselves if it wouldn't be better, things bein' what they were, to see if Grinner had any openings in his own organization."

"So they changed sides."

The big man grunted. "No surprise, really. They're criminals after all, not soldiers and certainly not saints. No surprise," he said again, frowning, "but that won't stop me from bustin' some of those fools' heads and carvin' out my own thoughts on the matter in their flesh, if given the chance."

"Forgive me," the swordmaster said, "but...with so many of your companions changing sides..."

"Why didn't we?" the big man asked. "No offense taken, swordmaster, it's a fair question, one I been askin' myself a lot lately while I been spendin' my days tucked away in the back room of some shitty little tavern or another, my nights spent creepin' around like some mongrel bitch afraid someone'll come along and give me a good kick." He shrugged. "Most times, understand, I can creep with the best of 'em, but I can't say I enjoy havin' a whole city out lookin' to poke a couple of holes in me, see what comes out. Anyway, I guess I figure that there comes a time a man has to stand for somethin', and I'm too old to be lookin' at starting over. Besides, the boss was always good to me, took in a drunk fool who spent his days beatin' the shit out of people for coin only to spend it on the nearest whore or the nearest drink, and made somethin' of me."

"Oh?"

"Sure," Urek said, grinning again. "Understand, I'll still have a drink from time to time, and I reckon beatin' the shit out of people is a large enough part of the job, but Hale gave me a family, and that's somethin' a man like me ain't ever thought to have. The men you see here—and those out on their own errands—feel much the same. We don't mean to give up on the boss so easy, and that bastard Grinner might be sittin' pretty now, but so do those noble ladies when they go to those travelin' shows, see a bear in a cage." He leaned in, an eager light in his eyes, "But if that bear finds his way out, or if, maybe, some foolish bastards with more loyalty than sense *let* him out...well, all the pretty words and likely lies in the world ain't gonna keep him from feastin' if he's of a mind. And in my experience, swordmaster," he said, giving Darrell a wink, "the bear's always of a mind."

"You mean to break him out." It wasn't really a question, but Urek decided to answer anyway.

"We do," he said, then scowled. "Though how we're to go about doin' that is what we ain't quite figured out yet. Oh, sure, the boy here's got hands that'll pick any lock and please any woman, but we've been doin' some scoutin' of the castle, and unless we can turn invisible like some stage magician he wouldn't get anywhere near close enough to the boss's cell to use 'em."

Darrell frowned, sharing the man's frustration, for he had been to the castle on a number of occasions himself. Ever since May's capture he'd been trying to think of some way of freeing her without killing several innocent guardsmen who were only doing their duty or, more likely, bringing half the soldiers in the city down on their heads. So far he had come up empty. "There must be another way," he said, though whether it was to the big man standing before him or to himself he couldn't have said.

"Maybe," Urek said doubtfully, "but if there is one, I ain't seen it. Still, I'm not known for my brains. Maybe you can figure somethin' out where we couldn't. It's why we come lookin' for you, after all. Figured you'd want that son of a bitch Grinner laid horizontal as bad as we do after the lies he's been spreadin' about you and yours. Was thinkin' maybe you might know of somethin' we ain't thought of yet. What I can tell you is that ain't no amount of coin we can lay hands on, nor fancy lies gonna get us in there. Whoever could be bought has been bought already, and Grinner's got much deeper pockets than ours. As for lying," he sighed, shaking his head, "that fucker could give lessons. So," he said, raising an eyebrow at Darrell, "what about it, swordmaster? Got any idea of how we can get in the castle and get the boss and lady May back?"

The man said it lightly, as if he was half-joking and didn't expect Darrell to have any solution. The problem was that he *did* expect it—Darrell could see the hope in the man's dark eyes. The swordmaster gave a sigh of his own, wishing he had something to give the man, but hope, unfortunately, was in short supply these days. "I'm sorry, but no. I've been thinking about it since they were first taken and, so far at least, I haven't come up with anything."

Urek grunted as if he wasn't surprised, but Darrell noticed the slumping shoulders and frustrated expressions from the other men in the room. "Well, that's alright then," the big man said, and Darrell respected him all the more for the fact that he spoke with a

A Sellsword's Mercy

confidence the swordmaster knew he didn't feel for the sake of his men. "We'll just keep on lookin', and either way I'll be glad to have a man of your skill at our side when the blood lettin' starts."

Darrell nodded. "I will do what I can, you have my word."

Urek grinned. "A man's word don't go very far around here, swordmaster." He studied Darrell, seemed to consider him, then shrugged. "But I think yours just might, which is a relief." A troubled look crossed his features, and he knelt, pretending to check Darrell's bandages. "I ain't stopped and told the lads as much, old man," he said in a voice barely loud enough for the swordmaster to hear though he was less than a foot away, "but I'm thinkin' that, the way things stand, we're all pretty well fucked. That Grinner is a bastard, but the world loves its bastards more than any king ever did, and that's a fact. I know you don't know me from anybody, and I don't expect you trust me anymore'n you have to, considerin' you're laid out like a pig for market and surrounded by a bunch of bastards who spend their lives thievin' and muggin' and worse. But I wonder if I couldn't ask you a favor, if you've a mind to hear it."

"I'm listening," Darrell said, pitching his own voice to a whisper to match the big man's tone.

Urek grunted, rubbing at his scruffy chin as if embarrassed. "Don't expect it'll amount to shit all, anyway, what with some mage from olden times out creatin' the gods alone know what kind of fuckery and Grinner bringin' his own brand to bear on us…I'd say we're all pretty well headed to the grave. The way I figure it, the best we can hope for is they put us in a box before they bury us, and even that's a long hope at best."

Darrell considered trying to say something to give the man some comfort, but he did not. Whatever else the big man was, he was no fool, that much was obvious, and he would see through any such attempts easily enough. "You were going to ask a favor?" he prompted instead.

The big man nodded, obviously uncomfortable. "Now it comes to it, I feel a fool to ask. But, you see, these fellas here…well, I won't lie to you and say they're good men that deserve savin' but…well, they're *my* men. You understand? I've been with 'em for some time now, and though they're handy enough when their enemy's lookin' the other way, sleepin', or, best of all, dead, they ain't made for the kind of shit storm that's comin'. When the real killing starts—I don't say *if*, mind, but when—I was wonderin' if you couldn't..." He trailed off, shaking his head in frustration.

Darrell met the man's eyes. "I will do whatever I can to protect them. If it is within my power, I will keep them safe."

Urek sighed heavily, a wide grin of relief spreading on his face. "Well, now, that's alright then."

He started to rise, but Darrell grasped his wrist, forestalling him. "You were a soldier once, were you not?"

The big man's eyes clouded over, as if remembering something he'd rather have forgotten. "Yeah, I suppose I was."

"Why did you quit?"

Urek studied him for several seconds then gave him another wide grin. "We got an army of monsters marching at us, swordmaster, and there's better than even odds we'll all be corpses long before they get here on account of our own army has turned against us." He let out a quiet laugh. "Who says I quit?"

He rose, glancing around at the other men gathered standing around the room, noting their expressions. Darrell knew that they'd been too far away to hear the words they'd shared, but their faces said that they knew the gist of them well enough.

"We stick with you, Urek." The words came from a man with a hook-nosed whose name Darrell had not been told. "And if the gods decide to fuck you over then they'll have to fuck us all over."

Urek grunted. "I wouldn't worry about it none, Shadow. If the gods got the sense they gave a pig, they'll stop long before they make it to your ugly mug."

The other man grinned wide at this, as if Urek had just paid him a compliment, and the youth, Osirn, stepped forward. "He's right, boss. You've always done right by us, and...and, well, we want to do right by you too. Besides, you're not, you know, like the only one that wants to get Hale out of that dungeon."

The big man sighed. "No, I don't suppose I am at that, lad."

Another man started to step forward and Urek pointed a thick finger at him. "Not one more damn step, you. Much more of this, I'll start bawlin' like a baby, and I reckon I'll have to kill the lot of you. Shit, ain't you bastards got anythin' better to do than stand around gawping and prattlin' on like old hens?"

The hook-nosed man, Shadow, grinned. "Well, boss, you told us to wait here with you. You said—"

"Damn what I said!" Urek roared. "All of you go find somethin' to occupy yourselves before I start decidin' I need some sword practice and you're the likeliest targets."

"You forget, boss," Shadow went on, "I've seen you swing that sword of yours—way I figure it, the safest place for us to be is right in front of you."

Urek scowled, and the man hurried over to the other side of the room to where a small table sat, followed by the others, but Darrell didn't miss the smiles and signs of barely suppressed laughter on their faces as they did.

"Now then—" the big man began, but he cut off as the door swung open, and they all spun to see the woman, Beautiful, walking inside. "Gods, Beautiful," Urek said, "but you scared me half to death. Tell me, what's the point of havin' a secret knock, if you don't use it?"

The woman saw that Darrell was awake and let out a surprisingly girlish squeal of joy, rushing to his side and completely ignoring the big man who stared at her with a dumbfounded expression on his face. "You're awake!" she said, and Darrell was able to answer with no more than a grunt of barely suppressed pain as she lifted him up—none too gently— and examined the bandage on his side. "Blood's seeped through," she said in a threatening voice, as if offended that Darrell's blood had dared leak out of him. Truth to tell, he was a bit offended by it himself, but he was too busy focusing on not screaming in pain at the rough treatment to say so.

Frowning thoughtfully, she unwrapped the bandage from his side, studying the wound. Darrell himself chose not to look. He'd seen enough wounds on his body to know what it would look like well enough. Besides, there was always something disconcerting about it, about seeing a hole where your flesh had once been. It wasn't an easy thing to realize that whether you lived or not— something he still wasn't wholly convinced of considering the way the woman handled him—you would always be missing a piece of yourself, a piece that was once there and now was not.

"Now, Beautiful," Urek tried again, talking in a slow, hesitant way as if the last thing he wanted just then was to get in to an argument with the woman but he'd reluctantly decided that a point needed to be made. "I understand you're in a rush to help your new friend here, and truth is I've taken a bit of a shine to him myself, but about the secret knock—"

"Oh, to the Fields with the secret knock," Beautiful said in a distracted, emotionless voice as she poured something—not the fire powder again, thankfully, for that surely would have pulled the scream out of Darrell that was even now so close to the surface—on his wound and began to rub it in. "And what good would it do anyway, Urek, considering the gods cursed door wasn't even locked."

The big man frowned at that as if only just realizing it. "I'm sure I locked it when we came in and—"

"And now Shits is out front, filling up a glass of water and complaining about how he has to do everything around here. Everything apparently," she said, finally turning to look at the big man, "except locking the door."

Urek looked as if he wanted to say more, to press her on the importance of their hiding place remaining secret, perhaps, but he heaved a sigh that showed he'd decided it wasn't worth it and remained silent.

"Now this," the muscular woman said to Darrell, leaning over him and brandishing a small vial of liquid, "is for the pain. It will make you sleep, for a time, but sleep is important for the healing process. Then, when next you wake, you'll feel all better." She spoke as if to a small child, her voice full of reassurance, comfort, and it was strange to see such a tone come from a woman of her stature.

"Thank you, lady," the swordmaster said, "for all your help—you are truly a kind woman." Beautiful beamed at that, and Darrell noticed several of the men in the room nod approvingly out of the corner of his eye.

The woman's cheeks flushed, and she shyly avoided his gaze, as if embarrassed, as she examined his side. Finally, she risked a glance up at him, as if she would speak, but before she could get a word out, the door slammed open again. Someone—Darrell wasn't sure who as his view was blocked by the wide-shouldered, muscular woman leaning over him—let out a shout of surprise, and they all spun, including Beautiful.

The man, Shits, rushed in. "Boss," he said, out of breath, "I've got news."

Urek grunted, staring at the door as if it had personally wronged him and then transferring the look to the man. "What about the damned secret *knock*, Shits? And damnit but we have *got* to start locking the door. Anyway, what are you rushing about as if your ass is on fire, shouting for all the world to hear? Might as well hang a sign up front that says, *Hideout here, come get us.*"

"But, boss," the man said, breathing hard, his forehead covered in sweat, "you need to hear this. It's about Hale."

"Well?" Urek demanded as the other men began to gather around. "What about him? I tell you, if that son of a bitch Grinner has done for the boss, he'll pay for it ten—"

"The boss ain't dead," the man interrupted.

When the big man spoke, his voice was quiet, and the swordmaster detected a hint of resignation in his tone. "Go on then, Shits. I reckon you better tell us what you know."

The man took a deep breath. "Don't have to tell you, boss. I can show you. Or, rather, he can." He motioned to the door and for the first time Darrell and the others noticed another man standing anxiously in the doorway.

"Damnit all," Urek said, scowling, "we're gettin' more custom than a brothel runnin' a free day, and that's the truth. Who's your new friend?"

"I don't know him," the man admitted, "but he was outside in the common room of the tavern, asking after the swordmaster and—"

"And you figured it'd be a good idea to *let him in?*" Urek demanded, incredulous. Suddenly, the air in the room rang with the unmistakable sound of drawn steel, and several of the criminals moved forward, long knives appearing in their hands as if out of nowhere. Even Beautiful let off her ministrations and stood, grabbing the nearest thing that could be used as a weapon—it just happened to be a thick oak chair that Darrell would have struggled to slide across the floor let alone pick up—and brandishing it over her head as she moved between Darrell and the newcomer.

"You'll not take him," she hissed at the stranger, and once again the swordmaster was uncomfortably reminded of the possessiveness of a child defending a new favorite toy.

The man standing in the doorway blanched, and Urek gestured to two of the men. "Grab him and close the door—and for the gods' sake lock the damn thing will you?"

The men rushed to do as they were told, and the newcomer let out a strangled yelp as he was jerked inside the room and unceremoniously thrown to the floor. His eyes were wide, wild, and he backed up along the floor, looking at the closing door like it was his only hope of salvation.

"Boss, wait," the man, Shits, said, "it ain't—"

"Quiet now, Shits," Urek said, his voice full of cold, hard menace and for the first time since meeting the man, Darrell saw no trace of the easy affability the man usually showed. "There's a fella here that needs to do some explainin' and fast, but it ain't you—not yet anyway. But don't think we won't be havin' a conversation about this later."

The other man—no doubt knowing his boss's moods better than the swordmaster—chose to remain silent, nodding like a chastised child and throwing the man sitting in the floor what might have been an apologetic look as Urek stalked forward. "Osirn, Shadow, you're on the door," the big man said over his shoulder. "Any bastard comes through you don't recognize, you poke him so full of holes he'll never need to pull his trousers down to take a piss again, you understand?"

"*Yes sir,*" the men said in unison, rushing to comply with an alacrity that would have been impressive in trained guardsmen. Darrell began to see that, however rough and disorganized the group appeared on the outside, they knew their business well enough.

"Now then," Urek said, kneeling in front of the wide-eyed stranger, his thick arms resting on his knees. The posture showed his muscles well enough, somehow made him appear even larger than he already was as he crouched over the other man, and the swordmaster was impressed by the surprising amount of subtlety the big man displayed for all his self-deprecation. After all, those thick arms, those knotted fists—scarred from the gods alone knew how many street brawls—seemed fully capable, just then, of tearing the newcomer apart limb from limb, if the big man took it in his mind to do so. "Why don't you tell us just who you are, stranger," he continued in a voice that sounded like two boulders rubbing against each other, "and why you've chosen to visit us unannounced on this fine evening. And I'd do it quick, were I you. I bore easy, you see, and when I'm bored I've a tendency of gettin' a bit…well, let's call it unruly."

The man swallowed hard, glancing at Darrell as if hoping he might save him, and the swordmaster was struck by the vague feeling that he knew the man, had, at least, seen him somewhere before. "S-sir," the man stammered, "I-I…that is, I'm sorry f-for coming u-unannounced." The big man's face seemed to cloud over in preparation of a coming storm, and the stranger's next words came so fast as to be almost unintelligible. "M-my name's Eric, s-sir. Captain Festa sent me, to find the swordmaster. I don't mean no harm, I swear by the gods I don't."

"Sorry friend," the big man said, shaking his head. "But I don't know no Captain Festa." He rose to his full height, staring down at the man, and again Darrell was reminded of a lion, this one tensing in preparation to strike.

"Wait," the swordmaster said, and they all turned to him. "Festa is a friend. It is he who ferried your men and Avarest's soldiers to Perennia."

Urek frowned, considering that. "Big bear of a fucker that's all dressed in animal furs?"

Darrell nodded, not missing the heavy sigh of relief that escaped the newcomer. "Yes, that's him. Festa is a friend." Not precisely true, and he wasn't entirely sure a man like Festa allowed himself friends, but it was close enough and, friend or not, Darrell trusted the temperamental captain.

Urek grunted. "Well, boy," he said, turning to look down on the sailor, "seems the swordmaster's given you a reprieve from seein' what your guts look like. Thing is, I'm a real curious type, see, my late wife, well, she always told me my curiosity'd get me into trouble, but I've still yet to find the knack of lettin' it go. So I tell you what—you start tellin' me why this Captain Festa of yours sent you, and maybe if I like what you got to say I won't let Shadow there use you for target practice."

He gestured to the hook-nosed man who gave the stranger a grin that was anything but reassuring as he held up two thin blades, an eager expression on his face.

"He's an ugly bastard I'll admit," Urek said to the scared sailor, "but I ain't never seen somebody can lob a knife as true as him." He leaned a little closer to the man, as if confiding a secret. "It's on account of he likes it so much, understand. Makes a game of it, aimin' for this part or that one. Gods, when he's of a mind, I reckon he can stretch his pleasure out for a few hours at the least and with night coming on…" He shrugged. "Well. Ain't much else for him to do, is there?"

"C-Captain Festa sent me," Eric said, "to find the swordmaster. He told me to tell him that if he needed any help from us regarding getting May out of the dungeons, then he'd have it."

Urek frowned, looking at Shits. "You said he knew somethin' about Hale. What does this have to do with—"

"In his hands, boss," Shits said, and Darrell didn't care for the troubled expression on the man's face.

The big man must have seen it as well, for some of the affected menace left his features, replaced by an almost pensive look as he turned back to the sailor, noticing, for the first time, the crumpled yellow parchment the man held. "I guess you'd better give that here," he said, holding out his hand with visible reluctance.

The stranger handed the parchment over tentatively, the way a man might give a piece of meat to a caged lion, ready to snatch his hand back lest the beast decided to add a bit extra to its breakfast. From where he lay, Darrell couldn't see the parchment, but he could see enough of Urek's face—darkening with each passing moment—that his stomach fluttered uneasily.

When the big man finished, he looked haggard and tired. "You can put the chair down, Beautiful," he said in a quiet, lifeless voice. "Unless you're intent on killin' the messenger."

The woman did as she was told, offering no argument as she studied her leader with a sickly, worried expression.

"What is it, boss?" Osirn asked, trying and failing to see over the taller man's back.

"Trouble is what it is," the big man answered, still in that voice that was empty of emotion. He offered the swordmaster the parchment, and Darrell found that he did not want it, did not want to read whatever was written there. But among the lessons the years had taught him, he'd long since learned that avoiding the truth didn't change it, so he took the paper, telling himself that the slight tremor in his hand was a side effect of the wound he'd suffered.

A fairly skilled artist had drawn a picture on the front of the parchment, one that contained two faces, and the swordmaster knew well enough what it meant even before he scanned the words with a growing sense of panic. "Oh gods be good." He levered himself to his feet, his fear allowing him to ignore, to a degree, the dull, nearly crippling pain that ran through his side as he did.

"You have to rest," Beautiful protested, but even her normally stern voice sounded weak and uncertain to the swordmaster's ears.

"There's no time to rest," Darrell said, meeting the big man's eyes. "There's nearly no time at all. I thank you for saving me, but I have to go. I have to…" He shook his head, trying to order his thoughts, "I have to find Thom."

"Thom?" Urek asked. "Who's that now?"

Darrell wiped a hand across his mouth, finding that it was suddenly terribly dry. "Thom's a friend. And the gods help me—he's in love."

He could see by the big man's pained expression that he knew at once what he meant. "Alright, where are we goin' to find this Thom then?"

Darrell swallowed hard, and he only barely noticed the parchment slipping from his numb fingers. "On Festa's flag ship, or so I hope. If he's seen this…" He trailed off, not sure how to finish. Then the full meaning of the man's words made it through his jumbled, troubled thoughts, and he met his eyes. "Wait. We?"

"Well, why not?" Urek said, nodding, his own expression grim. "We hang around in this inn much longer, we'll probably end up killin' each other. Anyway, we just now got you on your feet…" He paused, looking at the wavering swordmaster with a humorless smile. "After a fashion, anyhow. I don't expect Beautiful would thank me for it, if I let you go off and get yourself killed now."

The man said the words lightly enough, but Darrell knew what they meant, just as he was sure that the big man knew it too. Urek was risking his life—as well as the lives of those he'd called his family—to see the swordmaster safely to Festa's ship and, in doing so, he was throwing his lot and the lot of those with him in with Darrell. The swordmaster met the big man's eyes, and an understanding passed between them. "Thank you."

Urek grunted, obviously uncomfortable with gratitude.

"But...wait," Beautiful said in an almost desperate voice, "you can't. You need the medicine I brought, for the pain. It will put you to sleep, but you need it to get well. Tell him, Urek, don't let him—"

"Easy, lass," the big man said, studying the swordmaster. "It seems to me that ain't nobody in this world goin' to make this fella here do somethin' he doesn't want to, not with him still breathin' anyway. Besides," he continued, turning to her, "you get to our age, Beautiful, and pain's an old friend that greets us in the mornin' and lays down with us at night. Ain't that right, swordmaster?"

There was a question within that question, and Darrell knew it. The man was giving him one more chance to call it off, one more chance to listen to Beautiful's advice and take the medicine and let sleep, the great healer, do its work. "Yes," Darrell said, nodding resolutely. "That's right."

"Alright then," Urek said, and it seemed to the swordmaster that there was an added note of respect in those simple words. "Come on then, lads and ladies. Let's go find us a ship."

CHAPTER EIGHTEEN

Aaron ducked under the swiping claw of his assailant, his shining sword tearing through the creature's midsection. As with the others he'd fought, the creature's body offered no more resistance than air, as if he were trying to somehow kill the night itself. When his sword sliced through it, the shadowy form disintegrated like a thin patch of fog before a great wind. But the sellsword felt no victory at that, for he had been fighting the creatures for a long time now—just how long he had no way of knowing—and he knew that, soon enough, the creature would reassemble itself, appearing with the horde of its fellows surrounding him without any noticeable wound only to hurl itself at him once more.

Movement from his left caught his eye, and Aaron spun, guided more by instinct than sight, and narrowly avoided what looked like a long tentacle, as black as night, that smashed the ground where he'd stood only seconds before. He let out a cry of anger and frustration, bringing his blade down and hacking away the offending tentacle and it vanished into nothingness a moment later.

Knowing that to stay in one place for too long meant death, the sellsword immediately picked a direction and charged. It didn't matter much which way he went, for the shadows were all around him now, their teeming masses stretching as far as he could see in that dark world, their nightmarish forms displaying every possible shape and size. The one he came upon had four arms, two on either side, and a large, pitch black horn protruding from its forehead, but Aaron's blade did its work, and the abomination joined its fellows in whatever place they went before rematerializing minutes later.

Something else lashed out at him, and he brought his blade up only just in time to block a massive club that seemed to have been forged from the darkness itself. He grunted as the impact slid him back, nearly knocking the blade from his hands. He made use of the moment of peace this afforded him, glancing around desperately for his horse. He thought he saw a flicker of white off in the darkness to his right, but it could have been no more than his hopeful imagining, and it didn't matter in any case, for if that was the horse then it was far too distant for him to reach it before he was cut down or crushed by the horde of creatures.

He'd lost the beast some time ago—an hour, two, he couldn't be sure—had been knocked from it to the ground. He'd nearly died then as the creatures pressed in on him, seemingly eager to destroy this invader in their newly-conquered world. He'd felt himself being crushed under the weight of their numbers, but the armor had protected him from their attacks long enough for him to get his feet under him once more.

He'd thought the armor ridiculous at first, but since the fighting had begun, Aaron had been given ample opportunities to be thankful for its presence as it shielded his body against the worst of his opponents' attacks. Yet the armor did nothing for the weariness seeping into his muscles, a weariness beyond anything he'd imagined possible, and he took advantage of the brief moment of respite to get control of his ragged breathing.

He heard something move behind him and started to turn, but his exhausted body wasn't quick enough to avoid the claws that raked at his back. The armor protected him from the sharp talons, but the impact was still powerful enough to send him stumbling forward, and he fell to one knee. He told his tired limbs and muscles to rise, but they had been overused, his body aching from the battering it had taken, and his legs were slow to respond. He'd only just regained his feet when something massive hit him from out of the darkness with the force of a charging horse, and he screamed in surprise and pain as he was thrown from his feet. He hurtled through the throng, passing through the bodies of his attackers as if they weren't there at all, the only evidence that he'd struck them a revolting warmth that suffused his body where he touched them, one similar to what he'd felt when touching the great tree.

He hit the ground in a roll, the breath exploding from his body, and more by luck than design he came to rest on one knee once more. He shook his head in an effort to clear the dizziness he felt and hissed at a sharp, dagger-like pain in his chest. A rib cracked then, maybe two. *Can't keep this up for long.* And that was true enough. The armor had served him well, but it was covered in deep grooves from the talons that had scored it, not to mention several dents—the one from that last blow spread all the way across his chest—and it wouldn't be long before it failed. Not that he thought it mattered much—the way things were going, his body would fail him long before the armor did, for his muscles had long since stopped screaming from overuse. Instead, they mewled in quiet voices, without the strength left even to protest the demands he made of them.

The secret lies with Tianya, Co said. *This is her world, her fears that you fight, and you cannot defeat them without her.*

She'd said much the same several times now, but saying something cost a man—or a floating ball of light, as the case may be—nothing. It had been all Aaron could do to keep from getting butchered by the teeming creatures—he'd had no chance to try to make his way back to the base of the massive tree where, even now, he could hear the child moaning in the distance. "Shouldn't...have...lost the damned horse," he muttered, hissing with the effort of leveraging himself to his feet. The creatures, he knew, would not stop coming—they never did—and sure enough the space that his flying passage had cleared was even now being filled with more of them. Dozens. Hundreds. Enough to get the job done, at any rate. More than enough.

Your horse, Co said, her voice full of energy as if she'd just had some incredible idea, the excitement from which she could barely contain. *Call it.*

"Oh, there's plenty of things I'd like to call it," Aaron muttered, "asshole among 'em. I swear that bastard threw me on purpose."

Not that, the Virtue snapped, *and do you really think now is the best time to be telling jokes?*

Aaron backed up, forcing his exhausted arm to raise the blade he carried as he watched the creatures drawing nearer. He hoped it was just his imagination that made it seem as if the blade had lost some of its brilliant luster, but he didn't think so. "Maybe not the best time," he said, "but probably the only one. The dead only have the one joke, Firefly, and it isn't a very funny one."

Gods be good, Aaron, call the horse!

Suddenly, one of the shadows separated itself from the others, gliding toward him with a deceptive speed, and Aaron swung the shining blade, taking its taloned hand off at what he took to be its wrist before his back-swing passed through the place where it neck was, and it vanished. "And just what in the Fields am I supposed to *call* it?" he demanded. "I don't know the damn thing's name!"

It doesn't matter, the Virtue hissed back, *just call it anything.*

Aaron rolled his eyes, and was about to say something when another of the shadows rushed forward, and the next several moments were a desperate struggle as he pushed his body to its limits and beyond. Finally, he found an opening and lunged, the sword leading, and the creature dissipated into the air. "Ah fuck it," he said. *"Spot! Come here, boy!"*

He waited a moment, scanning the area where he thought he'd seen the horse, but nothing happened. "See, Firefly?" he said. "This isn't a story-book and—" He cut off as a flash of white—unmistakable now—came charging toward him, plowing a path through the shadows and scattering them like chaff.

Less than a minute later, the horse stood in front of him, regarding him as if wondering what had taken him so long to call it. "Son of a bitch," Aaron said. "You mean you could have done that the whole time, and you've been standing over there taking your ease while I'm getting my ass kicked?"

The horse only stared back at him, but there was a smugness in its eyes Aaron didn't care for. Still, for all the power of its rush and the damage it had wrought on the enemy's lines, the horse hadn't made it through the charge unscathed. Three long, bloody cuts ran down its side where one of the shadows had clawed it, and there were several crimson scratches along its muzzle. A bellow came from the darkness, and Aaron spun to see one of the massive, towering forms—probably the bastard that had struck him—bearing down on them. "We're going to have a talk about this later," the sellsword promised, then he climbed onto the horse—his horse, he supposed—grunting at a sharp pain from his ribs. "Come on then," he croaked, grabbing the reins and turning the horse in the direction of the tree looming in the distance. "Let's go save us a crazy little girl."

CHAPTER NINETEEN

"What's happening to him?" Adina demanded. The last few hours had been torture as she listened to the sellsword's grunts and hisses of pain, watched his body jerk from time to time as if from some invisible blow, and noted his shoulders slowly sagging more and more from exhaustion. But the last noise that had issued from the sellsword's throat hadn't been a growl or a grunt at all, but a scream so full of pain that her skin had grown cold. "What's happening to him?" she said again, hating the desperate whine in her voice but unable to contain it.

"He is losing," said the Speaker. Though his own worry was clear in his tone, Adina wanted to scream at him, to rail at him that he was a liar, to tell him that he knew nothing, but it would do no good, and she knew that he was right in any case. Whatever Aaron was fighting, he *was* losing, she need only look at his body, to listen to his ragged breathing to know the truth of it. So instead of giving in to the urge to yell and condemn the Speaker, she turned back to Aaron, grasping his free hand in hers.

"Princess," the Speaker said, "there is something I must tell you." His voice sounded troubled, sad, and Adina turned to look at him. *Oh gods*, she thought, *what now?* Though the Akalian was expressionless as usual, there was something about his posture, about the way he stood so erect, that made her think he was reluctant to share whatever news he'd learned.

"Is it something to do with why that other Akalian came in a few hours ago?"

The Speaker nodded. "Yes. I had thought to wait to tell you, thought that, perhaps, the battle here would be decided, one way or the other, but I fear we are running out of time, and I dare not keep it from you any longer."

"Keep what from me?" Adina said, a flutter of apprehension rising in her along with the certainty that, whatever news the Speaker had, she did not want to hear it. "And what do you mean we're running out of time?"

The Speaker winced. "Perhaps, I misspoke, for it is not only we who are running out of time, but also the city of Perennia."

Adina frowned. "Surely, you don't mean Kevlane. I know that the tournament in Baresh must be starting soon but…" She trailed off, unsure how to finish.

The Speaker shook his head slowly. "The tournament in Baresh has begun already, but that is not of what I speak. There is another danger which the city faces, one that, though not as terrible as the threat the magi represents, is still capable of causing great harm."

"What threat?" Adina said. "Have the creatures—what you call the Lifeless—attacked the city? Because when we left everything was fine."

The Speaker nodded. "You left, Princess, and that is much of the problem. Queen Isabelle may mean well enough, but your sister does not have your strength, your courage, and with you, Aaron Envelar, and the others disappearing, she has been begun to rely on other less…trustworthy individuals."

"But who?"

"You are familiar with the crime boss, Grinner, the man recently stylized as a councilman in the queen's court?"

"Of course," Adina said, realizing what the man was alluding to, but she shook her head even as she thought it. "Grinner's a swine, and I have my suspicions that he had something to do with Aaron and the others being taken, but Isabelle is smart enough not to listen to him. Besides, May is there, and she knows better than anyone what kind of man he is—he wouldn't dare try any tricks, not with her in the city. She's smarter than him by half, and he knows it."

"Perhaps you are right," the Speaker said, "but the lady May Tanarest has been thrown into the dungeons, as has Councilman Hale."

Adina stared at him, incredulous. "No. No, you must be wrong. What possible reason would Isabelle have to imprison them? That doesn't make any sense."

"Yet that is exactly what has happened, Princess, of that I can assure you. I don't know the details, but it seems it was done at Councilman Grinner's command."

For a moment, Adina was so shocked and confused by the man's words that she could find none of her own. "But…how…" *I am enough.* She forced down the panic welling up inside her and took a slow, deep breath. "And you're sure of this?"

"Yes," the Speaker said. "Of this much, at least, I am sure."

"But what of General Yalleck? Surely, he wouldn't have let Grinner—"

"General Yalleck has not been seen," the Akalian said. "Not since the councilman's…rise to power. I believe he has sequestered himself with Avarest's troops."

Adina shook her head in frustration. She wanted to blame the general, but found she didn't have it in her. After all, the man must have seen what was happening well enough and supposed—no doubt rightly—that his life would be forfeit if he remained in the castle. He was a stranger in a strange city, and she couldn't fault him for not laying down his life to protect it. That, however, was no excuse for her sister. "Grinner must have tricked Isabelle somehow, lied to her or threatened her or…I don't know."

"The report I received said that the queen has not been coerced in anyway, that she has come to rely on Councilman Grinner for reasons yet unknown."

"Damnit, Isabelle," Adina whispered. "What are you *doing?*" She did her best to order her frantic thoughts, forcing herself to slow down and think the situation through. Whatever was happening in Perennia, it was clear that Grinner was at the heart of it, and she doubted it was merely coincidence that he'd made his move right when she, Aaron, and the others had disappeared from the city. That meant that it had been planned. She supposed Grinner might have found some way to lure Aaron and the others out of the city, some excuse, but how could he know Kevlane's

A Sellsword's Mercy

creatures would be waiting in the woods, unless… "Oh gods," she said, her heart galloping in her chest. "Grinner is working with Kevlane."

The Speaker nodded. "Recent events seem to indicate as much, though what this Councilman Grinner might hope to gain by allying himself with the magi, I cannot imagine. Boyce Kevlane is not a man to share victory, nor is he one to make deals and compromises. Whatever agreement he and the councilman have reached, you can be sure that the magi will consider it obsolete as soon as it—and by extension the crime boss himself—has stopped being useful. Councilman Grinner does not know what force he meddles with."

"True," Adina said, nodding. "But that will do us little good as, if Grinner gets his way, we'll all be corpses long before he gets what he deserves." She knew, then, what she needed to do, what she *had* to do. She turned and glanced at Aaron where he still knelt. She'd wiped the blood away from his nose minutes ago, but a fresh runnel had appeared, tracing its way over his tightly-pursed lips. She knew well what he would say, even the tone he'd use. *One man isn't worth the world, Adina, no matter who he is and especially not me.* Except, she supposed, that he'd find a second to spit or grunt, maybe growl in between words. At another time, the thought might have made her laugh, but she couldn't have been further from it just then. "I love him," she said, nearly pleaded, as she turned and looked at the Speaker through eyes misting with tears.

"I know," the Akalian said, and there was such compassion, such understanding in his voice that she could not stop the tears from coming, and she bowed her head, wiping at them furiously. She was a princess, now a *queen*, had been chosen as the leader of Telrear's gathered armies despite her reluctance. She could not afford to falter, to be weak. *I am enough,* she told herself, but this time the words sounded false in her mind, and the tears that ran down her face were not just tears for Aaron. They were for Isabelle and May, for Hale and for the woman, Beth, now dead and gone, and for all the people of Telrear.

But if she were honest with herself—and the last several weeks and months had forced her to be honest with herself more than she might have liked—the tears were for herself most of all.

For the decision she now faced, the choice that had to be made. She could not even deny the choice altogether, for to do so would be making a choice just the same. Even worse, avoiding tough decisions was a coward's way out. Her father had taught her that truth long ago, and the years had not changed it, for all that she might wish they had.

She wept then, burying her face in her hands and letting the tears fall as they would, hoping against hope that some miracle might occur, might keep her from the decision she would make. But the world, it seemed, had no miracles to spare. She felt alone in her grief and indecision, terribly, completely alone, and so she started with surprise when she felt a gentle hand on her shoulder. She looked up to see the Speaker watching her. The man's face was unveiled, not just of the black cloth that often covered it, but of the placid calm that was the Speaker's second mask, hiding all but his strongest emotions from his face.

In that moment, he did not look like the Speaker of the Akalians, the leader of a group of elite warriors which even the hardiest, bravest souls spoke of in quiet whispers, as if somehow naming them would bring their wrath. He did not look like a man who had lived for centuries, or the possessor of the eighth Virtue, a great magic that even the most creative of storytellers had never thought might exist. He looked, instead, like a man. One whose heart was breaking, and the anguish and grief that twisted his face were a match to her own. Seeing his pain there, plainly writ on his features, Adina's own emotions rose in answer, and she brought the man into a tight embrace.

For a time, the two only stood there, each wetting the shoulder of the other with their tears and neither of them aware of it, each only taking what comfort they could in the knowledge that they were not alone in their pain, their grief. Then, the moment passed, and Adina stepped away.

She turned back to Aaron, studying the set of his jaw, his hand where it gripped the withered woman's own. He was strong—the strongest man she'd ever known, yet strength would do him little good in the land in which he traveled. He was kind, too, kinder than he'd ever let on and possessed of a compassion that wasn't due only to the Virtue he possessed, no matter what he'd claim—but what good was kindness in a land of nightmare?

The choice is simple and you know it, a part of her mind said, and it was all Adina could do to keep from crying out, railing at the voice to shut up, shut up, just *shut up.* The voice didn't stop though, but went on, each word like a dagger in her heart. *You cannot help him here—his fate will be his alone, and there is nothing you can do to stop or change it. But in Perennia and its outlying regions are thousands, hundreds of thousands of people that are counting on you. Without you, their fate is certain. With you, they may have a chance—however small—of weathering the coming storm, of coming out the other side of it beaten and battered but* alive.

She had to leave him; she knew that. *And if he dies while you're gone?* another part of her mind asked. *What then? Will you weep for him? And what good are tears to the dead? I think you know well enough what Aaron would say of that too.* Yes, she did. The dead were dead already, and no amount of weeping or wailing would make them rise again.

"Do you know what you ask of me?" she said, looking up at the Speaker. "What it is you make me do?"

The Speaker watched her for several seconds then gave a slow shake of his head. "Forgive me, Princess, but I cannot take even that much of the burden from your shoulders. You see the choices as I do, and no doubt their possible repercussions as well, but these choices are not of my creation. If it were within my power to take this burden from you, I would, but I cannot. I can only tell you that I, too, faced such a choice, many years ago. I made it amid the swirling sands of the desert instead of towering trees, but made it I did. All I can do is tell you that, whatever your decision—even should that be no decision at all—I will not fault you for it, nor condemn you."

"But what should I *do?*" Adina pleaded.

"I don't know," the Akalian said. "For what it's worth, I will tell you that I believed, at the time, that the decision I made was for the best, that the only way I could protect my wife, my daughter was to abandon them."

"And now?"

The Speaker shook his head again. "Now, I don't know. In leaving them, I saved their lives, saved my own, but I left them—and myself—nothing else. I thought, at the time, that there was no other choice to be made, but now I understand that my wife and daughter were left with their lives but without a husband, without a father, and that my choice stripped from me everything but the breath in my lungs. If my long years have taught me anything, Princess, it is that the years come and go, and there is no one living who can say, truthfully, that they have no regrets for the choices they've made."

Adina took a slow, deep breath. Tears threatened again as the choice she would make crystallized inside her mind, but this time she forced them down. There would be time later for tears and hopefully comfort too—gods let there be time—but that time was not now, and she feared that if she started crying once more, she would never stop. "I...I need to talk to the others."

The Speaker nodded. "They wait for you in the meeting room."

Adina frowned and started to speak, meaning to ask the man how he could have known that she would want to meet with them and, knowing, how he could have arranged it without leaving the room, but she did not. The man had done so one way or the other, that was all, and it made little difference how. So instead she only gave him a nod, stepping forward to give him a hug. "Thank you."

"Forgive me, but I have done nothi—"

"You were here," she said, meeting his eyes, "sometimes that is enough." She crossed to the door and opened it before pausing in the doorway. She turned back to look at the Akalian. "Please...take care of him, Speaker."

"I will do what I can. You have my word, Queen Adina."

***

The Speaker watched her go, watched the door close behind her, but his mind was far away, lost in a distant memory, looking down at a sleeping young baby, her limbs hidden beneath a tight swaddle to protect her against the cold desert air. It was an old memory, and it bore the faded wrinkles that only time and much handling brought, like a letter that has been read over and over until the parchment upon which it's written begins to flake and tear, and the ink itself begins to fade. An old memory, one full of pain and grief, yet a cherished one for all that.

"Call me Raenclest," he said to the empty doorway. On a whim, he raised his hands, staring at them. Hands that had wielded weapons of all kinds, hands that had killed when killing needed doing, but hands, also, that had held a small child, had comforted her when the unnameable fears of a child came upon her. "Call me Raenclest."

CHAPTER TWENTY

Balen was not a religious man. He didn't spend his days bent in prayer or smelling incense and reciting words to invoke the gods' blessing. But he prayed now as he rushed through the city streets, dodging people when he could and bowling them over when he couldn't. Religion, he figured, was a lot like swimming. He'd known plenty of men—sailors too, the silly bastards—who cared as little for swimming as he usually did about religion. But have a man take a tumble off the ship in rough seas, have him fighting for breath as the waves crashed around him, and that same man changed his thinking quickly enough. In fact, Balen imagined that if the bastard could go back and spend the entirety of his life waking up every morning and going for an hour long swim he would and do it gladly.

Religion, he thought, was a lot like that to some people, and he supposed that in the end he was no less fool than the drowning man, for now that something terrible had happened—and something even more terrible looking to follow it, if these sons of bitches in the street didn't get out of his *way*—he found that he got religion pretty quick. He prayed to every god whose name he could remember and once that was done—it didn't take long, truth be told—he started making up new names, figuring there were at least some kind of odds he'd land on one, after all there were a lot of gods...at least he thought so. He figured if he just kept at it maybe he'd chance on one willing to listen—one that'd maybe had a reservation set aside that had canceled at the last minute and was bored enough to pay attention to poor old Balen.

He saw the city docks in the far distance, little more than vague outlines on the horizon, and he ran on, regretting the ambitious amount of drinking he'd done the night before. He'd come to the city this morning, hungover and, if he was honest, being a bit of a bastard as he always was the day after a particularly large bout of drinking. Ostensibly, he'd left Festa's ship to discover what news he could about May and Hale, but that wasn't the real reason.

The fact was, he'd been out every day since their capture, combing the city in search of anything that might help to secure their release, and his hands had come up out of that well dry enough times for him to know that there wasn't any water to be had. The truth was far simpler. He'd been finding himself growing annoyed by every word out of another sailor's mouth, every joke or complaint about the weather—the bastards were always complaining about the weather, figured it was their gods given right as sailors, he supposed—and thought it a good idea to find a reason to get off the ship before he ended up throwing one of them overboard or, more likely, being thrown overboard by Captain Festa who was not known for his patience in the best of times. And these, any fool with eyes could see, were far from the best of times.

He'd been minding his own business, or at least as close to it as he ever got, listening to some fancy-dressed merchant prattle on to a not-quite as fancily dressed woman about all the coin he had and all of his earnings, considering how fun it would be to push the man down in one of the mud puddles that crowded the streets following the night's rain, when he'd seen it. Or maybe it was more accurate to say he saw *them.* A dozen flyers tacked on the wall of a nearby building, and a quick glance around had showed him that the other buildings were likewise decorated. Well, Balen wasn't much on looking for signs from the gods, wasn't big on omens for coming disasters. The way he figured it, there were so many of those that the gods would be too busy making omens to make any trouble at all, if that's what they wanted—but he wasn't blind either, nor could he ignore the feeling of dread that rose in him long before he was close enough to make out what the flyers said.

Not the announcement of wedding or a birth, that was sure. Balen knew enough about the world to know that no news traveled like bad news, and whoever had tacked the parchments on the wall—many of them now hanging crooked and askew from the wet following the rain—had wanted this news to move with the speed of a lightning strike. And so he'd given off trying to find a way to trip the fat merchant without appearing to mean to and instead had walked to the nearest paper, each step feeling strange and disorienting as if he was in a dream.

Some part of him had known what he would find there, had seen the two familiar faces in his mind even before he was close enough to see anything, and so when he drew close enough to read the parchment he felt at once a great sense of shock and outrage as well as a grim resignation. He tore the paper he'd looked at off the wall, crumpling it up and throwing it into the street. Blame his dark mood or blame the drink of the night before, but he'd ripped all of the flyers from one building and was halfway through the next, growing angrier with each, before he thought of Thom.

The older man was hanging on to his reason by a thread now, like a particularly skilled—or stupid—sailor walking on the edge of a ship, showing off for his crew mates. The news this parchment contained wouldn't be enough to tip him over—instead, it would send him hurtling through the air and down into the depths like the finger flick of some malicious god.

And so Balen had done what any sensible man would have done under the circumstances—he ran. And, as the air rasped in and out of his lungs, as a sharp, stabbing pain developed in his side, he decided that running was a lot like religion too. By the time he made it to the docks, he was covered in sweat. The ache in his side had traveled to his chest, but he was alive, at least, so that was something.

Give it time, a dark part of him thought, but he did his best to ignore it as he rushed down the docks toward Festa's ship, the last place he'd seen Thom, calling on the last bit of his energy, or at least telling himself he was. He was fairly certain he'd used up the last bit ten or fifteen minutes ago, and his body just hadn't realized it yet, his mind too busy running through likely scenarios—all bad—as they sprang in his thoughts at random, unwelcome visitors but not ones you could easily kick out either.

A Sellsword's Mercy

Balen might not be a religious man, but he *was* a superstitious one, and one of the universal truths he'd always believed was that trouble came in threes. The first, he supposed, had come in the form of the shot of liquor that bastard Benjy had put in front of him the night before, and he felt a fresh wave of pity for Pater, making time as he'd been with Benjy's sister. There wasn't any denying that bastard had a mean streak in him, but Balen had figured one drink, what's the harm? Well, the harm had been that one drink had led to another, then another and before Balen knew it he was sitting under the tavern's table arguing with his own feet. He still wasn't sure who'd come out ahead on that one, and he supposed it didn't matter.

The second trouble was obviously the flyer—plastered all over the city and looking like nothing to Balen so much as a victory flag for that bastard Grinner. The third...well, he thought he knew all too well what the third would be, especially if Thom had caught wind of what was happening. "Hoy, Balen!" Someone yelled, and Balen waved a dismissive hand as he ran—or, at least, did the closest approximation of which his body was now capable—past.

"Not...now," he wheezed over his shoulder, "can't you see I'm...busy dying?"

He walked up the ramp to Festa's ship and froze, all his panicked thoughts leaving his head to be replaced with new panicked thoughts. The captain stood on one side of the deck, his arms crossed across his chest, flanked by four sailors, and gods if that bastard Benjy wasn't among them, showing no ill-effects of the night before. They were all doing their best to look threatening—and putting on a pretty poor show of it, so far as Balen could see, as they each held the small, curved knives used on ships to cut lines, and those weren't of any particular danger unless you found yourself being a rope. He tracked their stares to a group of what looked like near a dozen men standing opposite them on the deck, the group weathering the sailors' attempts at scowls with an idle disregard that said they'd seen worse and weren't impressed.

And, surprise—or maybe no surprise at all, the gods being possessed of a particularly cruel brand of humor—but the third trouble turned out to be something completely different after all than what Balen had suspected. For there was no denying that the group was trouble, all hard-bitten men that looked like the type that spent their time in dark alleyways, sharpening their blades and making lists of men they wanted to kill.

Balen considered finding something else to do—he thought hiding behind some of the crates on the deck sounded pretty promising—until the strangers decided to leave but reluctantly decided against it. There was Thom to think about, after all, so for possibly the first time in his life, Balen dismissed the survival instinct which had, to that point, if not kept him out of trouble, at least kept him alive, and walked onto the ship to stand beside the captain and the other sailors.

No one so much as glanced in his direction, a thing for which he was incredibly grateful, as they were all too busy listening to Captain Festa talk—which was to say roar, the man did little talking. "—Don't know what you're doing here, and I don't much care. But by the gods, if there's going to be violence on my ship, I'm going to be the one doing it, is that clear?"

A big man at the front of the other group sighed, rubbing at his head as if embarrassed. "Yeah, sorry about that, Captain. The last thing we want is trouble." He turned to scowl at a man beside him who was even bigger than he was. "It won't happen again."

"Well, he should know that's not how to treat a lady," the other man huffed, and there was something strange about his voice which made its way past Balen's frantic thoughts, but he dismissed it as unimportant.

"Maybe he should and maybe he shouldn't," the first man said, sighing heavily, "but we didn't come here to teach lessons on manners, did we, Beautiful?"

Beautiful. Balen cracked a smile at that. Whatever else the men were, it was clear they enjoyed giving nicknames to their mates as much as the sailors did, and with just as much dubious accuracy, for the man to which the first spoke was anything but beautiful. Strong, sure, if the width of his shoulders and the size of his hands—as large as dinner places—were any indication, but Balen didn't think there was enough coin in the world to make even the most experienced whore able to say he was beautiful with a straight face.

Balen guessed that the man growing so big, so muscular, was his body's defense against all the name-calling he must have suffered in his youth. After all, it was hard to make fun of someone for being ugly when their fist was in your mouth, and he suspected the big man had done his fair share of punching over the years. For one, his hands were calloused, his knuckles scarred and red as if he spent his time hitting anything that came…well, to hand. For another, his face itself looked like it had been carved out of stone by some particularly enthusiastic—if not skilled—mason, all hard edges and sharp angles, and when the man bared his teeth in frustration, Balen couldn't help but notice that he had few enough left to bare. He felt his unease increase, for men generally didn't get their teeth knocked out by spending their lives being polite, and the smile on his face faltered a bit.

"You want we should fetch him up, Captain?" one of the sailors asked, and Balen wondered what the man was talking about until he realized that the sound he'd been hearing—one he'd taken to be the fluttering of his nervous heart—was actually the unmistakable sound of a man thrashing in the water beside the ship.

"Leave him," Festa spat. "The bastard could use a bath, and the gods know I'm tired of his mouth myself."

The sailor nodded and then winced, clearly not wanting to say anything more but deciding he'd best do it. "Thing is, Cap, Fingers ain't a particularly good swimmer and…" He hesitated as Festa turned to glare at him. "Well, that is…he might drown."

"You got a point coming soon, sailor?" the captain demanded, and the man swallowed, shaking his head and subsiding into silence.

Festa watched him for a second more, possibly, Balen thought, considering throwing him over the ship to give the thrashing, unfortunate Fingers some company, but finally he turned back to stare at the group of strangers. "Anyway," he said, looking at the big man with the missing teeth, "I reckon I'm sorry for any disrespect the man gave you, lady, just so long as we understand that throwing my mates overboard is a particularly favorite pastime of mine, and one I don't intend to share."

Lady? Balen thought, confused, the smile on his face giving a twitch, and he watched in shock as the big man dropped into a gods forsaken *curtsey,* trousers and all. "That's quite alright, Captain," he said, and Balen realized with a shock what had bothered him about the man's voice. It was the fact that it wasn't a man's voice at all but a woman's.

"No damn way." The words were out of his mouth before he could stop them, and he realized as everyone turned to him that, in his surprise, he hadn't just said them, but nearly yelled them.

The man—*woman, Balen, damnit, she's a woman*—started to scowl, and Balen felt his knees grow weak as he saw the dinner plates attached to her wrists begin to ball into fists. "You got something to add, Balen?" Captain Festa said, and whether the warning in his voice was meant to make Balen aware of the threat from the captain himself or the woman, the first mate couldn't say.

"N-no, Captain," Balen said, "I was...that is...I stubbed my toe, is all." He sketched the best bow he could in the direction of the woman. "It's a pleasure to meet such a ...well, beautiful woman, lady."

Her scowl abruptly turned into a wide grin that was somehow more frightening than her frown had been, and she curtseyed to him this time. "Thank you, sir, the pleasure is all mine. And may I ask the name of such a fine-mannered gentleman as yourself?"

Balen nearly snorted at the thought of himself as a gentleman, but he managed to force it down as she might misunderstand, and thinking of what those fists of hers could do to his face if she took it in mind to use them provided ample motivation. A problem averted then, but judging by the look dancing in her eyes, Balen thought there was another one on the way, and he felt as if he'd somehow been pulled into one of the stage plays he'd seen in his youth, only there'd been no women left to play the part of the blushing maid, and the fool who'd been in charge of things had cast a temperamental she-bear instead. "M-my name's Balen," he said, all too aware of the fact that the eyes of everyone on the ship were locked on him, "and you're...Beautiful."

"Why thank you," she said, smiling again, and Balen quickly looked away from her gaze, since he'd been told once that, if a man encountered a predator in the wild, he should never make eye contact with it.

"Well, if you two are done," Festa growled, turning to the big man who was, apparently, the leader of the group, "then maybe you won't mind telling me why you're on my ship."

A Sellsword's Mercy

"No offense, Captain," came a familiar voice, and Balen was shocked when the swordmaster, Darrell, stepped from where he'd been hidden from view by the woman and the group's leader, "but I have tried to explain. Urek and the rest of these men—and woman—saved my life. I was still recuperating when we heard of the queen's decree, and I feared for Thom. Given the fact that you had sent a man to search for me, I didn't think it would prove a problem if I should show up."

"Sure, swordmaster," Festa said, "I sent a man after you, and that's a fact. What I didn't know is that you'd be bringin' some of the city's most low-down scoundrels with you." Balen winced at that, glancing at the group to see if today was going to be the day that what luck he had was finally going to run out. But none of them seemed angry, at least. A hook-nosed man in the back was the only one holding a weapon—a cruel dagger that looked sharp enough to cut air—and he was currently using it to trim his fingernails. The big man, Urek, only shrugged, as if the captain had a fair point, and Balen let out an audible sigh of relief, wincing as Festa snapped him a dark look.

"In such times as these," Darrell said, "a man must find his allies where he may."

Festa hocked and spat. "True enough, swordmaster. Now, since we're all done introducing ourselves and tugging on each other's dicks, why don't you tell me why you're cluttering up my ship with all these dirtfeet?" As he finished, he gestured to a skinny youth standing at the back of the group who looked to Balen as if he was about to lose his lunch and then some. "And best be quick about it—that kid there pukes on my deck you've my word you'll all spend the rest of the day swabbing it until I can see my reflection."

"I came to check on Thom," Darrell said. "Once I heard the news...I thought he might do something rash."

"And I don't figure you'd be far wrong," the captain said, "about that at least. Thing is, Thom ain't heard nothin' of the kind, not yet."

Darrell frowned, clearly confused. "But how could he not? Why, there are so many flyers posted throughout the city, not to mention the queen's criers going around yelling it at the top of their lungs—we passed several such on the way here—that a man would have to be blind and deaf to miss it."

Festa barked a laugh. "Sure, blind and deaf or, as is the case here, locked in his cabin below decks."

The look of surprise that came over the swordmaster's face was no doubt a mirror to Balen's own, but the big man, Urek, only bellowed out a laugh that Balen thought would be what it sounded like if the clouds decided to rain stones. "I fancy," the captain continued, grinning and obviously pleased by the reaction his words had caused, "that if you listen closely enough, you can hear him shouting to be let out even now."

Once the captain mentioned it, Balen realized that he *had* heard someone yelling, screaming to be freed, but he supposed he'd chalked it up only to his own inner, terrified self when he'd walked onto the boat.

"Though," Festa went on grudgingly, "we *will* have to open the door sooner or later—Thom'll need to be fed, and the gods know his skinny ass ain't got much fat to spare. Once *that* happens, I suspect we could measure in seconds how long it takes him to learn of it, considerin' that some of my sailors wag their tongues more than a couple of old hags sittin' around knitting sweaters and talking about how things used to be different." He glanced between Darrell and the big man, Urek. "So, what's the plan, swordmaster?"

The older man winced. "I had hoped you might have one."

"*Hoped?*" Festa said, grunting. "Hope ain't got no business in plannin', swordmaster. Hope is what a man does when the plan fails. Still, I suppose I ought to thank you for bringing these others with you—if things go the way I think they will, I reckon that fella there'll be needin' that blade of his for more than for pickin' his teeth and looking ornery. Not a habit I'd recommend, anyway. The gods know there's enough ways for a fool to die in this world without cutting his own throat trying to look scary."

Urek turned and scowled back at the man with the blade who gave a sheepish look before sliding the knife back into the sheath at his side. "Well then," the big man said, grinning as he stepped forward and offered Festa his hand. "From one soon to be dead fool to another, Captain, I'm glad to have you on our side."

Festa grunted, "I'll say the same back to you, stranger, but don't be offended if'n I keep my purse locked away from here on out."

Urek laughed again, his thick chest shaking with mirth. "Oh, I wouldn't have it any other way, Captain. If it was too easy, it'd take all the fun out of the thing. Now," he said, clapping Festa on the back, "why don't we go work on this plan of yours and figure out how we're all going to be meetin' the God of Death." Either the captain didn't feel the stranger's hand for all the furs stacked on his thick frame, or he'd taken a liking to the man, for he didn't explode into violence as Balen had expected, but only nodded and led the men below decks.

"Oh, relax, you old bastard!" he heard Festa bellow from down below a moment later, presumably at Thom. "Get some rest—you been lookin' like death on a bad day, at any rate!"

Balen couldn't make out the first mate's reply, but he was barely listening. He was busy replaying the conversation in his mind and doing his best to avoid the appraising eyes of the woman, Beautiful. "Gods," he muttered under his breath, "we're all gonna die."

One of the sailors standing beside him must have heard, for he laughed, giving Balen a nudge with his elbow that made Balen want to kick him in the stones. "Judgin' by the way that woman over there's lookin' at you, Blunderfoot, I'd say you'll be beatin' us all to Salen's Fields."

"Except maybe you, if you keep runnin' your mouth," Balen snapped, but the man had clearly received worse threats from more threatening men—he worked on Festa's ship, after all—and he only grinned as he walked off to get back to his duties.

"Bastard," Balen muttered, but his heart wasn't in it. It didn't matter much which of them won the race to Salen's Fields, if race it was. Unless Festa, Darrell, and Urek came up with some miraculous plan, they'd all be getting there soon enough.

CHAPTER TWENTY-ONE

May stared at the chunk of stale bread that would be her dinner, or, she supposed, breakfast—in the darkness of her windowless cell such things had lost their meaning—trying to decide which mouthful might have the least amount of mold. In the past days, she had spent much of her time shocked that she had been reduced to such a state, swallowing each piece of bread and struggling to keep it down as she lamented the woman of power—envied by so many in the Downs—that she had once been.

That fiery-haired woman seemed an utter stranger now, not even one that she had ever met, only perhaps that she'd heard stories about. Certainly, such a woman had more pressing concerns, more important decisions to make than which side of bread held the least mold and, therefore, was less likely to make her violently sick. Still, for her, it was not a decision to make lightly—she had done so before, and had understood the foolishness of it as she sat huddled in the corner of her cell, spewing the contents of her stomach up in a foul flood. It was not a mistake she would make again, so she ate slowly, methodically, and without relish.

"How you doin', lass?"

The voice came from the cell across from her. She recognized it, but it still sounded strange and alien to her ears. This was a man the fiery-haired woman had known, and he had no business with what she had become. She did not answer him, had not answered for some time now when he asked similar questions. In the end,

A Sellsword's Mercy

there was no point. Talking would not unlock the cell door, would not turn the moldy bread into a feast, nor allow her to forget what she had become. Talking, interacting with another person, would only make it worse, only make her remember all that she had been, all that she had lost.

So she remained silent and, after a time, the voice gave up its questions, as it always did, and there was only the darkness, only the suffocating, yet somehow comforting silence. She heard the sound of the dungeon door opening, and her eyes went wide, her heart thundering in her chest. She knew that sound, and it—along with the torchlight that accompanied it—at once sent fear and longing rushing through her. For the sound and the dull, ruddy orange light brought food, yet it also brought pain, and so she hesitated, tentatively leaning toward the bars of her cell then back again until she finally lost her nerve and skittered into the corner, her eyes wide and wild as she waited to see what would come.

The torch-light grew closer, bobbing in the grip of whoever held it aloft, and as it did her heart beat harder in her chest until it felt as if it would surely burst free. A man peered inside, and at first she didn't recognize him, for she had been sure it would be either one of the few guards—she knew their faces well now—who brought her food or, if she was unlucky, Grinner himself. This man was neither of those, though, and he rubbed at the salt and pepper stubble on his chin furiously as if barely able to contain some unknown but powerful frustration. "May?" he said, narrowing his eyes as if having a problem seeing her. As well he should—she'd chosen the corner for a reason, had crawled into it often when she'd heard the dungeon door open in the hopes—always vain—that Grinner, when he came, would forget about her if he didn't see her.

"Good luck, Captain Gant," the other prisoner said. "Our May Tanarest is in a bad way and not too fond of idle chatter these days."

May noted the captain's frown, and felt a thrill of fear, pushing herself further into the corner as if wishing she could disappear into it. She couldn't, of course, she'd tried often enough to know. Deep down, she knew this man was her friend, that he would not hurt her, but what she knew and what she *felt* were two very different things. After all, didn't the guards who accompanied Grinner wear similar frowns?

The captain must have seen something of her fear in her face. His frown deepened, and he walked closer, peering inside her cell. She knew well enough what he must see—a frightened animal abused for too long and now afraid of anyone it came across. A creature, in truth, not so very unlike those poor young girls the old her had once pulled off the streets, giving them new clothes, a new job. A new life. She wished someone would do the same for her, prayed for it every day, but she knew that they would not.

Even if help was coming—and she doubted very much if anyone would go through the trouble for a wasted woman such as herself—then she would be dead long before it arrived. Grinner had promised her as much, and for the first time in her life, she'd believed him. She could not even hope that the guards might come and arrest him, as they would have done in Avarest if only they'd known where to find him, for the guards *worked* for him. She'd seen their faces often enough when Grinner was beating her—unhappy faces, displeased with their task but silent for all that—to know it.

"May?" the newcomer asked again, holding the torch aloft, and his breath hissed out as he took in her appearance. Not that she was surprised. She was a horror to look at—filthy rags for clothes, torn where Grinner's whip had done its work, long, striped wounds wherever her skin showed, and bruises covering her cheeks as if her face had taken it in mind to have a fight with a wall and been too stupid to give it up. "Gods, what has that son of a bitch done to you?" the captain demanded, and May was unable to keep the mewl of terror from escaping her throat at the anger in the man's voice.

"It's alright, May," the captain said. "Don't you know it's alright? I wouldn't hurt you. I'm your friend—you know me."

It wasn't alright, nothing had been alright for a long time. May could have told the man as much, if she possessed the courage, but she did not, so she only remained silent, watching him.

"That bastard has a lot to answer for," the captain said.

"But will he?"

The captain turned to regard the prisoner who'd spoken. Hale stood, though not to his full height, for May knew that the beatings he'd taken had left their mark, and he could not stand as tall, as straight, as he once had. "What's that?" the captain asked.

"Will he answer for this? For *her?*" the big man growled, gesturing at May, and despite spending the last days being beaten to within an inch of his life, his words carried a strength born of anger.

May could only see the captain in profile, but she saw him open his mouth to speak, saw him hesitate and close it again. Finally, he shook his head. "I don't know. All I can promise you is that, if it's left up to me, that son of a bitch will pay tenfold for every bit of harm he's inflicted on her."

The big man grabbed the cell doors in his massive hands as if he would rip them apart—and looking at the naked anger on his face, at his arms and shoulders, thick with tensed muscle, May almost believed he could. "But it's not up to you, is it?" he said. "You're only a loyal castle guard in fancy armor, pretty enough to look at, I reckon, but no more heeded than the barks of a favored hound. Oh, queenie throws you a bone sometimes, sure, but she wouldn't trust you to counsel her any more than the mutt."

The captain's body tensed, and for a moment, May thought that he would strike the big man through the bars of the cell. "I serve my queen loyally, criminal. That's something you could never understand."

Hale hocked and spat. "And the people of Perennia? Those poor sons of bitches countin' on you and yours to protect them. Do you serve them, too?"

"Of course I do," the captain hissed.

The big man nodded thoughtfully, cocking his head as if to study the man before him. "Well, that settles that then—you really are a fool. I had my suspicions, understand, but I like to give a man the benefit of the doubt, when I'm able."

"Me, a fool?" Captain Gant demanded. "*Me?*"

"Yes *you,*" Hale continued, "and you shouting about it ain't gonna change the truth of the thing. Tell me something, Captain. Does the army march on Baresh?"

There was a hesitation before the other man answered and when he did his voice was low, angry. "No."

"And what will happen, do you suppose," the crime boss went on, "if it continues not to march? Do you reckon that dusty old wizard will forget all about us? Maybe decide that instead of destroying the world he'll take up candle making?"

May watched the captain's jaw working, as if he'd swallowed something he didn't like. "No, I do not."

Hale nodded. "Well, Captain, then why isn't the army fucking *marching?*"

The other man seemed to slump at that, as if his shoulders were too weak to hold themselves up any longer. "The army waits...on the queen's order."

The giant barked a laugh, seeming bigger now even as the captain grew smaller. "The queen orders the army, sure. And who orders *her?*"

Brandon Gant let out a heavy sigh. "Grinner."

Hale grunted. "Maybe not a complete waste of your father's seed, after all. So then, Captain, if you know keeping the army here means certain death for all those poor saps depending on you and yours to keep them safe, then how, exactly, are you serving them?"

The captain seemed to consider the man's words for a long time then finally he shook his head. "The queen's order—"

"Ah, fuck the queen's order," the crime boss spat disgustedly, leaning back from the bars as if he'd given up on the captain. "You can wipe your ass with it for all the good it's doing—shit, if you did maybe we'd all live a bit longer."

"And what do you know of it?" Brandon snapped. "Any of it? You're a criminal, a bottom-feeder of society who hurts others for his own benefit. Do you expect me to believe you care about them, any of them?"

There was a sound that May couldn't identify at first, a raw, rasping sound, and it took her a moment to realize that the crime boss was laughing. "Gods, but you really are a fool. I don't give a shit about those people out there, Captain. I'd be willin' to rob, cheat, or kill every one of 'em if it got me out of this cell. The difference is I *know* what I am. You, on the other hand, sit back and tell yourself that you're a good man, a protector, maybe. Shit, you probably think of it right before you go to sleep, console yourself about the fact that you're on the wrong side of forty, still single without any kids of your own, without anything to show for your life, but oh at least you're a *good man.* I haven't known many good men in my life, guardsman—my line of work doesn't exactly give me much opportunity, and I wouldn't want it anyway. From what I've seen, good men got a way of dyin' young. But either way, I've met enough of 'em in my time—killed a few too, matter of fact—to know that good men don't sit back and watch the world burn. They don't strut and posture and declare their anger while they watch innocents—if there is such a thing—slaughtered like cattle."

Captain Gant seemed to wither with each word from the crime boss, and May wanted desperately to scream at the big man, to tell him to stop. There was no use torturing the man so, for even if he *did* try to do something it would accomplish nothing but having him thrown in a cell beside the rest of them. But even now, she could not bring herself to speak, and so she only watched as some part of the captain, some belief he'd had in the world, died.

Hale, though, wasn't finished. He leaned forward again, gripping the bars, his bruised and bloody face—nearly unrecognizable now, from Grinner's attention—pressed tight against them. "I may be the only criminal here, Captain. The only murderer, sure, the only thief. But the gods know I ain't the only liar." He spat at the captain's feet then shuffled back to the far end of his cell, seeming weaker now that the anger of the moment had left him. Once he reached the wall, he half-sat, half-collapsed with his back against it. May could see little but his eyes. A dark man, full of dark truths. She hated him then, for torturing the captain so, but she also loved him, for saying what she could not, for being brave enough to stare the truth in the face no matter how much it must have hurt.

"Go back to your room, Captain," the crime lord said, not sounding angry at all now, only tired. "Tell yourself whatever lies you need to and go on with your life. Leave the dead to the dead."

A sound that was somewhere between a laugh and a moan escaped the older man's throat, and he lifted his hanging head to stare at May. "I had to sneak in here to see you," he said in a voice that was little more than a whisper. "The guards wouldn't let me come—they were under strict orders to keep me out. Grinner's orders. I had to lie to the guard on duty, tell him that Grinner had demanded his presence elsewhere." He shook his head in disbelief at this, as if he still couldn't believe it. "I came…" He hesitated, and when he finally did speak his voice was even quieter, little more than a whimper. "I came to tell you…they've scheduled your execution." He shot a quick glance at the crime boss. "Both of yours. It's to be the day after tomorrow. At noon."

Hale gave a weak laugh from where he sat, his arms slumped over his knees. "We know, Captain. That bastard Grinner didn't waste any time coming down here and gloating about it. Now, go on for the gods' sake and let us get some rest—we've got a big day comin'."

The captain turned to May, and his face looked haggard, as if he were near death himself. He opened his mouth to speak, hesitated, and closed it again. Then, he turned took a step toward the dungeon's exit and looked back at her. There was such pain, such grief and impotent anger on the man's face, that through all of her own pain, her own fears, May felt her heart reaching out to him. "I'm sorry," the captain said. "I...May, I..."

"I know," she said, and the captain started in surprise.

Hale grunted a laugh. "Well, you got her talkin' again and that's somethin' at least. Though based on the acid I normally get from her, I don't suppose I ought to thank you for it."

Brandon didn't turn to look at the crime boss, only stared at May, his mouth working as if he would speak, but no words came.

"I know," she said again. "You have done what you can, Brandon. I thank you for it. Now go. Leave the dead to the dead." She turned at that, turned her back on the captain, on Hale in the cell opposite her own, on the whole world beyond her small, sad place in it. The captain tried to speak again, tried to talk to her, but she did not answer, for there was nothing to say, and eventually he walked out, leaving her alone once more. May found that she felt a sense of relief when he was gone. Perhaps, it was as Hale had said, perhaps the dead had no place among the living. She thought of Silent, of Adina. She thought of Thom. *Look after them,* she prayed, with no real hope that anyone was listening. *Look after them when I'm gone.*

CHAPTER TWENTY-TWO

"Can't say as I like this none, Princess," Wendell grumbled as he smoothly ducked under a tree branch, a cry of surprise from behind him announcing that the Parnen captain had not been so quick.

"None of us like it, friend Wendell," Leomin said, rubbing at his forehead where the offending branch had struck him. "But you, in particular, have made your position quite clear over the course of the last hour."

"Well, I *don't* like it," the sergeant said again, realizing and not particularly caring that there was a sullen note to his voice. "Leaving the general with those...those *people*. Not to mention Caleb. Oh, that Speaker fella seems friendly enough, I'll grant you, but the others won't so much as say one word to me."

"Surely, you can't be serious," Seline said from where she walked in front of him, frowning over her shoulder. Wendell appreciated a good-looking woman as much as the next man, and this one was fine enough to appreciate, at least from behind—he ought to know since there'd been little else to look at for the last hour except for trees and more of them—but it was clear she had a mean streak in her, and he didn't envy the Parnen the future arguments they'd inevitably have. "They've taken an *oath*," she continued, "to not speak."

"Sure," Wendell said, nodding, "and once or twice, when I was younger and a bigger fool than I am now, I took an oath to only be with one woman, but that ain't stopped me from visitin' brothels when I've a mind."

"I imagine," the woman said dryly, "that, in the case of such an oath as that, the woman leaving you because you're a fool absolves you of any oathbreaking."

"How'd you know she said that?" Wendell said. "You using some kind of weird Virtue power on me?"

The woman blinked. "I...yes. That's exactly it. There's no other way I could have ever reached such a conclusion than to use a mystical power from ages past."

He grunted. "Well, I'll thank you to keep it to yourself. I've already had to deal with Leomin cuttin' our card games short every night to take a bedroom tussle with some new woman or another; oh sure, handy enough, I reckon, if you ain't got the money to pay for the night's entertainment, but I want no part of it."

The woman glanced over Wendell's shoulder, raising an eyebrow at Leomin. The Parnen had stopped too and was busily studying the ground as if the answer to life's great mysteries lay scattered in the shin high bracken at his feet. "A new woman every night, is it?" she asked.

Leomin shifted anxiously, refusing to meet her eyes, and Wendell did his best to hide the grin that came on his face. Let them chew that over some, and it'd serve the bastard right for all the trouble he'd put him through. The Parnen muttered something about it not being every night, and the woman's scowl deepened.

Wendell watched happily, wishing he had a chair, maybe a beer to go along with the show that was about to start, but Adina, who'd been walking in the front, had noticed they'd stopped and walked back to find them. "What is it? What's happened?"

"Nothing yet," Wendell said, pretending not to see the angry look the Parnen shot him. "But give it a minute or two."

"Forgive me, Princess," Gryle said, "but Sergeant Wendell was expressing some...doubts about our course of action."

Adina sighed. "We've been through this, Wendell. We can't do Aaron any good back there, and you know it. Besides, don't you want to rescue May?"

It was Wendell's turn to fidget. "Well, of course I do, Princess. It's only...well, shit, when I was a kid I wanted a pony and one of those long caps with the stars on 'em like the actors wear when they're playin' a magician." He sighed, remembering. "Never did get the pony, nor the hat neither. Wantin' ain't enough to make a thing happen. If it were, I'd be laid up in Sallia's bed instead of traipsin' through the woods with you all." Adina frowned at that, and he cleared his throat. "No offense, o'course."

"Of course," she said without inflection. "But we discussed this back at the barracks, Sergeant, all of us, at length."

"Just don't seem right," Wendell said, "leavin' the general and the boy. Especially not with those bastards."

Adina raised an eyebrow at him. "In case you've forgotten, those 'bastards' saved our lives and, what's more, have sent two of their number to escort us safely back to Perennia. The same two," she said, gesturing to the black clad figures that stood silently at the sides of the company, "who are listening to your opinion on them even now. As for Caleb, he and the Speaker thought it best that he stay and help plan the attack on Baresh, given the nature of his bond with the Intelligence Virtue, and considering that we intend to march into what looks to be a hostile city and stop an execution that—by all accounts—is supported by its rightful ruler, it's probably best he stayed behind anyway."

Wendell couldn't argue with that. He'd been at the meeting and had spent his time trying to find a reason to stay himself but, unfortunately, had come up short. Sure, staying with the Akalians had its own risks, but once the headsman's axe started swinging back in Perennia, well, the blade wouldn't much care whose head was on the block. "Sure, they saved us, Princess, in the clearin'. I'll be the first to admit it. And I'm grateful and all but...well, when I was a kid, see, my father raised pigs."

The princess only stared at him, and Leomin let out a soft, barely audible groan. "Pigs," she said.

"That's right," Wendell agreed. "Pigs. Not many, understand, but enough that when some celebration come up—weddings and birthings mostly, ain't a lot else to do in a small village—there'd be bacon for any man, woman, or child as wanted it."

"I'm sure that was quite nice, Sergeant Wendell," Gryle began hesitantly, "but I'm not certain if now is the best time—"

"There was one time, I remember," Wendell said, casting his mind back through the years, "when I was checkin' on 'em, feedin' 'em and the like as it was one of my chores, when I found one of the poor bastards dead, all cut up and missin' chunks and covered in bloody teeth marks, like somebody had taken it in mind they wanted some bacon but weren't ready to wait for the cookin' of it. You'd be amazed how much a pig'll bleed," he said, shaking his head, still amazed at the memory. "I'd never seen anythin' like it at the time, and I ran to my da as if that dead pig was an army marchin' down on us." He shrugged. "I was a kid, understand, and I guess I had it in mind that they was bandits as done for the pig, a whole slew of 'em just sittin' in the forest surrounding our little village. Lookin' back, it seems ridiculous to think it was the work of bandits."

"That makes sense," Leomin said, obviously relieved to find an excuse to avoid Seline's glare. "After all, a group of bandits would hardly chew on a pig like that."

"Exactly," Wendell agreed, "they'd chew on a bunch of 'em." He didn't notice the Parnen's frown of confusion, didn't see him open his mouth as if to protest only to close it again. "I ought to have known better—a single pig ain't gonna feed an army of bandits no matter how it's split. Anyway, point is I showed it to my father, and he told me weren't no bandits done the deed at all, but a coyote, probably a pack of 'em. We set out the next mornin', him with his bow and me with mine. My father was always a fine tracker—best in the village, shit, best in all of Telrear you ask me—and it weren't but the work of a few hours to find 'em. Well, long story short—"

"Or long," Leomin muttered.

"Well, either way, we killed the coyotes one and all, saved those pigs from bein' butchered like their buddy, and I reckon they were probably just about as grateful as pigs can be."

"Which is to say not at all," the Parnen captain said.

"Right," Wendell agreed. "Anyhow, we saved those pigs sure enough, took out those coyotes that would have been the death of not just them but the other livestock in the village if left alone, or so my da said. 'Course, that didn't stop us from eatin' those same pigs when the next Fairday came around."

Leomin groaned. "In the name of the gods, the Akalians don't *eat* people, Sergeant."

"And how would you know?" Wendell said back. "Look, I ain't sayin they do or they don't—all I know is what savin' my father and I did that day, we didn't do for the pigs. Maybe you're all right, and the next time we see the general he'll be right as rain, bitchin' and snappin' at everybody around 'em. You know, his old self. And the boy, may be he'll keep on being weird. But, then, if either comes up with a couple of bite marks in 'em well...don't say I didn't tell you. No offense, lads," he said, turning to speak to the Akalians who only watched him silently. Escorts to see them safely to Perennia, the Speaker had said, but Wendell didn't much care for the look of them, figured if a coyote could stand upright and walk on two legs he'd be giving him a look just about the same as those Akalians were now. A look he didn't deserve—the gods knew he'd been nothing but nice to the bastards.

"We can only do what we can do, Sergeant," Adina said, and there was a sadness in her voice that told Wendell he wasn't the only one that regretted leaving the general behind. "We must hope that Aaron is able to win whatever battle he fights, just as we must hope that we reach Perennia in time and are able to do something to rectify the situation that Grinner has caused. Now," she said, looking at each of them in turn. "Are we ready? We have little time to waste if we hope to be of any help to May and Councilman Hale."

Wendell nodded along with the others, if a bit grudgingly. Adina was right in the main, of course. They couldn't stand aside while May was executed, but that didn't mean he liked it. It seemed to him that far too much of their plan relied on hope. And he could have told them—if they'd listened—that he'd shown up at plenty of brothels with nothing but hope in his pockets, and he'd been disappointed every time. But he didn't think it was what they wanted to hear just then, so he walked on, trudging after the others toward Perennia and whatever horrors awaited them there.

CHAPTER TWENTY-THREE

Something struck the horse from the side, and it stumbled, barely managing to keep its feet. Growling, Aaron lashed out with his blade, striking the offending shadow then bringing the sword back to slice through the next closest. He'd been riding toward the tree for what felt like hours, but they'd yet to reach it. Still, he'd thought they'd been making good time, could see the giant tree getting closer, before the creatures piled in thick all around them, forcing them to first slow down then stop altogether.

The horse was trained well, and it lashed out with its hooves. Where those thunderous impacts fell, shadows turned into dust, but despite the horse and Aaron's efforts, it wasn't long before they were both covered in fresh cuts and scrapes, each small enough wounds on their own, but taken as a whole, they threatened to leech the strength from Aaron. His sword felt impossibly heavy in his hands, as if someone had decided to strap a boulder to it, but still he fought on, raising it again and again, his muscles burning and feeling loose, disconnected.

"Come on then," he rasped to the horse as he struck at another shadow. "If we don't get out of here soon, we're done for."

The horse seemed to hear him, for it kicked out with its back legs, destroying several creatures that had been rushing at it, then began a labored charge forward, its muzzle flecked with crimson foam, its eyes full of pain and anger both. Aaron did what he could to keep the shadows off the beast, swinging as fast and as well as his exhausted body would allow, but more than once the nightmarish creatures made it through, and the horse screamed in a voice that sounded all too human as their claws cut bloody furrows down its side.

Aaron risked a glance up at the tree, stretching up into the black sky past his sight, saw that they were getting closer, and urged the horse on. The Virtue floated at his side, a floating ball of magenta light once more, and lighting their way the best she could. "Not much further, boy," Aaron said to the horse, though he didn't know if it understood him, didn't know, in truth, if it even *was* a boy, but such a thing as that was the least of their problems.

The creatures were pressed in thick around them, all manners and sizes, and despite the beast's efforts, the sellsword felt sure that they would be bogged down again. Instead, the horse continued to push its way forward with a shocking determination, and finally they burst free of the knot of shadow that had surrounded them. A clear path opened in front of them so that Aaron could see the girl sitting huddled at the tree. "*Come on!*" he yelled, and the horse seemed to give its own bray of agreement, charging forward as best as its exhaustion and wounds would allow as the shadows closed in on either side.

Aaron began to believe that they would make it, after all, were no more than a few dozen feet—seconds on the horse—away from the girl and the tree, when suddenly dozens of shadows appeared from either side of the massive trunk. He lost sight of the girl altogether, and felt a moment of impotent anger. There weren't that many of the creatures considering how much he and the horse had slain in the interminable amount of time they'd done battle with them, but plenty enough to slow them down, to waste their time so that the army of darkness behind them could catch up and finish its work.

He was trying to decide what to do, what he *could* do, when the horse leapt. He had not thought horses capable of roaring, but this one did even as its powerful legs carried it upward, over the top of the first row of creatures. Aaron had a flash of hope, thinking that they would clear them, but the hope was quickly shattered as he realized that, for all the horse's efforts, they were going to land in the middle of the creatures. At the apex of its jump, however, the horse seemed to buck, and before he knew what was happening Aaron was flying through the air, up and over the heads of the waiting shadows.

He struck the ground hard, the breath getting knocked out of him for what felt like the hundredth time in the space of an hour, and he rolled to a jarring, painful stop only feet away from the girl. Looking at her, he saw to his dismay that where once her wrist had been stuck into the tree, now her entire arm up to the shoulder was, and the black, pulsing lines had spread across her neck and one side of her face. *Speak to her Aaron,* the Virtue said, *you must make her understand, make her realize that the creatures are no more than the products of her own fears. You must show her how to vanquish them.*

Aaron had no idea what in the name of the gods the Virtue was talking about, but he decided that he had to try. "T-Tianya," he wheezed. "You have to let it go. Your...fear. You have to let it go."

"I cannot," the little girl said, her voice sad and pitiful. "I don't know how."

Letting out a hiss of pain, Aaron worked his way to his feet and turned back to see the horse kicking wildly, destroying the shadows seemingly by the score, but he felt his heart drop as he saw what must have been thousands more closing the distance with impossible quickness. They would be on the horse in another few moments and, once they were done, it would be his and the girl's turn.

He spun to Tianya, grabbing her shoulder. It was hot, the skin fevered to the touch, but he resisted the urge to let go. *"Listen,"* he growled, "what are you afraid of? That you have failed, that you *will* fail? Everyone fails, Tianya. It's a man's—a *woman's*— willingness to try again that makes her brave."

The girl met his eyes, her shame writ plain across her features, and when she spoke it was not in the voice of a child but of the woman he knew. "I failed them. They all died to that...that *thing* and I ran. I was...afraid."

The horse let out a scream of pain, and Aaron risked a glance back at the battle. One of the creatures was hunched on the beast's back, its talons disappearing into the horse's sides, but the horse gave a mighty buck, and the shadow went flying. Turning back to Tianya, Aaron forced a calm into his voice that he did not feel. "Of *course* you were afraid," he said. "Who wouldn't run, when facing a monster like that behemoth Kevlane made?"

"They died because of me," she said, as if she hadn't heard him. "I might as well have killed them myself."

Aaron growled, growing angry now, and his grip on the young girl's shoulder tightened. "Are you so vain that you'll take the credit for every dead man on earth? Is every soldier lying in their graves your responsibility then? Every corpse in every cemetery put there by your hand?"

"They were my *men*," she said, her face wretched with guilt. "And I abandoned them."

"Sure you did," Aaron said, "you ran and because of it you're alive. They didn't, and they died, died fighting for not just your cause, but *their* cause. You did not force them to be there, Tianya, and taking the responsibility for all their deaths, claiming them as your own, steals the meaning of their sacrifice."

"What *meaning*?" she spat, anger sharpening her unfocused gaze. "They are all dead, Aaron Envelar. Dead and gone, all of their efforts, all of my own, come to nothing but dust. What meaning may be found in any of it?"

Aaron shook his head. "There's something I've learned, Tianya, something I'm still learning. Meaning doesn't come with victory, with winning whatever battle we set ourselves. Meaning comes from fighting it to begin with. Those men who died did so for a cause greater than themselves, because they believed in something bigger. In the end, the fact that they lost means nothing. They stood where other men would have run, they fought where others would have begged, and they went to their deaths with courage. We can all hope for little more than that."

She seemed to consider his words, to be thinking them through, and Aaron felt a surge of hope. He was beginning to say something else when suddenly the air was pierced by the horse's terrible scream. The creatures were climbing all over it now, raking at it with their claws, biting into its flesh with their teeth. It gave another great kick, knocking many of the creatures loose, but not all, and then it seemed to turn its head, seemed to meet Aaron's eye, as if to tell him that it had done all it could, that it was sorry it couldn't do more. Then, in another moment, the shadows swarmed over it like ants, and the horse vanished from view.

"*Nooo!*" the sellsword bellowed, surprised by the fury and sense of loss that rose in him at seeing the beast brought down, for it had been his companion in this nightmare world, standing with him against the inevitable darkness, and he bared his teeth in a rage that did not come from the power of the bond but one that was entirely his own. "You bastards!"

There was a flurry of motion as the shadows feasted and in mere seconds they separated once more. Where the horse had been, there was no sign. No blood to mark its passing, not even so much as a single white hair to show that it had ever been there at all. For the horse was no real creature of blood and muscle and bone, but the girl's imagining, a dream. And though dreams could die as well as men—and did so at least as often—the most terrible thing about their passing was that, when they perished, there was no evidence that they had ever existed at all, no corpse for the dreamer to mourn, nothing but an emptiness where something grand had once been, nothing but an awful stillness where once it had breathed.

"Dreams die, Tianya," Aaron rasped, his voice harsh with fury. "Men die. All we can do is to make sure that, when they do, they don't do so for nothing." *Good men try.*

Aaron, don't—

But whatever the Virtue had been about to say was drowned out by Aaron's own roar, an answer to the horse's final cry, a recognition of the death of yet another dream in a world that could ill-afford the loss. Then he raised his sword and charged into the shadow.

He hacked at the creatures of nightmare with abandon, swinging his blade first this way then that, demanding more of his bruised and battered body, more speed, more strength. Deep down, he knew that the burst of energy his anger had given him would be the last of its kind, but he did not care. He saved nothing, held back nothing, and he fought better than he had ever fought before. He slew the shadows with a blade shining brilliant white, cutting them down in droves like some avenging god come to wreak a divine retribution.

But even as he did so, he knew that he would not, *could* not win, for those he slew in the light rose again in the darkness. Still, he fought on anyway, the breath rasping in his lungs, for he now

A Sellsword's Mercy

understood that the definition of a man, the truth of him, was not in the battles that he had won, but the battles he had chosen to fight. And for one of the first times in his life, Aaron fought not in reaction to some wrong, but because he chose to. Because the battle before him was one worth fighting, worth dying for, if that was what required, and slowly the anger that had fueled his charge changed into a sort of peace, a contentment in knowing that however it ended—and that ending seemed clear enough—he had done something worth doing.

He drove deeper and deeper into the heart of the shadow until, standing before him, was one of the great behemoths of darkness, so tall that he couldn't see where it ended. He didn't hesitate, just charged toward it, his blade leading. Unlike the smaller shadows, there was resistance when his blade met what served as the creature's ankle, but Aaron grit his teeth and kept going, the brilliant blade cutting a furrow across the shadowy limb, the wound leaving a burning trail of white in its wake.

The creature let out a great roar, a massive hand swiping down at him, but he dove to the side, rolling just out of its grasp. Then he was up and running again, burying his blade deeply into its leg once more. Another roar, this one greater than the first, and Aaron felt, more than saw, the great weight of the creature's bulk shifting, swaying like some huge tree preparing to topple to a woodsman's axe.

He kept up his attack, hacking away at the creature as if, by defeating it, he might somehow defeat all the darkness not just in this dream world, but in all worlds, might, in conquering it, lay waste to the evils that plagued the lives of men and women from the moment they were born. Suddenly, the creature gave a great lurch and began to fall. He dove out of the way, and after what felt like an eternity, the creature landed with a great, silent *whumpf,* crushing thousands of its allies beneath it. The impact made Aaron's teeth rattle in their sockets, and he felt as if some malicious, giant child had picked him up and started shaking him. But soon it was over, and when he rose from the ground, he rose bloody, as full of pain as most men were full of blood, but smiling for all that.

He continued to smile even as three more of the great hulks seemed to materialize in front of him, even as weak arms raised his sword in front of him, forced to grip it two-handed now to be able to lift it at all, for though it was a sword forged in a dream, made from it, dreams, Aaron was beginning to learn, had their own weight. The creatures began taking their lumbering steps toward him, and in between their feet milled thousands of their smaller brethren.

"*No.*"

For a moment, Aaron was so consumed by his own thoughts that he believed the word had come from his own mouth, some last denial before the end came upon him. It wasn't until it came again, stronger than the first time, that he realized it wasn't his voice at all, but a woman's voice, full of power. The creatures must have heard it too, and they hesitated, appearing unsure for the first time, shadows who had once been confident in their own preeminence quivering uncertainly at the rising of the morning sun.

"*No!*" The voice came a third time, and it was not a whisper or a statement now, but a shout, a roaring greater than any that had issued from the mouths of those towering monstrosities of darkness. This time, the shadow creatures did not hesitate, but backed away as if hurt or scared, their limbs coming up as if to ward off some unseen blow.

Aaron turned, his weary legs nearly giving out beneath him, and was shocked to see that where the young girl had once crouched, now stood a woman. He recognized her as Tianya at once, and she seemed to him to be the best version of herself, not plagued by the fears and doubts that latched onto the living, but standing straight and proud. A soft, white light glowed around her, *through* her, as she stared out at the throng of shadows creatures surrounding her and the sellsword, her anger a palpable thing.

"*This is my place,*" she said, each word resonating and echoing through the air. "*And you are not welcome here.*" She raised her hands above her head and, as she did, the light that suffused her seemed to travel out from her into the world itself, pushing back the darkness. The shadows shrank away even farther, as if somehow they might avoid their fate, but shadows have no place in the world of light. "*Be gone,*" she said, and brilliant white light erupted from her in a wave, rushing in all directions. Many of the creatures turned, tried to flee, but there was no escaping it. When the light touched them they wailed and vanished until it was only Aaron and the woman and the tree, standing tall and proud now, majestic and beautiful.

"Well," Aaron said, wavering drunkenly. "That's a fancy trick." He wasn't aware he was falling until he was down on one knee. Now that the fight was over, his wounds dragged at him, great weights that he could not shrug off.

"You're weary," Tianya said, coming to stand in front of him, and to Aaron's amazement the shadow world that had surrounded them was changing. A pale sun shone in the sky, weak now but growing brighter with every second. All around him, the unidentifiable ground of darkness was quickly giving way to lush, green grass that spread out in a ring with the woman its center. He even thought he heard the distant sound of a bird calling and another answering.

Still, whatever changes were being wrought on the world were not being worked on him, and now that the immediate danger had passed, he felt every scrape, every blow, and it was all he could do to keep from shouting in pain. "Weary?" he said, giving a breathless laugh. "Nah. I'd say I passed weary a lifetime ago."

The woman gave a laugh of her own, a mellifluous laugh that was at once comforting and somehow fey. Aaron raised his head with an effort, studying her. "You've changed," he said. Not much of a compliment, maybe, but his breath was a short rasp in his lungs, and he didn't trust himself to manage anything more.

She smiled, and though she was a woman now, he could still see traces of the girl she'd once been in the expression. "So have you."

Aaron grunted. "Sure. I'd say it's safe to say I've got a few more scars anyway."

"That's not what I meant," she said, her smile still well in place, "and I think you know it."

"I don't know what you're—"

"Oh *shut up,* Aaron," a voice said as the magenta ball of light materialized beside him. "You know good and well what she means. You can play the tough asshole when you're out drinking with your soldiers, if you want, but here, we know better."

Aaron stared back at where the battle had taken place. Now, bushes and trees shot out of the ground, though none matched the might of the one tree, *Tianya's* tree, that loomed over all, not a menace now, but a savior. A protector. Still, his memories were not so easily erased as the darkness, and he sighed. "Not tough?" he asked. "I thought I did alright."

"Gods, but if I had feet I'd kick you in the shin," the Virtue snapped. "And save that scowl for someone who'll be impressed by it—I'm not."

"Fine," Aaron growled. "I've changed, so what? What difference does that make right now?"

Tianya cocked her head at him, studying him strangely. She waited for him to meet her eyes, then she gestured expansively to the world that was growing rapidly around them. "I cannot speak for anyone else, Aaron Envelar, but for me, it has made all the difference in the world. It has been the difference between light and darkness, life and death." She knelt before him, bowing her head. "And I want you to know that I am eternally grateful for what you have done. I know well what it cost you—what risks you took—and I know better still that I deserved none of them. I do not know how I could ever repay you for the kindness you've shown me."

Aaron winced, suddenly uncomfortable, and he thought it said something about him—probably nothing good—that he felt more at home with people trying to kill him than trying to thank him. "You can start by standing up. I'm no god or king. Just about as far from it as anyone could be, in fact."

She smiled, but he was grateful to see that she *did* stand. "Perhaps, Aaron Envelar. Perhaps. But I know of no one else who would do for me what you have done."

Aaron started to say that it had seemed like a good idea at the time. The problem, of course, was that it hadn't. It had been a shit idea with a shit plan, and he could not explain—even to himself— why he had done it. A thought struck him, and he frowned. "What of the horse?"

A troubled expression flickered across Tianya's face, but it was gone in another moment. "A piece of me, Aaron Envelar, my mind, perhaps, or what the priests call my soul."

Aaron nodded slowly. "I liked him."

She smiled, and there was something sad about it. "So did I. Or, at least, I think I did—I cannot be sure for even as I stand here speaking with you my memory of it fades. Still, you should know that, in other circumstances, I might have something to say about your assumption that it was a he."

Aaron shook his head, confused. "But I saw it die. If that was a piece of you..."

"Yes," she said, nodding. "The road to change is never easy, and few battles are won without casualties. I fear that piece of me is gone forever, but do not mourn it too terribly. Such creatures are born all the time in our hearts, fighting those most terrible of foes for us—grief, anger, fear, hatred. And my *Sugar* is not the first to be conquered by the enemies she faced, nor will she be the last."

That gave Aaron several questions, but he asked the one that bothered him the most. "*Sugar?*"

She smiled, and once again he was reminded of the little girl who'd sat by the tree. "I had a dog once, as a child. The sweetest animal I had ever met before or since with a coat of pure white. My mother said, when she saw her, that she looked as if she had been dipped in sugar."

Aaron grunted. "Right."

"But enough of my past," the woman said. "We need now look to our future, to the future of Telrear itself. I fear time is running out."

He didn't like the sound of that. "Time? Why do you say that?"

The woman frowned, gazing at the sky as if searching for some answer. "Say, simply, that the real world has not paused to wait on us while we tarried in this one. I fear, Aaron, that you may have risked more than you know in saving me. More than just your own life."

A sinking feeling came to the sellsword's stomach, and his first thought went to Adina, some unknown fear rising within him. But that was ridiculous, of course, for Adina was safely sleeping. He had checked on her only...but he had no way to finish that thought, for he realized that he could not have even begun to guess how long he'd been here, fighting Tianya's demons, her fears. He would have been no more surprised to hear that it had been ten minutes as he would have been had someone told him a year had passed while he battled. He started to rise, not sure where he would go or what he intended, only that he couldn't stay here doing nothing. But, as was so often the case, the body had demands of its own, no matter how much the mind and the heart might yearn for something different. His weary legs refused to take his weight, and he sank back down, sweating and gasping from the simple act of trying to stand.

"Fields take it," he swore.

"Your wounds steal your strength," the woman observed, compassion filling her voice as she stepped closer.

Aaron stared at her as she moved near him, and despite the fact that she had clearly changed, he couldn't help feeling uneasy at being so vulnerable at her feet, a woman who had, not so very long ago, tried to kill him and his friends to get what she wanted.

She seemed to see the content of his thoughts, for a hurt look crossed her features, but only for a moment. "I am no healer, Aaron Envelar. Once, I thought I was, one great enough to heal the world, but I was shown the truth when Kevlane's monstrosity slaughtered my men before my eyes, when I fled into the darkness, thinking only of my own safety. I denied the truth then, refused it, but you have made me see it clearly enough. My life has been one of hurting, not healing, yet in this place I can be something more, something better."

She reached out, taking Aaron's hand. An unnatural, but not unpleasant warmth radiated from her touch, suffusing him and traveling through his body. And where it went the pain vanished. "Thank you, Aaron Envelar," she said, and as she spoke a haze seemed to come over his eyes, the world of green and light all around him blurring and becoming indistinct. "Not just for my life, but for giving me the chance to do good."

Each word was quieter than the last, as if she spoke to him over some great distance. Though she did not move, and the grip of her hand in his remained. Aaron's eyes felt heavy, and he found them closing of their own accord as she continued to speak. "There are many shadows in the world, Aaron Envelar...much darkness. But you have shown me that the light can still win...Thank..."

***

"...you..." she finished, and Aaron's eyes snapped open. For a moment, he had a terrible sense of disorientation as he realized he no longer knelt in a field of green grass, but beside a bed. He still felt the pressure of the woman's hand in his and looked to see her lying in the bed as she had been. His gaze traveled to her face, and she smiled, an expression that was at once both weary and content. "Now…go," she said aloud. "There is…little time."

Aaron rose from where he knelt, his body stiff from the time he'd crouched there. Stiff, but no more than that, for the pain of the wounds he'd suffered had vanished as if they had never been, and he found his muscles practically surging with energy as if he'd awoken from a long, restful sleep.

"The gods, it seems, can be kind, after all."

The sellsword spun at the sound of the voice to see the Speaker of the Akalians standing by the door of the small bedroom. "Welcome back, Aaron Envelar," the man said, bowing his head. "I must admit that I feared you might never awaken."

"How long have I been…gone?"

"I cannot say for certain," the Speaker said, apologetically. "I can only say that, since I found you, you have spent nearly twenty hours here, without moving."

Twenty hours, Aaron thought wildly. Nearly a full day gone. Another thought struck him, and his heart sped up in his chest. "Where are Adina and the others?"

The Speaker winced. "She stayed with you as long as she could, Aaron. It was no easy thing, I assure you, for her to leave you in—"

"Where are they?"

The Speaker sighed. "News reached us from Perennia. I'm afraid it isn't good. It seems Councilman Grinner has, for all intents and purposes, taken over rule of the city, the queen now turned into little more than his pawn. Lady May Tanarest and Councilman Hale have been taken prisoner, and an execution has been scheduled for them both."

"An *execution?*" Aaron asked, stunned. He couldn't believe it. How could everything have gone so wrong in such a short time? "How is that possible?"

The Speaker shook his head. "I do not know, Aaron Envelar. It seems that Councilman Grinner had been planning the coup for some time, and once you and the others were away from the city, he moved quickly. One of my brothers brought me news, only a few hours gone, that apparently Councilman Grinner saved the queen from an assassination attempt by two of Hale's men and, since then, she has grown increasingly reliant on his counsel."

Once you and the others were away from the city. Aaron thought back to the men that had attacked him in Perennia what felt like a lifetime ago. He'd been so busy since then that he'd given it little consideration, but he remembered one of them calling him "Silent." Had they been men from Perennia itself, they would not have done so, for here he was known as General Envelar, the Leader of the Ghosts, and savior of the city—gods help him. There were few enough who still called him by the name he'd been known as in Avarest. May, of course, Hale, and Grinner. That meant that one of them was involved in the assassination attempt, and given recent events, it seemed clear it had been the old crime boss. He had lured the others out of the city into an ambush, had tried to have Aaron killed. Fueled with rage, Aaron had done exactly what the man wanted, abandoning the city to Grinner's designs as he went into the forest in search of blood and death.

"Gods, I've been a fool."

"You did what you believed best, Aaron Envelar," the Speaker said.

Aaron shook his head, angry with himself. "That's no excuse, Speaker. I think you've lived long enough to know that thousands of corpses, rotting in their graves, were put there because of one man doing what he thought was best. The fact that he thought he was doing what was right is little consolation to the living and none at all to the dead."

His frantic thoughts raced, turning the situation over, and he grunted as he realized it was even worse than that. Grinner had known Kevlane's creatures would be waiting in the forest, and that meant that he'd been in contact with the mage, had formed some alliance with him. Taking the thought a step further meant that anything they'd discussed in the council, their plans and strategy, had no doubt all been told to the magi, handed up to him on a silver platter.

"We have all been fools," he said, and it was no more than the truth. They had brought a wolf into their midst, had dressed him in fine clothes and treated him as they might a man, but he was a wolf just the same, and what right did they have to act surprised when he behaved according to his nature?

It was necessary, Aaron, Co thought back. *Without Grinner, we could never have held off Belgarin's first attack. You had no choice.*

That was logical, inarguable, but it did nothing to dispel the guilt that he felt, that the others—Adina especially—would feel. And with the thought he realized where Adina had gone, where she *must* have gone. "She left, didn't she?"

The Speaker did not ask who he was talking about, only nodded. "Yes. Queen Adina and the others left for the city several hours ago. Saving for Caleb, who has elected to stay and assist with planning the assault on Baresh."

If there even is *an assault,* Aaron thought. He bared his teeth, fear for Adina and the others making him angry. "And you let her go?"

The Speaker cocked his head at him as if he'd just spoken a different language, one which he did not understand. "She did not ask for my permission, Aaron Envelar, and I am not sure I could have stopped her, even if I wanted to. And even if I could, I would not, for Queen Adina made her choice. Who am I, then, to tell her she is wrong?"

Aaron started to speak, a scathing comment on the tip of his tongue, but he hesitated. The Speaker was right—even past his fear, his worry for Adina and the others, he could see that. Of course, she would have gone to the city, would have been intent on doing what she could to save it and never mind the risk to her own safety. "And the execution?" he asked. "When is it meant to take place?"

"At dawn," the Speaker said. "One hour hence."

One hour. Nowhere near enough time to make it to the city, and Aaron knew it. *Gods, May, I'm so sorry.* He felt a wave of despair threaten to overwhelm him, but he forced it down. He might not be able to make it to the city in time, might not be able to save May and the others, but he could only do what he could and hope to the gods for some miracle. *Good men try.* "I'll need my sword."

"Of course," the Speaker said. "This way."

They started to leave, but Aaron turned back at the threshold, looking to the woman in the bed. She gave him a weak, exhausted smile. "Go," she said. "I will…catch up. When I can."

"Okay," Aaron said. "And do me a favor. If you fall asleep…maybe dream about rainbows and bunny rabbits, huh?"

She grinned. "I'll try."

The sellsword nodded and followed the Speaker out of the room.

Minutes later, sword in hand, Aaron stepped out of the barracks and into the morning light, shielding his dark-accustomed eyes. The Speaker faced him, an Akalian on either side. "Most of our brothers are out patrolling the area in case the Lifeless should find their way here," the Speaker said for at least the third time since they'd left Tianya's room. "Will you not give me but a few minutes' time to call them back?"

Aaron was shaking his head before the man had finished. "Thank you, Speaker, but no. These two here will do, and I thank you for it. I don't think half a dozen more will make much difference one way or the other." But that wasn't the only reason he refused to wait. The truth was, he didn't' think they had minutes to spare. It was all too likely that they were out of time already.

The Speaker clearly wanted to argue, but only nodded. "I will look after Tianya and the boy. We will follow as quickly as we may. Go with the gods, Aaron Envelar, and be careful. This fight, dangerous though it may be, is not the true one, and it will do the world no good to be saved from the snake's bite only to find itself in the lion's mouth."

Aaron gave the man a grim smile, the anger he felt at Grinner and his men roiling within him. But it was his anger, his to control, and he nodded tightly. "Thank you, Speaker," he said, staring into the forest. "But careful is just about the last thing I intend on being." Then he was off and running, the wind whipping at his face, the two Akalians following after him, twin shadows in the early morning light.

CHAPTER TWENTY-FOUR

When it came, the day inside the dungeon cell was like any other. Outside, the weather might have been hot or cold, the sun shining brightly or the clouds blocking it from view. The wind—if wind there was—might have carried buoyed on its breath some whisper of the secret the coming day held. But if the air held a spark, some heady premonition of what was to come, it never made its way down into the dungeon. Here, the air was as it always was—thick and cloying, somehow greasy, smelling of dirt, despair, and worse. And if there was any sound, any omen to announce what awaited the day then it came in the always-present moaning of those poor lost souls who shared the dungeon with her.

It was a day like any other, full of broken hope and stolen dreams, and it was the day May would die. She did not rail at the thought of it, did not bellow at the injustice, nor add her voice to that unearthly, piteous chorus. At least, not any more than usual, for she, like the others, had become a moaning, desperate beast, so full of pain that she could not have told a healer—had he asked—what it was that hurt, for the hurt was all over now. Each bruise, each dried tear, had fused together so that they were no longer separate pains at all, but one great aching despair, and in this way, she had become like the prisoners in the cells around her.

All, that was, save for Hale. The man had suffered greatly in the past days, his body beaten and misused, but he alone still stood tall in the face of what he had endured, keeping his feet against a furious storm that had long since scattered and broken his companions. May loved him for his strength, his courage, for being able to hold on and shout his defiance into that raging tempest. She loved him, and she also hated him, for his refusal to break, to submit as she and the others had, serving as a stark reminder of what she had once been, of what had been ripped from her.

Even now, he sat with his back against the wall of his cell, his arms draped over his knees. Had one not been able to see the wounds covering his body she would have been forgiven for thinking he could have been relaxing in some tavern somewhere, had sat down to play a hand of cards, perhaps. He did not speak, only studied her with his dark-eyed gaze. And in that gaze was a question.

He'd studied her often of late, in just such a way, his dark eyes measuring, weighing, and for this, too, she hated him. For the question his eyes held was one she did not want to answer, not even to herself. *Are you broken?* those eyes asked. Even now, so close to the end, the answer came reluctantly, but she forced herself to give it.

Yes.

Are you beaten?

Yes.

Will you fight, when the time comes?

She sneered at that, a flicker of anger rising in the cold despair filling her. "Fight with *what*?" she rasped, unaware she was going to speak out loud until she did so. "Fight *who*?" A woman could not fight shame, could not conquer despair. They were opponents for which there were no weapons and against which there was no victory. Was she to wield a sword against injustice, against evil? Such things could not be slain with a blade or bow, and even if they could she was not the one to wield it, for her arms were as weary as the rest of her.

But if the crime boss heard her, he chose not to answer, only continued to study her with that dark, terrible gaze, with those eyes that held no pity, no sympathy for what she was, what she had become. Those eyes which did not give her answers, only questions, and asked them without remorse or compassion, battering her with them even as tears began to form in eyes she had thought long since dried up.

Do you want to die?

She quailed from the question, pushing herself further into the corner of her cell and jerking her eyes away from the crime boss's visage as if, in doing so, she might somehow avoid the piercing question, as one trained in such things might avoid the blade of a sword.

"Damn you," she hissed, oblivious of the spittle that flew from her mouth as she did. The crime boss still did not speak, did not so much as move at all, as if he had been carved from stone, put there, across from her, as another form of torture, to serve as a counterpoint to her own pitiful state, to show her what it meant to endure.

Do you want to die?

Who in the name of the gods did he think he was, to ask such a question? Even in her wretched state, she felt a spark of indignity at it. She would not have thought that she could still feel such a thing, had thought that the depravities to which she had been subjected had stripped her not only of her dignity but of the memory of it as well. But the spark vanished as quickly as it had come, extinguished by the creeping despair that had settled over her, for such despair was a jealous companion and did not suffer others in its place.

Do you want to die?

She let out a sound that was somewhere between a snarl and a moan. What difference did it matter what she wanted? The day had come. Even though she did not know what hour it was or how long left there was to wait, she knew that much. Soon, perhaps even now, the guards would be on their way to fetch her and the crime boss, their manacles hanging at their belts, their swords drawn in case she or Hale put up any fight. She could have told them, had they asked, not to bother with the last. What fight she'd had had dimmed along with her red hair. It was not a question of whether she would fight or not—her only fear was whether she would be able to walk, when the time came, whether she would be able to put one foot in front of the other, knowing full well where the path she trod would lead.

But doesn't it always? a part of her asked without much curiosity or any sort of feeling one way or the other. From the moment a child was born, she set her feet upon a path. There were none—not scholars or profits, not even priests—who might tell her all the twistings and turnings of that path, but they all knew well enough where it ended. The only question was how many obstacles the girl would face, how many heartaches, how many pieces of herself she would lose, to win the right to reach the path's end.

Adina gone, Aaron gone, and no sign of either. Both of them gone and most likely dead, along with Gryle and Leomin, even the boy, Caleb. All taken, and she able to do nothing about it at all. She, a woman who had once fancied herself a power, believed herself capable of nearly anything she set her mind to. But she had learned the lie of that, had been taught it over the past days.

Even Thom, if he still lived, was doomed along with the rest of Perennia, the rest of the world, for Kevlane would come, sooner or later, and his creatures would come with him. And then would begin the slaughter. May could do nothing to stop it—no one could. It was, she'd realized some time ago, inevitable. All things died, after all. Why should the world itself be any exception?

Do you want to die?

At least it would be an end. When the slaughter came, when the streets ran red with the blood of Kevlane's victims, of Grinner's victims, there would be great pain and sorrow. She did not doubt that many would stand and make of themselves heroes, but they would die just the same. Everyone would die, and there would be none left who might sing the song of their glory. It would be a time of terrible agony, terrible loss. Perhaps, the world itself would weep cold tears upon witnessing the massacre, but she did not believe that it would.

Either way, however unbearable the agony of what was to come, the city would not have to endure it for long. Sooner or later, it would be over. No longer would men and women go to sleep in fear for themselves, their children. No longer would smiths and merchants pause in their work, casting troubled glances east, toward Baresh. All fear, all worry would be no more. It would be a brutal, cruel end, but it *would* be an end.

Do you want to die?

"Yes," May answered, and this time there were no tears winding their way down her face. "*Yes.*"

CHAPTER TWENTY-FIVE

Adina paused on the edge of the forest, staring at Perennia in the distance, across the wind-swept fields. From this far away, the city looked beautiful, its white walls shimmering in the morning sun as if thousands of diamonds had been embedded there. The castle reached proudly into the sky, a testament to the great things of which men, working together, were capable. Seen from here, it might have been some castle out of the storybooks her nurse or her father had read to her when she was a child. Inside, she could almost imagine great knights and ladies dancing and laughing together.

If it *were* a story, there would no doubt be treachery, some evil man with which to do battle—there always was. But in such a story, the end was certain even as you began reading it. Some unknown girl or boy would rise up, proving themselves and saving the kingdom. They would be heralded far and wide for their courage, their resourcefulness. Perhaps, there would be a celebration, a feast. Either way, no matter how dark the tale became, at its end, the castle would still stand, and those within its confine would remember how to laugh, how to dance.

But this was not a story, and there was no knowing whether the evil that had come upon the city would be vanquished, or if she and those with her would only die in the attempt. Perennia might look picturesque from here, but she knew that when they drew closer, they would be able to make out the blood-stains on the ramparts, stubborn proof of the battle waged here only months before when her brother, Belgarin, had brought his armies to conquer and had only been beaten back by the sacrifices of hundreds of lives.

Such beauty always came at a cost, and when one drew near, its flaws inevitably presented themselves. The thought made her sad, but she put it aside. Her companions stared at the castle as if their thoughts echoed her own, all no doubt considering, too, the distinct possibility that they would not live through the day. *They need a leader,* she thought, and following on the tail of that, *you are enough.* She turned to the Akalians who had accompanied her and the others through the forest in case Kevlane's creatures attacked them. "I thank you for the escort," she said, bowing her head to each of them in turn. "Please, return to your brothers with my blessing."

Wendell frowned. "You sure about that, Queen?"

Adina nodded. "They have their own battle to fight, Sergeant, for Kevlane's creatures might, at any moment, discover the barracks. If they do, I'm sure the Speaker will need all the help he can get to hold them off. Besides, with what we intend, two men—no matter how skilled—are unlikely to make a difference in any case."

The scarred sergeant grunted. "Don't know that I agree with that, Majesty. Seems to me that one man's enough to stab a fella aimin' to kill me. Think that'd make a pretty big difference, least so far as I'm concerned. There's a couple of whores, too, I imagine'd be put out by it."

"And if Kevlane's creatures *do* find the barracks, with Aaron still helpless as he tries to help Tianya?"

Wendell winced. "Right, well, I hadn't thought of that. I guess maybe you've got the right of it, after all." He shot a sidelong glance at the two Akalians. "Leastways, if they haven't eaten him already," he muttered.

Leomin rolled his eyes, opening his mouth. Adina suspected it was to tell Wendell for the near-hundredth time that the Akalians weren't in the habit of eating people, but she gave him a small shake of her head, and the Parnen subsided. "Very well," she said, meeting each of their eyes in turn. "Then we are in agreement."

"It will be very dangerous, Majesty," Gryle said, coming up stand beside her and gazing out at the distant city. Adina studied him with a small smile. The months since they'd met Aaron and begun their quest had changed everyone, and the chamberlain was no exception. Where once, he might have been terrified at the prospect of the coming violence, his voice quavering as he spoke, now he did so without inflection, simply making an observation. There was a hardness in his gaze, a determination Adina had rarely seen that would have shocked her not long ago. She wondered if he thought of Beth. Her death had affected them all, but Gryle had been closest to her. He had spoken little of the events that had occurred since Aaron found him in the inn, and Adina felt a stab of guilt that she had not taken her friend aside and talked it through with him. There was no time to do so now, but she promised herself that she would when this was all over. Assuming they survived it.

"Yes," she agreed. "It will be dangerous."

The chamberlain nodded, his expression calm and without fear. "Say," the sergeant said, "you reckon the Speaker and those other fellas might need some help? I could—"

"No, Sergeant," Adina said, unable to keep the smile from her face. "I think that they'll get along well enough without us."

He grunted, shrugging as he studied the distant city. "Well, it was only a thought."

"I'm sure," Adina agreed. She turned to take in all of them with her gaze. Gryle, the man standing proudly, standing tall, so very different a creature than the man he'd once been. Wendell, gazing at the city as if it was a snake that might bite him, but not fleeing for all that. Leomin and the woman, Seline, standing side by side, close enough that their shoulders were touching. An unlikely pairing, Adina thought, but one she was glad to see nevertheless. "Are we ready?" She waited for each of them to nod. "Alright. Then let's go."

CHAPTER TWENTY-SIX

The crowd in the city square was larger than any Balen had ever seen; it seemed to him as if the entire population of the world had come to see the execution. Men, women, and children were crammed together so tightly that they couldn't turn without bumping several other people. To Balen, it was as if they weren't individual people at all, but one great heaving beast, and if the stares and expectant voices—loud, excited voices that combined into a thunder of indecipherable words—were any indication, this beast was hungry.

Just looking at that churning mass of humanity made Balen break out in a cold sweat. He'd never done well with crowds. Sure, on a ship, sailors were stuck with each other for weeks, sometimes months on end, but they, at least, weren't strangers. Not necessarily friends—the gods knew a ship was full of more arguments than a brothel with only one customer—but on a ship a man had enough room to walk around, to stretch his limbs and maybe even spit if he'd a mind without hitting somebody square in the face and getting himself in a fight.

Not that anyone would be able to so much as raise a fist in such a tightly-packed crowd. Balen wasn't even sure how the poor bastards managed to breathe. He glanced over at his companion, but if the older first mate felt any anxiety at the thought of entering that throng, he didn't show it. Instead, Thom's face was creased with hard, angry lines, the way it had been since he'd heard the news. After he'd finished shouting, of course, and

Balen—with the help of the others—had managed to convince him that maybe rushing headlong into the city, knocking every guard he saw over the head, wasn't the best way of saving the club owner.

It hadn't been easy going, that—some of the more unfortunate sailors had fresh bruises to show for their troubles and one a black eye that reminded Balen of a rotten fruit—but they had eventually managed to calm the older man down long enough to tell him their plan. He hadn't said much, only stood there looking like a storm cloud ready to burst, and Balen had breathed a sigh of relief when he'd finally agreed to it.

"Well," Thom said now, in a snarl that sounded more like it came from the throat of a wolf than any human. "Let's get down there."

"Sure," Balen agreed. "But how?" He said the last with a wince, not wanting to anger the old man any further—he himself had some fresh bruises, and he wasn't keen on feeling the first mate's fists again, if he could help it—but unable to imagine how they would be able to force their way through so many people to the front, where it had been decided they would need to be.

"Come on. I'll show you."

Balen sighed—careful not to do so loud enough for the first mate to hear—then followed him as he stalked purposefully toward the crowd. Thom didn't waste time on any social niceties such as "excuse me" or "pardon me," not that Balen suspected he would have been heard over the roar of conversation that filled the city square, anyway. Instead, he took the more direct approach of shoving people out of his way as if there was a chest of gold at the front of the crowd, and he meant to have his share of it.

Balen followed in the man's wake, murmuring apologies to the angry men and women they passed. After a few minutes, he looked up, trying to gauge how far they had left to go, but he could see nothing past the heads of those gathered around them.

He was still trying to catch a glimpse of the wooden platform when he heard a grunt of anger, and his attention snapped to where Thom had pushed the most recent man out of the way. This one, though, wasn't satisfied with an angry look and reached out to grab the first mate's shoulder. "What the fuck do you think you're doin'?" he demanded.

He was a big man, looked to Balen like maybe he spent his time juggling boulders, but if that gave the first mate any hesitation he didn't show it. Thom turned, and his knee shot up between the man's legs with no more expression on his face than a man might show swatting a fly.

The man, though, had expression enough for both of them, his eyes going wide as he screamed in shocked pain. His hands went to his fruits as if they'd caught fire and he was trying to put them out. Balen shouted him an apology before following after the first mate who was already plowing ahead, and a moment later the big man—and his sore fruits—disappeared in the crowd.

"Fella probably didn't want to have children anyway," Balen commented, but the first mate gave no sign of hearing him, and Balen decided that was probably for the best. The big man might not have wanted children, but Balen himself wasn't quite sure on the issue one way or the other and would just as soon keep his options open.

By the time they made it to the front, he was sweating heavily, unbearably hot, and he figured that if there was a place of perpetual torment as some priests believed Salen's Fields was, then he'd gotten there without so much as a sign post to guide his way. The people nearest them frowned and shot them sullen glances, not surprising, he supposed, considering that Thom had pushed them aside the way a man might push away undergrowth in a forest and with even less thought than that.

Balen did his best to not meet their eyes directly, keeping an apologetic look on his face, and hoping none of them decided to make a fuss. He was still concentrating on not getting punched or stabbed—he'd had enough of the former for one day, thanks to the first mate, and had no intention of ending it with the latter, despite the fact that there was a better than even chance he'd do just that—when his gaze lighted on the wooden platform at the square's center.

A chill ran down his spine at the sight of it. It was just plain wood, wood that could have been used to craft any number of things—beds or chairs, maybe a crib to hold a baby in. But it was none of those things; this wood had been crafted for death, shaped and made for it, and Balen felt a sense of unease as he stared at it, as if he was somehow being watched and not in a friendly way.

Ridiculous, of course. Wood couldn't stare, and it certainly couldn't think, but that did nothing to settle Balen's queasy stomach.

A simple platform, big enough to hold eight men, maybe more, considering one of the poor bastards would be kneeling with his head on the stout block of wood in the center of it. Balen found it difficult to fathom that soon, less than an hour from now, May and Hale would be marched up onto that platform and—unless he and the others managed to stop it—their blood would stain that freshly-cut wood crimson. He had a moment, then, when he felt as if he was dreaming. Surely, it couldn't be real. Surely they could not have come to such a place as this. But the scowling people around them were real enough, and the sensations running through him, burning one moment, freezing the next, were also real. So, too, was the man standing beside him, staring at the platform and the block on it as if they were creatures, mad dogs, maybe, that needed to be put down.

"It's alright, Thom," Balen said. "We'll save her."

"We'd better," the first mate said, his gaze unwavering. "Because this much I promise you, Balen, whatever happens, I'll die before she does, and I'll take as many of these sons of bitches with me as I can."

Balen swallowed hard. If there was a better way to kill a conversation, he'd never heard it, so he decided to start looking around for the swordmaster, for the sailors and Urek and all the others who would be spread out in the crowd, waiting for their moment. He thought he saw a flash of Beautiful's face, but it could have been no more than a product of his own fear, for the woman had been eyeing him like a piece of meat since they'd met, one she intended to devour, given the opportunity.

The swordmaster himself, he knew, would not have arrived yet, for he'd gone in search of captain Brandon Gant. Balen didn't know if he had managed to find him or not, but he prayed he had and that the captain had agreed to work with them. They had little enough chance as it was, if the captain did get involved. If he didn't…well, better not to think of that. If he didn't, Balen could spend eternity in the Fields thinking it over. After all, it wasn't as if the dead had jobs to get to.

CHAPTER TWENTY-SEVEN

May looked up at the sound of footsteps in the dungeon corridor. She did not shrink away as she so often did, for one surprising side-effect of her impending death was she was no longer afraid of something so small as the scuff of a boot on tightly-packed earth, nor the ruddy glow of torchlight in the dark. Eight guardsmen filed in front of her cell, two carrying torches. Six lined themselves in front of Hale's cell while two stood in front of her own. She felt vaguely offended at that, but she couldn't really blame the guards. She'd heard it had taken nearly a dozen guards to arrest the big man in the first place, and more than one had been forced to visit—or be carried—to a healer after.

One of the guards turned to her, regarding her with eyes that were not unkind, a vaguely troubled expression on his face. "It's time, May Tanarest. Are you ready?"

May nearly laughed at that. How, exactly, did a woman prepare for her own execution? Did she do her hair differently, spend hours combing it? Did she exercise, maybe, in hopes of slimming her figure before being put on display in front of so many people? The thing about being executed, she'd found, was that it had a tendency of stealing a person's motivation to keep up with her appearance.

She did not answer the man, for there was no answer she might give, no words to express the combination of despair and relief that mingled within her. Instead, she only rose on unsteady legs that threatened to give way beneath her.

Despite her instincts for self-preservation, May forced one foot forward, then the other. It was the hardest thing she'd ever had to do, yet it was also the easiest, and she wondered if soldiers, marching to their deaths, had feet so heavy, wondered if their steps, too, seemed to glide over the ground with a shocking, almost scary ease.

She reached the cell door, and the guard nodded. "Please turn around," he said, "with your hands clasped behind you."

May did as she was told. Over the past days, she had grown accustomed to doing what she was told, saying whatever she was told to say, no matter if it were true or not. It didn't always keep the whip at bay, didn't always keep Grinner from showing his displeasure with his knotty fists, but sometimes it did.

The cold iron of the manacles touched her wrist, and she jerked in surprise. "S-sorry," she stammered, scared she would upset the guard. "I-it startled me." The truth, of course, was that it hadn't startled her at all—it had terrified her. She thought she had never felt anything so cold as the touch of that metal on her skin.

"Don't worry about it," the guard said, clapping the manacles closed. "Most people jump the first time they're put on."

May wondered at that, and some small part of her, the part most resembling the woman she'd once been, felt sorry for the man. What a life it must be to spend your days bringing men and women to the dungeons and throwing them in cells, often not knowing whether they were truly guilty or not and having no say in what finally happened to them. It seemed to her a cruel profession, as cruel to the man who worked within it as any who he ever imprisoned. A man would either have to be one of the best, strongest people she could imagine, or, she supposed, one of the meanest.

"Okay, that's good," the man said, and he didn't seem cruel to her, only tired and more than a little sad. Not sad at her plight particularly, she thought, but sad, perhaps, that the world was a place in which his role was necessary. "Now, be still for a moment."

She waited, fighting the urge to tense her back in case he decided to hit her after all. Then she heard the metallic clank of the cell door opening, a sound that she had longed for in the past days. And now that she heard it, she was glad; though the freedom she was offered was not the freedom for which she had hoped, it was still freedom. Or would be. Soon.

"That's just right," the man said, speaking as if to a child or a lunatic, slowly, with each word clearly enunciated. "Now then, I want you to take two steps back and one to the side, do you understand?"

May swallowed. *Two steps back and one to the side. Two steps back and one to the side.* She felt a thrill of panic surge through her. "W-wait. I-I'm sorry. Which side?"

"Ah, shit. Two steps back and one to your left, understand?"

"Y-yes." She waited, expecting some other instructions.

When the guard did speak there was pity in his voice. "You can move now, Lady Tanarest." That pity, so unexpected, struck her like a blow, putting a crack in the armor of resignation she'd erected around herself that no amount of pain or harsh treatment, where no questions from Hale—or his damned eyes—had been able to penetrate.

"Well, perhaps you should be clear on what you want," she snapped, and her eyes went as wide as those of the two guards must have. But she found she wasn't done. "I'd hate to do the wrong thing and force you to kill me without an audience—the gods forbid they miss their show."

She heard a grunt that might have been laughter from behind her and knew it was Hale. "Move now, Lady Tanarest," the guard said, and when he spoke this time there was no pity or compassion in his voice, only a cool hardness. *Great,* she thought, *you find a guard who treats you like a person instead of some feral animal, and you bite his head off for it. That'll teach him.*

She did as she was told, feeling the sudden surge of anger-fueled strength leaking from her, as if she were a wineskin that had burst open, spilling its contents onto the floor. She was outside her cell now, staring at the dungeon wall.

"Now, remain still and do not move."

She felt one of the two presences behind her depart then heard another man giving the same instructions to Hale. She realized they would be escorted to their execution together. *Don't worry, ladies and gentlemen, it's all part of the show.*

"*Careful,*" one of the guards hissed. "You saw what he done to Jessum."

Another grunted. "Jessum's a fool that spends too much time with whores and not enough with his sword."

"Maybe," the first said, "but I doubt he'll be doin' much of either now. Fool he might be, but he's a cripple for sure."

"There'll be no trouble here, will there, big guy? We're just gonna go on a stroll, you and me. How's that sound?" If Hale answered, May didn't hear it, but she tensed in expectation.

There was the sound of something falling, and she felt a rush of fear, thinking that the big crime boss had decided to attack the man, after all. She craned her neck, but could make out nothing save for the forms of some of the guards standing in front of the crime boss's cell. "See there?"

The guard who'd spoken said, laughing, "Fucker can barely stand, let alone fight. Councilman Grinner has done for him right enough—my pa always said even the meanest dog'll learn not to bite, if you show 'em who's boss. Now, on your feet, you big bastard."

Someone let out a weak groan, and a wave of despair washed over May as she realized it came from the giant. Although she had grown to hate the crime boss's staring, silent visage, hated the way it had always seemed to measure her, she realized then that she had also come to rely on it in. Whatever else he was—admitted crook, thief, and murderer—Hale was a man of seemingly inexhaustible strength. And without having known she was doing it, May had come to rely on that strength in the last days. To hear those tortured, pitiful moans from the crime boss made her feel weaker and, what's more, afraid.

"Oh, stop your damned blubbering," the guard spat. "You two help him up for the gods' sake. Dangerous is he?" The man laughed. "I've seen cows more dangerous than him, though I'll admit he's as big as one anyway."

Please, Hale, don't do anything stupid, May thought, but she realized that some part of her wished he would, wished that he would surprise the guards—and her as well—and show them that his strength had no limits, after all. But there was no cry of surprise, no scream of alarm, and soon she heard the metallic *snick* of Hale's own manacles as they closed around his wrists. "Alright, Lady Tanarest. You can turn around."

May turned and let out a breath she hadn't known she was holding as she saw, with relief, that he only stood there placidly, making no move to attack the guards. But her relief was mixed with a bitter sort of disappointment. Even Hale, it seemed, could be broken. The club owner felt a wave of sadness at the thought, for though the big crime boss was not necessarily a kind, or even a good man, he was one from whom she'd always known what to expect. Seeing him as he was now was like seeing some great beast of the jungle, lying in a cage with barely enough room in which to move, wasting away, all its nobility, its majesty, being stripped away one day at a time, being bought and paid for with each coin that changed hands as villagers came to gawk at it so they might have a story to tell their friends. A story of the great beast they had seen, one that had once been capable of slaughtering men by the dozens. Once, but no longer, for the beast had been broken. Tamed.

May was so focused on the disappointment, the unexpected sense of loss, that she didn't realize the guard who'd laughed at Hale was speaking for several seconds. "...be a crowd out there, all come to see justice done. They'll be shoutin' and hollerin', maybe throwing fruits, vegetables and such, but you two just stick to your best behavior, and we'll do what we can to keep 'em calm. This thing is happenin' whether you want it to or not. Don't bother tellin' me you're innocent or that we've got the wrong man or woman. That decision's been made already, and it wasn't mine or these others here who made it. So you just act right, stay calm, and we'll get this thing done with as little fuss as we can, and maybe when you see Salen, he'll listen to you holler about innocence, now how'd that be?"

May nodded, her heart racing. She had thought that she'd prepared herself for this moment, this day, but the truth was a woman could never prepare herself for giving up her life, the only thing that made her *her*. She wanted to tell the man yes, she would do as she was told, but she found that the words stuck in her mouth, simply too big to utter.

"And you, big fella?" the guard said. "We gonna have any problems today?"

Hale remained silent, and May saw he was out in the hallway now, supported by a guard on either side. His head lolled, but whether it was a nod of agreement or a sign of exhaustion, she couldn't have said. Still, it seemed to satisfy the guard and he gave a short nod of his own. "Alright then. Let's get this thing done."

With that, the man turned, holding his torch aloft, and May followed him out of the dark dungeons to that far greater darkness which awaited all women and all men when their time came.

CHAPTER TWENTY-EIGHT

Adina did her best to project a presence of authority and strength as she strode up to the gate, her companions behind her, but her stomach fluttered nervously, and her hands were slick with sweat. Would the guards even let her and the others in? Or would they attack the moment they identified themselves? If things were truly as bad as the Speaker said—and she had no reason to doubt him—there was no telling how the guards at the gate might react to her and the others seeming to show up out of nowhere. She just had to hope that the men stationed there were loyal to Isabelle, not Grinner, had to hope, further, that there was still some distinction between the two.

"Morning, miss," one of the four guards said. "What can the city of Perennia do for you and your companions?"

"You can let us through," Adina said, forcing an air of authority into her voice that she did not feel. "And it is not miss, but Majesty. I am Queen Adina, and I have—thanks to the help of my friends—narrowly avoided an attempt on my life and their lives as well to return here and once again take up the fight against the mage, Kevlane."

The guard's eyes went wide as she spoke, and he looked as if he weren't sure whether to draw the sword at his side or kneel. Adina studied him and the other three, holding her breath as she waited to see what choice they would make.

Finally, the man dropped to one knee, bowing his head, and Adina breathed a sigh of relief. A moment later, the other guards followed suit. "Forgive us, Princess Adina," the one who'd spoken said. "We did not expect you this morning, but it is good to see you returned, of course, and safely at that. What can we do for you?"

The man's tone was subservient, even helpful, but she didn't miss the fact that he'd called her "Princess" not "Queen." She hoped it had been only a slip, nothing more, but the butterflies that had gathered in her stomach when she approached the gate fluttered restlessly. "I have heard that May Tanarest and Councilman Hale are to be executed," she said without preamble, schooling her features to look imperious. "Is this true?"

"Regretfully, yes, Princess," the man said. *That word again. It means nothing, Adina. Relax.* "Lady Tanarest and the councilman have been interrogated by the queen's questioners and found guilty of treasonous plotting including the downfall of Perennia and the kingdom of Isalla as well as conspiring in an assassination plot on the queen herself."

Hearing the words out loud from a man who believed them as opposed to the Speaker who only told her what news he'd heard made Adina feel as if she had woken to a world where everything had been turned upside down. For a moment she could do nothing but stare at the guard in mute shock. A second later, she felt the urge—very strong and very hard to resist—to slap the man across his face for his ignorance, but she did not.

Instead, she took a slow, deep breath, steadying her anger and her frayed nerves, and when she spoke she did so in a reasonable tone, one that, she hoped, also demanded obedience. "May Tanarest and Councilman Hale have been accused unjustly, guardsman. There are none more loyal or more instrumental in our fight against the mage, Kevlane, than they. The execution must be stopped at once until we can launch an investigation into what has truly occurred." *An investigation,* she promised herself, *that will end with Grinner's neck bent beneath the executioner's axe.*

The guard's brow furrowed in confusion. "But, Princess Adina, begging your pardon, the investigation was done by the queen's very best, and it is said that the two admitted to all manner of evils."

"Then the investigation was wrong, and I intend to launch one of my own."

The man nodded. "As you say, of course, Princess. If you like, I can escort you and your companions to the queen, and I'm sure—"

"There's no time for that," Adina said. "Finding them innocent will do Lady May and Councilman Hale little good if they are already dead. Now, where is the execution to be held?"

"At the city square, Majesty," the guard said, "but, forgive me, Princess, I do not think it wise for you and your...friends to go there."

"No?" Adina said, letting a note of warning enter her voice. "And why is that?"

The man winced uncomfortably. "Excuse me for saying so, Princess, but there have been many rumors circulating around the city since you and General Envelar...left." *Abandoned,* was the word Adina suspected he meant, but she let it go. "Many people are scared, and it is an easy enough thing, in my experience, for fear to turn to anger, given the right conditions."

"And you believe that within the city exist the 'right' conditions?"

"Apologies, Princess," the guard said, bowing his head to her, "but if ever there was a city close to destroying itself, it's Perennia. I don't mean to offend you, but...many believe you and the general deserted us in our time of need or...or that you're traitors in league with Isalla's enemies."

Adina nodded slowly. "And you, Guardsman?" she asked. "What do you believe?"

The man hesitated, but finally met her eyes. "I'm a simple city guard, Princess. Such high matters are beyond me. But once, when I was first starting out, I worked with an older guard who had served under your father. He'd retired from His Majesty's household guard, and only offered his services from time to time, but I guess I looked at the man like something of a hero, serving under so great a king as your father was, the gods bless and keep his soul. I asked him..." He paused to give a soft laugh. "Pestered him, if you want to know the truth, about his time in the castle. At first, he was reluctant, but finally he began to tell me stories. Some of those stories, Princess, were about you. You were young then, but the man spoke of you highly, said that you had a heart to match even that of your father, and that you were always kind to him and the other guardsmen."

He paused for a second, and Adina waited to see if he would say more. Finally, he shook his head. "No, Princess. I do not believe you a traitor, nor a deserter, and believe that whatever reason you had to leave the city as you did, you and the general, I believe it must have been a good one." He seemed to come to some decision, and nodded, his face set. "Whatever help you need from me, Princess, you'll have it."

Adina smiled. "Thank you, Guardsman. I know that these are troubled, uncertain times, but I assure you that you do your queen and your homeland a service by helping us. Now, if you would allow us to pass—we must stop this execution before it takes place."

The man's face grew troubled. "The execution is scheduled but a half hour from now, Princess. I am not sure you can make it. I wasn't lying about the state of the city. There are some out there—more than a few—who, I think, might be tempted to violence should they see you in the open, and would no doubt attack you and your companions without giving you time to explain."

One of the other guards, who'd been waiting by the gate, stepped forward, an almost eager expression on his face. "I'll take them to the square, Marcus, if that's alright with you."

The first guard turned on the man, frowning. "Bow when you approach royalty, recruit. And I told you, you refer to me as 'Captain,' not Marcus."

The man's face grew sullen, but he nodded, sketching a distracted bow at Adina. "Sorry, *Captain,* but as I said I'll be happy to lead them there."

The guard captain frowned, as if considering whether or not to reprimand the man for his tone while Adina and the others were present, but apparently decided to save it for another time. "No, the streets will be dangerous, and if we want to get to the square, there's no time to waste. Hugh," he said, turning to address one of the other guards, a man with salt and pepper in his beard who held himself with the bearing of a veteran. "You and I will escort the princess and her companions to the square."

The man nodded, stepping forward. "You other two," Marcus went on, "watch the gate—we will return as soon as possible. Now," he said, turning back to Adina and the others, "Princess, are you ready?"

"Yes," Adina said, "and Marcus, is it?"

The man winced. "Forgive me, Majesty, but my mother and father were loyal subjects to your father, and they gave me his name. I hope that it does not cause offense…"

"Of course not," Adina said, smiling. "It is a strong name, a proud one, and it suits you well, I think."

The man's face went red at that, and he shifted uncomfortably before bowing his head again. "Thank you for your kindness, Majesty. Now, we must hurry if we're to have a hope of making it in time."

Adina glanced back at the others then nodded. "We're ready."

"Very well, Princess. We will do our best to protect you and your companions, but I cannot guarantee your safety, as much as I might want to. The city is a dangerous place just now, and we will have little time for stealth, as we will have to move quickly to get to the square in time. This way." He turned to start away, and the sullen guard stepped in front of him.

"Sorry, Mar—I mean, *Captain*. But don't you think someone should be dispatched to inform Queen Isabelle that her royal sister has returned to the city?"

"Fine," Marcus said, waving a hand dismissively, "do so then return to your post at once." He glanced back at Adina, waited for her nod. And then they were running.

CHAPTER TWENTY-NINE

Captain Brandon Gant was a man of simple pleasures—not for him the fine clothes and decadent meals that so many of the wealthy enjoyed or, at least, pretended to. He'd tried both, on occasion and always regretted it—the first always seemed to chafe and constrict him, and he'd spent that day in a life or death struggle, trying not to be strangled by his attire. The second always left his stomach roiling uncomfortably and guaranteed a night spent racing his unsettled bowels to the privy. He'd won every time, but the matches had been too close for comfort, and neither the food nor the clothes were experiences he cared to relive.

For food, he was a man who enjoyed plain fare: meat, potatoes, maybe some bread, and a nice cold mug of ale to wash it all down. For clothes, well, there had always been the uniform. The one he wore when going about his duties, or the dressier—but still relatively practical—one he donned when attending audiences with his queen or visiting dignitaries. Not that there had been many of the second of late—being at war with an ancient wizard with unimaginable powers had a way of reducing the number of a city's visitors significantly. As far as he was concerned, that was one of the few benefits of the whole thing.

Still, his feelings for the uniform were the closest he'd ever come to a real, genuine love. It wasn't the fabric itself, of course, that had always earned his admiration, but what it stood for, what it *meant.* The uniform was a symbol, a ward against the darker things the world had to offer—disorder, chaos, cruelty. And he, when he donned it, became a living, breathing symbol of the same, one of those blessed men whose calling was to bring order to the chaos, to bring law to the unlawful and justice to the unjust.

He had always put on the uniform with a sense of pride, a sense of a duty fulfilled, an obligation met. But as he fastened the top button of his collar and stared at himself in his room's simple looking glass, he realized that, for the first time, he felt neither of those things. In their place were feelings of guilt, of shame, as if the cloth had somehow become tainted. Hale's words echoed in his mind. *At least I am honest with myself. At least I know what I am.*

Brandon had always been sure he knew himself, knew what he stood for, but since speaking with the crime boss, he was no longer so certain. For the first time he could remember, the uniform didn't seem to fit right, as if it had been made for someone else. He frowned at the man in the mirror. Not elderly, not yet, but getting there quicker with each passing year.

All those years, all that time, and with little enough to show for it. No wife to weep when he died, to throw herself on his grave and cause a scene. No children to carry on his name, to face their lives armed with the lessons their father had taught them. Only him and the uniform. The eyes that stared back from the mirror didn't look like his eyes at all, not like the eyes that he'd seen on so many other mornings just like this one. *Not just like this one,* a voice whispered in his mind. No, maybe not, but this part, at least, was the same.

Yet the eyes staring back at him were the eyes of a stranger, those of a lonely old man who would die sooner or later, leaving no mark on the world to show he had ever been there at all. He'd spent a lifetime of service to a king or a queen, and never before had he felt those years had been wasted. But as the task he'd been given loomed ahead of him, he felt that waste now.

He forced himself to stand straight, but it did little to change the appearance of the old man in the looking glass. "You will do your duty," he told the elderly stranger. "That, at least, you will do."

The stranger didn't disagree, didn't argue, and he chose to take his silence as agreement. The problem, of course, was that where once his duty had been as clear as the sky on a cloudless

A Sellsword's Mercy

day, now it seemed murky and uncertain. He would do his duty, yes, of course he would. But what, *exactly*, did that *mean?*

He'd spent the last days hoping, *praying,* that someone—Swordmaster Darrell, perhaps, or the sailor, Thom—would come to him, would demand that he release May. He had imagined the conversation a thousand times, imagined doing his best to calm them, to reason with them, to explain that he was only obeying his queen, doing his duty. But even in his imaginings the words had always sounded false, more like an excuse than a reason, and he had not been able to convince them.

You must help, these figments had told him, *you must.* And again he would explain to them that he could not, that, if given the choice, he would have stood with them…but he had his *duty,* surely they must understand *that.* They hadn't though, and in these imaginings—visions felt like a better word, for never before had the conjurings of his mind felt so real—they had tried to reason with him, to convince him.

The scenes had always stopped there, perhaps because he himself had been unsure whether their pleading would be successful or not, but Brandon hoped that, in that dream world if nowhere else, they had been. He had waited for just such a visit, had expected it each time he ventured forth from his rooms, had even found himself looking for excuses to do so, but none had come. And perhaps that was for the best, after all.

Since he and Councilman Grinner had butted heads about his treatment of May, the captain had felt watched, followed. There was no proof to it, for each time he turned when walking through the castle or down the street, sure that he would find someone watching him, there was nothing. No one. Yet the feeling did not leave him, and he had been a guard long enough to trust his instincts. And if someone *were* following him, it seemed clear enough who had sent them. For all his faults—and there were many—Councilman Grinner had never struck Brandon as the type of man who allowed many uncertainties into his life or who didn't pay attention to things or people—people such as a certain willful Captain—who might cause him problems.

And was it any great surprise, after all, that Brandon *hadn't* seen them? The men and women like those Grinner would send on such a task were those who were accustomed to sticking to the shadows, to staying unnoticed. Men and women who had spent their lives as criminals, scraping a living off the unwary and unfortunate and scuttling back to the darkness whenever a true threat presented itself. As much as he hated to admit it, Brandon knew little of such things, for his life had taught him how to deal with the blade he saw coming, but it had done nothing to show him how to see the blade in the first place.

Yes, perhaps it was best that the swordmaster or the first mate had not come to him asking for help, for he suspected that they would have never reached him anyway and, if they did, their lives would have almost certainly been forfeit. He looked out the window and saw the sun high in the sky. For the first time in his life, he was late for an assignment. *Gods, but if only I could miss it entirely.* He cleared his throat, straightened his collar a final time, and gave himself a brisk nod, full of a confidence he did not feel. "You will do your duty."

***

Brandon waited for them in the castle courtyard, outside the dungeon entrance. So he wasn't the only one running late. While he waited, he looked over at the castle gate in the distance—the point at which they would begin the long walk to the city square. Or, at least, the point at which *he* would. He suspected that May and Hale had walked that path a thousand times already in their minds, and however difficult they might have imagined it, Brandon doubted they were fully prepared. But, then, is anyone ever really prepared to die?

People lined the street outside the castle gate. Even from this distance, he could see the tense postures of the guards, their hands close to their swords as they regarded the milling crowd. Ridiculous that they should be so on edge, but he didn't blame them. On a normal day, the men, women—and, he was sad to see, plenty of children too—who lined the street might be kind enough. Bakers and merchants, candlemakers and blacksmiths, cobblers and clerks and their families. But today, they were none of those things—today, they were a bloodthirsty mob, and Brandon had seen enough during his years in the guard to know that when a man got blood on his mind, it didn't matter all that much whose was spilled, just so long as it was.

He supposed the crowd would follow them all the way through the city to the square. It wasn't enough to witness the execution itself. No, later, when bragging to friends and family about having been there, they would be able to boast they had seen the two condemned step out of the dungeons, maybe even got so lucky as to watch a lone tear fall from faces etched with despair.

The metallic sound of the lock to the dungeon's door drew his attention, and he turned, glad for an excuse to look away from that gathered throng. When the door opened, Brandon was confronted with the face of a guard he didn't recognize. No real surprise—he didn't recognize most of them now. Councilman Grinner had replaced men who had served for years with his own people, citing the queen's safety as a reason to dismiss men who had, time and again, shown their loyalty to Perennia and its ruler. As if such men would ever dream of harming her, but then neither he nor, he suspected, Grinner, ever thought they would.

The guard gave what might have been a grunt upon seeing Brandon standing there then the briefest of nods before stepping out of the dungeon and moving to the side. At another time, another place, Brandon might have rebuked the man for the clear lack of respect, but he did not do so here. It would have served no purpose, and, besides, if the man decided to carry his disrespect further? What could Brandon actually do? Nothing, of course, as the man was Grinner's through and through. The crime boss would ensure that he was well taken care of either way, and one of the things Brandon had learned long ago, when taking his first position as a leader of men, was that you never made a threat you couldn't carry out. There was no faster way, he'd always thought, to destroy your credibility. *Except, maybe,* he thought sourly, *to watch your kingdom taken over by a crime boss, the guards who were meant to protect it replaced with criminals who know nothing of protecting, only pain.*

So Brandon remained silent, watching as the guards filed out of the dungeon, flanking the two prisoners. There was a roar of excitement from the distant crowd as they saw that the day's entertainment had finally arrived, and Brandon clenched his jaw to hold back his building anger. He stared at the two, a club owner and a crime boss, both come to help a city they knew nothing about, to save people they had never met, and both thanked for it with their deaths. As terrible as they had looked in the dungeon, as pitiable, they looked much worse standing in the daylight, for the sun exposed the truth quicker than any questioner might.

The big crime boss was a wealth of bruises and cuts, his clothes ripped and torn in dozens of places with bloody wheals showing on the flesh underneath. His face, too, was a mass of bruises, one eye swollen completely shut, and he took each heavy, uncertain step as if he might fall at any moment, the two guards flanking him forced to hold onto his arms to keep him upright.

But it was the sight of May that broke Brandon's heart. The once proud woman with her fiery hair and temper to match, cringed away from the light, shrank from it, as if she had spent so much time in the shadows that she had become one of them and feared the sun's touch. Like the crime boss, she was filthy, her body covered with cuts and bruises and marks from the whip's attentions. But it was her eyes that struck Brandon most—eyes that were frightened, and confused, and somehow feral.

Another roar went up from the crowd, and Brandon snapped his head around, glaring at them despite the fact that they were too far away to see his expression and would not have heeded it even if they had. Today was their day, a day of destruction, and they knew as well as he that there was no fighting it. His heart heavy, he turned back to the two prisoners. *We make of them animals, so that what we kill is no longer a man, a woman, and in so doing we believe that we absolve ourselves.*

When the final guard had exited the dungeon and was closing the door behind him, Brandon nodded to the first who had emerged, the impromptu leader, he suspected, of the grim procession. "They look half dead already. Gods, could you not have even given them a bath, some fresh clothes?"

The man grunted, hocking and spitting. Not quite at Brandon's feet, but not away from them either. "It'd be a waste of soap—duds them up all you want to, clean 'em if you want, but their heads will be rolling soon enough either way."

Brandon's patience—already stretched to the breaking point—shattered at the man's casual disregard for the solemnity of the occasion. Before he had time to think better of it, his fist lashed out, catching the man in the nose. The guard cried out in surprise, stumbling, and would have fallen had one of his comrades not been there to catch him. His face twisted with rage, blood seeping from his unnaturally bent nose.

He started for his sword and Brandon held up an admonishing finger. "I would consider your next choice carefully, were I you. You see, you might wear the uniform of a guard, but that doesn't make you one, just as it doesn't mean you know how to use that sword you carry any better than a farmer might." Brandon shrugged. "Maybe these others can stop me before I kill you, but I doubt it, and even if they do, I suspect your boss won't look kindly on any man who dared to come in the way of the day's work." The man hesitated, his anger and fear warring on his face. Brandon gave him a humorless grin. "But who knows? Maybe I'm wrong. Why don't you go ahead and draw that blade, and we can find out together."

The man stood frozen with indecision, then glanced at his companions, looking for help. But the mention of the crime boss had been enough to curtail any assistance they may have thought to give, and they only stared at him mutely. Finally, the man gave a hiss of impotent anger, turning back to Brandon. "You'll pay for that, *Captain*."

"Maybe," Brandon agreed. "But it seems you won't be the one to collect that debt, at least not today." He leaned closer to the man, and didn't bother trying to keep the satisfaction from his voice. "Clean all the filth off a man, duds him up however you want, but a coward is still a coward. And wipe your nose—you're bleeding all over your uniform."

The man's face twisted in renewed fury, but he did nothing as Brandon had known he would not, only bringing his hand to his nose in a vain effort to staunch the flow of blood. The captain was surprised to note, however, that one of the other guards seemed to be trying to conceal a smile at his fellow's plight, and he thought he recognized the man, not as one of Grinner's lot, but a young guard who had been granted his post only recently.

That gave him an idea, one last chance—not a good one, not really, but the only one. "Very well," he said, turning away from the man with the broken nose to look at the young guard. "I commend you on successfully removing the prisoners from the dungeon and bringing them here. As captain of the guard, it is now my duty to see them to the square. Guards have already been posted throughout the city to keep the crowds back, and so you are relieved of duty, all of you."

The young guard hesitated, suddenly unsure, and Brandon saw a light of recognition, of excitement in his eyes as he realized what Brandon was trying to do. He opened his mouth, though whether to agree or disagree Brandon couldn't have said, for the bloody-nosed man spoke first. "Oh, that's quite alright, *Captain,*" he said, making the last a curse. "After you having only recently reminded me of the importance of ensuring the Councilman's pleasure, I would be foolish—*we* would be foolish," he paused to shoot a meaningful look at the other guards, "to risk rousing his ire by not seeing the thing done and done proper. You see," he continued, smiling a bloody smile that made Brandon want to strike him again, "the Councilman, well, he'd be just all tore up, if he knew that we didn't make sure justice was done."

Brandon watched the excitement go out of the young guard's eyes, and he had a moment of regret for striking the other man, for making of him an enemy, but only a moment. The truth was the man had been an enemy already, never mind the uniform he wore, and the pleasant memory of the feel of the man's nose cracking beneath his fist was one he would take with him to the grave. "Fine," he said, shooting May an apologetic look she didn't seem to notice. "Then let's not waste any more time—we're already running late, thanks to you."

"Not our fault," Grinner's man said, and Brandon felt a fresh surge of anger as the man rubbed the arm of his uniform across his nose, soiling the fabric with blood and snot as if it was a simple garment of no worth. "The big fucker here can barely stand—so much for Hale's legendary strength, eh?" He looked at the others, and there were a few answering chuckles. Quiet enough, without much feeling, but far more than Brandon would have normally accepted, and again he was struck with how much the world had changed and in how short a time. He would have had such men as this flogged at the least for making a joke of the thing. A man's death, whoever that man might be, was never something to jest about.

"Just shut up and come on," he growled. And with that, they began what would be one of the longest walks of Brandon Gant's life.

CHAPTER THIRTY

Despite the guard captain Marcus's warnings of danger, Perennia's streets were practically deserted, and Adina only saw a few people as they made their way into the city. The captain himself ran at the front while the other guard, Hugh, brought up the rear of the procession. Those few they did pass, however, paused to watch them, their expressions suspicious if not openly hostile. Adina wasn't sure whether they did so out of the normal curiosity such a group of people, running through the city and escorted by guards, might cause, or because they recognized her or one of her companions, and she had little time to consider it in any case.

The captain set a brisk pace, moving quickly enough that soon Adina could hear Gryle's ragged breathing beside her as he struggled to keep up. But the chamberlain did not complain, and his features were set with a grim determination. She had the thought that, just then, the chamberlain would have run until he passed out, if that was what it took to save his friends.

Still, for all their haste, Adina was all too aware of the minutes slipping by, and prayed to the gods that they would arrive in time. They'd been traveling for twenty minutes at least, and she was preoccupied with another prayer—at least the fifth of its kind—when the captain came to an abrupt halt, and she only just managed to avoid running into him.

She started to ask why he'd stopped, but there was soon no need as four men with blades rushed out of an alleyway, blocking their path. She recognized one of them as the overeager guard from the gatehouse. He was panting heavily, his face covered in sweat, but his mouth was twisted into a cruel sneer.

"Recruit," the guard captain said, his tone ringing with authority, "what is the meaning of this?"

"Oh, take your 'recruit' and your 'captain' and be damned, *Marcus*," the man spat. "As for what this is," he said, grinning as he glanced at the men on either side of him, "well, I think you know that well enough."

In answer, the captain drew his sword, and the quiet, deserted street rang with the sound of steel leaving scabbard. "I will say it once and no more after—leave this place and get out of our way, or we will be forced to cut you down."

The man laughed. "Is that supposed to frighten me?" he asked. "The fact that you got a sword? Turns out, we got some too."

Adina studied the men, and though they wielded blades, they were dressed in trousers and jerkins, not the uniforms of the guards. Grinner's men then, she did not doubt, as was the guard from the gate house. "This man works for Grinner, Captain. That much is clear."

Marcus nodded without taking his eyes away from the men in the street. "We outnumber you nearly two to one. It's still not too late to walk away from this thing breathing—the next time we ask, our blades will do it for us."

The man laughed again. "Outnumber us, do you?" he asked, looking over the group. "And what a little army you are too, huh? A fat man who looks like maybe he ate one of your number, two women, a Parnen who thinks the height of fashion is hanging bells in his hair, and a dried up old sergeant? That what we're supposed to be scared of, *Captain?*"

"Captain." This voice didn't come from the man in the street but from Hugh, the other guardsman who stood at their rear. Adina looked behind her to see several more armed men spilling into the street. For his part, the guard captain didn't so much as turn from where he studied the man who'd once been under his command.

"How many, Hugh?"

"Six, sir."

Marcus nodded, and Adina was impressed with the guard captain's calm. A worthy name for him indeed, and she promised to tell him as much again—assuming they survived what was coming.

"Now then," the criminal said, "I reckon that ought to even us up a bit, Captain, what do you say? So how about you just go on ahead and put down your weapons, and we'll get this thing done civil. I ain't set on killin' you, understand, but it ain't exactly gonna break my heart, neither. As for the princess here," he said, looking her up and down as if she was a piece of meat he was considering purchasing at market. "Well, might be she can make it out of this thing with all her royal bits still in their royal places, too. All we mean to do, see, is bring her to the boss—figured he might want to have a conversation with her."

"What do you want to do, Princess?" Marcus asked, turning and glancing at her over his shoulder, and by the look of anger on his face and in his tone she thought it was all too clear what he wanted.

Adina frowned. "The only conversation I intend to have with Grinner is the one that takes place before his execution."

The traitorous guard hocked and spat. "You sure about that? And what about the rest of you? You all so keen to die on account of the princess can't be bothered to sit down and talk with the likes of us criminals?"

In answer, Wendell drew his own sword and went to stand beside Marcus, the scarred sergeant choosing, for once, to let his actions speak instead of his words. Gryle followed a moment later, his fists clenched at his sides. Leomin and Seline went to stand beside Hugh, facing the others who had appeared at their backs.

"Well alright then," Grinner's man said, shaking his head. "It's your blood—I reckon you can decide whether it gets spilled or not." He gestured to the men beside him, and they started forward. Adina drew her own blade and went to stand with Hugh and the others.

"Get it done fast," she said, loud enough for all of those with her to hear, "we haven't much time."

There was a shout from one of their attackers, and as if on cue, they all charged forward. Adina braced herself, gritting her teeth in anticipation.

"Stop." The word struck with the power of a lightning strike, and every one of the onrushing men froze as if commanded by one of the gods. Adina saw Leomin staring at them, sweat beading on his forehead, a look of intense concentration on his face.

The men stood as still as statues in the street, their eyes glazing over, and Adina and the others only stared at the Parnen in astonishment. "Can't...hold it...for long," he hissed.

"Don't worry, love," Seline said, drawing the short blades at her side. "You won't have to." There was a sudden blur of motion, and one of the six screamed as she appeared behind him, burying her blade in his side. She was on to the next one before the first had even had time to hit the ground, slicing his throat, and Leomin began to growl with apparent effort at holding the men still.

There was a wooden, creaking sound, and Gryle walked toward the four men in front of them. Adina's eyes widened as she realized he was carrying a horse cart over his head.

One of the their attackers started to move, as if breaking whatever hold Leomin had placed on them, but then the chamberlain brought the full weight of the cart down on him, powered by his incredible strength. There was a crushing, squishing sound, and Adina felt her gorge rise in her throat as she stared at the bloody mess on the cobbles. Gryle brought the cart back up, moving toward the next man, and Adina turned away in time to see Seline pulling her blades free of the last of the group at their backs who collapsed on the ground at her feet.

It was all over in an instant, and despite the fact that she knew the power they carried, Adina found herself staring at the three in awe. But for all her surprise at the speed with which the violence had occurred, she, at least, had possessed some sense of what her companions were capable of. The guard captain hadn't, and his shocked gaze shifted between the corpses, his eyes wild. "I...I don't understand," he breathed, his voice little more than a whisper.

"No, Captain," Adina said, pulling her eyes away from the massacre and turning the captain so that he faced her. "And, right now, I don't have time to explain it to you. Know only that Kevlane's dark sorcery is not the only magic in the world—there are other forces at work, and many of those forces, such as the ones you have seen here, are on the side of good."

The man nodded slowly, his eyes still glazed over as if he was dreaming. "A-alright," he said. He cleared his throat, shaking his head in a visible effort to gain some control over himself. "Hugh." The man didn't answer, still staring wide-eyed at the corpses in the street. Veteran he might be, but there were few in the world who had seen such swift carnage as he had just witnessed.

"*Hugh*," the captain said again, louder this time, his voice ringing in the preternatural silence of the street. Some ingrained part of the guardsman, accustomed to responding to such an authoritative tone, must have heard the captain's words despite the shock he felt, and he finally turned to look at the captain.

"S-sir?"

"Take your position, we need—" The captain's words cut off as the sound of a bell filled the air. Adina had never heard a sound so terrible as the sound of that bell ringing. Her heart lurched in her chest. "Is that—" she began, knowing the answer to the question even as she started to ask it.

"Noon," the captain confirmed, scowling in the direction of the bell tower as if it was somehow in league with Grinner and the dead men littering the street.

"We are too late then," Gryle said, his tone full of disbelief.

"What do we do now?" the Parnen asked, staring at the bell tower as the last peel of its ringing echoed in the air.

Adina was at a loss for what to tell him. She glanced at the woman, Seline, thinking that, perhaps, she could use the Virtue of Speed to make it to the square in time but quickly dismissed the idea. The woman looked exhausted, and her breathing was labored from her fight—if fight it could be called—with the criminals. Just then, it looked as if it was all she could do to remain standing.

Still, Adina had to believe there was *some* way of helping May and the others. In the stories she'd heard so often as a child, things often grew dark, seemingly hopeless, but in the end good always triumphed, always found a way.

This is no storybook, she chided herself, *and you are no child to be comforted by pretty fancies. You are a princess—a queen—and you are* enough. "What do we do? We go anyway—perhaps the execution is running behind, and even if it isn't..." She didn't finish the last, for she saw in the slowly building anger in the faces of those around her that they knew what she would say, felt it as well as she. If they didn't manage to save May and Hale, then at least they would make sure the two did not venture into Salen's Fields alone.

CHAPTER THIRTY-ONE

Darrell pushed through the people in the street, trying and failing to quell the panicked urgency rising in him. There was a chill in the air, but he was sweating profusely, a product of an hour spent forcing his way through the multitude gathered to see a man and a woman die. Despite his recent wounds he was possessed of an almost manic energy as he shoved people to the side, driving further and further into the shouting crowd.

Soon, he could make out the castle, could even see what he thought were the captain and other guards gathered outside the dungeon. They started toward the gate, and as they drew closer, Darrell craned his neck to see them over the men and women crowding the gate—the most dedicated of the audience, those who had fought their way past their fellows for the dubious honor of being the first to lay eyes on the condemned.

Briefly, a space opened in the crowd, and he caught a glimpse of the captain in his dress uniform. The man had a grim expression on his normally jovial face, as if he were contemplating murder, and the other guards that walked with him, surrounding the two prisoners and blocking them from Darrell's view, looked tense. Not that the swordmaster could blame them, as they were about to venture into a street flooded with a river of humanity, one that could easily overpower the guards spaced intermittently along the street to keep it in check.

Grinner must have mobilized the entire city guard as well as a generous helping of soldiers from the gathered armies, but the guards and soldiers were still outnumbered a hundred to one at least. If the people decided to start the execution early, to rush the two prisoners and take out whatever fears and frustrations the past months had caused in them, Darrell knew—as the other guards must—that those meant to keep them in order would be no more successful than a shield crafted of paper would be at staying a blade.

The grim procession reached the gate, and the guards stationed there opened it, closing it back again with what seemed to Darrell to be indecent haste, as if the thousands of people that had gathered might decide that an audience could easily enough become an army and rush through the gates, intent on seizing control of the castle and, thereby, the city. The guards needn't have worried though, for the men and women who'd come to see the execution were content to shout angry threats and curses at the two prisoners. The bravest in the crowd hurled rotten fruits and vegetables, never mind the fact that, like Darrell, they almost certainly couldn't see anything of the two prisoners for the guards that surrounded them.

The rotten missiles struck the guards and the captain, and soon Brandon's fine dress uniform was covered in slime and filth, but from what Darrell saw the man didn't so much as notice, his eyes cold and hard and far away. The swordmaster was trying to meet that stony gaze when one man from the crowd—particularly outraged or particularly thirsty for blood—abandoned his fellows and rushed toward the procession, brandishing a knife.

Brandon Gant reacted at once, spinning and thrusting a finger at the man. "*Blade!*" he bellowed in a voice that somehow managed to cut through the shouting multitude.

The guards on that side reacted, spinning, and Darrell noted that one of their number had a bloody nose, obviously broken. The guards drew their swords and faced the onrushing man. At the sight of them, he seemed to think better of his plan, and came to a stumbling stop, dropping his blade.

A second later, the bloody-nosed man lunged forward and drove his sword through the man's gut, and what he obviously lacked in skill he made up for in cruel enthusiasm, ripping the blade free and driving it in again in a shower of crimson. He grinned grimly as the man struggled weakly at the blade that pierced him, as if to pull it out, then the guard jerked the sword back, and the man crumpled to the cobbles of the city. *Gods, but that was ill done,* Darrell thought, and judging by the angry shouts of the crowd they thought so too. Several of those in the front surged forward against the guards that tried to hold them back, threatening to overwhelm them, but the swordmaster barely noticed.

His attention was fixed on May and Hale, the two prisoners having finally become visible when the guards stepped away to meet the onrushing threat. The two had clearly been beaten repeatedly, and judging by the long, bloody weals on their flesh and their clothes—torn in dozens of places—someone had taken to them with a whip. Darrell thought he knew well enough who that would have been, but pushed down his anger with the efficiency of long practice. There would be a time for anger, for revenge, but this was not it.

Still, the sight of the two of the prisoners was not one easily banished. Hale leaned heavily on a guard for support, the much smaller man obviously struggling under his weight, and the crime boss's eyes seemed clouded, as if not seeing anything at all. The swordmaster pulled his gaze away from the grim spectacle with a will, looking to where Captain Gant strode toward the bloody-faced guard who even now stood over the dying man, watching him with a small smile on his face.

Brandon growled something Darrell couldn't hear, grabbing the other guard by the shoulder and roughly shoving him back toward the prisoners, and the swordmaster didn't miss the look of pure hatred the guard gave the captain as he took up position among his fellows. The captain didn't notice, however, for he was turning to the man on the ground, kneeling beside him and ripping a piece of his own sleeve free, pressing it against the man's wound in an effort to slow the bleeding. "*Healer!*" the captain shouted. "*Is anyone here a healer?*"

Darrell noticed for the first time that a muted, sullen silence had settled over the gathered people, and the captain's voice rang out clearly in the morning air. At first, no one answered, and the swordmaster reflected that men and women who dedicated their lives to preserving life would not be drawn to the spectacle of its taking, but no sooner had the thought occurred to him than a heavy-set, middle-aged woman stepped out of the crowd. "I'm a healer," she said, glancing nervously at those around her as if she'd just stepped into a church and claimed herself a heretic and was only waiting to be stoned to death.

"Help him," Brandon said. "I'll cover the cost."

He rose, his hands bloody, as the woman moved forward with a surprising speed and dropped beside the wounded man to begin ministering to him. As she did, Darrell saw the captain glance down at his hands, covered in so much blood that he might have been wearing crimson gloves. Then he looked at his uniform, seemed to take in the ripped sleeve, staring at it as if he couldn't fathom how it had come to be torn. Then a hard resoluteness entered his eyes, as if he had come to some decision, and he wiped his hands on the front of his uniform, covering it in crimson streaks and irrevocably ruining it, continuing to wipe at it, studying the fresh stains on the fabric with a cold expression.

In a few seconds, however, the moment passed, and the healer turned from where she'd been working on the wounded man. "Captain?"

At first, the man didn't seem to hear, and she had to repeat herself before he turned to her. "Yes?"

"I'm sorry...h-he's dead."

The captain stared at her as if unable to comprehend her words. "Dead?"

"Yes," the woman said, "I'm afraid...his wounds were too grave. Had I perhaps been at my shop..." She trailed off, leaving the rest unsaid.

Brandon studied her, and though his expression did not change, Darrell thought he saw something die in the man's gaze. He gave a sharp nod. "Very well. Thank you for your kindness. What is your name?"

"Tilda, sir," the woman said, her voice timid.

"Thank you, Tilda," Brandon said again. "I will find your shop and bring payment as...as soon as I can."

The woman protested weakly, saying something about how she had done nothing and therefore was owed nothing, but Darrell was hardly listening, nor was the captain. The man turned to look at the crowd, his expression hard and set, as if carved from stone. "Two deaths, this day was promised," he said, nearly growled, into the morning air, "and now in our foolishness we have given it more than it was owed." His eyes swept the crowd, and where his gaze touched they seemed to recoil. "You will have your spectacle, your *show*, but let us have no other lives wasted today."

His gaze swept the crowd, and Darrell was surprised when none shouted in disagreement or anger, but only watched him quietly. The swordmaster rose to his full height, craning his neck in an effort to meet the captain's gaze. For a moment, Brandon's gaze hesitated, and Darrell thought, but could not be sure, that they locked eyes. Then, without another word, the captain turned and walked back to the head of the procession, sparing a glance that promised retribution for the bloody-faced man as he passed.

Did he see me? Darrell thought to call out to the man despite the risk of attracting the attention of the other guards, some, if not all, of whom he suspected to be Grinner's men. But a moment later the decision was taken from him as the procession started forward once more and, as if waiting on their cue, the crowd took up their cries, though he didn't miss the way those in the front shied away as the guards passed, fearful for their own lives after witnessing their fellow cut down so quickly. He thought they were right to be fearful. With what the city was quickly becoming, they should all be afraid.

He watched the captain, his heart going out to the man who had been put in such a situation, on the one side stood what was right, on the other a duty that he had spent his life committed to, believing in. *But did he see me?*

Frustrated, angry, and feeling more depressed than he could ever remember, Darrell began to push his way forward through the crowd, toward the city square where Urek, Balen, and all the others waited for what news he would deliver. He only wished he had something good to tell them, for the day had possessed more than its share of bad news already, and he hated knowing that the word he brought would only add to it, for no plans had been made. There was nothing more than a single glance, and even that might have been no more than his imaginings. *But did he see me?*

CHAPTER THIRTY-TWO

Urek stood with Beautiful in the crowd, a surprising amount of space around them. Everyone else was so pressed together that if one of them decided to take a piss, twenty would leave the square wet. Those around them appeared reluctant to draw too near, and he thought he knew why. Beautiful had decided that a lady, visiting such a spectacle as the one which they now attended, would have worn a dress and taken great pains on her appearance. Despite Urek's adamant refusals that had quickly turned to pleas, she stood beside him in a sleeveless dress, smiling as if she'd come out for a pleasant stroll.

Beautiful was big, possessing more muscle than he himself, and the effect of the sleeveless dress was such that she looked like some giant from legend, some ancient warrior god of destruction, always only a moment from erupting into unrestrained violence. The dress, as it turned out, did nothing to soften the image, for the only thing worse than an avatar of death standing beside you, at least in Urek's thinking and those gathered around them seemed to agree, was one who was obviously insane.

Thankfully, Beautiful took the extra space only as her due, a politeness the city's populous extended to a lady. As he stood there, the woman smiling at the stolen glances those nearest shot her—no doubt thinking those glances admiring, and completely oblivious of the stark, naked fear in their gazes—Urek wondered, not for the first time, why he hadn't stayed a soldier.

"*Noble populous of Perennia,*" a voice rang out, and Urek turned to see a man dressed in finely-cut clothes standing on the wooden platform that lay at the heart of the square, "*I wish to thank you for attending today's spectacle, for putting your own errands on hold to see justice done.*"

There were several answering shouts of approval, and Urek frowned. No matter what they told themselves, the crowd hadn't been drawn to the square with thoughts of justice and order, but with thoughts of blood, of the validation, the assurance one might find in watching another's life end and knowing that, however shitty their own life was, they, at least, still *had* one. Most of those gathered seemed to know it too, for though there were a few shouts of agreement, there weren't many, and most of those who called from the crowd did so to point out that it was already several minutes past noon, and no heads had rolled as they'd been promised.

The man answered these queries, his voice surprisingly strong despite his small frame, explaining that yes, they were running behind and that, yes, to everyone's obvious relief, the executions would still take place. The man droned on about other things, and Urek was only half paying attention, focused on looking for the swordmaster. The man should have been back by now, one way or the other, and Urek was growing increasingly sure that something had gone wrong.

"Such a fine day, isn't it, Sir Urek?" Beautiful said from beside him.

He turned to stare at her and realized, for the first time, that she had put on face paint. Such mixtures of herbs were often used by women of station to hide wrinkles or accentuate the lines of their faces, and he had seen them used to surprising effect before. The problem with Beautiful, of course, was that she had never used face paint, and even he knew enough to see that whatever she'd done, it had been wrong. Instead of softening the hard lines of her face—of which there were many—instead of lending it an air of femininity, the marks and red streaks looked like nothing so much as war paint. Another reason, no doubt, why the crowd gave them such a wide berth.

Urek was suddenly overcome with the impression that he had somehow stumbled into some play, yet knew none of his lines or the mark upon which he was supposed to stand. "Give it time," he said. "It's early yet." She gave him a small frown at that, pursing her nose in what she must have taken for a dainty way.

"Oh, but you must learn to enjoy yourself and not be so maudlin, Urek. We have been treated kindly all day, yet you scowl at everyone around us as if they were wild animals in need of being put down."

As far as he was concerned, that wasn't all that far from the truth for men and women who would willingly come to see another killed, but he didn't say so. He understood, too, that he himself was a criminal, a man who had killed people and taken what they had, but he, at least, did his own killing, his own taking. He didn't make a sport of the thing, some event where watchers might eat pastries while others bled out their last then go on to drink themselves into a stupor and spend the evening recounting stories of the thing to each other, as if they both hadn't been there and seen the same head leave the same shoulders.

Beautiful looked away, and he frowned at her, thinking. She'd always been...well, call it what it was and say crazy, but she seemed to be acting even more so than normal. If the swordmaster didn't manage to get in touch with the captain and, between them, contrive a plan, they'd be doing this the bloody way—a way that almost certainly ended in the death of him and his crew—and it would only be over all that much quicker if Beautiful decided to be a lady instead of a killer.

He distracted himself from his dark thoughts by looking around at the gathered people again, and was rewarded with what he hoped was the swordmaster's gray pony-tail in the crowd not so far away. A moment later, Darrell emerged from the crowd, pushing his way through with a look on his face like that of a drowning man who has managed, by luck more than design, to thrash himself onto dry land. An image that was further enhanced by the fact that he was soaked in sweat.

"Swordmaster," he said, nodding his head in acknowledgment. "I was startin' to think maybe you'd decided to miss the show, after all. Not that I could blame you."

Darrell frowned, staring over Urek's shoulder. "Is that—"

Urek gave a frantic shake of his head before Beautiful turned around. "Ah, Sir Darrell," she said, curtseying, "it's a pleasure to see you again. Fine day, isn't it?"

The swordmaster glanced between her and Urek, a bemused expression on his face, but he must have noted the warning stare the big man gave him, for he only gave a graceful bow in return. "A pleasure to see you as well, my lady."

She beamed at that, and a moment later she was looking back to the stage with all the eagerness of a child at a magician's show. Urek let out the breath he'd been holding, stepping away from Beautiful and toward the swordmaster, and speaking in low tones. "Never mind that, for now. She'll snap out of it when the time comes." *I hope.* "So, where do we stand?"

The swordmaster dragged his gaze away from Beautiful and her dress with an obvious effort and winced. "I tried, and I can't be sure but...I think we must assume that, for the interim, we are on our own."

The big man grunted. "I wouldn't worry about it, swordmaster. It was a slim chance at best, anyway."

Darrell sighed. "I suppose you're right."

Urek nodded. "The bloody way it is then." He raised one hand over his head and made a slashing gesture to let the others know they'd been unable to reach the captain. He just hoped that everyone had managed to get into their positions as they'd planned, the crowd making it impossible to know for sure. He made the gesture again for good measure, stretching his frame as much as he could in hopes of being visible above the mass of people.

He was just about to do it a third time when he noticed several of the nearby people staring at him strangely, and he let his arm fall to his side, giving them a shrug. The people watched him warily, as if he was as crazy as the thickly-muscled woman in the dress beside him. Considering what they were about to do, that probably wasn't all that far from the truth.

The swordmaster said something else, but his words were drowned out by a roar from the crowd, and the mass of people to the left of the platform parted to allow room for what looked to be nine guardsmen as they escorted the two bedraggled prisoners toward the executioner's block. As if he'd been hidden and only waiting for his cue, the executioner stepped up onto the platform from the other side, gripping the handle of a double-bladed axe in both hands. The man wore a black hood that covered his face as was custom, and Urek's mind, suddenly alive with a thousand, random thoughts as the reality of what they were going to do set in, noted that the executioner must surely begrudge the hood of his station. After all, with the city in such a mood, the man could have gone to any brothel—following the proceedings—and no doubt not had to pay a single coin for a night's entertainment.

The executioner said nothing, only walked to stand beside the block upon which Hale and May's necks would soon rest, if Grinner had his way. He waited, his dark visage seeming to study his would-be victims as they were led up and onto the platform by their guard escort, whose job was made more difficult by a sudden volley of rotten fruit and vegetables raining down on them from the crowd.

Urek was shocked to see Hale—normally as steady and sure as a pillar made of stone—trip on his way up the stairs, as if his legs had simply given up beneath him, and the two guards that had been holding him on either side were forced down to one knee as they caught his full weight, only just managing to keep him upright.

Beautiful shouted from beside him, and he spun, suddenly sure that seeing their boss in such a state had awakened the rage for which she was known and that the blooding would start sooner than they'd intended. Instead, he was stunned to see her reach down to pick up a rotten cabbage from where it had fallen at her feet. She studied it as if she didn't know what it was for a moment, then she flexed her massive arm and threw it, where it exploded on one of the guards' backs, making the man stumble from the force if it. The woman proceeded to let out a shriek of delight and clap her hands, caught up in the spectacle of the thing, and Urek felt another knot of unease form in his stomach.

Against all likelihood, the guards somehow managed to get May and the big crime boss up and onto the wooden platform, standing them at one end of it. Urek turned to the swordmaster. "Now?"

Darrell frowned, not turning away from the platform as he shook his head. "Not yet. He will want to be here for this, will want to witness it himself."

Urek gave a frown of his own, wondering at who the swordmaster meant. But he didn't have to wait for long to find out as the crowd on the other side of the platform began to part and what appeared to be at least twenty guardsmen formed an avenue. *Gods,* Urek thought, *two dozen at the least.* With the nine that had escorted the prisoners, that made more than thirty men, not even bothering to count all those stationed in the crowd in a vain attempt to keep order.

Through the lane the soldiers created marched a man Urek recognized all too well even with the silver mask he wore. Grinner walked calmly, confidently, like a man who owned everything around him and knew it. If things hadn't already been strange enough, the crowd erupted into cheers at the sight of him, yelling their thanks for him rescuing the queen from the assassination attempt, calling him "savior" and "hero."

Urek listened to their shouts of admiration in disbelief, thinking this was a sure sign the world was doomed—that a man such as Grinner, a man who had spent his life murdering, backstabbing, and cheating any who got in his way, could be hailed as a savior.

Grinner, though, didn't seem surprised in the slightest, appearing to take the crowd's adoration as his due as he made his way toward the platform and up its steps. He walked to stand in the center, turning to face the crowd, and the shouts of approval continued until he finally raised a hand, bidding them to be silent which they did with a swiftness that disgusted Urek.

"Ladies and gentlemen," Grinner said. "Loyal subjects of Perennia and Her Majesty, Isabelle. I must ask for your forgiveness, for though I might be able, in some small capacity, to shield the queen from the blades of those who would do her harm…" He paused here, basking in the nearly manic shouts of gratitude that erupted from the gathered people. "I can do little, I fear, for those stresses and problems which come with her position. As such, Her Royal Highness will not be attending this most important matter with us today, for she is sequestered in her rooms, recovering from the ordeal of the last few weeks."

There were angry hisses at that and more makeshift missiles flew from the crowd at May and Hale. Urek saw the faces stretched in rage and incoherent hate, and sighed. Not only would they be taking on city guardsmen who outnumbered them several times over—even with Captain Festa and his sailors—it seemed that they would be taking on the city itself when they attempted their no doubt ill-fated rescue.

He took a slow, deep breath, and turned to the swordmaster as Grinner droned on. He waited for the man to give him some signal that the thing would begin, waited with his hand ready to grasp the sword concealed by the cloak at his back. He knew it would not be long now.

***

The big man's anxiety was a palpable thing, but Darrell paid it little attention. Nor did he bother to listen to the empty platitudes and poorly-veiled boasts of the crime boss. Instead, his eyes were fixed on Captain Brandon Gant who stared out at the crowd from his position on the platform, an unreadable expression on his face. *Did he see me?* Darrell thought for what must have been the hundredth time.

He stood there, praying to the gods that the captain would look in his direction, would give him some sign, as the man's gaze swept the crowd, though whether he was looking for any possible threats or for Darrell himself, the swordmaster didn't know. Finally, the captain's eyes did lock on him, and there was no question of it now. He gave one single, short nod, almost imperceptible, but it was enough, and the swordmaster felt a flicker of hope rise in him. They still had no plan, their chances were still almost nonexistent, but they would have help. "Come on," he said to the big man, "let's get closer to the front."

Urek nodded, pulling Beautiful along, saying something about being closer to the show and how a lady such as herself deserved a better view. Whatever that was about, it got the woman moving, and Darrell didn't have time to ponder it—he was too busy watching the captain. They were still making their way to the front when Grinner finished his speech, and the people around them erupted in riotous applause, as if the man wasn't a man at all but some benevolent god come to the city to save it.

Give me just one chance, Darrell thought, thinking not just of May and Hale, but of Aaron and Adina, still missing, of Wendell and Leomin, of Caleb, and all the others who Grinner had betrayed. *Just one chance, and we will show them that even a god can bleed.*

CHAPTER THIRTY-THREE

Balen didn't normally consider himself a coward, but he realized, standing beside the first mate, staring at the dozens of guards and listening to the crowd cheer Grinner's words, that maybe that wasn't completely true. That maybe, given the right circumstances, all men could be cowards, and if ever there were circumstances for it, these were certainly them.

So far, at least, Thom hadn't charged the platform, but there had been a panicked moment when the guards had first led Hale and May onto the stage. When the first mate saw her, Balen was sure the festivities were going to begin ahead of time. The older man had made a strangled sound of inarticulate rage, his body going rigid with fury, and Balen had been prepared to restrain him. Or, at least, to try. He was fairly sure—given the experiences of earlier in the day—that it would take far more than just him to keep the first mate back, if he took it in his mind to charge the platform in some suicidal attempt to save his lover.

Which, Balen supposed, is exactly what their plan—such as it was—entailed. But if he was going to die, he consoled himself with the fact that at least he wouldn't be doing it alone. Unless, of course, all the others had decided it was a lost cause and abandoned him and Thom to their deaths. Ridiculous, of course, but that didn't keep him from looking around frantically in search of his companions.

He let out a heavy sigh of relief when he saw the swordmaster, Urek, and the woman—was that a *dress* she was wearing?—

standing in the front row not far away. He couldn't imagine what had possessed the woman to wear such a thing, knowing full well the fighting—and most likely dying—that they'd be doing soon enough, but he supposed that, at the least, the men in charge of burying her wouldn't have to go looking for something to dress her in.

She chose that moment to turn and saw Balen staring at her, gave him a wink and a girlish wave that sent his heart racing for all the wrong reasons, before turning back to stare at the podium. *Gods be good, Blunderfoot,* he thought, *you're doomed one way or the other.*

***

Captain Brandon Gant was angry. He'd woken up angry, had dressed and gone to escort the prisoners angry, and events since then—such as that fool killing a man when he'd clearly decided against rushing them—had done little to improve his mood. He'd spend the day—and the days before it, if he was being honest with himself—mulling over the big crime boss's recriminations, vacillating between righteous indignation and self-pitying acceptance. He had still been debating with himself as they made their way out of the castle gate, until he saw Darrell in the crowd, studying him with what had felt like a question.

It was a question that left Brandon Gant feeling unsure, unsteady, and it was one to which he'd had no answer. But standing on the platform, listening to Councilman Grinner prattle on about "justice" and "traitors," his anger had grown into a full-blown rage, and the answer to the question the swordmaster's eyes had asked—the same question he had asked himself a thousand times over the last few days—became clear. He would abandon his duty, abandon a life spent in service, branding himself a traitor and irrevocably so, because, in the end, it was better to be a good man than a loyal one.

All of which would most likely be moot, as he didn't see much chances of finishing the day—or even the hour, come to it—alive. Eight guards shared the platform with him, not to mention the executioner himself, a man who looked all-too comfortable with the double-bladed axe he carried and one that, Brandon suspected, wouldn't be too pleased at some man putting himself between him and the deaths he'd been promised. And if Brandon somehow managed, with the others' help, to survive the first thirty seconds of what was coming, the dozens of guards scattered throughout the audience and standing around Grinner would rush the stage and put an end to all Brandon's doubts and worries quickly enough.

He was so lost in thought he didn't realize that all those gathered were waiting on him until one of the men nearest him nudged him with an elbow. Then Captain Brandon Gant, Commander of the City Guard, once proud defender of King Marcus himself, and until now at least, loyal servant of his royal daughter, Queen Isabelle, stepped forward before the waiting crowd, and if any rational thoughts made it past that jumble of emotions which he felt, then they were traitorous ones indeed.

CHAPTER THIRTY-FOUR

May listened to Captain Gant recite her and Hale's crimes in a sort of daze. Nothing mattered anymore. Not the dreams she'd once had as a child, nor the visions she'd had as a woman of how her life would be spent, not even the fear that she had felt cowering in the dungeons, a wretched, pitiable creature. She was all of those things: the hopeful child, the confident woman, the frightened wretch, and yet she was none of them. She did not even feel any connection to the woman who now stood on the platform in the center of the city, surrounded by thousands who had come to watch her death. She *was* that woman, but she was *not* her at the same time. She was a being without form or substance, a witness that floated above the scene, watching events unfold impartially and without any feeling one way or the other.

In that daze, nothing reached her, nothing seemed to have any real meaning. At least, that was, until the captain burst forward with a shout, and gave the executioner a hard kick to the midsection. The hooded man hadn't seen the blow coming, and the double-bladed axe flew from his hands to land on the wooden platform with a *thunk* as he flew off the stage, crashing into several surprised people in the crowd.

One of the guards at her back gave a shout of surprise as the captain drew his blade and spun, driving the steel through the nearest—the man with the bloody nose—who let out a grunt of shock and agony, toppling to the ground as the captain ripped the blade free.

There was a moment of frozen disbelief, one which the guards on the platform, the people standing in the square, even the captain himself, shared. Then everything happened at once. Several guards rushed forward with their blades drawn, intent on cutting the captain down, but they'd barely made it a step before Darrell, the swordmaster, leapt onto the stage and ran at them. He spun among their attacks like some dervish, his sword licking out to cut one guard on the wrist and, an instant later, striking another in the ankle. The guard screamed and toppled as his severed foot was no longer able to keep him upright.

Despite the swordmaster's skill, it looked as if he would be overcome by sheer weight of numbers, but then a knife flashed through the air, embedding itself in the throat of a guard who'd been coming up behind him, and the unfortunate guard stumbled back, his hands going to his throat. May spun to look at where the knife had come from to see a hook-nosed man she didn't recognize standing in the crowd and smiling grimly, another blade already raised to throw. Whether he got the throw off or not she couldn't have said, for he was blocked from view as a big man climbed on the platform, followed an instant later by what looked to be another man even bigger than he was, this one—and if ever she thought she was dreaming surely it was now—wearing a dress.

A roar came from behind her, and May turned to see the crime boss, Hale, rise to his full height, knocking away the two guards who held him on either side as if they were children. He turned to her, grinning madly. *It was all an act,* May thought wildly, *nothing but an act. And where have his manacles gone?*

She watched, stunned, as the giant crime boss grabbed the closest guard and slammed his forehead into the man's face. There was a crushing, *crumpling* sound, and the man let out a gurgle as he collapsed. But Hale was already moving on to the next. He grabbed the man's shoulder in one hand, burying his fist in the guard's gut. The air exploded from the guard's lungs in a *woosh*, but Hale wasn't finished. He took hold of the guard's ankle and—with seemingly no effort at all—lifted him above his head and threw him through the air where he soared over the heads of the nearest people and landed somewhere in the crowd, out of May's sight.

Grinner shrieked in rage from where he stood beside the platform, and the guards gathered around him started forward only to have more people materialize on the stage as if from nowhere—sailors, judging by their attire—to block their path. The sailors fought with a surprising viciousness, using the small, cruel knives they carried on the onrushing guards. But for all their fervor, May could see they would not hold out long against the better-trained and equipped city guard. Even as she watched, one was cut down, a guard's blade carving a bloody ruin into his chest.

The unfortunate sailor fell away screaming and another man May thought she recognized—*Balen,* a part of her confused mind thought vaguely, *that's Balen*—leapt onto the guard's back, bearing him down onto the wooden platform and burying a knife in the guardsman's throat. The first mate looked nearly as terrified as the guard he'd ambushed, but he didn't hesitate, charging the next closest guard and kicking him off the steps and into other guards trying to climb the platform.

May blinked dully. Once, the woman she had been would have known exactly what to do, but she had become something else, been *made* something else by her time in the dungeon, and she only stood, waiting for what would happen. She felt a tug at her wrists where they were manacled behind her back and craned her neck to see a man—a boy, really, as he looked to be no more than fifteen—grasping at her manacles. "J-j-just a minute, m-m-ma'am," he stammered. "T-the manacles are old, so it makes them a bit t-trickier."

May frowned, opening her mouth to tell the stranger, whoever he was, to leave them, for surely when Grinner saw her free he would punish her for it, but a second later there was a metallic rattle and the manacles fell to the platform at her feet. *Too late,* she thought, a stab of panic piercing the fog that had settled over her thoughts. *He'll see. He'll see, and he'll be so angry. He's always angry.*

She saw a guard rushing toward her, his sword raised. May knew she should run or hide, should do *something,* but she only stood and watched her death come. The man was only a few steps away from her, would be on her in another moment, when someone barreled into him, tackling him to the platform. The newcomer was wiry, with a thin frame packed with corded muscle, and when the guard tried to rise the stranger grabbed his head in his hands and slammed it down onto the wooden platform once, twice, three times.

The guard's struggles stopped after the third impact, and the wiry man had just begun to rise when another guard emerged from the crowded melee on the platform, swinging his sword. The thin man cried out in surprised pain as the blade sliced a gash into his arm, and he stumbled away. As he did, his face turned so that May could see it, and she gasped. *"Thom?"* The words came out in a rasping croak, and if the man heard he gave no sign. He clamped a hand over his wound, hissing in pain.

The first mate started to turn to his attacker, but before he could another guard charged him, tackling him to the ground. The guard jerked a dagger from his belt, raising it over his head to strike. Thom lashed out wildly, hitting the man in the wrist and sending the knife flying to where it landed only a few feet in front of May.

She stared at the knife, her mind trying to process everything that had happened, everything that *was* happening. Then a strangled hiss from the two struggling men snapped her back to the present. The guard had his hands wrapped around the first mate's throat, and despite Thom's wiry strength, the guard had all the leverage, and the first mate was unable to break his attacker's hold. His face was turning a deep red, wheezing sounds coming from his throat, and it wouldn't be long before he lost the ability to struggle altogether.

The guard screamed in shock and agony as the knife buried itself deep into the meat of his shoulder. May stared down at her hands where they held the blade's handle, baffled and disappointed at once, for part of her didn't remember moving, didn't recall bending down to scoop up the knife from where it had fallen. As for her disappointment, it came from the part of her that *did* remember, the same part that had aimed for the back of the man's neck, and would have ended his life, had his struggles with the first mate not caused him to move at the last second.

The guard swung a backhand at her, striking her in the face with enough force to send her stumbling away. He rose from the wheezing first mate who appeared to be close to unconsciousness. He growled incoherently, ripping the blade free of his shoulder, and stalked toward her.

She watched him come, cupping her hand against her face and staring at Thom, her thoughts racing, the pain of the blow having served to banish the fog that had settled over her mind. Thom was alive, but barely, his chest rising and falling almost imperceptibly. He had come to save her, and he had nearly died and, what was worse, she had come close—far too close—to standing there and watching it happen. Anger blazed within her, the heat of it scouring away the filth, the desperation and hopelessness that her time in prison had grown within her, and she let it have its way, let it burn away the pathetic *thing* Grinner had made her, the wretched creature she had let herself become.

"Come on, you bastard," she hissed at the guard, and the sound of her own voice, raised in defiance, helped to wipe away the last vestiges of her despair, not that she thought it would do her much good, in the end. The guard was wounded, but he was also well-trained and armed with a knife, while May had no training and a quick glance around the platform showed that there was no weapon near to hand. So she faced the man, a silent snarl on her face, aware of the irony that she would discover her will to live only to be executed after all.

"Fucking bitch," the man spat, brandishing the blade coated with his own blood. "I'll kill you."

"No. You won't." The guard spun at the sound of the new voice, but not quickly enough to avoid the axe blade that cleaved through his neck.

Hale let out a growl as he kicked a foot into the dead man's midsection, ripping the axe free as the body went tumbling along the platform, leaving a trail of blood to mark its passage. Then he turned to May. Battle raged all around them but, for the moment, the two of them existed within a small pocket of calm. The crime boss walked to her, looking her up and down. "You alright, lass?"

"Oh yes, I'm glorious," May said sarcastically, but she didn't bother trying to hide the grin that spread across her face. The odds were still stacked terribly against them, and chances were they'd still die before the day was over, but she couldn't help the pleasure that filled her now that she had, once again, found herself. She studied Hale. Before, he had seemed only inches from death, but his strength, if it had ever been gone, had returned to him in full, and he stood covered in the blood of the gods alone knew how many of Grinner's men, the double-bladed executioner's axe looking natural in his hands. "It was all an act then?"

The crime boss grinned, shrugging his massive shoulders. "Maybe not all. I'd be lyin' if I told you I minded those two bastards carryin' me here, gave me time to take a rest. But it seems I'm not the only one who was actin'," he said, eyeing her. "Gods, lass, I have to admit you even had me fooled."

May snorted. "I had myself fooled." Her expression grew solemn. "Thank you. For helping me. For bringing me back."

Hale grunted. "Ain't no cause to be thankin' me, lass. The place you went, can't nobody in this world bring you back from but you. Now—" He paused as a guard separated himself from the melee on the platform and rushed him. Hale stepped to the side, dodging the man's blow and swinging the axe with an almost contemptuous ease. Ribs cracked as the axe caved in the guard's chest, and he collapsed in a shower of gore. "Anyway," the crime boss said, glancing around the platform and speaking as if nothing had just occurred, "save your thanks. From where I'm standin', it looks like we'll be seein' that fucker Salen and his Fields soon enough."

May followed his gaze and had to admit that he was right. The sailors were doing what they could to keep the guards from gaining the platform, but for every guard they brought down, two sailors followed him into death. On the platform itself, Brandon Gant and the swordmaster fought back to back along with a big man and the other wearing the dress, but the four were being surrounded as a few of the more intelligent guards avoided the stairs at which the sailors waited altogether and climbed onto the platform.

May glanced to where Thom still lay unconscious, her mind racing to try to find some way to make it off the platform alive with the first mate. She was still struggling to come up with a solution when a horn sounded, and she spun to see armed men pouring into the square from the distant street. Fifty or more at the least. "Oh gods."

"I'd hold on that too, lass," the crime boss said, looking at the approaching forces. "Whatever you've got to say to the gods, I reckon you'll be able to say it in person."

"There's got to be some way," May said desperately, not sure if she was arguing with the crime boss, her own thoughts, or the world itself.

Hale grunted. "There is—we run."

"Run?" May asked.

The big man nodded. "That's right, lass, you heard me." He gestured to the oncoming soldiers with the bloody axe. "Those fuckers there ain't gonna be content to come up here and ask what all the fuss is about, I promise you that much. They're here for blood, and they'll have it one way or the other. Now, we have to go."

"And abandon the others?" May asked in disbelief.

"Yes, *abandon* them," Hale growled. "Don't you get it, woman? They came here to save you—those men dyin' over there have died for nothin' if you just sit around waitin' for somebody to come and lop off your head. Now, let's go." He grabbed May by the shoulder, trying to lead her toward the edge of the platform, but she resisted.

"No," she said, glancing at the unconscious first mate, the man she loved, that she had hoped in her wilder imaginings to one day marry. "I won't leave him."

Hale bared his teeth, glancing between May and Thom's prone form. Then he let out a growl of anger and frustration. "Wait here."

Before the club owner could protest, Hale waded forward, into the thick of the melee, the axe he wielded flashing out with shocking speed. He carved a bloody path through the men surrounding Darrell and the others. While he did, May ran to Thom, checked his pulse, and was relieved to find it strong and steady. *Damn fool is as tough as leather and as stubborn as a mule,* she thought, wiping at a tear that had come to her eye.

"Alright then." Hale said, walking up. The big man she'd seen climb the platform stood with him, but next to the crime boss's giant frame he almost looked small. The stranger was covered in blood—more than a little of it his own judging by the cuts on his chest and arms—but he was grinning wildly, as if there wasn't a place in the world he'd rather be. To the right of him stood the man wearing the dress, only, now that May was closer, she realized it wasn't a man at all, but the biggest woman she'd ever seen.

"That's the one there," Hale said, stabbing a thick finger at Thom. "Get 'em up and get 'em out of here. To the ships, if you can."

The newcomer started to answer, but cut off as a guard rushed at him from behind, growling a curse and brandishing a bloody sword. The big man started to turn, but May realized he was going to be too late, and felt a thrill of fear that quickly turned to surprise as the woman in the dress lashed out with shocking speed, her fist connecting with the onrushing guard's jaw. There was an audible *crack* and their attacker stumbled away, but not quickly enough to avoid the woman grabbing him by his shirt and pants and lifting him above her head as if he weighed no more than a child.

The guard had enough time to grunt in surprise before she brought his back down on her knee, and there was another *crack*, this one louder than the first, as his spine snapped. Growling with disgust, she turned and hurtled the unfortunate guard into the melee, knocking down two more that were engaged in fighting the sailors. "We're *talking* here!" she screamed, then turned back to May and the two stunned men, a contented smile on her face.

The woman's companion stared at her as if at a loss for words, swallowing hard. Then he turned back to the big crime boss, clearing his throat. "Sure, boss. Whatever you say. But what about you?"

Hale grunted, shaking his head before looking away from the woman. "Don't you worry about me, Urek. I ain't no blushin' maid lookin' for a knight in shining armor to save me, and you'd be a shit excuse for one even if I was. Now, you just get yourselves and your crew out of here and do it quickly. I don't want to be hearin' nothin' about how one of you took it in your mind to be a hero and got your fool ass killed, you understand?"

Urek grinned wider, nodding. "Gotcha, boss. Don't be a hero. Don't get my fool ass killed." He turned to the woman, "Alright, Beautiful. You heard the boss. Now, if you want to go ahead and grab the—" He paused as the woman's face began to twist into a scowl. "Well," he continued, clearing his throat, "whatever it is you wanna grab, that is. I'll grab this bastard here—totin' bodies, after all, is a man's work."

Her smile returned at that, a girlish, innocent smile that was more than a little disturbing considering the mask of blood covering her face. "Whatever you say, Urek."

The man breathed an audible sigh of relief and lifted Thom as if he weighed nothing, throwing him over one shoulder. "Alright," he said. "Let's get the boys and get out of here." He turned back to Hale. "Where do you want us to meet you, boss?"

Hale grinned. "I'll find you—I found you the first time, remember?"

The crime boss's words must have touched on some powerful memory, for Urek suddenly nodded as if at a loss for words. "Boss...I never did thank you for..."

"No, you didn't," Hale interrupted in a growl, "and that's one of the reasons you're still breathin'. Now, go on and get it done—there's no more time to waste."

Urek looked as if he still wanted to say something, but he only nodded. "Yes, sir." He started away, toward the least crowded edge of the platform, but paused when Hale spoke.

"And Urek."

"Sir?"

"Thank you." The words came out in a deep growl, as if difficult to say, and judging by the way Urek's eyes went wide in surprise, they weren't words the crime boss said often.

"Of course, sir," he said. Then he and the woman were gone, moving toward the edge of the platform.

"Alright then," Hale said, turning back to May. "Now, it's time to go."

May still hesitated, looking after Thom where he hung without moving from the criminals shoulder as they climbed down the platform's edge. "But..."

"Never mind your 'buts,'" Hale said. "That man of yours risked his life to come here and save yours—either he'll die or he won't, it's in the hands of the gods now, and you bein' cut down for being too stupid to move ain't gonna help him one way or the other."

"And this Urek," May said, allowing the crime boss to lead her away. "You trust him?"

She could only see the crime boss's face in profile, but she didn't miss the grin—not the wild grin he showed while fighting, but a contented, peaceful one. "Like a brother." He seemed to realize what he had said and turned on her. "If you ever tell him I said that, lass, I'll finish what the executioner started, you understand?"

May recoiled in surprise at the vehemence in the man's tone. "I understand."

"After all," the crime boss said, giving her a wink as he jumped from the platform and offered her his free hand, holding the axe up with the other, "I've already got the axe for the job."

CHAPTER THIRTY-FIVE

Balen understood, vaguely, that he was in trouble. He knew he should move or do something, but the blow to the head had left his thoughts scrambled, fragmented, and there was a ringing in his ears that made it nearly impossible to think. He'd made it to, *This is bad,* when the guard on top of him raised his knife, intending to bury it in...well, somewhere. Balen was pretty sure wherever it was, he wouldn't be thanking him for it.

He watched the knife start downward with foggy disbelief. A man shouldn't die so confused, should he? Surely, he ought to know what was happening. It became a moot point soon enough, however, as a blade seemed to come out of nowhere, severing the guard's wrist. The knife—as well as the hand it was attached to—went flying away out of Balen's blurry sight.

The guard tumbled away—maybe to go hunting for his hand—and the swordmaster's face appeared above Balen. Darrell offered him his hand, and Balen took it, allowing himself to be pulled to his feet. "Thanks for that," he gasped.

The swordmaster only nodded, glancing around the platform. "We need to go."

"Go?" Balen asked. "But what about May and—"

"Already gone, both of them," Darrell said, giving Balen a half-smile that did nothing to banish the exhaustion on the man's face. "I saw them leave while you were busy lying down and taking a rest."

"Leave?" Balen asked. He knew he sounded like a child, mimicking the swordmaster's words, but also just aware that he couldn't stop. "Leave where?"

The swordmaster shook his head. "I don't know, and it doesn't matter. Anywhere will be better than here."

"I notice that bastard Grinner's gone," Balen said, scanning the platform.

"Yes," the swordmaster answered. "As soon as the fighting started."

Coward, Balen thought with venom, but mostly because he'd had the same idea himself when the blades came out. "And what of Thom? I seen him, not so long ago—bastard was fighting like a madman, but I lost track of him in—"

"Gone as well. Along with Urek and his crew."

"You sure that was a good idea, letting him go with them?" Balen asked uneasily.

Darrell raised his eyebrow, his eyes never leaving the first mate as his sword flicked behind him, slicing the throat of an attacking guard and sending him stumbling away. "I was a bit preoccupied at the time. Besides, if when we find Thom he's had his pocket picked, well, I'll call that a more than fair trade. Now, come on before those reinforcements get here."

Balen followed the man's finger to see dozens of armed men rushing toward the platform. They would have reached it already had they not had to plow through a panicked crowd of thousands of people, all seeming to decide the best course of action was to run directly in to one another. "Oh gods," he breathed.

"Not gods," Darrell said, "but they'll decide our fate quickly enough if we don't get out while we can."

Balen nodded at that, and they began to fight their way toward the opposite end of the platform, Balen shouting at the few remaining sailors to retreat but not taking the time to see whether they listened or not. It was a near thing still, as they were forced to fight their way through several guards who had managed to gain the platform. But despite how exhausted he looked, the swordmaster made quick work of them and soon they were on the ground and running as if the Death God himself were on their heels. Which, Balen figured, was just about the truth of it.

CHAPTER THIRTY-SIX

By the time Adina and the others arrived, the city square was in chaos. The large crowd who had come to watch the execution still stood in front of the platform, but, they seemed to have lost all interest in the spectacle. Instead, they either talked in angry, raised voices, or stood around with dazed expressions, as if they'd just awoken from a dream and had yet to figure out where they were or how they'd come to be there.

Adina hesitated, apparently trying to decide what to do. Sergeant Wendell took the opportunity to coax some air into his heaving lungs. They'd spent nearly the last half hour at a dead run, and he had decided that drinking and whoring weren't such good exercise, after all. He'd promised himself during that grueling run that, should he survive the day, he would cut down on both and start training more, consoling himself with the knowledge that the one benefit of charging to what was almost certain death was that he doubted he'd live long enough to break his oath.

"Gods, what happened here?" Adina breathed, but no one seemed inclined to answer, and Wendell didn't blame them.

It was clear enough that the crowd had got more of a show than they'd bargained for, and there were several unmoving forms lying in the crowd, probably trampled by their fellows, many of which had run past Wendell and the others as they drew close to the square. The unmistakable smell of blood filled the air, and Wendell took a moment to thank the gods that he hadn't been in the middle of that crowd when whatever had caused the panic had taken place.

"With your permission, Majesty," the guard captain said, turning to look at Adina, "let's go find out."

Adina nodded, her face grim. "Lead on, Captain Marcus."

His expression set, the man started to push his way through the dazed people toward the platform. Wendell watched the others start in after him, shaking his head. "Ain't no damn way I'm going in there," he muttered to himself. "A man'd have to hate himself an awful lot to—"

"Sergeant Wendell!"

He looked up to see the Parnen looking back at him, a question on his face. He gave a long sigh. "Fine, yeah. Alright," he said, "I'm comin.'"

It didn't take long until they were surrounded by people on all sides, their progress coming nearly to a halt by the press of bodies. "Gryle," Adina said, having to yell to be heard over the shouts of the crowd, "if you'd be so kind?"

"Of course, Majesty," the chamberlain said, taking up a spot in the front of the group and pushing his way forward. Wendell didn't expect it would make much difference, but when the chamberlain began pushing at those in front of them with his Virtue-enhanced strength, it turned out that there was some extra room after all, and they began to make better time as Gryle scattered men and women before him like chaff.

People studied them as they made their way through the press of bodies, and Wendell overheard mutterings of "princess," and "the Parnen." He didn't much like the angry, threatening tones, nor the sullen looks they were giving him and the others.

"Uh, Princess," he said, glancing around them nervously as he walked after the Parnen. "I think maybe this ain't such a good idea, after all." But if Adina heard she gave no sign, and soon they made it to the executioner's platform.

Blood and bodies littered the area around the executioner's block, corpses stacked on top of each other in piles as if someone had dropped a coin, and they'd all went for it at once.

"Gods be good," Leomin said, staring at the bodies.

"Come on," Adina said, heading toward the platform's stairs, her expression dark. "Let's see if Hale and May are here." She didn't say dead, but then she didn't have to, and the sergeant and the others followed her, their own faces grim.

***

Wendell turned over another body, jumping back in shock when what he'd taken for a corpse let out a groan. And if a scream escaped him, well, surely such a thing was understandable, given the circumstances. "Sergeant Wendell?" Adina said, rising from where she'd been checking another body and hurrying to him. "What is it?"

"This one here's alive, Princess," he said, swallowing hard, his heart galloping in his chest. "Well," he added, staring down at the deep gash in the guard's side, "after a fashion."

Adina crouched down beside the moaning guard, turning his face toward her. "Sir? Sir, can you hear me?"

Slowly, the man's eyes began to focus, and he saw her crouched over him. "You," he hissed, his lips pulling back into a bloody snarl. "This is your...fault. *Traitor.*"

Adina recoiled as if slapped, too stunned to speak, and Wendell found himself growing angry. "Look here, fella," he said, "the princess here ain't done nothin' but try to help the city. Goin' around callin' innocent folks names, it ain't no surprise you're lyin' here all cut up and bloody."

The man sneered at that and started to say something, but broke into a coughing fit, blood and spittle frothing from his mouth. His eyes closed, and Wendell thought he'd have the last word in that argument, whether he wanted it or not, but then the guard captain appeared at his side along with the others. "Guardman Nicholas?" Marcus asked in disbelief.

The wounded guard's eyes flittered open at the sound of his name. "C-captain Marcus?"

"Yes, it's me, Nick," Marcus said, kneeling beside the man. "What happened here?"

The guard's eyes went from the guard captain to the princess. "Y-you're...with the...traitors?"

The guard captain shook his head. "Not traitors, Nick. We've been lied to, all of us. That bastard Grinner's tricked the whole city.

The princess has come to help us. Now, can you tell me what happened here? Where are the prisoners?"

"T-they came out of n-nowhere," the guard said, his eyes growing unfocused once more. "So many...the prisoners...escaped."

His eyes fell closed again, and the captain leaned forward, grabbing the wounded man's shirt. "Where, Nick? Where did they go?"

"I...don't know. The others...went after them. Don't know...where..." He trailed off then, and his body slumped as his eyes closed for the final time.

"*Damn*," the captain hissed, laying the body down with a gentleness that surprised Wendell. When he turned back to look at the others, his eyes were hard. "I've known Nick for years. He was a good man, a loyal one. Grinner has a lot to answer for."

"Yes," Adina said, "and I promise you, Marcus, that he *will* answer for what he's done. But we must find May and Hale. They, as much as anyone, will be instrumental in explaining the crimes for which Grinner is guilty."

The guard captain gave a short, angry nod. "Yes, of course, Princess."

Wendell shot a glance back at the crowd in front of the platform and was met with dozens—hundreds—of angry sneers. And had the crowd been so close, when they'd climbed onto the platform? He didn't think so, but he couldn't be sure. "Princess—"

"But how do we find them?" Leomin asked. "It's a big city, after all, and we can't search all of it, certainly not as quickly as Grinner and his men can."

Adina glanced at Seline, raising an eyebrow in question, but the other woman shook her head, clearly frustrated. "I couldn't—not so much. I'm not...I'm not very good with it yet. I get really tired, more tired than I thought possible and after the fight with those men that attacked us..."

There were dark circles under her eyes, and her face looked a bit sunken, as if she was coming down with something. Adina must have seen it too, for she only nodded. "That's alright," she said, glancing around the square. "Maybe we can find someone else who knows where they went or..."

"Princess," Wendell said, still eyeing the crowd, and there was no question that they were slowly coming closer now. "Whatever you intend to do, we'd better do it and soon. Seems to me we've overstayed our welcome."

The princess and the others followed his gaze to the gathered people, noting their sullen glances for the first time.

"Perhaps they know something," Gryle ventured uncertainly. "If we only explain to them what has really happened and..."

"You ask me, Chamberlain," Wendell said in a low voice, "they ain't in a mood to listen."

"The sergeant's right," Adina said. "We can't stay here. We'll split up. Leomin, you and Seline take the western side of the city and be sure to check the ships—they might have sought refuge there. Gryle, you and I will search the north. Sergeant, you go with Captain Marcus and Hugh and check the south."

"Princess," the captain said, "I don't mean to be difficult, but do you really think it's wise to go off on your own?"

Adina gave the man a smile with no humor in it. "I won't be alone, Captain. I'll have Gryle with me—you've seen what he is capable of. I'm sure he'll be able to handle any trouble we run into." Wendell could see by the chamberlain's expression he didn't necessarily share the princess's confidence in him, but he said nothing.

"Adina," Leomin said hesitantly, "are you sure—"

"No," Adina said, "I'm not sure, but there's no time to argue it. Every second we waste here is a second we can't help May and Hale." She looked at each of them in turn, giving them a chance to object, if they wanted to. Wendell himself didn't like the idea, but he couldn't think of a better one, so he remained silent. When no one else spoke, Adina gave a nod. "Now go, and the gods keep us all."

Wendell glanced at the bloody carnage on the platform. *Gods keep us all? Well, seems to me they've been doin' a pretty shit job of it so far.* But he followed the two guardsmen as they left the platform, hoping the crowd wouldn't choose this moment to attack, hoping they would find the club owner and the crime boss in time. But most of all he hoped they hadn't just doomed themselves, for if the city was a great, hungry beast in search of a meal, they'd just managed to split themselves up into nice, bite-sized portions.

CHAPTER THIRTY-SEVEN

May was exhausted. It seemed they'd been running forever with no end in sight. Hale led the way, taking one alley then another, never hesitating—as if he'd memorized a map of Perennia. Which, she supposed, he probably had. A crime boss such as Hale would want to know his way around the city, would want to know what parts of it were best for ambushes or escaping the guards. But his seemingly remarkable knowledge did nothing for the waning strength in her legs as muscles she'd had little cause to use in the dungeons screamed in protest.

If their grueling pace affected the big man at all, he didn't show it, running on as if he could do it forever, his breath strong and even, a cruel counterpoint to May's own ragged gasps. "W...where are we going?" she managed.

"The docks," the crime boss called over his shoulder. "I figure that'll be the best place for now and if things really do go to shit, well—" he gave her a wink, grinning as if he was having fun, "—then we can always go on a little boat ride."

May frowned. She might not be as familiar with the city as the crime boss seemed to be, but she knew enough to be well aware that they were heading in the opposite direction of the docks and had been for some time. She said as much, and the big man nodded.

"Sure," Hale agreed. "Whatever else that bastard Grinner is, he ain't a fool, and I reckon he'll know that's where we'll head. The quickest way between two points might be a straight line, but you ask me, that'll also be the quickest way to our graves. Better to lead them on for a bit, make 'em think maybe we're making a break for the city gate."

Well, there was no arguing with that, so May only followed after the man as he led the way down another alley. They hadn't encountered any resistance yet which surprised her. The few people they'd passed had gotten out of their way quickly enough when they saw the bloody axe the giant carried. But Hale was right about one thing—Grinner was no fool—and it seemed to her that if he was smart enough to know they'd go for the docks, then he might well be smart enough to know they wouldn't head there directly, might expect them to do exactly what they *were* doing. But she had no better ideas, so she ran on, forcing her aching legs to take one more step, then another.

She didn't know how long they ran, she was too concentrated on trying to breathe past the stitch that had risen in her side to pay much attention, but eventually they came out on one of the city's main streets. "Alright then," Hale said, "time to head to the—" His words turned into a grunt of surprise as what May was sure was at least a hundred armed men piled out of the alleyways in front of them, spilling into the street.

"*Shit,*" Hale growled. "Turn around, lass, we'll lose them in the alleyways."

Fear lending her energy, May spun to do just that but froze as more men filled the street behind them as well, and soon they were surrounded. The two prisoners and the men gathered around them only stood in silence, studying each other, then a familiar figure wearing a silver mask came to stand in front of the armed men.

Although she couldn't see his face, May could hear the satisfied grin in the old crime boss's voice. "Lose us in the alleyways, will you?" He shook his head, letting out a soft laugh. "Come now, Hale. Surely, you are not foolish enough to believe you could escape me so easily. There are thousands of ears in the city to hear your steps, thousands of eyes to mark your passage, and all of them belong to me."

Hale grunted, and if he felt the thrill of fear that had overcome May, he showed no sign. "Too bad none of 'em have a spare face for you then, eh?"

Grinner visibly tensed. "Make what jokes you will," he hissed, "you'll be dead soon enough."

"Maybe," Hale agreed, "but you'll still be an ugly bastard." Then, in a low voice, barely loud enough for her to hear. "The door, lass. Give it a pull, why don't you?"

At first, May had no idea what he was talking about, her thoughts scrambled from her shock at how quickly their doom had come upon them, but saw they stood next to a shop door, the sign hanging over it marking it as a tailor's place of business. Not trusting herself to speak, May tried the handle and found it locked. *Of course it would be,* she thought angrily. The tailor had no doubt closed to go see the execution, just like so many others in the city. "It's locked."

Hale grunted. "Good thing I brought a key then," he said, his eyes still not leaving Grinner. "You'll want to take a step back."

May did, about to ask what the crime boss meant by "key" but then she saw clearly enough as he exploded into motion, swinging the axe quicker than she would have thought possible. The wood around the door handle shattered in a shower of splinters. "Give it a go now, lass," he said, "might be it'll open for you this time."

"You can't be serious," Grinner called from down the street. "You think to what, exactly, take shelter in a tailor's shop? Well, I suppose it will serve as a grave as well as anywhere else."

"Never mind him," Hale said, "just go on."

May swallowed hard, and pushed at the door. It slid open without any resistance. "It's open."

"Well, that's alright then," the big man said. "Now, go on inside, see if there's a back door."

"Enough of this!" Grinner yelled. "Your little sideshow in the town square will avail you nothing, just as this will avail you nothing. You will still die, Hale. This ends today."

"That so?" Hale called. "Well, if you're so keen on seein' my blood, then why don't you get a blade and come on up and take it, old man? Might be my axe can finish what your assassin started with your face."

"I have no need to sully myself fighting you," Grinner spat, "I have men to do that work for me."

Hale yelled something back, but May was inside the tailor's shop now, and his words were muffled. She hurried around the room, searching behind racks of shirts and dresses, for some means of escape. She saw a door behind the counter and felt hope blossom in her chest only to wither a moment later when she saw that the door led to a small, windowless office. With a curse, she spun and hurried back out into the street. "There's no other door!" she said, unable to keep the rising panic from her voice.

The big crime boss nodded. "Too much to hope for anyway, I guess. Now, just get yourself back inside, lass."

May frowned, swallowing past her fear. "But what about you?"

"Me?" Hale said, glancing at her, a humorless grin on his face. "Well, I'll watch the door then, won't I?"

CHAPTER THIRTY-EIGHT

Aaron arrived at Perennia's gate to find only one guard there to greet him, a young man that stepped forward uncertainly, paling visibly at the sight of the Akalians flanking the sellsword. "W-who goes there?"

"General Aaron Envelar," Aaron said. "You'd best just let us through, lad."

The guard hesitated, clearly wavering between his duty and his fear. Finally, he seemed to settle on duty, drawing his sword. "General, you have been deemed a traitor by the city of Perennia, and I must ask you to come with me."

Aaron raised an eyebrow. "You're serious?"

The guard licked his lips nervously, but managed a nod. "Yes, General. I must...I must escort you to the dungeons."

Aaron sighed, shaking his head. "Well, alright. Come on then."

The man hesitated, shooting an anxious glance at the Akalians. Finally, he seemed to screw up his courage and took a step forward. "Sorry, General, but until all of this is sorted—"

He never got to finish what he'd been about to say. Aaron lunged forward, drawing the blade at his back and using the sword's handle to strike the guard on the temple, and he collapsed at the sellsword's feet. "Sorry about that, lad," Aaron said, stepping over the unconscious form. "You'll have a headache in the morning, I'd wager, but at least you'll be alive. For a day like the one this one promises to be, you'll be getting off light."

Inside the city, Aaron paused, closing his eyes and calling upon his bond with the Virtue of Compassion. The power came easily this time, more easily than ever before. Perhaps, the time in Tianya's dream world had somehow increased his control of it. When he opened his eyes, the buildings and the street looked gray and lifeless. He could see through their blurred forms, as if they were hardly there at all. Scattered throughout the city, he saw thousands upon thousands of magenta glows, marking the city's people. "Come on, May," he said, searching, "where are you?" He filled his mind with thoughts of the club owner, her fiery red hair, the temper that matched it so well, the confidence and self-assurance that she wore like a cloak. Soon, one of glowing beacons seemed to shine brighter than the others.

Aaron let out a breath he hadn't known he'd been holding. Still alive then. Whatever had happened, she wasn't in the city square—that much, he knew. What's more, he noted another glow near her, and he quested out with the power of the bond, finally recognizing the gruff crime boss, Hale. Both, it seemed, had escaped their execution, but for how long? For with the power of the bond he could also make out what looked like a hundred or more men surrounding the club owner and the crime boss, and it didn't seem all that likely that the city had decided to throw the two of them a party.

Another thought struck him, and he turned his thoughts to Adina. He knew her well, the smell of her, the smile she gave only to him. It didn't take long to pick her out among those multitudes filling the city. He breathed a sigh of relief as he saw her, alive and well, but one that was cut short when he realized that she was traveling in the direction of May and Hale, and those hundreds of men that surrounded them.

"*Shit*," he cursed.

She's heading right for them, Aaron.

Aaron grunted, turning to the Akalians. "This way." And then they were running again.

CHAPTER THIRTY-NINE

Hale stood inside the door frame of the tailor's shop, cutting down Grinner's men with a strength and speed that was hard to fathom. May had already last count of the number the crime boss had slain, the number of times Grinner's men had been forced to drag the corpses of their comrades out of the way before they could come at him again.

Hale stood in a widening puddle of blood, growing bigger with each sweep of his axe, yet still he fought on, striking down each man that came within his reach with an efficiency of motion that reminded May of a lumberjack at his trade.

But efficiency of motion was where the similarities between the two ended. Unless, that was, lumberjacks laughed as they went about their work, a deep, resonating laugh that sent chills down May's spine despite the fact that the crime boss was on her side. His axe went up and down, from one side to the next, leaving corpses in its wake. May had thought, a dozen times at least, that surely the man must grow weary, that sooner or later even his strength must have an end. But if it did, they had not reached it yet, and he was just as deadly with the axe now as he had been over half an hour ago when the killing began.

Outside in the street, May could hear Grinner screaming with impotent rage, urging his men on. But here, at least, his words, his lies, did him little good. The axe held a truth of its own, one that could not be bent or swayed, one that could not be changed or dissembled. And so men came and men died, and the last sound they heard before they were sent to Salen's Fields was the sound of the giant's laughter.

May was tempted to think Hale wasn't a man at all, but a god inside a man's body, come to the earth to seek a bloody celebration, so well did he fight. Yet, for all his incredible skill, for all his unflagging strength, the crime boss had not had it all his way. More than a little of the blood gathered at his feet was his own. It oozed from a dozen cuts, all relatively minor on their own, but May knew that, given time, the amount of blood loss, if nothing else, would finish him.

Still, none of these small wounds were what worried her the most. Instead, it was the deep puncture in the crime boss's left shoulder from where one of Grinner's men had impaled his own comrade—killing him before Hale's axe could—to strike the crime boss. The steel had dug deep into Hale's shoulder in a spurt of blood before his axe gave answer, cutting his attacker down. The laughter *had* faltered at that, giving way to a grunt of pain and surprise, but only for a moment, and then it had started once again, and for all the strangeness of it, May had been glad when it did.

The man couldn't go on forever, this much she knew. She'd tried to think of some way to help, to give him a moment to rest, but so far she had come up empty. After all, the door wasn't big enough for two people to stand abreast—no doubt the reason he'd chosen it in the first place. The only other option was to replace him altogether to give him time to rest, but such an act would require Grinner and his men to give them a minute or more of a break, and she thought it more likely that Nalesh, the Father of the Gods, would appear to lend his aid than for Grinner to allow them a moment's respite. Not that it would have mattered in any case, for May was a woman who knew well her strengths and her weaknesses, and she wouldn't have lasted ten seconds in that doorway.

So she only stood and watched Hale go about his grizzly work, waiting for the time when he would inevitably fall, and Grinner and his men would come in to claim their prizes. Thinking of that moment—as sure as the sun would rise the next day, though she would never see it—filled her with a great sadness. Not for herself, or at least, not *just* herself, but for the giant crime boss too. She had known the man for years, had known him to be a thief, a liar, and a murderer, and the truth was that he *was* all those things, but he was also the man who stood when others would have run, who laughed and roared while others would have whimpered and pleaded.

A criminal, yes, but a man who faced the monsters alone, knowing, surely, that sooner or later the monsters would win, but fighting them anyway. And though May knew he would have denied it, she knew that he stood in that doorway not just for himself, but for her, too.

He was her savior, a man who accepted wounds and let his own blood flow so hers wouldn't. At least for a little while longer. She wished desperately that she could somehow reverse years and treat him differently, knowing now what he was. But, of course, she could not. Time moved how it would, and not even Hale's prodigious strength could stand against it when it chose to march. So May watched; she watched, she worried, and she waited for the end to come.

CHAPTER FORTY

Adina and Gryle ran through the city streets, their eyes scouring the alleys and sidestreets in search of any evidence marking the club owner and crime boss's passage, their ears listening for any noise that might alert them to the presence of the escaped prisoners but, so far at least, they had seen nothing. And with each moment that passed without finding the two, Adina felt her urgency grow and, at the same time, a dark resignation, one that she forced down each time it rose unbidden into her mind.

Grinner had hundreds of city guards, and hundreds more of his own men at his disposal, while she and the others numbered only four—six including the guard captain, Marcus, and his fellow guard, Hugh. What chances did they have, then, of finding the club owner and crime boss before Grinner or his men did? *Never mind the chances,* she thought, *you will find them, that's all. Because they need to be found, they need help, and you...you are enough.*

She consoled herself with the fact that they had not yet been forced to deal with any of Grinner's men, and that was something to be grateful for. They had been searching for some time now, and the fact that they had been lucky enough to not run into some of the crime boss's men—no doubt doing the same—was surprising to say the least. *Not that surprising,* a voice inside her head whispered, *not if they have already found that for which they searched.* Adina decided to ignore the voice and the harsh truth it carried, choosing instead to believe that they had only been lucky thus far.

She turned down an alley, giving no thought to where it would take them only meaning to cover as much ground as possible. She was so deep in thought, in her own worry, that her attention slipped for a moment. She didn't realize anything was amiss until Gryle grabbed her arm, halting her forward motion as efficiently as a brick wall.

"Princess," he said, and Adina followed his troubled gaze to see three figures standing at the opposite end of the alleyway, bared steel in their hands. Adina felt a rush of fear, but Gryle only stepped in front of her, and when he spoke his voice was calmer, more confident than she'd ever heard it before. "Stay behind me, Adina," he said, using her given name for the first time Adina could ever recall.

The three figures moved closer and, as they did, the one in the center became visible, and Adina let out a cry of surprise and relief, the fear and uncertainty that had been building in her shattering apart like glass before a smith's hammer. "Aaron!" She ran to him, hardly aware of the two Akalians at all as she pulled him into a tight embrace, and he let out a laugh as he stumbled in surprise. "You're alive," she said, pulling him close.

"I am," he said, grabbing her shoulders and gently pulling her back so that he could look into her face. "I'm so thankful to find you okay. When I awoke, and the Speaker told me where you had gone, I was scared that…" He shook his head. "Never mind."

Adina grimaced. "Aaron, about us leaving, I didn't mean…"

"Forget it," the sellsword said. "You did exactly as you should have done—as a princess, as a queen would. And Gryle," he continued, nodding as the chamberlain walked up, a sheepish expression on his face.

"Aaron," the other man said, nodding, clearly embarrassed.

Aaron grinned. "We're going to talk about those heroics later, Chamberlain, I promise you, but for now there's not time." He turned back to Adina. "We have to get to May and Hale—now."

"I know," Adina said, frustrated. "We've been out searching, but I hope the others are having more luck than we are because we haven't seen any sign."

"The others?"

Adina nodded. "Leomin, Seline, Wendell, and two guards we met at the gate. We split up, thinking we'd be able to find them sooner but so far…" She shook her head.

"That's alright," Aaron said, glancing to the left wall of the alley as if seeing something beyond it, and Adina thought that, for a moment, his eyes shone a bright purple. "I know where they are."

"Then we can go and help them. Grinner's men are out looking for them too."

Aaron nodded. "Of course we can go, but Adina," he said, turning back, "May and Hale aren't alone. I think Grinner and his men—a lot of them—have found them already."

He stared at her, and Adina thought she saw a question in that gaze. It was the sort of question one might pose a queen, a question of priorities, of the greater good. However, just then she wasn't a queen but a friend, and one of those closest to her needed her help. "We go," she said, answering the sellsword's unspoken question. "If there's any way to help Hale and May, we have to do it."

Aaron nodded. "I thought you'd say that. Let's go."

***

Aaron ran with Adina at his side, the Akalians flanking them, and Gryle bringing up the rear. As they ran, the sellsword wondered if he should have lied to Adina, should have come up with some excuse to lead her away from Grinner's men. True, such a deceit would have meant the certain death of May and Hale, and Adina might never have forgiven him—he would certainly have never forgiven himself. For May had always been a friend to him, not just a friend at all really, but family. A mother to fill the space his own had left behind when Kevlane murdered her. A sister to tease him when he grew melancholy or brooding.

Aaron had left the choice to Adina, but he had known well enough what she would choose. It was who she was, why the world and its people needed her so much. He only hoped he didn't come to regret it. He slowed to a stop as he neared the end of the alleyway in which they ran. "It's here," he said to Adina. "They're around this corner. Are you sure?"

She studied him for a moment, then finally nodded. "Yes."

He grunted. "Alright then—let's go save the city."

Although Aaron had some idea of what they would find, he was still shocked. Hundreds of armed men crowded the street, some wearing the armor and trappings marking them as city guardsmen, and others wearing crude linen pants and shirts, carrying weapons ranging from swords to daggers and even clubs. Grinner's men, criminals all, standing with the city guard as if they belonged there. They were gathered around what looked to be a tailor's shop, and though Aaron could not see past them, he could hear the sounds of fighting—and dying—taking place somewhere beyond his view.

"*Gods,*" Adina breathed behind him, and Aaron couldn't blame her. The sheer number of armed men was daunting, but even more so was seeing the criminal and guardsmen allied against a common foe. *Hang on, May,* he thought. *We're coming. For whatever good that will do.*

The armed men had their backs to Aaron and the others, but one of them chose that moment to turn and look down the city street. He gave a shout of surprise at the sight of the sellsword and his companions, and soon all of the men nearest them were turned, raising their weapons. A voice, one he recognized, yelled something in an authoritative tone and the men began to step to either side, opening a path through which walked a familiar form, though Aaron had a moment of confusion when he saw the silver mask. "*The Silent Blade,*" the man hissed, and the sound of that voice left little doubt to his identity. "The traitor has returned, it seems, to finish what he started."

"Grinner," Aaron said, and though anger rose in him at the sight of the man who had tried to kill him and all of his friends, it was a cold anger, sharp and deadly to the touch, and one which he controlled instead of one that might control him. "I am no traitor, but, then, you know that already, don't you? After all, it was you who lured me and my friends into the forest, you who made a deal with Kevlane to kill us all and doom the city."

A few of the guards shared troubled glances at that, but Grinner only laughed, shaking his head. "Ridiculous, of course. No, Aaron Envelar, word has filled the city of your treachery, yours and that of those you would call friends. The queen herself has seen the truth of it and has condemned May Tanarest and Hale to

A Sellsword's Mercy

death. It is only through treachery, no doubt instigated by more of your comrades, that the sentence has not yet been carried out."

"Word has filled the city, huh?" Aaron said. "And I wonder whose men spread that word." But he could see that whatever moment of doubt several of the guards had experienced, it had passed at the mention of their queen.

"The queen has no more time for your lies than I do, *General Envelar*," Grinner hissed. "And it is good that you have come—you will die along with the other traitors." He gave a sharp gesture, and hundreds of men began moving toward Aaron and the others, their faces grim, their blades raised.

"Those of you loyal to Queen Isabelle," Aaron called, knowing it for a lost cause but deciding he had to try anyway. "You have been deceived." He jabbed a finger at Grinner, "That man is the traitor, not us, and he has fed you a belly full of lies. Kevlane is still out there, plotting Perennia's downfall. With each moment we waste fighting each other he grows stronger. Can you not see the truth of it?"

I don't think they can, Co observed.

"Alright then," Aaron said, bringing his own blade up, "If that's the way you want it."

"*Wait!*" Such was the power of Adina's voice, the authority in it, that everyone froze and turned to her. She did not quail beneath those gazes, did not look anxious or afraid, but stood proud, gazing out at all those gathered. "I am Princess Adina, royal daughter of King Marcus. Many of you have heard of me, know well what I have done—what *we*—" she continued, gesturing to Aaron and Gryle where they stood beside her, "have done to keep this city safe. We have lost friends, have risked our lives, and we have done so gladly, for Perennia, Telrear, is a place worth fighting for—worth dying for, if that is what is required."

She paused to take a breath, and Aaron glanced between her and the crowd, saw some of the guards hesitating, torn between their loyalty for their queen, the trust she had seemed to place in Councilman Grinner, and Adina's words.

They're close, Aaron, Co said, her voice excited and anxious all at once.

Yes, Aaron thought, *but not close enough.* Through his bond with the Virtue, he could feel the men hardening their hearts, preparing themselves for the grim task of cutting down one of royal blood. They heard her words, but they did not feel them, did not recognize, fully, the truth of them. Struck by an idea, Aaron reached out and placed a gentle hand on Adina's shoulder. *We will make them feel, Firefly. We will make them understand.*

Aaron, Co said, *I...this has not been done before. I don't know if it is even possible.*

But Aaron did not respond, for he was concentrated on shaping the power of the bond, of reaching out to take hold of the storm of emotions that raged within Adina—righteous anger at Grinner for the deaths he had caused, fear for her friends and herself but, most of all, sadness for a city, on the brink of destruction, one she would do anything to save.

Adina let out a small gasp as the power of the bond touched her, and she glanced at Aaron uncertainly, who only gave a sharp nod back. "Tell them," he said through gritted teeth, straining under the immense pressure of using the power in such a way, "they will hear you."

"Citizens of Perennia," Adina said, turning back to the armed men, and each word carried with it the weight of her feeling, the weight of her truth. "General Envelar, myself, and these others have done everything we have to protect you, to protect this city. It is the reason you signed up for the guard, isn't it? You did not sign up to hurt, but to help, not to kill, but to save. Will you now allow this, this *creature,*" she said, gesturing at Grinner, "to make a farce of your duty, of your sacrifice? To make of you no more than a blade for him to wield as he would? Would you have him make of you a murderer?"

The men hesitated at that, the guardsmen among the group frowning and glancing at each other. "Perennia does not need more corpses," Adina went on, her voice ringing out, "we do not need more blades. We need *men,* men like yourselves who would sacrifice everything to protect their families, their home. Perennia needs you, guardsmen," she said, her gaze roaming the faces of those gathered, "will you answer her call?"

"Enough! You have heard your queen's wishes," Grinner screamed, his voice a high shriek. "*Kill them!*"

Still the guards hesitated, unsure, but Grinner's men, at least, did not, and dozens of men separated themselves from the guardsmen with a roar, charging at Aaron and the others. "Stay back, Princess," Aaron said grimly as he, Gryle, and the two Akalians stepped up to meet them. "You have done your convincing—now it's our turn to do ours."

CHAPTER FORTY-ONE

May watched as the axe flashed down again, burying itself in the forehead of the latest man to brave the doorway. Grunting, the crime boss gave the corpse a kick, and it tumbled out into the street, knocking several of the nearest men down. Hale still fought on, as implacable as a mountain, but in the last fifteen minutes the club owner had begun to see the exhaustion and the man's wounds—exactly how bad May couldn't say, for she could not see the front of him—take their toll. His parries were no longer as fast as they had been, and not five minutes ago she had cried out as she saw the crime boss stumble, a sword piercing his stomach. She had thought surely he would fall then, *had* to fall, but somehow Hale had kept his feet, grabbing the man who'd impaled him by the back of his head and smashing his own forehead into the man's face, leaving it a bloody ruin.

He bled freely now from several deep cuts, and his laughter had turned to dry, croaking rasps not long ago. His clothes were stained crimson from the blood he'd shed mixed with his own, as if he had taken a bath in the stuff, yet though he wavered from time to time as if drunk, his axe blade was always there to meet the next attacker, reaping a bloody harvest of all who dared come within his range.

May watched with a sort of grim fascination as the axe tore through the belly of the next attacker, and the man collapsed in the doorway in a pile of corpses that had once again begun to accumulate in the street in front of the shop. Suddenly, the flow of attackers ceased, and May's heart leapt as she heard Aaron's voice. *Thank the gods,* she thought, her relief so strong that she felt dizzy. *He's alive, after all, thank the gods.* A moment later, her relief doubled when she heard Adina speaking to the gathered guardsmen.

Hale grunted. "Knew the son of a bitch wasn't dead." He turned to look at her, and May gasped as she saw the full extent of the his injuries. He bled from dozens of cuts, many deep, and May couldn't fathom how he was able to stand, let alone fight. "Well," the crime boss said, "looks like they've forgotten all about us. Just as well, that. I could use a bit of a sit down."

He walked inside the shop, wincing with each step, and May grabbed a wooden chair from behind the counter and set it in front of him. Hale smiled. "Thanks, lass." He eased into the chair carefully, as if even that small movement caused him great pain, then laid the axe—its handle coated in as much blood as the blade itself—across his lap. "I don't guess there's any whiskey or ale in this place, is there?"

May had spent the last hour or so rooting through the shop looking for anything that might help them, and she shook her head sadly. "No," she said, but that gave her an idea and she hurried behind the counter, retrieving the needle and thread she'd seen earlier. "Now, let's see what we can do about your—"

"Leave it, May," Hale said, holding up a hand to forestall her. "Just for a minute." He looked away from her then, back to the doorway and the piles of the dead he'd left. "Not a bad day's work, anyway. Still, it's too damn bad about the whiskey, though I guess I can't be surprised. It's been that kind of day." He leaned his head back in his chair and closed his eyes, his hands still on the handle of the axe. "Let me know if they come back, won't you, lass? I'm going to just catch my breath."

Nodding, May hurried to the door and looked out. She couldn't see much, for a wall of guardsmen stood with their backs to her, blocking what was happening from her view, but from time to time she saw blood fly into the air, and she could plainly hear the sounds of fighting. *Gods, don't let them die now, please. Not when I've just gotten them back.*

***

Adina watched in amazement as Aaron and the two Akalians cut a bloody path through Grinner's men. Aaron had always been skilled with the blade, but he was even better now than when last she'd seen him fight, better, even, than the Akalians who fought on either side of him as they drove their way deeper into Grinner's army of thieves and thugs.

The sellsword flowed in and out of his opponents' strikes like wind given form, dodging even blows he couldn't have seen coming with a preternatural ease. From time to time, his sword lashed out, the movement like a part of some intricate dance, and when it did men died. The man made killing an art, and it was at once beautiful and terrible to behold. Flanked by the two Akalians, he seemed unstoppable, and what few criminals managed to find their way past them, more by luck than design, Adina suspected, were greeted by the chamberlain who stood not far away from her.

Gryle had broken off the door of a nearby shop and wielded it like a club, battering anyone that came close and sending them hurtling through the air, their broken bodies crashing down among their fellows. Dozens of criminals were down in less than five minutes of the fight's start, with more following their comrades to Salen's Fields every second. Watching their allies get massacred, Grinner's men began to show fear, several of them pushing their way through their fellows to get further away from Aaron and the deadly Akalians, and Adina wasn't surprised.

They were criminals, after all, not trained guardsmen—those, thankfully, still hesitated, not joining the fight—men and women who had spent their lives preying on the weak, counting on the elements of surprise, brutality, and numbers to survive. But here, now, their numbers seemed to mean nothing, and the only surprise was the efficient, shocking violence with which their comrades were cut down.

Adina saw the moment when things changed, the moment when what had been an army bent on blood became instead a crowd of terrified men trampling each other to get away from Aaron and the black-garbed figures. Soon, there was no one left to fight, no one left to kill, and Aaron and the Akalians stood surrounded by dozens of bodies, facing the guardsmen and, in front of them, Councilman Grinner who gaped at the bloody spectacle, his body rigid as what little remained of his men fled past him.

"*Impossible,*" he said. "Fight them, you cowards! Stand and fight!" But he might as well have said nothing, for all the attention the criminals gave him, and soon he stood in the street facing Aaron and the others, the guardsmen at his back, his own men scattered.

***

"Oh, by the gods, I can't believe it," May breathed, watching the criminals rushing past the guards and into the alleyways, the faces she was able to see twisted in fear, their eyes wild like those of hunted animals. The guards still made no move, only stood still in the street. "Hale," she said, "I don't…I don't think the guards are going to attack. I think…I think we're going to be okay."

The crime boss didn't answer, and May turned to see him still sitting with his head back, his eyes closed, his hands gripping the bloody haft of the axe. "Hale?" May walked back into the tailor's shop. "Hale, didn't you hear me? I think we're going to live to see tomorrow, after all…" She trailed off, noticing, for the first time, how very still the crime boss was. His chest did not rise and fall with his breath, did not move at all.

"Oh, Hale," she said, tears filling her eyes. "I'm so sorry."

But the crime boss did not respond, and the only answer she received was in the form of the small, knowing smile that still sat on his face. Whatever his final thought had been, she supposed that, at least, it must have been a good one.

***

"Well?" Grinner demanded, turning to the guards behind him. "What are you waiting for? Kill them! Your queen demands it!"

"They don't work for you, Grinner," Aaron said, walking closer, his bloody sword held down at his side. "They never did."

"*Don't you hear me, you fools?*" Grinner screamed, his anger giving way to fear as he stepped back, watching Aaron approach. "Kill them! In the name of your queen!"

The guards still did not move, did not so much as answer, and Grinner tried to push his way through them, but for all their unresponsiveness, they stood like a wall, barring his way. Shooting a glance over his shoulder, Grinner made a terrified, mewling sound in his throat as Aaron drew nearer. He moved as if to run around Aaron, but one of the Akalians stepped forward, bringing the old crime boss up short. He tried the other side and was met with the second black-garbed figure, moving up to bar his path.

"W-wait, Silent," Grinner said, his breath rasping in his chest. "Just wait a second. I can help you—we can help each other." The sellsword did not respond, only kept walking closer. "*Damnit, you fool!*" Grinner screeched. "Think about this, about what you're doing!"

"I have, Grinner," Aaron said, his voice calm and cold. "I've thought about this for a long time."

With a hiss of rage, the crime boss jerked a cruel knife from somewhere inside his tunic and rushed Aaron. The sellsword brought his blade up, striking the crime boss's wrist with the flat of it, and Grinner screamed in pain as the knife flew from his fingers. The older man stumbled backward, his hand clamped around his wrist, and Aaron followed, in no hurry now.

"J-just *wait,* damn you," Grinner said again. "I did what I thought was best, can't you see that? For everyone, for Perennia and Telrear both." He stumbled away, toward the wall of a nearby shop, and Aaron followed him. Grinner screamed, his breath coming in ragged pants, and he pulled his mask free, throwing it at Aaron even as he turned to run, but the implacable guardsmen stood on one side, the Akalians on the other, and there was nowhere left for him to go.

Aaron took in the old man's ruined face. "Our crimes always catch up to us, Grinner. No matter how fast he is, how hard he tries, no man can outrun his reckoning when it comes."

Grinner growled, an inarticulate, wordless sound, and swung a fist at Aaron. The sellsword avoided the blow easily, leaning his head back so that it passed in front of him, then kicked the crime boss in the stomach. The breath exploded from the older man, and he slammed into the wooden wall of the building, crumpling to the ground in a gasping heap. "T-trial," Grinner croaked, "t-there must

A Sellsword's Mercy

be a trial. Y-you cannot kill a man without proving he's g-guilty first."

Aaron laughed. "I'm not sure what gave you that idea. It seems to me you've killed plenty and planned on killing plenty more. Where were their trials, I wonder? Besides, Grinner, your guilt is writ plain for anyone with eyes to see it."

Grinner gave his own laugh then, a desperate, wretched thing as he looked up at Aaron, one ruined eye weeping a clear substance onto his face. "You are a fool, Aaron Envelar. You always were. And when Kevlane comes with his army, you and everyone you care about will die."

"Maybe," Aaron said, grabbing the crime boss's lank hair and pulling him up, slamming his head against the wooden wall of the shop. "But however it ends, I'll be here to see it. You'll just have to guess."

He replaced his sword in its sheath and drew one of the blades at his side. The crime boss struggled against him, screaming, his wide eyes studying the blade with a sick fascination, but Aaron slammed his head against the building again, and his struggles weakened. "M-mercy," Grinner gasped in a weak voice. "H-have *mercy*, Aaron."

Aaron cocked his head, studying the man. "This is mercy." The crime boss started to say something else, but whatever it was going to be turned to a wet, gurgling sound as the blade opened a bloody furrow across his throat. Grinner's eyes went wide with disbelief, as if even now he could not believe such a fate had come upon him, and he wavered drunkenly, his mouth working as if he would speak, but a moment later he collapsed at the sellsword's feet.

Aaron felt no joy as he watched the man breathe his last, no pleasure, only a vague relief at a job done, one that had been long overdue. He thought of the countless men and women who had suffered and died because of the crime boss's machinations, thought of all those living who would carry the scars of his cruelty.

Aaron let out a heavy, tired sigh. "This is mercy."

CHAPTER FORTY-TWO

Boyce Kevlane finished reading the letter again, a mixture of emotions crossing his features, and, at this moment at least, they *were* his. Here, within his personal quarters, if nowhere else, he could wear his own face instead of that of Belgarin. Soon enough, every man, woman, and child would come to know his true face, would come to fear it. For the tournament had been progressing well, his days spent watching over the proceedings, wearing the face of the dead king, his nights filled with the working of the Art on those men and women who had come for the tournament, turning them into creatures, *his* creatures, adding scores to his ranks.

Given how close he was to having an unstoppable army at his command, the letter's contents should not have bothered him. Yet, they did. A minor setback, nothing more, but however useless, it was a victory for Aaron Envelar and those others with him, and that thought rankled the magi more than he would have thought possible.

So when he looked up at the man standing before him, his face was twisted with anger. "Your master, it seems, is dead."

The muscled bodyguard's eyes went wide at that, his face twisting with emotion, and more than Kevlane thought such a man might feel for his charge. "D-dead?"

"Oh yes," Kevlane said, rising from his chair and moving around his desk. "Dead. It seems that Aaron Envelar himself slit his throat for him."

The man's mouth worked soundlessly for a moment, and when he spoke his voice was low, scared. "But...what will I do now?"

"Oh, do not be so upset," the magi said, coming and placing a hand on the man's shoulder. "You are a big man, strong, capable." He grinned. "I'm sure that we might find something for you. For where one master dies, surely another might fill his place."

The man's eyes went wide as he realized exactly what the magi's words meant. Kevlane nodded to Caldwell who stood at the side of the room with the creature, Savrin, only recently returned from his hunt of the sellsword in the forest. A failure that had been also, for Kevlane had never expected the cursed Akalians to show up, to throw in their lot with Aaron Envelar and the others. A setback, but one that, he told himself, would not matter, in the long run.

He stepped away, walking toward the window as the creature moved forward. Kevlane was so lost in thoughts of vengeance, of the terrible devastation he would wreak on the sellsword and his companions, as well as the Speaker and his ilk, that he hardly noticed the big man's screams as he fought—quite uselessly—against the creature. In another moment, the screams cut off. "Put him with the others," the magi said. "I will see to him soon enough."

"Of course, Master," the advisor said, bowing deeply, but Kevlane was already turned back to the window, staring out at the darkness. Tomorrow, the tournament would continue, his work would continue, and soon, he promised himself, the world would know all too well what he had wrought.

CHAPTER FORTY-THREE

Aaron stared at the pyre, the flames rising far into the night, and though the towering blaze illuminated the field surrounding it in a ruddy glow, it did nothing to chase away the shadows that crowded in his mind. He wasn't sure how he felt staring at the flames as they licked at the body within. Was it sadness? Relief? Did he feel anything at all? He had known Hale for many years, and the man had tried to have him killed more than once. That should have been enough to guarantee some satisfaction at the sight of his body feeding the flames, but he had also saved May, had given his life to do so, and so as he departed the world he had left a great debt at Aaron's feet, one the sellsword could never repay.

"The boss always wanted it this way."

Aaron turned at the sound of a deep voice to see a big man standing before him, one he didn't recognize. Behind the stranger stood several others, the biggest woman he'd ever seen, a man with a hawk-nose, and a youth who shifted restlessly from foot to foot. "Do I know you?"

"No, Silent, you don't, but we know you well enough," the man said, offering his hand. "The name's Urek, and if you don't mind, I reckon I'd like to shake the hand of the man that did for that bastard Grinner once and for all."

Aaron grunted and shook the offered hand. He expected the man to squeeze in an effort to show his strength, as so many men—particularly men of his size—did, but he surprised him with a handshake that, though firm, was surprisingly gentle. "You worked for Hale then?"

"Aye," the big man said, and Aaron didn't think it was a trick of the firelight that made it appear as if the man's eyes were misted over. "He was the boss, alright, and a better one a man couldn't ask for." He snorted, glancing behind them where thousands of men and women had gathered to pay their respects to the dead crime boss as well as those others who had died because of Grinner's crimes, those whose bodies now fed the other pyres spread out before them. "I think he would've shit, he'd seen this. Still, the flames are right anyway—boss always said that when he died he wanted his body burned. Told me the worms were fat enough already, he didn't mean to give 'em any free meals." He snorted, rubbing at his eyes. "He was funny like that. A simple man. But complicated too."

Aaron nodded. "Yes. Yes, I think he was."

Urek smiled. "He always liked you, Silent. Respected you—it's why he tried to have you killed so much, you know."

"I'm glad he didn't like me anymore than he did then—some of those times were far too close for comfort."

Urek laughed, clapping Aaron on the back. "Well. I just wanted to let you know, I appreciate what you did—we all do. If you ever need anything, all you got to do is ask around for old Urek, how's that? You do that, well, we'll do what we can for you."

"We?" Aaron asked.

The big man rubbed a hand across his unshaven face, shaking his head as if embarrassed. "It's the damndest thing, but well, we've got a lot of criminals without a fella to call boss floatin' around now. And you know enough of us to know we ain't no good at all without someone to tell us what to do."

Aaron nodded slowly, realization dawning. "And so that's you then?"

The man hocked and spat. "Not by choice, I'll tell you that much. But sure, I suppose it is. For now, anyway."

Aaron couldn't help but grin at the man's obvious discomfort. "So you'll be the one telling everyone else what to do then."

"Seems that way. Though the gods alone know who'll be tellin' me." He clapped Aaron on the shoulder once more, then turned and walked away, the others following after him. Aaron watched the man go, thinking that Hale would have been happy with how that had turned out, at least.

He turned back to the flames, watched them dance, and reflected that it was a strange thing about people—they were always more, and always less, than you thought they were. Hale had been a criminal, a murderer and a thief, but he had also been a hero. Queen Isabelle was a ruler of a nation, the daughter of a man widely considered the best king Telrear had ever known, and yet she was a coward. Thinking of her, he glanced at where she stood flanked by guards, looking small and weak and afraid.

Once they had gotten the guards under control and hunted down those of Grinner's men who they could find, they had marched to the castle, Adina brimming with barely controlled rage at what her sister had allowed to happen. Adina had rebuked her, had told her that her actions might well have doomed all of Telrear. Aaron had expected the queen to argue, to defend herself, but she had only sat in her throne and weathered Adina's scorn. Even when the princess had informed Isabelle that she was to make no more decisions without first consulting her, still she had not argued, and the expression that came to her face was not one of anger or offense, but of unmistakable relief.

Aaron thought about that as he gazed at the pyres, thought about a lot of things, thousands of questions and so few answers. He watched the fire burn down until there was little left but ash and glowing embers. Then someone touched him on the shoulder, and he turned to see Adina standing there. Behind her stood May and the first mate, Thom—the two holding hands as if, after their ordeal, they didn't dare let go of each other—Leomin and his new woman, Seline—and what a shock *that* had been—and Gryle. Save for them, everyone else was gone, the field that had been packed with people the last time he'd looked up now deserted and empty.

He had the vague memory of Wendell muttering something about being tired and needing some sleep, but he thought it all the more likely that the sergeant had decided that now was as good a time as any to pay for the pleasure of a woman's company.

"Aaron?" the princess said. "Is everything okay?"

He gave her a small smile, then let his eyes take in the others. "Not yet, but it will be. We'll make sure of it."

"So we will go to war then?" Gryle asked. There was no fear in the man's voice, no recrimination or discontent, only the question.

"We're already in a war," Aaron said, gripping Adina's hand and starting away from the fire. "It's time we started fighting it."

**THE END
OF
BOOK SIX
OF
THE SEVEN VIRTUES**

BY JACOB PEPPERS

To stay up to date on the next release and hear about other awesome promotions and free giveaways, sign up to my mailing list. For a limited time, you will also receive a FREE copy of *The Silent Blade,* the prequel to The Seven Virtues, when you sign up!

Go to *JacobPeppersAuthor.com* to claim your rewards now!

Once again, Dear Reader, we have come to the end. I hope you enjoyed spending some more time with Aaron, Adina, and all the others. To figure out how the story ends, pick up your copy of *A Sellsword's Hope*, the seventh and final book of The Seven Virtues, today!

If you enjoyed the book, I'd really appreciate you taking a moment to leave an honest review—as any author can tell you, they are a big help.

If you want to reach out, you can email me at JacobPeppersauthor@gmail.com or visit jacobpeppersauthor.com. You can also follow me at Facebook or on Twitter.

I can't wait to hear from you!

Note from the Author

Another part of the journey is finished, dear reader. We have traveled far and seen great, terrible things together, but we are not quite done—not yet. If you are tired, do not fret, for I, too, am weary. Let us pause here, then, to gather our breath, our strength, for I believe that we will need it soon. The end is close now, so very close.

Look, up ahead of us. Do you see the chasm? Can you make out the bridge traversing it?

That is the path we must take—there is no other. Please, do not ask me if it will hold our weight, for any comforting words I might offer would ring false, and whatever else passes between us, let there be truth. Let there be that, at the least.

I can't promise that we will make it across—I can only tell you that others have come before us to this place, that they traveled this very bridge, crossed this very chasm. As for what transpired once they reached the other side…that is something we will discover soon enough.

What's that? You hear the sounds of fighting? Yes, come to it, so do I. Soon, I fear, things will be decided one way or the other, never mind our presence. But still we will be there to see it. That much, at least, we will do. Just another moment and…

I'm sorry? You believe I hesitate? Now, at the brink?

Fine—yes, I know, truth and truth only between us. Very well, I hesitate. But do you not feel it? Do you not know that we have reached the very edge of things? The very end?

Whatever Aaron and his companions face on the other side, whatever fate seeks them even now, there will be no second chances. What waits for us there, on the other side, is truth and that only. Perhaps, it will be the death of Aaron and his companions—perhaps they will win through. But no matter how things fall we will bear witness to the death of hope, for what comes is final, as all true endings are, as all true endings must be.

I see that you are impatient to cross, to lend what support we may to Aaron, to Adina and the others. Very well—I will lead you, for a poor guide I would be should I let you make the journey alone. But, please, just another moment.

Just one more moment...to catch my breath...

About the Author

Jacob Peppers lives in Georgia with his wife, his son, Gabriel, and their three dogs. He is an avid reader and writer and when he's not exploring the worlds of others, he's creating his own. His short fiction has been published in various markets, and his short story, "The Lies of Autumn," was a finalist for the 2013 Eric Hoffer Award for Short Prose. He is the author of the bestselling series, The Seven Virtues, as well as The Nightfall Wars, and The Essence Chronicles.

Printed in Great Britain
by Amazon